Doña Nicanora's Hat Shop

Kirstan Hawkins

HUTCHINSON

LONDON

Published by Hutchinson 2010

2 4 6 8 10 9 7 5 3 1

First published in Great Britain in 2010 by
Hutchinson
Random House, 20 Vauxhall Bridge Road,
London SW1V 2SA

www.rbooks.co.uk

Addresses for companies within The Random House Group Limited can be found at:
www.randomhouse.co.uk/offices.htm

The Random House Group Limited Reg. No. 954009

A CIP catalogue record for this book
is available from the British Library

ISBN 9780091931704

The Random House Group Limited supports The Forest Stewardship
Council (FSC), the leading international forest certification organisation. All our
titles that are printed on Greenpeace approved FSC certified paper carry the FSC logo. Our
paper procurement policy can be found at www.rbooks.co.uk/environment

Typeset by
Palimpsest Book Production Limited, Grangemouth, Stirlingshire

This book proof printed and bound in Great Britain by
CPI Antony Rowe, Chippenham, Wiltshire

Doña Nicanora's
Hat Shop

Kirstan Hawkins studied anthropology at Edinburgh University and has travelled extensively in her work in Africa, Latin America and Asia. She carried out fieldwork for her degree among the Ashaninka Indians of the Peruvian Amazon, and for Ph.D. she spent time in the altiplano of Bolivia.

[dedication to come]

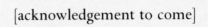

[acknowledgement to come]

One

The town of Valle de la Virgen lies at the bottom of a deep gorge, which, surrounded by eucalyptus trees on its upper slopes, descends into dark, boggy, luscious forest inhabited by humming-birds, snakes and howling monkeys. Despite its legendary beauty, the town is largely untroubled by visitors as the buses descending into the valley are in the habit of dropping off the road, making tourism a precarious business for the locals. The church, built by the colonial ancestors of the present-day inhabitants in honour of the Virgin of the Swamp, houses a weeping effigy, and is said to be one of the finest examples of the architecture of its day and an inspiration for the work of the great master, Marrietti.

Travel books on the area have little to say about Valle de la Virgen, mentioning briefly that, while fabled for its intoxicating charm and historical interest, the town remains an elusive tourist destination, reachable only by treacherous road or through dense forest marsh. One out-of-print guide even suggests that Valle de la Virgen is a creation of local legend retold in occasional travellers' tales, and that the road simply descends into impenetrable swamp.

*

The town's only foreign visitor arrived one day in the back of Ernesto's pickup truck and, much to the consternation of Ernesto's mother, failed to leave. Doña Nicanora was at first less dismayed by the arrival of the dishevelled stranger in her front yard than by the sudden reappearance of her son, who only three months previously had been given a lavish send-off at great expense and relief to the town. It was her youngest daughter, Nena, who first alerted Nicanora to the return of Ernesto and to the presence of the stranger who was about to be mauled by their dog in the yard.

'Come quickly,' Nena shouted breathlessly, running into the kitchen, where her mother was squatting over a basin, peeling potatoes. 'Ernesto is back, and he's brought a strange man with him. Lucho is attacking him. I think it's because he smells.' Dropping the potatoes, Nicanora ran outside to quell the commotion, calling the dog off whilst trying to find the words with which to begin to admonish her son.

The uninvited guest was standing in the dry dirt of the tiny bric-a-brac-filled yard, surrounded by squawking chickens and looking bewildered. He was dressed in a stained orange shirt and dirty blue jeans, and had a battered red and black bag hanging from one shoulder. His hair was as long as Nena's, his beard looked tangled and he gave off an unwashed, milky odour. He needs to be taken straight to Don Bosco, Nicanora thought. The man was holding a small book, which he was flicking through nervously. A crowd of children had gathered nearby and were nudging each other and

2

giggling, pointing at the stranger. Nicanora straightened her stained apron and pushed her hair from her face in an effort to appear respectable in front of the visitor.

'There are plenty more where he came from,' Ernesto said proudly, presenting the foreigner to his mother as the answer to her financial problems before passing out at her feet.

*

Doña Nicanora had not had an easy life, and the furrows she had dug over the years were beginning to show on her once smooth, dark face. At the age of forty, with one dead husband, two children buried, and her three surviving children remaining at home, things were not getting much easier. Ernesto's desire to leave home and build his future in the city had come as a source of great comfort to her. She had begun to despair of his ability to apply himself to anything remotely sensible, and feared that his drunken antics in the town were starting to sully her own reputation.

Having ridden away on a donkey, with a fire in his belly and a determination to seek his fortune in the city, Ernesto had now returned home in an old truck with a fire in his balls and a determination to seek a cure, having received a sound dose of the clap in Dolores's Karaoke Bar in Puerta de la Coruña. Ernesto's ambition to become a city businessman had ended on the same drunken night. By the close of the evening he had exchanged his life savings for the battered truck and acquired the foreigner, who at the time had seemed to be a good business proposition. The foreigner, who had been hanging around Puerta de la Coruña for a few months, was apparently seeking a quieter location in which to spend some time and was offering 'top dollar' for the privilege of sleeping on a

3

local floor. Ernesto, whose business sense had been sharpened at his mother's breast, could not let the opportunity pass him by.

Ernesto had already sought the help of several quacks in Puerta de la Coruña and was now prepared to place his faith in the traditional cures of his hometown. After a day of berating and beating by his mother failed to relieve him of his symptoms, managing only to elicit a confession as to the source of his ailment, he finally agreed to be taken by her to meet the new young doctor who had recently, and inexplicably, turned up in town. Doña Nicanora, who was always ready to try out an innovation, had been anxious to make the doctor's acquaintance since his arrival. Ernesto's problem presented itself as an opportunity through which to do so. These are certainly unusual times, Nicanora thought to herself as she marched her son off to the clinic, two strangers arriving in town within a few weeks. It must surely be an omen.

*

Dr Arturo Aguilar was spending another morning of solitary contemplation in his pristine white clinic. He was enjoying the glimmer of the sun on the whitewashed walls and felt strangely proud of the freshly painted sign at the front, which told the townsfolk that the clinic had been brought to them out of the goodness of the hearts of the people of Japan. Fresh from college and with a keen interest in history, Dr Aguilar had come to see his year's posting in the backwater as a challenge, an opportunity to understand a people whom modernity had seemed to pass by. He was looking forward to trying out the array of cures that he had studied during his history of medicine course, and had been eagerly awaiting a visit from a patient for some weeks.

The doctor was awoken from his reveries by the sound of Nicanora's remonstrations as she dragged her son up the path. By the time his patient reached the threshold of his clinic Dr Aguilar had been able to make his diagnosis. He believed himself to be a liberal and open-minded man. After administering a large shot of the antibiotics supplied to him by the provincial health authority, he covered Ernesto's body in warm jam jars to see whether there was in any truth in the belief that they would suction out the remaining fever, before hanging him upside down by his feet — resisting Doña Nicanora's suggestion to hang him by his *cojones* — as a brief experiment to see whether the force of gravity could draw the lust out of a man's loins. By the end of the visit, the doctor found that he had agreed to Nicanora's request to take her son on as his assistant, partly out of gratitude for having received his only patient and mainly out of fear that Ernesto's mother exuded a presence and strength of personality that suggested she might be adept in the art of witchcraft.

*

Over the ensuing weeks, the foreigner, who became known to the townsfolk as the Gringito, or little foreigner — a reference not to his height, which was a match for any of the men of the town, but to his pitifully wasted appearance — became a fixture of Doña Nicanora's household. At first, Nicanora, bemused by the Gringito's desire to do nothing all day but sit in her front yard smoking, playing with his unsightly beard and picking his teeth, decided that he had probably had to leave his village because his mother had thrown him out of her house on account of his bad manners and suspect personal hygiene. She worried that the Gringito, who appeared to

5

be quite harmless, might do something unpredictable in the middle of the night, like suck the fat out of her body while she was sleeping and sell it to a cosmetics factory in the United States to make into lipsticks. She had heard of these things happening, indeed her neighbour's sister-in-law had died of such an affliction after sitting next to a gringo on a bus.

But the arrival of the Gringito had also brought an unexplained tranquillity to her household. Nena, who at twelve years old was always difficult to keep occupied, appeared to have adopted him as a sort of pet and now spent her time when not at school trying to teach him new commands and tricks. She had managed to convince him to stand on his head in the yard for an hour balancing a cup of water on his feet, 'to make the rains come early'. She had him repeating for hours on end long lists of fictitious words, made up for his benefit, which were slowly evolving into a secret language between them. She had even tried to teach him to spin cotton backwards, much to Nicanora's amusement. Isabela, whose main occupation over the past year had been teasing the neighbour's son, had shifted some of her flirtatious attention to the Gringito and was consequently spending more time at home helping her mother. For the sheer amusement of seeing the Gringito's cheeks redden as she swept past him, making sure her bare flesh brushed against his, Isabela would spend hours at home helping her mother with the cleaning, cooking and washing. Ernesto, as Nicanora observed to Fidelia, also appeared to have uncharacteristically settled down. However, it was the young doctor to whom she felt indebted for this transformation.

'Nicanora,' Doña Fidelia warned her as they sat together in the market one day, 'you're my neighbour and my friend and what

6

hurts you will also hurt me. You must have heard what people are saying. It's very odd, two strangers suddenly turning up from nowhere in a space of a few weeks, and both seem to have something to do with your Ernesto.'

'I don't know what you mean,' Nicanora said, feeling the sharp significance of Fidelia's barbs.

'You must be careful, is all I'm saying,' Fidelia replied. 'You can't go giving food and shelter to any old foreigner Ernesto decides to drag into your house.'

Doña Nicanora, wary of Fidelia's propensity for jealousy, omitted to tell her friend that the Gringito was now paying her more money a week for his board and lodging than she could possibly earn in months at the market.

'But Fidelia,' she replied, 'we must help strangers and then when we come to make a journey someone is bound to help us in return. Besides, what harm can he do? He's a friend of Ernesto's. The boy has calmed down such a lot since he arrived home with this foreigner, you must have seen how he's changed. He's now working for the doctor, and he has his own pickup truck.'

'Nicanora, don't be fooled,' Fidelia retorted. 'Your boy is wild, just like his father. He always has been and he always will be, pickup truck or no pickup truck. He has no sense for what trouble he may cause with his goings-on. Remember those disgusting giant lizards he dragged out of the swamp to sell to us as guard dogs – they ate all my chickens and killed your goat. He has no sense and no self-control. Who knows what further trouble he'll bring to this town? I tell you, Nicanora, there are many children running around with his hooked nose. And that doctor must be a simpleton as well, otherwise why would he spend his days hanging around here with your boy rather than making money from the people in the city?

And what do you know about this Gringito anyway? Where does he come from?'

Nicanora, choosing yet again to ignore the various insults that peppered Fidelia's conversation, had to confess to her neighbour that she knew very little about her house guest. The Gringito appeared to lack any ability to converse in an understandable way with anyone except Nena, who had somehow been able to make sense of the sentences he occasionally tried to put together with the aid of the battered little book he kept in his pocket. What was more, she had no interest in knowing anything about him, sticking in this instance to her mother's philosophy of 'What you don't know can't trouble you.'

'All I'm saying to you, Nicanora, as a friend and neighbour,' Fidelia continued, 'is, be on your guard. These foreigners aren't always what they seem. I told you about my poor husband's sister. She went to the city to sell her vegetables and arrived home a mere shadow of herself after sitting next to one of these gringos. During the night she started to piss blood, then she got thinner and thinner and within a month she was dead. The gringo had drained the life out of her, and he took her fat back home with him to make into soap. All I'm saying, Nicanora, is be careful of this Gringito.' Nicanora had heard this story many times before, and had dismissed it as fanciful nonsense dreamed up by Fidelia's in-laws, but recently the significance of the tale had begun to grow in potency.

*

Despite her worst fears, life had become immeasurably easier in Nicanora's household since the arrival of the Gringito. The money he supplied was helping to keep food on the table, finally pay off

8

Ernesto's numerous debts, buy Nena's school books and hold the moneylender at bay. And now she found she had enough left over to begin to refuel her dream of opening Valle de la Virgen's first ever hat shop. In the middle of the night she started to see scenes of the grand opening. She could visualise the queues of anxious people waiting for the latest fashions to arrive from the city, and the sheer beauty of the hand-made hats that she would bring to the town. She would wake up with a long-forgotten but familiar voice repeating in her head, 'Nicanora, it is your destiny,' as if the ancestors were trying to tell her that she finally had a purpose.

Knowing instinctively that location is of the utmost importance to the success of any business, Nicanora had her eye on the small shop on the corner of the plaza, opposite the church and near the mayor's office. It was the only premises suitable for her exclusive merchandise, its interior lending itself perfectly to the display of elegant hats. Being in the main square it was passed by everyone en route to the market, or taking the road out of town. The only obstacle that lay between her and her dream was that the shop was owned by Don Bosco the barber, had been for over twenty years, and the afternoon meetings at Don Bosco's shop to discuss the events of the day were a greater tradition among the men of the town than paying homage to the Virgin herself. She even ventured to discuss the hat shop with a few friends and neighbours, to test out the level of demand that existed for such an establishment. Her idea was met with stupefied derision.

'You're becoming as bad as that son of yours,' Fidelia warned. 'Nicanora, you're not a young woman. I notice new wrinkles appearing on your face every day. You can't go gallivanting back and forth to the city to buy ridiculous hats that will only fall into the swamp the first time we wear them. Be content with what you

9

have, as I am, and, God willing, your children will look after you. Nena studies hard, she'll probably grow up to be a teacher if she doesn't ruin her eyes reading before she's old enough. Isabela, well let's hope she'll marry a rich man, she'll certainly have to get married soon if she carries on the way she is. And Ernesto − of course the less said about him the better, but perhaps he'll finally leave home one day and stop bleeding you dry. Anyway, where would you get the money from to start up such a thing?' And there Fidelia had the last word. Even the moneylender would refuse her any more capital. In her feverish half-sleep, Nicanora worked out that if she could keep the Gringito with her for a few months she would have time to convince Don Bosco to retire and sell the shop, and to save enough for a down payment on her first consignment of hand-made Italian Borsalinos, the finest hats in the city.

Two

Doña Nicanora and Don Bosco had a history, a history that they had both worked hard over the years to forget. Don Bosco had considered Nicanora to be a great beauty in her youth, an idea that Nicanora had dismissed as an illusion created by his poor eyesight. More than twenty years on, he still believed her to be the most beautiful woman he had ever known.

In her early days, Nicanora had enjoyed the attention that Don Pedro Bosco lavished on her. He would walk her to the market every morning, talking with passion of the day he would turn his barber's stall into a respectable business in the plaza. She listened to his plans in apparent awe, laughed at his ridiculous jokes and toyed girlishly with his affections. He waited for her every Sunday afternoon outside the church to walk her round and round the plaza, buying her numerous useless presents from the stalls. His particular favourites were the brightly coloured balloons, which he bought from the old balloon seller who mysteriously appeared every Sunday morning and then vanished at the end of the day back to her unknown village.

Nicanora would return home from her afternoon strolls laden

with the most luxurious and bizarre objects her suitor could find: sugared apples and toffee bananas, watermelon slices and carved mango on sticks, paper windmills that spun in the breeze, raffia dolls and wooden dogs whose heads nodded in agreement every time Don Bosco spoke, tinted glasses that he put on her to make the world look pink and hopeful, and scented balms that were made from the fat of the *tigre* that roamed the forest, bought for her to protect her 'beautiful and succulent lips'. Don Bosco would walk her home, picking fruit and bunches of flowers along the way, talking of the day that he would make her the envy of the town. Nicanora listened and laughed, never indicating that she had the slightest understanding of his intentions. Nicanora's Sunday exuberance was always expertly deflated by her mother as soon as she entered the house.

'How long are you going to lead that poor man on for?' her mother scolded. 'What are you going to do when he finally asks you to marry him?'

'I haven't thought about it,' Nicanora lied.

'Well, you had better start to think about it, my girl, because he is bound to get around to asking you sometime, the hopeless fool. You've been parading yourself in the plaza with him for the past two years, like some careless hussy. Everybody has seen you. If you break his heart, people will find it hard to forgive you. He's well liked.' Nicanora managed to ignore her mother's warnings, convinced that Don Bosco had taken so long to buy the barber's shop that it would never really happen, and that even if he did he would still never manage to pluck up the courage to ask her to marry him. Besides, she was young enough not to care what anyone thought of her. She knew her future lay elsewhere.

Don Bosco had worked tirelessly to save up the money to buy

the lease for the shop in the plaza, which he believed to be the finest building in town. It was owned by the family of Doña Teresa, as were all the best properties in Valle de la Virgen. The purchase of the shop involved some very unpleasant dealings with Doña Teresa's great-nephew, Rodriguez Ramirez, who had recently arrived in town to look after the affairs of his great-aunt. The memory of the negotiations still caused Don Bosco acute pain. The haggling went on for over two years, during which time Don Bosco took great care in his courtship with Nicanora to reveal gently his intentions towards her and to convince himself that she returned his feelings. Don Bosco was certain that if he could secure the business and show Nicanora that he was destined to be a man of standing, she would agree to marry him.

Don Ramirez was asking for more than money. Recognising Don Bosco to be a man of future influence, he wanted the barber's commitment to act as his friend and ally in all his political endeavours, an agreement that Don Bosco steadfastly refused to make. Every time Don Bosco came close to achieving the amount agreed, the price of the shop inexplicably rose, taking it just out of his reach again. Finally, desperate to buy the business and terrified that Nicanora would think he was no longer serious about her, he agreed to the terms set out by Don Ramirez. The next day the shop was his. Don Bosco had never breathed a word of what he had done to anyone.

The day that Don Bosco held the keys to his shop in his hand was the proudest and happiest day of his life. The following day marked the beginning of a lifetime of loneliness, sadness and regret. He told only his friends Julio and Teofelo of his plans, and they helped him work through the night to prepare for the occasion, filling the shop with bunches of wild flowers gathered from the forest. The following morning, Don Bosco ran to meet Nicanora to secure his final triumph. He led her, laughing and blindfolded to the plaza, and revealed to her the flower-strewn interior of the shop. Then, on bended knees, he offered her a corner of the business from which to sell her woven shawls, if she would agree to be his companion on his life's journey.

At the age of eighteen, Nicanora did not consider that Don Bosco's life journey would take him or her very far, and certainly not in the direction that she wanted to go. He was ten years older; and kind and attentive though he was, she thought him far too settled and contented with his lot in life. Besides, she had a secret lover who was much more exciting, although a good deal less respectable than Don Bosco. Nicanora had dreams, which certainly did not include a barber's shop. She was determined that she would not spend the rest of her life rotting in a corner of forgotten swampland when there was a world full of cities and adventures just waiting for her.

Nicanora first met Francisco during the fiesta of the Virgin. Francisco was everything that Don Bosco was not. He was tall, and handsome, and full of the danger and carefree vitality of youth. He was the cousin of one of Nicanora's neighbours and had recently set up a business in the river town of Puerta de la Coruña, 'cleaning the filth from the shoes of the rich'. He told Nicanora he was saving enough money to buy a ticket to travel to a distant and exotic location on one of the many boats that came and went along the river. Francisco offered to take Nicanora with him. After a day of festivities which involving countless bottles of beer and vast quantities of *aguardiente*, Francisco and Nicanora made their way into the forest to pay their own tribute to the Virgin, a state that was very quickly lost to Nicanora. Francisco disappeared back to Puerta de la Coruña two days later, promising to return in a few weeks. Nicanora was convinced that she now knew what love was. She could not get the thought of Francisco out of her mind. During her Sunday strolls with Don Bosco she started to imagine that it was her secret lover who was buying her presents and flowers and talking about the future. She managed to close her mind during the long musings about the barber's shop and to imagine that it was her lover talking to her about travelling on boats and visiting foreign lands.

'Don't you ever want to get out of here?' Nicanora once asked, coming back to earth during one of Don Bosco's ramblings.

'Why would I?' he replied. 'When everything I want in the world is right here in the plaza with me.' He gently squeezed Nicanora's hand and her heart missed a beat and then died a little.

Francisco started making frequent visits back to the town, always being careful to meet Nicanora in the forest. Nicanora went to great lengths to ensure that her lover remained a secret, the clandestine nature of their meeting adding to the passion of their moments together. Her mother, who had an unnerving sixth sense, announced to her one day when they were working together on their small plot of land: 'These leaves help to stop babies coming when they are not wanted, and these ones help them come out quickly once they are there.' Nicanora had no idea why her mother had suddenly decided to impart this information to her. She supposed that she must be priming her for marriage and no more was said on the matter. Nicanora kept quiet about her plans to leave, until one day Francisco arrived saying that he had almost saved up enough money to buy their tickets to paradise. He convinced Nicanora that she should leave with him when he returned to Puerta de la Coruña the following day. The day that Francisco offered Nicanora her ticket out of town was the day that Don Bosco clinched the deal on the barber's shop.

Nicanora was so filled with excitement at the prospect of leaving with her lover to discover the mysteries of the world, and with fear at the thought of the perilous journey ahead, that she hardly listened to Don Bosco's prattling as he led her blindfolded to the plaza to show her the great surprise. She did not listen as he told her that the shop would always smell of flowers as long as she was near it, and she did not hear him say that he no longer needed dreams now that he held the keys to their future happiness in his hands. It was only when he got down on his knees in front of her that she realised what he was finally asking of her. She looked down at the man staring lovingly up at her, his legs half buried in flower petals, his eyes smiling with a spirit and warmth that made her heart question her head for the first time, and said nothing.

'Everything I have is yours,' he said, laughing with pride. She stood looking at him. He got up, dusting the petals off his trouser and held her hand. 'You never thought I would manage it, did you? But look – I have – it's mine,' he said, dancing with delight. 'I mean it's ours, if you will have me,' and he bent to kiss her on the cheek. She stood silent.

'So will you, will you have me?'

Nicanora said nothing.

'Will you have me?' he asked again.

Still she was silent.

'I can't,' she said finally, in a whisper.

'What can't you do, my love?' Don Bosco replied, holding on to his self-deception to the last.

'I can't. I'm sorry. I just can't. I can't marry a barber.' He stared at her.

'What did you say?' he asked, almost inaudibly.

'I . . . I can't marry a barber,' she repeated.

He looked at her and then looked at the floor. He tried to speak, but the room resounded with her words. In an instant the shop was transformed. Where there had been bunches of flowers and petals strewn over the floor he now saw a mess of rotting vegetation that needed to be cleared away. Where there was a future home and happiness, he saw a small dingy shop that had cost him his life savings and for which he had signed away his integrity forever.

'Why?' he said finally. 'What's wrong with marrying a barber?'

'Nothing,' she said 'I didn't mean . . .'

'Would you marry me if I were a tailor instead?' he asked, as if all the wrongs that had been done in the last minute could be undone with a swift change of career.

'I don't know. I don't think so,' she replied candidly.

'Well, I'm pleased to hear that it isn't just barbers that you have such distaste for. But you will marry a shoeshine boy?'

'I don't know,' she said, tears of shame now pouring down her cheeks.

'At least marry someone worthy of you,' he said gently and squeezed her hand for the last time. She ran out of the shop and home to tell her mother that tomorrow she was leaving to travel the world. He locked the door, pulled down the shutters, sat among the flower petals and wept.

★

Francisco and Nicanora did not make it to the boat. They got as far as Francisco's small rented room on the outskirts of the town, from which it was possible to see the ferries coming and going, along with Nicanora's dream for her future. Despite his promises, Francisco always remained one month's work away from having the money to buy their tickets.

The first couple of months in Puerta de la Coruña were ones of blind happiness for Nicanora. Even though they were living in a damp, dark room with nothing to cook on and nowhere private to wash, she enjoyed the excitement of having her own home and she thrilled with the touch of Francisco's beautiful body at night. All day, while he was out working, she would long for the smell of his sweat and the touch of his warm dark skin against hers. He would return home with little presents from the market where he sat cleaning shoes, and with stories of the people above the feet he spent his day staring at, which made them both breathless with laughter. He would imitate the voices of his clients and the way they stood looking down on him, and he would tell her glorious lies about the generous tips that they promised him next time they came to the market. He assured her he would be able to buy the tickets within a month.

The tickets never came. At first, she willingly forgave Francisco for his inability to move their lives forward at the pace she had hoped for. She reprimanded herself for being too demanding, her mother's last words to her before she left home still ringing in her head: 'You always were an impetuous and impatient girl. It will be your downfall,' After the first few months, the thrill of lust began to be replaced by the gnawing disquiet of distrust. Francisco started to return home later and later at night, apparently too exhausted from his day's work to stay awake long enough to even begin to satisfy her desires, although usually just long enough to satisfy his own. He would lie lifeless, snoring in her arms, as if the passionate and caring husband of the first few months of their marriage had now been replaced by an overgrown baby with the sour stink of booze, rather than the sweet smell of the breast, on its breath.

Nicanora blamed herself. She was not beautiful enough or a good enough lover to keep her husband interested. Francisco would complain that he was simply too exhausted from his long hours of work to able to be both a good worker and a good husband, and that the pressure to save up so much money so quickly was affecting his manhood. Nicanora sensed the resolve in Francisco to leave the security of his wretched life dissolving with the midday heat of the river town. His absences, which at first only encroached into their nights together, soon began to stretch into days at a time. Nicanora was certain that if she could take Francisco away from the monotony of the life they had so readily slipped into and from whatever temptations were pulling him away from her, the beautiful young lover from the forest would be restored to her. She made up her mind to change their fortunes by not only selling her woven shawls at the side of the road during the busy afternoons, but cleaning the houses of the rich in the mornings.

After six months of hard labour, she had gathered enough money to buy two single tickets to Manola, from where she understood they could sail to anywhere in the world. When she presented the money to Francisco, she lied as to how she had come by it, so as not to make him feel he had failed. She told him that a wealthy elderly patron whose house she had been cleaning had died suddenly, and that his family had given it to her as a thank-you gift. She was surprised at how readily he accepted the unlikely story. They celebrated their good fortune with a feast of roast chicken, throwing liberal quantities of beer on the ground to thank the Mother Earth for her help along the way. The next day Francisco went out proudly with the money in his pockets to buy the tickets, and did not return for three days.

Nicanora had not told Francisco about the bouts of sickness that she had been having for a few months, which at first she put down to the stench of the busy streets. The monthly bleeding, which initially she was relieved to be without, showed no signs of returning. Despite there being scarcely any food in the house, a growing belly had begun to accompany the sickness. She wanted to keep her condition a secret from Francisco until she had saved enough money to buy the tickets, worried that the thought of the added responsibility of a baby would put him off leaving forever. She convinced herself that she could quite as easily look after a child on a boat as she could in a dingy little rented room. He only commented on how life in Puerta de la Coruña must be agreeing with her as she was looking fatter than ever. When Francisco finally returned home after his three-day absence, he came carrying a handful of coloured stones and a pocketful of foreign coins, offering no explanation for his disappearance.

'And the tickets?' she said expectantly.

'I bought them,' he said, unable to meet her eye. 'I did buy them.'

'Well, where are they?' she asked, thinking he was playing a cruel game in which she momentarily saw all hope disappear before he finally produced the promise from his pockets. It was no game. It was the start of her life's disappointments.

'I lost them,' he said.

'Lost them?' she repeated. 'How could you lose them?'

'I just did. In a game. It was a chance, a chance to win us the tickets around the world.'

'You gambled them?'

'It was a good bet. I knew I could win. I had already won these,' and with a sheepish grin he put the stones and coins down on the table in front of her. 'They told me I could sell them. They're rare gemstones – look at the colour. Have you ever seen stones that colour before?'

Nicanora picked them up, green and blue flakes of paint peeling off as she turned them over in her hands. She had never felt rage like it before, not even when conversing with her ancestors. She threw the stones on the floor and flew at him. She grabbed him by the shirt and shook him. She reached for his hair, trying to pull it out by the roots. She slapped his face and then sank down, sick and exhausted.

'We'll try again,' he said, still unable to look at her. 'I'll get the tickets. It'll be all right, I promise.' Then he left the room and disappeared for a week.

*

Nicanora was determined not to give up. She could not face the shame of returning to Valle de la Virgen with a child and no husband, to be chastised by her mother and neighbours for having failed so easily. And she could not face looking every day into the eyes of the man whose feelings she had so carelessly toyed with. She made up her mind that whatever it took she would save enough money to buy the tickets to transport them to a world of hope. For the next three years, Nicanora sat on the streets selling her weavings while Francisco drank, gambled their money away and filled her belly every year with another child. It was during this time that the idea of the hat shop first came to her. She had seen the groups of mountain women who made their way down the treacherous pass for an opportunity to sell their produce in the markets of

Puerta de la Coruña, their bowler hats perched meticulously on their heads. She remembered how, as a child, her mother would tell her stories about life in the mountain village from which her ancestors came, and in particular how she would lament the poor standards of dress in the swamp town to which her husband had brought her. 'In the village where I was born,' her mother would say, 'no self-respecting woman would dream of stepping outside without her smart black bowler on her head.' Or she would click her tongue after her neighbour had walked past bare-headed and mutter: 'Where I come from you could tell the sort of woman your neighbour was by the state of her hat.'

Nicanora would challenge her mother as to why she had let her own standards drop so low and had abandoned her own precious bowler. Her mother would simply reply, 'It doesn't do to stand out from the neighbours. I don't want them killing me with their envy.' It was true. Nicanora had never seen anyone wearing a hat in Valle de la Virgen, with the exception of Don Bosco, who always wore a smart black trilby sent to him by his brother Aurelio to go with his Sunday suit. Don Bosco would not walk out without it, even on the most stiflingly humid days. 'It stops the mosquitoes biting my head and stealing my thoughts,' he explained to Nicanora as the sweat dripped off his face during their Sunday strolls.

For many months now Nicanora's daydreams had been drifting unchecked back to the safety of her hometown. No longer did she wish to be transported to foreign parts and exotic locations. She craved the comfort of her mother's house, and with a regret that was too painful for her to acknowledge, she thought of how one day she might still set up her business in the plaza, selling her shawls, if she could bring herself to look humiliation and sadness in the face.

Her decision was made the day a travelling salesman stopped by her roadside stall. He stood for a long time looking at her woven shawls, touching them gently, running his fingers over the fine fabric of the weave. At last he spoke to her.

'You're very clever,' he said, 'these designs are works of art. Where did you learn how to do them?' Nicanora, at first thinking he was making fun of her, did not answer.

'They really are beautiful,' he said again. 'I like them for my shop. The colours and patterns are exquisite. But I'm afraid I would never be able sell them to the ladies in the city. These are peasant clothes.'

'So what do the women in the city wear?' Nicanora asked, feeling both indignant and deflated. The man pulled some pictures out of his pocket. The photos were of women in glittering jewellery and elegantly laced skirts, and all wearing the most glorious hats. She could not take her eyes off them. She ran her fingers over them as if trying to conjure the hats out of the photographs and into the reality of her world. She imagined herself returning home in one to prove to the townsfolk and above all to her mother, that despite what they thought of her she had made something of her life, and that she could dress like an elegant city woman.

The man stood quietly observing her. 'Would you like one?' he asked finally. 'I have one here in my bag. I will give it to you in exchange for your shawls.' He bent down to undo his travelling case and pulled out a pink box. It contained the most exquisite hat Nicanora had ever seen. It had a soft, delicate sheen that subtly changed colour in the light, transforming itself through shades of pink and blue. It was trimmed with a lace that looked as if it had been woven from diamonds. Nicanora could not bring herself to touch it.

'It's yours,' the man said at last, coaxing her. 'I could sell it for a fortune. It comes all the way from Europe, handmade in Italy. You can have it in exchange for all the weavings you have.' Nicanora knew, in that moment, that destiny had tapped her on the shoulder.

Her mind was now made up. She could no longer stand the squalor and disappointment of her life in a single rented room with only Francisco's lies to support her and the children. She would face her mother and anyone else in Valle de la Virgen who might wish to judge her. She no longer felt she had to hide from the man whose goodness she had spurned and whose hopes she had destroyed. She knew who she was and what she was worth and it was far more than the life she was living now. In a moment of inspiration she knew where her destiny lay. She would bring joy and elegance to her hometown. She would save every penny she earned, and one day soon she would open Valle de la Virgen's first ever hat shop, and this was the jewel in her collection.

She rushed home and gathered the results of her hard labour and handed them over to the man in exchange for the pink box. He tipped his hat to her as he departed and wished her a life full of surprises. She packed a small bag, and with the precious hatbox in her hand, a baby on her back and her children beside her, she made her way home for good. It was only when she arrived at her mother's house, beaten and worn after three weeks travelling and with sick children to nurse back to health, that she realised she had been cheated. She had tentatively peered inside the box, but it was wrapped so beautifully in soft pink tissue paper and tied with ribbon that she wanted to leave it in its pristine state until she presented it to her mother. When she finally opened the box to reveal to her mother the woman she had become, she found a plain straw hat on which sat a bright pink plastic rose. It was the only possession she had to show for her three years' toil on the streets of Puerta de la Coruña.

Several months later, Francisco arrived back from one of his many long absences wandering the area in search of profitable work to find another miserable and hungry family living in their rented room. It took him several hours to recognise that the sleeping children were not his own. It was only when their mother returned home and pleaded with him not to hurt them that he realised they were strangers and that his family had disappeared.

*

Nicanora put her mind to feeding the rapidly growing appetites of her children. She continued to weave her shawls, which she hawked around the surrounding villages, but nobody ever again picked them up with such tenderness and appreciation as the man who had shown her that perfection could exist in a single object. She set up a small stall selling fruit and cooked food for the men who passed through the market on their way to and from the estate and their small plots of land. The money she earned was barely enough to pay for the food to feed her family. Her dream and the straw hat were safely locked away – alongside her cherished hopes for her children – in a mental box marked 'Life's unfulfilled promises'.

She saw Francisco only one more time. He arrived suddenly one night at her mother's house some years later wearing a smart suit, and regaled a wiser Nicanora with stories of how he was on the brink of making his fortune from his endeavours in gold prospecting, pig farming, matchmaking and storytelling. She listened to him with no more interest than she had listened to her mother's warnings in her youth. He stayed for one last night, a night in which some of the passion of their first few months together was rekindled for old times sake, and then disappeared the next day promising to return with the money to change his family's destiny. Nicanora sensed that she would not see him again. She did not expect, however, that his body would be found three days later splattered at the foot of the cliff. He had been seen the day he left by one of the townsfolk, who had passed him stumbling drunkenly near the cliff edge, shouting about the great future he was about to give his wife and children. He left one lasting reminder of his visit. Nine months later Nena was born. As Nicanora stared into the eyes of her freshly delivered bloodstained daughter, she knew that Francisco had on his final journey been able to leave her with the most precious gift possible.

*

Don Bosco in the meantime resigned himself to a lifetime of bachelorhood and the removal of unwanted beards. He seldom ventured outside his shop, sleeping in the small room above and trying hard to keep himself out of the affairs of the town. His self-imposed isolation was thwarted by his natural good humour and charm, which despite all his efforts to the contrary drew people to him. Within a couple of years the barber's shop had become known as the place to seek solace and advice for all manner of misdemeanours and problems, ranging from neighbourly disputes to marital infidelities. It was Don Bosco who settled the long-running and deeply felt quarrel between Don Julio and Don Alfredo over whose goat should be allowed to be tethered to the post situated equidistantly between their houses. Don Bosco finally came up with a compromise position, allowing each of them access to the post on alternate days and declaring Sunday a rest day for the post, during which time both goats wandered freely into Don Teofelo's yard, causing another grievance that took a further year to settle.

Don Bosco's barber's shop became the unofficial meeting place of the men of the town. They would gather to watch and commiserate over the ritual humiliation of the national football team played out on the rickety black-and-white television, which at popular request had been installed in the corner of the shop, whilst airing their grievances against the goalkeeper, the president and the mayor. 'He should be shot,' was the usual cry that echoed around the shop, directed towards all three.

For over twenty years, Don Bosco's had been the place where the disgruntled and disaffected would meet and talk confidently about how, if they were mayor, they would do things differently. Nobody could understand why, when the first free elections took place, Don Bosco refused to stand. Despite the insistence of his patrons that nobody would vote against Don Ramirez unless he gave his public support to a challenge, Don Bosco stood firm. He simply said that he wanted a life of peace and quiet away from the ups and downs of politics and that he was better suited to the business of cutting hair than cutting remarks. 'Why don't you stand yourself?' Don Bosco would challenge the more belligerent among them, to which nobody could think of a better response than that they were either too busy or too unreliable to take on such an important task. In truth, nobody was prepared to make a challenge to the family who owned the homes they lived in. Don Bosco, on the other hand, who owned his business and had no wife or family to support, apparently had nothing to lose.

Don Bosco and Doña Nicanora maintained a respectful distance from each other over the years, exchanging pleasantries whenever their paths crossed as if nothing had passed between them. Don Bosco's playful remarks always left Nicanora with an uncertain aftertaste, unsure whether they were meant as a sour compliment or a sugary insult. 'And how is your exuberant brood?' he would ask with interest as she passed by with her screaming and giggling children. 'They do you proud, my dear Nicanora,' he would add, surreptitiously pressing sweets into her children's clammy, searching little hands. On other occasions he would compliment her, saying, 'My dear Nicanora, your children are just like little rose blossoms, with the possible exception of Ernesto.' He would bend down and pinch the children on their cheeks before Nicanora had a chance to wipe away the dirt and food that had invariably stuck to their faces. Or he would stop with a remark such as, 'You must be so proud of Ernesto. My dear Nicanora, there can be no greater sacrifice than to give your life to the rearing of our great nation's future intelligentsia.' Then, checking himself, he would ask with a gentle look of concern, 'But you, Nicanora, you're content and keeping well, I trust?'

Nicanora always left her encounters with Don Bosco with a confusion of emotion. In all their years of pleasantries, neither she nor Don Bosco had ever mentioned the events that had passed between them and neither had ever made any reference to Francisco. The regret that Nicanora felt for the arrogance of her youth, which had led her to tread so roughly over the feelings of a man whom with the wisdom of experience she now recognised was kinder than any she had known, had troubled her over the years. And yet she felt unable to move beyond their casual banter and offer the apology, which although it could never change their past, would at least give her heart some peace. Instead she usually replied with formality, saying something like, 'As well as can be expected under the circumstances, thank you, Don Bosco,' never really sure which circumstances she was referring to.

Until the day he died, Francisco remained blissfully ignorant of the full details of the history that had preceded his marriage to Nicanora. But it was Don Bosco who had been there when Nicanora had needed him most. He had quietly and discreetly helped with the arrangements for Francisco's funeral, making sure that the ceremony was carried out with solemnity and dignity. Francisco's body had been too dismembered, picked about by carrion, to be fully recovered from the valley after the fall. And so, Nicanora had lain Francisco's suit in the coffin, along with the old stones and coins he had brought back for her from his first gambling trip, and said a final farewell to the illusion that had taken away her youth.

Three

Life at the clinic was becoming a little more settled for the young doctor, who had quickly established a comfortable daily routine with his assistant, Ernesto. As soon as Arturo heard the first rumble of the pickup's wheels making their way along the potholed mud road, he lit the gas burner and placed a pan of coffee on top, knowing that by the time Ernesto reached the clinic the thick, strong, sweet brew would be ready. By this point in the mid-morning he had carried out his daily check of the medicine cabinet, swept the rotting vegetation and dead insects off the clinic floor and polished the microscope, a parting present from his father. Even though Arturo had no work to give to Ernesto and was paying him a substantial portion of the allowance that his father had sent him off with, he was extremely grateful to have a companion to talk to.

At first, nobody had paid much attention to the arrival of the young doctor in town. His presence had not been noticed for at least ten days, when he was eventually spotted in the market trying to buy fish and potatoes during the annual shoe fair. Dr Arturo Aguilar had arrived in the middle of the night, on a donkey from

Rosas Pampas arranged for him by Ramon, the mayor's assistant, and had spent the first week of his stay in Valle de la Virgen lying on the floor of the clinic in a feverish state, only occasionally venturing outside to vomit and relieve his twisting and watery bowels in a small pit latrine. Ramon visited him on his first day, bringing him a few supplies of fruit as a welcome present, a box of medicines sent by the district health authority and a mound of forms to sign and paperwork to fill in. Ramon had been so appalled by the state of the new arrival as he lay moaning on the clinic floor that he at first suggested taking him to see the medicine man. Realising that this was inappropriate under the circumstances, he then decided to leave the young doctor to his own devices and hope he would soon sort himself out.

Ramon mentioned to a few of his neighbours that a sick doctor had arrived. Some of the more interested and concerned townsfolk wandered close to the clinic to try and catch a glimpse of him and to offer a variety of concoctions known to be good for troublesome bowels, including a plate of papaya seeds, a dish of cold fish soup, a variety of herbal teas and a half-drunk bottle of Coca-Cola. Fear that the doctor might have brought a highly infectious disease with him from the city prevented them from getting too close. When Arturo finally emerged from his malaise, the only sign that he had had any visitors was the little line of offerings left at the end of the path, which by the time he stumbled across them were swarming with ants. It was only after the first appearance of the young man in the market that word really began to get around and rumours and suppositions started to spread. Once Arturo had recovered from his bout of dysentery, brought on by drinking the rancid water served to him in the guise of coffee at his guest house in Rosas Pampas, he made a diligent effort to get to know his surroundings and make his acquaintance with the townsfolk visiting the market every day.

He struggled considerably in his early encounters with the market, his initial approach having been to go there with some thought in mind of what he wanted to buy. The market, it seemed, always had other ideas for him. During his first week of recuperation he had gone there with a growing desperation to buy fish and vegetables with which to prepare a nutritious meal, only to be confronted with row upon row of stalls piled high with old boots and a range of sandals made out of used car tyres. Three months later, when the soles of his shoes had completely rotted away, he realised with regret how foolish he had been not to stock up with boots when the opportunity of the annual shoe fair had presented itself. There appeared to be no rationale to what was on offer on any particular day of the week, or in any particular week of the month. The market always took a perverse pleasure in thwarting his plans, and after several weeks of disappointment and frustration he finally decided to give in and leave his shopping to serendipity. The only certainty was that if he had an idea in mind of something he wanted to buy it would not be available on the day he wanted it and usually then for some time to come. If he desired fish, the stalls would abound with goat. If he wanted rice, there would be no end of dried pasta. When he finally decided to content himself with buying only the fruit that grew in abundance in the vicinity and was the one item consistently on offer, the fruit sellers suddenly left town for a month. For two weeks they were replaced by an influx of mountain women on their annual pilgrimage to sell dried llama foetuses, along with the neat alcohol, Camel cigarettes and little pink and white sweets that were intended as offerings to the unpredictable Mother Earth in exchange for the wandering souls of sick children, which she was so often inclined to devour if her insatiable hunger and sweet tooth were not appeased.

*

Arturo greeted his assistant with two steaming cups of coffee in hand. He looked forward to this point in the morning, when he could sit down with his assistant and learn more about his new surroundings.

'Ernesto, good to see you,' he said warmly. 'Before we start our work, there is something I want to ask you.'

Ernesto was a little surprised by the doctor's suggestion of work. In over a month of their routine, work had not been mentioned. Not liking to point out this inconsistency in an arrangement that suited him just fine, Ernesto had not ventured to raise the subject either. Arturo sat down on the step of the clinic, handing Ernesto the coffee. 'Tell me,' he said, 'tell me again the story of the Virgin of the Swamp. Is she really in the church, as people say? Why is the church always locked?'

Ernesto noticed a slight change in the mood of the usually cheerful doctor. He seemed suddenly to be a little pensive, even sad. On several occasions over the past few weeks he had asked Ernesto why nobody ever visited the clinic. Ernesto tried to reassure him, suggesting that it was because nobody ever got ill; but this answer did not satisfy the doctor, who replied that if this was the case, it begged the question of why the authorities had sent him there in the first place. On this morning the doctor seemed particularly agitated.

'Well, the story goes like this,' Ernesto began. 'The old priest who went missing in the swamp told it to me. He lived in the church

33

for about ten years. He was a missionary — he told me he came from Italy. He spent a lot of time talking to the old people, and he had read all the history books that were written by our great-grandfathers.'

'History books,' Arturo said now with more enthusiasm in his voice. 'Where are they, Ernesto? Can I read them?'

'When the priest disappeared, I was just a boy,' Ernesto continued. 'The books disappeared with him. As many people in the town couldn't read, nobody was very bothered about them going missing — except for Don Bosco. But the disappearance of the priest was a mystery — he went without a trace.' Ernesto paused for a reaction from the doctor, but there was no response. Arturo just stared ahead at the line of trees that marked out the edge of the forest.

'Some say he was eaten by the spirits that wander the swamp at night,' Ernesto continued. 'Others say he simply left in the middle of the night and went abroad. He took the books with him, and they say he sold them along with photographs of the Virgin weeping and became a very rich man.'

'Have you ever seen the Virgin weep?' Arturo asked, a note of scepticism in his voice.

'The priest was the only person in over fifty years to have seen that happen,' Ernesto said, enjoying his new status as a voice of authority. 'Nobody has been able to see the Virgin for years. We are only allowed to look at her during the fiesta, but we haven't held one for over ten years now. The mayor keeps the church locked for security, because the Virgin is so valuable.'

'I've been waiting for the mayor to return ever since I arrived,' Arturo said. 'I was going to ask him to unlock the church for me to see inside. Do you think he would?'

'I doubt it very much,' said Ernesto. 'Because the priest took photographs of the Virgin, people say there is now a curse on the town. This is the reason why our children get sick,' he said, contradicting himself, 'why people die on the road, why the tourists never come here, and why we remain poor. The mayor says it's because of the curse that he keeps the Virgin locked away. It is said that the Virgin will only weep again once all is put to right, after the foreign priest stole her tears,' Ernesto continued.

The doctor suddenly had a sick feeling in his stomach. He had never experienced loneliness before, and was still struggling to identify the emotion that had been starting to gnaw at him for the past few weeks. As he gazed out at the unforgiving forest he felt more insignificant and more alone than he could ever remember. He longed to be home. He missed his mother. He missed her cooking. He was sick of eating the stewed fish he prepared alone at night on his single-ring gas stove. He was tired of people whispering about him behind his back as he wandered around the market, and he was frustrated by people misunderstanding every word he uttered even though they spoke the same language as him. He even found himself missing the long philosophical arguments he had had with his father about the pros and cons of democratic government and whether the peasants really deserved the vote. He missed going to the *Cine* on a Saturday afternoon and being able to discuss with his friends the latest movies brought over from the United States. Most of all, he missed Claudia, his forbidden love. And yet there was another and far more disconcerting feeling growing inside him that was slowly beginning to compete with his homesickness. It was a sense of a new-found freedom, a freedom to explore who he really was and who he wanted to be; Above anything, he simply wanted to be accepted, to be a part of things, and for the first time in his life to stop being a stranger. He was growing tired of waiting for the day when a patient might show up unexpectedly at his clinic.

'So what do people here say about me?' Arturo asked.

'Well, people here like to gossip. I wouldn't take any notice,' Ernesto said.

'Really, Ernesto,' Arturo replied, 'do you believe all this nonsense you have been telling me this morning? You're young and a man of the world, you've travelled – well, at least as far as Puerta de la Coruña. I've been here for over a month now and not a single patient except you has entered my clinic. First you tell me to wait until people get to know me. I've been to the market every day and greeted people and introduced myself, and still nobody comes. Then you tell me that nobody is ill and that I will have to wait for the next plague to hit, and now suddenly you tell me that people are actually dropping down like flies because of some curse put on them twenty years ago because of a priest who probably got drunk and fell into the swamp.'

Ernesto was a little shocked by the sudden emotion that had entered into the doctor's usually placid voice. 'Well, I wouldn't worry about it, doctor,' he tried to reassure him again. 'Nobody really minds you being here.'

'But Ernesto, don't you understand?' Arturo replied. 'I don't want to be sent home by the authorities for not doing my job properly. My father would never forgive me. Claudia would despise me –' Here he stopped himself. 'I don't know what I'm going to do.'

'What's wrong, doctor?' Ernesto asked, suddenly worried that this was the point at which the issue of work was going to be raised. 'Is something worrying you?'

'Yes, something is worrying me, Ernesto,' the doctor replied in a calmer voice, glancing at a piece of paper he had been holding in his hand. 'Tell me, Ernesto, what's the mayor like?'

'The mayor?' Ernesto replied. 'The mayor is a very difficult man.'

*

The mayor, to Ernesto explained, had held his post for the past twenty years, nobody having yet been bold enough to challenge him. He had arrived in Valle de la Virgen as a young man, the great-nephew of Doña Teresa, the señora who lived in the large house set back from the road, whose family owned most of the land around the town. The story was told that he had been sent by his father to help look after his great-aunt, having been forced to leave the family house after an incident that had brought shame to his parents. The elderly people of the area still talked about the times when they had had to bend down and kiss the feet of Doña Teresa and her husband Don Pedro whenever they ventured into town. That was before the peasants' revolt, and the land reforms brought in by the new revolutionary government. Don Pedro had died of a heart attack at the shock of hearing news of the revolution, although this had proved to be an unnecessary response, as nothing had really changed afterwards. Doña Teresa kept her house and most of the best land in the hills surrounding the town, paying the families who worked her estate meagre wages to grow her coffee for her. Only the most difficult and uncompromising pockets of swampland had been turned over to the peasants, so that they could grow their own crops. Living in constant fear of the riots that had swept other parts of the country at the time of the revolution, Doña Teresa had refused ever to leave her house again. This had also been

37

an overreaction, as the townsfolk had never contemplated rioting, considering it to be an unnecessary ostentation and a waste of valuable energy. Doña Teresa was now an old woman – Ernesto estimated she must be in her eighties or even nineties – but she had not been seen by most inhabitants of the town for nearly fifty years.

'And the mayor?' Arturo asked again. 'What sort of a man is he?'

'Well,' Ernesto replied. 'He's very large. And he always gets his own way.'

'What am I going to do?' the anxious doctor said. 'I've just received a note from Ramon saying the mayor will be returning soon and I must prepare myself for a visit. Apparently he will want to see "what a busy and thriving clinic we have here".'

Ernesto thought about the situation in silence.

'Don't you think', the doctor continued after a while, 'that maybe the reason you don't get any visitors to this town is not because of some curse put on you because of a drunk priest, but because the people here are so unfriendly to strangers? Look at how you treat that Gringito of yours. From what you tell me, your sisters tease him mercilessly, and nobody has made any effort to get to know anything about him.'

'That's true,' replied Ernesto, 'but he is a little strange. Even stranger than the other foreigners I saw in Puerta de la Coruña.'

'Well, yes,' Arturo replied, 'he certainly does sound a bit odd.'

*

Isabela entered the house in her usual style, tweaking Nena on the ear as she breezed past, making her young sister squeal with pain and look up from her school books. After smiling at the Gringito, who was sitting on a blanket in the corner, she sat down at the table. Turning to Ernesto, who had just returned home from his morning with the doctor, she demanded, 'So what has lazy arse been up to this morning?'

'I won't have foul language like that in my house!' Nicanora shouted from the kitchen. 'If you want to behave like a tramp, go out in the street and eat with the dogs.' If she could not so clearly remember the morning nineteen years ago when she had finally given birth to Isabela, after days of life-threatening struggle between mother and infant, Nicanora would have sworn that the girl could not possibly be hers. For one thing, Isabela was extremely beautiful. 'If you have nothing better to do, come out here and help me prepare the food,' Nicanora called to Isabela, who was performing a little dance for the benefit of the Gringito. Ernesto turned to his younger sister and fondly asked her what she had been up to that morning.

'Well, the teacher is on strike again,' she said. 'We've run out of chalk and somebody has stolen all the desks out of the schoolroom, so there is nowhere to write and nothing to write with. So I've been teaching the Gringito how to protect himself if he's attacked by a pack of wild dogs.'

'How did you do that?' her brother asked. Calling the Gringito to attention, she took Ernesto out into the yard to show him.

'Stand over there,' Nena demanded of the Gringito, who smiled kindly back at her, looking confused, and continued standing where he was in the front yard. Nena took the Gringito by the hand and led him into the middle of the dusty street that ran between the rows of mud-brick houses. Ernesto followed.

'Now, remember,' Nena instructed the Gringito. 'When I shout the word "tree" you must stand like this.' And Nena demonstrated being a tree, standing on one leg and holding her hands above her head. 'If you pretend to be a tree, they won't attack you,' she explained to her brother. The Gringito smiled benignly and lit a cigarette.

'Are you sure he understands what you're saying?' Ernesto asked.

'I think so,' Nena replied. 'I tried a demonstration run with Lucho this morning and it seemed to worked quite well.' Lucho looked up from the bone he was chewing on his small patch of turf in front of the house and growled, making it clear that he no longer wanted to play.

'Now, stay there a minute,' Nena called to the Gringito. She disappeared into the house, and returned a few minutes later with a piece of meat she had managed to steal while her mother was not looking.

Nena gave a piercing whistle. The pack of dogs prowling the lower end of the street stood to attention as she hurled the meat in the direction of the Gringito. A stunned silence filled the air for a few fleeting seconds, before being replaced by a howling and gnashing of teeth as the pack of dogs flew up the street past Ernesto and Nena in the direction of the uncomprehending Gringito.

'Tree!' Nena shouted.

Nothing happened.

'Tree!' Nena shouted again. Still nothing happened.

Suddenly, a look of horror crossed the Gringito's face as he realised what was about to strike.

'Tree!' Nena shouted again.

The Gringito suddenly raised one leg and wobbled precariously, flailing his hands above his head, as the leader of the pack flew through the air and grabbed one of his wayward limbs.

'*Por dios*, Nena!' Ernesto gasped, as the Gringito tumbled to the ground like a felled eucalyptus.

Ernesto grabbed a handful of stones and ran towards the Gringito, hurling them in the general direction of the pack. Lucho, suddenly awakened from his lethargy, decided to join the party and made for the biggest, ugliest-looking dog, which was just about to take a bite out of the Gringito's leg. The noise of the fray brought Nicanora running from the house, and with a few expertly aimed stones and words she sent the pack of dogs running in one direction and Ernesto, Nena and Lucho in the other, leaving the lone Gringito quivering on the ground.

Nicanora ran up to the Gringito to inspect the damage. There was a bloody gash in one arm, his shirt and trousers were torn to shreds, and he was making a whimpering sound. Nicanora helped the shaking Gringito to his feet and led him into the house, shouting to Isabela to boil up a soothing brew of camomile tea. Nicanora washed the gashed arm with warm herb-filled water and bound it with some clean cloth that she tore from one of Ernesto's shirts. After some time, and several cigarettes, the Gringito calmed down and stopped shaking. Nicanora made him lie down, covering him with a blanket and sat with him until he fell asleep.

Nena and Ernesto did not appear back home for some time. Nena was barred from talking to the Gringito for a week unless supervised by her mother, and Ernesto was made to sew up the Gringito's torn clothes. After a good sleep, their guest appeared to perk up and was even able to eat a large bowl of soup in the evening. Raising his head from his meal, he muttered something appreciatively to Nicanora.

'What did he say?' she asked Nena.

'He said that the chicken soup is delicious.' Nena giggled nervously.

'Oh,' said Isabela. 'Then I suppose we'd better not tell him that it's snake.'

*

After the tree incident, the Gringito started to spend less time in Nicanora's house and more time sitting in the plaza. He would leave the house when Isabela was around and, although always friendly to Nena, he became a little more wary of being the centrepiece of her antics. Nicanora began to notice him sitting on the bench at the side of the plaza in the afternoons as she made her way back home from the market. Sometimes she would stop and try to pass the time of day with him. Occasionally, he would be writing in a little note-book, but more often than not he would just be sitting in a trance-like state watching people hurrying backward and forwards on their way to and from the fields, the school and Don Bosco's barber shop. Gradually he began to spend whole days in the plaza without even returning to the house for lunch. Nicanora would see him set off in the morning on his long, circuitous routes, which consisted of any amount of detours to avoid the packs of marauding dogs that mercilessly prowled the side streets.

Then Nicanora noticed that he had shifted his attention from the bench at the side of the plaza to the old eucalyptus tree in the centre. It began with him sitting under the tree, smoking and reading. Nena would often sit and chat with him there on her way to and from school, and Nicanora started to send her down to the plaza at lunchtime with a bowl of rice and stewed fish. A scrupulously honest woman, Nicanora felt that, as the Gringito was paying for their food, he ought at least to be able to eat some of it. Don Bosco, who delighted in observing the daily comings and goings in the plaza, also began to comment to Nicanora on her strange house guest.

'Ah, my dear Nicanora,' he greeted her one day as she hurried past his shop working out her strategy for usurping his business. 'I believe we are indebted to your delightful Ernesto for having introduced yet another strange creature to our town. Hopefully, this one will not be as difficult to tame as those delightful giant lizards.'

Nicanora hated sarcasm, but Don Bosco's observations were always delivered with his irrepressible smile and a glint in his eye. Nicanora struggled for a suitably quick-witted reply and failed. Don Bosco was the only person in whose presence she became lost for words, the memory of their past never far from her mind.

'He's a foreigner. He's come a long way, and I'm very proud that he's decided to stay in my house during his time here,' she replied with an unnecessarily haughty air.

'And well you might be, Nicanora,' Don Bosco said. 'He's truly a great find. For how long do you think our humble town will benefit from his presence?'

'I don't know,' Nicanora said, not wishing to divulge her plans to keep the Gringito for as long as was necessary to make a successful bid for Don Bosco's shop.

'Well, I'm sure our good and honest mayor will be most delighted to be greeted by a chanting foreigner outside his office – that is, when he finally decides to grace us with his company again.'

The chanting to which Don Bosco referred had been a recent addition to the Gringito's daily repertoire of strange behaviour. It had started with short episodes of humming, during which time he sat under the eucalyptus tree cross-legged and with his eyes shut. Then one day Nena noticed, as she brought him his lunch bowl, that he seemed to be talking to himself and repeating the same strange words over and over again. After the humming and chanting episodes began, Nena also noticed a pungent smell wafting around the square as the Gringito sat smoking his cigarettes and burning little pieces of twig that he stuck into the ground around the eucalyptus tree.

Although his behaviour in the plaza seemed to be becoming more and more bizarre, he was much the same as he had always been in Nicanora's house, entertaining Nena, getting in everyone's way and smiling hopelessly when anyone asked him a question. Finally exasperated by the continual jibes made by Don Bosco, Nicanora asked Nena to find out from the Gringito what all this business in the plaza was about.

'Apparently he's on a journey,' Nena reported.

'What do you mean "he's on a journey"?' Nicanora asked irritably.

'That's what he said. He's on a personal journey.'

'Well,' retorted Nicanora. 'If he's on a journey, could you ask him if he could please move around a bit while he's making it. This sitting under the eucalyptus tree all day is disturbing the children and upsetting Don Bosco, and heaven knows what the mayor will say when he gets back. I don't want to have to deal with the consequences.'

'All right,' said Nena, who skipped off to the plaza to find the Gringito and suggest a more appropriate route for his personal travels.

When Nena got to the square, she found that the Gringito was no longer sitting cross-legged under the tree, but was now standing on his head. Deciding that either the world had turned upside down or the Gringito had finally gone mad, she went home to tell her mother.

Four

Arturo sat in the plaza reflecting on life. It had become part of his daily routine over the past weeks. He was becoming quietly accustomed to his contemplative existence and he was struggling with guilt over the intoxicating sense of freedom he was enjoying away from his mother's cloying affection and his father's unbending disapproval. In truth, he was relishing the liberation of having, for the first time in his life, nobody to tell him what he should think and who he should be. Indeed, nobody seemed to care that he was there at all. He was confused by the mixed sense of loss and relief he felt away from the hold of Claudia's charismatic charms, which in his youth had given him the strength to disobey his parents' wishes, always with the hidden safety of knowing that he was meeting with Claudia's approval. He sat gazing at the little square, a yearning growing in him to become a part of the life of the uncomplicated town: simply to be accepted for himself.

As usual, a group of men were seated at a table outside the barber's shop. They were eating watermelon and drinking beer, engaged in a lively debate. The only other sign of activity in the middle of the weekday afternoon was the gentle humming of the Gringito as he sat under the eucalyptus tree, and an emaciated dog who sidled up to the men only to be chased away with handfuls of watermelon pips. As yet, Arturo had not spoken to the men, beyond the exchange of a friendly nod and greeting, and they seemed to eye him with a wary suspicion. He felt a surge of warmth as he looked at them, trying to pluck up the courage to go over and make conversation. They were dressed just like the peasants he had seen everyday of his life as they flooded into the city to sell their produce in the large central market, which, as a boy, his mother had forbidden him from visiting.

'Don't get too close to them,' she would warn. 'They are crawling with lice and carry all sorts of diseases on their clothes that will make your fingers and toes drop off. There was a good reason why they didn't used to be allowed to ride on the buses,' she would deliberate loudly within earshot of their maid Doña Julia. Even at the age of six, Arturo would feel his eyes and face burn with the humiliation that Doña Julia accepted in dignified silence. Arturo remembered with clarity the lecture his mother had delivered to him one day after he had begged her to be allowed to go to the market, shopping with Julia.

'You are different from them,' his mother told him. 'It demeans you to be seen with them. Doña Julia should know that.'

'But she looks after me,' Arturo protested. 'She's kind to me.'

'She may be kind to you,' his mother replied. 'But she is not to be trusted. Give these people half a chance and they will stab you in the back. You must understand, Arturo, they are not like us. They think and feel differently from us. They are ignorant peasants, always remember that.' And Arturo always had remembered it, with an acute and profound shame.

The *campesinos* sitting at the little table outside the barber's were now drinking their beer in silence, staring at him. The emaciated dog had lost interest in the watermelon remains and had deserted the plaza to try his luck in the scrabble for pickings from the closing market. Arturo decided that now was the moment to break the deadlock. Apart from anything else he wanted to know whether anyone among them knew when the mayor would be returning. His resolve to try and start a conversation melted away under the steady gaze of the men as he approached. He felt awkward and over-dressed in the white city shirt and black trousers that Doña Julia had packed for him. He had worn them having set out that morning to try, yet again, to arrange a meeting with Ramon. As usual, when he had arrived at the town hall Ramon was nowhere to be seen. As he walked over to the men, one of them muttered something in an indistinguishable dialect and the others smiled and nodded in agreement. Suddenly, a small man with a balding head appeared in the doorway of the shop, holding a razor in one hand as he reached out to greet Arturo with the other.

'At last,' Don Bosco said, 'and I've won the wager that today would be the day that you would finally talk to us. You owe me five hundred pesos each,' he said, addressing the other men.

'So, tell us, what brings you to these parts?' Don Bosco continued, smiling amiably.

Surprised at the question, Arturo was momentarily stuck for a reply. His first inclination was to tell the truth and say that his father had sent him in order to separate him from his unsuitable attachment to Claudia, or that Claudia had sent him to separate him from his unsuitable respect for his father. He decided it was easier to say that he understood that the mayor had asked for him because the town needed a doctor.

'Indeed we do. Of course,' said Don Bosco, 'and I'm sure you'll be very good for us all. You are, indeed, just what we need here, an educated man.'

Arturo felt uncomfortable, uncertain whether or not Don Bosco was toying with him. 'Actually,' Arturo continued, 'I was wondering if you knew where the mayor's assistant is. He sent me a note yesterday and I need to make an appointment to see him. Do you know when the mayor will be returning?'

The men looked at each other. 'As far as I know the mayor left town on business a couple of months back. We're hoping he isn't lost in the forest,' Don Bosco said with a look that suggested no such thing. 'You're not acquainted with our mayor?' he continued.

'No,' Arturo replied. 'I've never met him.'

'Well,' said Don Bosco, 'that's a pleasure awaiting you. Don Teofelo here will take you over to find Ramon in a moment. But first, why not join us in a quick beer?'

'So, what were you thinking?' Don Bosco asked as Arturo sat down, a chair having been placed for him at the little table. 'We've been watching you for some time now, sitting there in the afternoons staring at our plaza, and although we all think it is a fine square ourselves – one of the best in the province by all accounts – we were asking ourselves whether it is interesting enough to warrant staring at for an hour. Don Teofelo here was wisely saying how the world that is so familiar to one man can look so different through the eyes of another. So I wonder, how does our little world look to you?'

'Actually, I was thinking how beautiful it is here. Different, but quite beautiful,' Arturo replied with sincerity.

'Yes, and more besides that, I'll wager,' Don Bosco replied knowingly. 'So you like what you see so far?'

'The church is like no building I have ever seen before,' said

Arturo. 'I'd love to see inside. I would give anything to be able to see the statue of the Virgin. Is she really in there?'

'That is what we would all like to know,' Don Bosco replied. The men looked at each other in silence. Don Teofelo cleared his throat nervously. After a pause Don Bosco continued. 'Perhaps the doctor could help us settle our little dispute. Seeing you sitting there in the square got us to discussing how times change. We seldom see visitors these days, and suddenly we have two, you and that odd fellow over there,' and Don Bosco nodded in the direction of the eucalyptus tree. One of the men who had left the table at the start of the introductions returned with a bottle of beer, which he gave to Arturo. Arturo, who seldom drank alcohol and never in the afternoons, accepted the beer gratefully.

'Our mayor, it seems, has great plans for our town,' Don Bosco said suddenly, 'and you, doctor, I suppose, are part of those plans. Don Teofelo has his views on the subject. Teofelo is a clever man, you know. He went to work in the mines when he was a young man, before he came and settled back here.'

'As you know, Bosco,' Teofelo said, 'I'm a modern man, I'm not against change like you people who have lived all your lives staring at this plaza and never seeing anything beyond its four corners.' Don Bosco winked at Arturo again, indicating that he was taking the insult in good spirit.

'Not all that "modern man" nonsense again,' Don Alfredo mumbled as he took a gulp of his beer. 'Having been in the mines makes you no more modern than the rest of us. I don't see what is so modern about going here, there and everywhere. I'm sure the beer is the same wherever you go. And anyway, if you are so modern and we are not, then why did you come back?'

'If it wasn't for people like me, with a bit of experience of the outside world, this town would be dead on its feet,' Don Teofelo retorted. 'My only concern now is what the mayor is up to. I tell you, changes are afoot. I keep telling you this but you're all too caught up in your little lives to listen.'

'Well, why don't you do something about it then?' Don Arsenio added to the debate. 'Especially as you're so much better than we are.'

'Now, now,' Don Bosco said, opening another bottle of chilled beer to cool readily heated tempers. 'But, Teofelo. We are not clear. What is your point?' asked Don Bosco. 'It seems to me you are confused. One minute you tell us how we are small-minded people who are stuck in our ways here and never open to change, and the next you tell us to beware because changes are afoot. I'm not sure you can have it both ways. I can't see how the arrival of a doctor from the city is a sign of disaster for our town, can you, doctor?'

Arturo was uncertain, but was spared the effort of answering as Don Teofelo cut in.

'My point is quite simple, even for you. All I am saying is, things should be done in the right way, and we need to be careful. What is the mayor's intention? That's what I'm asking. He's never shown any concern for the welfare of this town before. You people have a short memory. Don't forget his family owned the estate that sucked the lifeblood out of our fathers and grandfathers. All I am saying is that there are ways and means of going about things.'

'Well, I have never understood why Bosco here would never stand for mayor,' Don Alfredo said.

'Here, here,' Don Arsenio added in support of the suggestion.

'Well, I'm not sure about that,' Don Julio suddenly interjected. Everyone looked at him. 'I mean, I'm not so sure about progress. You say, for example, that a bigger school with a well-qualified teacher from the city would be a good thing for our children. On the other hand, I've heard of this happening in other places. The children start to see the world in a different way and they begin to argue with their parents and the next thing you know they're leaving in their droves, not just a few at a time. Eventually all you have left is a lot of old people sitting around on benches in the plaza discussing how sad the town is now that there are no young people left. Now, doctor, the question I am asking myself is this. If we've managed for so long without you, are we really going to be better off having you here? I only ask this out of interest. I mean no disrespect.'

'So, you would stop progress for our children because you're afraid of becoming a lonely old man?' Don Teofelo challenged him provocatively.

'Don Julio is only saying that because he's afraid of what a doctor might do to him,' Don Bosco added. 'He's been suffering from toothache for the past two months and I've offered to pull his teeth out. He won't have it, you know.' Don Julio smiled sheepishly at the doctor, revealing a row of black stumps. Arturo suddenly wished that he had paid more attention to his emergency dentistry classes.

'Well, I have never needed a doctor yet,' Don Alfredo said. 'The medicine man was good enough for my father and his father before him, so he's good enough for me.'

'Thank you, Alfredo,' Don Bosco said with a hint of impatience in his voice. 'I suppose the question we are posing to you, doctor, is this. Is your presence a good or a bad thing for our town? I suppose that is also what you are here to find out, is it not? You are most welcome and I am very pleased to make your acquaintance.' And with that, Don Bosco shook Arturo's hand again and disappeared back into the barber's.

'I'll take you to see Ramon now,' Don Teofelo offered.

Arturo stood up and shook hands with the other men. He then whispered quietly to Don Julio, 'If you come up to the clinic I promise I can take your tooth out for you without it hurting at all. I have an injection I can give that will stop the pain, you won't feel a thing.' Arturo was surprised at the confidence with which he offered a service that he had only ever performed once in his life, and then with much bloodletting and a good deal of screaming.

'That I will, doctor. It would be good to be free from the pain,' said Don Julio, holding his face. 'Thank you for your advice'.

Don Teofelo led Arturo away in search of the elusive Ramon.

*

Don Julio's promise to let the doctor sort out his aching tooth developed into nothing more than the subject of daily banter.

'And how is the tooth today, Don Julio?' Arturo would ask as he passed the barber's on his way to the market.

'Still hurting, thank you, doctor,' would come the reply.

'Good, good. Make sure you visit me soon, I'm waiting for you up there.'

The ritual came to an end one day when Don Julio proudly announced that the tooth was no more. The pain, so the story went, had become so unbearable that Don Julio had become completely delirious in the middle of the night and had tied a rope around his neck and started pacing the house in search of a suitable place from which to hang himself. His wife, hysterical with fear, had run to Don Bosco's house, waking up the neighbours in the process, screaming that her husband was possessed by a devil, or maybe even two. With great presence of mind, Don Bosco had rushed to Don Julio's house and yanked the offending tooth from his friend's head, apparently without spilling so much as a drop of blood. The story had become a favourite at the barber's shop, and Don Bosco was particularly fond of retelling the bit about how he had managed to restore health and sanity to his friend with the aid of nothing more than a good deal of common sense and a large pair of pliers.

'And so, doctor,' Don Bosco said to Arturo playfully, 'the old ways sometimes are the best, don't you agree?'

Arturo had almost forgotten about the mayor's threatened visit until one morning Ramon arrived at the clinic. He appeared just after Ernesto had gone home for lunch and before Arturo was about to set out on his daily walk to the plaza. He stayed long enough to deliver a letter informing Arturo that the mayor had arrived back in town and would be making an official visit to the clinic in the next week. He also handed him a little batch of letters that had been delivered by donkey a few weeks previously from Rosas Pampas, including a letter from Arturo's parents and a card from Doña Julia. Most disturbing of all was a note from Claudia written in a hurried scrawl implying that she was in serious trouble and warning Arturo that she would be leaving the city imminently.

Five

Arturo had first met Claudia at a family picnic party. They were both eight years old. Claudia had shown him that the world could be seen from another point of view entirely, and from the moment they met he had lived with the conviction that their fates were intertwined and that she was the person with whom he was destined to spend his life. His father had other ideas. Claudia was the daughter of a cousin of Arturo's father, several times removed. Her father had been a known communist agitator, a writer of dubious fiction, a womaniser and a drunk. Arturo's parents considered Claudia to be possessed with the same reckless spirit as her father. Although she was a frequent visitor to the house during Arturo's childhood, she was tolerated only because her mother – having eventually separated from her ill-chosen husband – had become a prodigiously influential civil servant with the power to make or break a man's career. Loretta Camacho was a force to be reckoned with. Under her protective matriarchal shadow, Claudia's untamed spirit ran riot throughout the Aguilar household, taking Arturo with her.

Arturo had been a timid child. Having no siblings, he was

overanxious to please his father, and lived in constant fear of the wrath he would encounter whenever he fell short of his father's expectations, which happened daily. In the presence of Claudia, he became filled with a confidence and a bravado that, both terrified and excited him, and which departed with Claudia as soon as she left the house. Alone, he faced his father's icy disapproval.

'Did you and that girl go into my study?' his father asked sternly, after Claudia had dared Arturo, yet again, to go into the forbidden room. 'You are nothing but a disappointment to us. You know that, don't you? You will be the death of your mother. If you ever dare to do that again, we will give you to the monks.' And Arturo was sent to his room in disgrace.

After Claudia's visits to the house, Arturo's parents started to notice that small items had gone missing. An old snuffbox that had belonged to Arturo's grandfather disappeared from the mantelpiece, and the cleaning maid was instantly sacked on suspicion of the offence. Then a little book with pressed flowers that Arturo's father had treasured since his childhood – and which he had foolishly shown to the children one day to impress Loretta – went missing from the bookshelf. After that, Dr and Señora Aguilar realised that countless small and insignificant items such as pens, teacups, notebooks, tablemats and ashtrays mysteriously vanished after a visit from Claudia and Loretta Camacho. Then objects started to go missing from Arturo's mother's bedroom: her tortoiseshell comb was suddenly nowhere to be found, neither were her favourite lipsticks; a little vanity mirror her mother had given her and other pointless trinkets given to her by her husband over the years all disappeared.

Arturo's father could not bring up the matter of Claudia's kleptomania with Loretta. He was greatly indebted to his cousin for her help in furthering his career and was also very proud of his connection to her. Under her patronage he had been given a place on all the important committees, with the added financial bonus of being made head surgeon at the Santa Maria Memorial Hospital, the most prestigious private hospital in the city and the one used by all the important generals, politicians and foreign diplomats as well as visiting dignitaries laid low by the demands of altitude and the excesses of formal state visits. Loretta Camacho's house calls became more frequent as her influence over Dr Aguilar grew. He provided her with a useful and authoritative voice on the various committees on which she had installed him, eloquently advocating the initiatives she supported even when he passionately disagreed with them.

Rather than daring to raise the issue of Claudia's thefts, the Aguilars started clearing away all small and extraneous items from the main rooms of the house and locking them in the cleaning cupboard before a visit was expected from Loretta and her daughter. Eventually, the hiding and rearranging of household knick-knacks became so tiresome for the domestic staff that it led to the threatened resignations of some of the most reliable amongst them. After that the Aguilars adopted a more minimalist approach to household interiors, keeping their ornaments permanently locked in the broom cupboard and starting a fashion that was much admired and copied by many in their social circle, with the exception of Loretta Camacho.

Despite the upheavals caused to the Aguilar household by Claudia's presence over the years, Arturo became increasingly besotted with her. By the age of twelve he was hopelessly in love. He became listless and unable to eat on the morning of a visit. As soon as Claudia arrived he would disappear with her into the far reaches of the house or garden, and she would fill his mind with notions of a life he would never otherwise have dared dream of.

'I'm going to do something great when I'm older,' she told him. 'And I'll only be able to love you if you come away with me and do something brave and daring as well.'

'Like what?' Arturo asked, breathless with excitement.

'I'm going to the lead the revolution,' Claudia said proudly. 'And if that doesn't work, I'll become a film star in Hollywood.'

'But my father wants me to stay here and be a doctor,' Arturo said meekly.

'Don't be such a baby, Arturo,' Claudia replied. 'There's a world out there, you know, in which people do heroic deeds. I'm not going to stay here and grow fat like your parents.'

It thrilled and terrified Arturo to entertain the possibility that his father was wrong and that there could be another view of the world. He was consumed with guilt at the exhilaration he felt after one of Claudia's long rants, which inevitably left his father lined up against the wall and shot along with all the other fascist pigs. Claudia was never very clear in her explanation of what a fascist pig was, except that she was certain that her mother was one and Arturo's father was another.

Claudia gave Arturo the courage to carry out unthinkably daring deeds, such as stealing swigs of his father's imported malt whisky when their parents were in the garden having their afternoon tea, or breaking into his father's study to look at the pictures of naked bodies that littered his medical books. Arturo never let Claudia know that the books filled him with the utmost horror and disgust, some of the bodies they giggled over having the most grotesque deformities and diseases imaginable. He became more and more convinced that the last thing he ever wanted to be was a doctor and spend his life looking at such monstrosities.

Arturo's friendship with Claudia came to an abrupt end one day when his father caught them in the study, Arturo with his pants around his ankles and Claudia with her blouse wide open. The adults had as usual departed into the garden to take tea, leaving the way clear for at least an hour. Claudia had convinced Arturo to take a swig of whisky before creeping up to the study, and he had impressed her by taking four, which had proved to be a fatal mistake, leading him to let his guard down completely, After ten minutes giggling at a book which contained pictures of pregnant women with huge breasts, Claudia had announced that she was now growing breasts herself and hers were much more impressive than anything in the books and she would show them to Arturo if he would take his trousers down and show her what lay beneath. Arturo, in a haze of alcohol, anticipation and fear, stood with his mouth open as she unbuttoned her blouse and showed him her small but perfectly formed breasts. He was transfixed. He reached out and touched them, gently, as if they were the shells of rare eggs about to break in his hands, and from that day on he was unable to get the image of Claudia's breasts out of his mind. Unfortunately, at the point at which Claudia had demanded her side of the bargain, Arturo's father had unexpectedly returned to the house to retrieve an important document. Arturo had been frogmarched to his room with his trousers still round his ankles and Claudia returned to her mother's charge with no explanation but that Arturo was unwell and would not be joining them again that day.

Arturo was forbidden to spend any more time alone with Claudia. At first their communication was carried out through hidden notes and furtive glances across the table during their parents' weekly tea parties. Then, at Claudia's instigation, they began illicit meetings in the park. Arturo would sit holding her hand, whispering words of adoration into her ear, while she would fill his head with radical ideas.

'Promise you'll marry me and have my children,' he begged her as he unbuttoned her blouse and gently felt inside.

'I can never marry you if you live the parasitic life of your parents,' she replied sternly. 'Show me that you're a man who follows his belief and I'll go anywhere in the world with you.'

Then, suddenly, at the age of sixteen, Claudia moved to the United States, and Arturo's secret world was torn apart. Claudia's mother had been offered the chance to take up further studies, followed by a prestigious posting in an American university. After finishing high school, Claudia had stayed on in the States, signing up to study politics and philosophy at one of the leading universities. Claudia and Arturo continued to communicate by letter. Arturo wrote long poetic declarations of his love and she replied with long philosophical tracts on the injustices of the world.

Her letters were at first cheerful, peppered with American slang: Hola, *Arturo*, como estas? *All's going great here, college is* awesome. But as they continued they became more strident in tone. *You know,* she told him in one letter, *the longer I am here in the land of the gringos, the more appalled I am by them and the way they've treated our country and those around us. It is clear to me that the gringos are our oppressors. They always have been and always will be. It's people like your father who continue their oppression with his supposed science, which he practises only for the benefit of the rich. I hope you will be strong enough to break away from your bourgeois life and follow a path towards truth and freedom, as I will.*

Arturo, who had been deliberating his future for some time, finally plucked up the courage to explain to his father his complete abhorrence at the idea of becoming a doctor. He was terrified by the sight of blood and although he never wanted to hurt his parents, he would rather be a historian or a writer. His father had become so apoplectic with rage that he had to be hospitalised for several weeks with a suspected stroke. Arturo wrote to Claudia in a confusion of guilt over his father's poor health and pride in being able to tell her that that he had finally found the courage to defy his parents' wishes and follow the life of a poet. Several weeks later he received his anxiously awaited reply.

My dear Arturo, Claudia wrote. *I have to tell you that I am very disappointed in you. I don't understand what good you think yet another bourgeois writer will do for our country. Don't you think there are enough already? Anyway, what do you have to write about? You have seen and done nothing. I have been reading a paper for our politics course on the function of the doctor in the fight for liberation. Although I don't understand medicine, I do understand the needs of our country. You may think I'm changing my mind, but it's just that my thoughts are getting sharper. If you were really brave you would become a doctor, challenge the Establishment that your father is a part of, and start to try and understand our people and the conditions they live in. I have to go now for my consciousness-raising group, and then to a party with some new friends. I'm sure you would love to meet them, they talk about these things all the time. Your trusted friend, as ever, Claudia.* Arturo read the letter over again looking for a hint of the tenderness and passion that he had poured into his own to her, and found none.

Devastated by Claudia's response to his decision to be a poet, and unable to defy his father's wishes any longer, Arturo resigned himself to entering medical school and trying to please the two people he loved and admired the most. He was not very good at his studies, easily distracted by irrelevancies, and he took longer than most to graduate. His contact with Claudia started to diminish over the years, with longer and longer gaps appearing between his letters to her and the replies he received.

Then, in the last year of his course, Claudia suddenly reappeared back home and Arturo's passion was reignited under her guiding hand. Claudia had taken a job teaching politics and sociology and was beginning to be associated in the newspapers with the frequent student demonstrations and teachers' strikes that were plaguing the university. Arturo's desire for her, fuelled by guilt at the liaison, was stronger than it had ever been. She terrified him, but she taught him to enjoy a pleasure beyond anything he had ever known. Secretly, sometimes playfully, sometimes tauntingly, in the darkness of the bushes of their teenage meeting place, she showed him how to be a man.

'Promise me we'll get married when I've finished my studies,' he begged, after each liaison.

'Take care,' she whispered back seductively, 'I believe I have the power to make you do anything.' Then, as they were getting dressed, she would chastise him. 'Remember, Arturo, there is more to life than personal satisfaction. You shouldn't get too attached.'

He would leave their assignation confused, intoxicated with the softness of her touch and the harshness of her words. He knew that any knowledge of his continuing contact with her was likely to kill his father, and yet when he was in her company he was possessed by a passion that was beyond his control.

Arturo's father had his contacts and eventually got wind of his son's renewed liaison with the young political agitator. Fortuitously, Arturo was coming up for his year after qualifying, in which he was required by the authorities to do twelve months' medical service in the rural provinces. His father started to ask around among his acquaintances for a suitably isolated location to which to arrange for his son to be sent, in the hope that this would break the affair with Claudia. Through a close friend of Loretta's he heard of a little-known and inaccessible town in need of a doctor. Within a month he had made all the necessary arrangements for his son's posting. Arturo's spirits were lifted only by Claudia's admiration for his dedication to serving the poor.

'I'm proud of you at last,' she told him. 'Arturo, promise me you'll never become a pampered professional like your father, taking care of the privileged classes and performing unnecessary operations for imaginary diseases resulting from their idle life.'

'But I'm only going for a year,' Arturo objected, never having really contemplated what Claudia's ambitions for him meant. He could not conceive of a life away from the comforts of his cherished home.

'Will you visit me?' he asked, quietly defying his father's wishes.

'I'll try and join you in your work, once I've finished mine here,' was all she said. 'Don't let me down.'

His father, on the day of his leaving, sent him off with a similar warning: 'I have pulled important strings to get you this job, son. Don't ever forget it. If you fail in your duties, I will never forgive you.'

With these parting words from Claudia and his father, Arturo left, secure in the knowledge that if he was to win the approval of one, he would lose the love and respect of the other for ever. He remembered with guilt how his mother had cried for three weeks before his departure, pleading with her husband not to be so harsh on their only son and to arrange for him to be posted to one of the towns close to the city so that he could return home at least once a week for a bath and to have his washing done. Arturo's father would not listen to any of it, saying that he had a simple choice between this posting and af five-year stint in the army.

Señora Aguilar was too distressed to say goodbye on the day Arturo left home. It was Doña Julia who hugged him and kissed him as he left, giving him a rich fruit cake she had just baked to help him on his way. As he kissed her goodbye, she pressed a tiny doll into his hand, telling him that if he took good care of it, it would look after him and would see that no harm came to him. With that, she wiped her eyes on a small lace handkerchief that Arturo had saved up his pocket money to buy for her as a present many years ago. The handkerchief looked as new and freshly pressed as on the day that he had proudly presented it to her. As he finally turned to leave, Doña Julia put her hand on his arm to draw him back to her one last time and said quietly:

'Arturo, you were always a kind boy and you'll be a good man. Don't be anyone's toy or puppet any more. Just be yourself.' It was not for some time to come that Arturo really understood her words.

Six

The mayor wiped his face with his shirtsleeve, dislodging a large drop of sweat from the end of his nose. He heaved his body into his swivel chair, which lurched at a forty-five-degree angle, threatening to tip its occupant onto the floor. He picked up the phone and shouted down the crackling line to his assistant: 'Ramon, has that bloody doctor arrived yet?'

'Hello, hello, who is that, is there anyone there?' came a faint and incoherent reply. The mayor slammed the phone down in a fit of rage. He was not a man to take an insult lightly and was still smarting from his humiliation in front of the insipid district officer at the hands of the People's Popular Participation Vigilance Committee, which the mayor preferred to call the 'bloody upstart peasant group'.

'Perhaps you would like me to let you know when I plan to fart next?' he had suggested during a heated discussion with their president, who had declined the offer, saying that would not be necessary as it did not come under the mandate of the PPPVC.

*

The mayor opened his office door and bellowed down the corridor to Ramon, who had already dutifully appeared, before the demand for his presence had been made.

'How can I ever expect to civilise this town when the bloody phones never work?' the mayor growled at his assistant. 'I've only been away for a few weeks — what's wrong this time?' But before Ramon could answer that rains and landslides in another part of the province had, once again, brought down the telephone lines and rendered Valle de la Virgen out of contact with the outside world, the mayor interrupted him with another tirade of fury before asking:

'What's that bloody noise?'

Ramon listened carefully to the usual cacophony of sound that milled around the decaying building, and replied diffidently, 'Which noise in particular is that, señor?'

The mayor's assistant always knew when his patron was in a fouler mood than usual because, as his temper rose, so did the quantities of spit that he sprayed as he spoke.

'That infernal humming. It's been going on all bloody morning.'

'Is it perhaps your ceiling fan?' Ramon enquired.

'It can't be the bastard ceiling fan, Ramon,' the mayor spat. 'That's been lying on my office floor since it tried to decapitate me this morning. I told you to get the damned thing fixed before I went away.'

During the weeks of the mayor's absence from the town, Ramon's work routine had become progressively slacker. His recent efforts to tidy the many piles of documents on his desk, which were about to create their own mini landslide, had resulted in the fatal loss of his list marked 'Essential things to do before the mayor's return'.

At least his memory had now been jogged about one of the twenty items on the list.

'It could be a cicada caught under the floorboards. Or perhaps you have a small sandfly caught in your ear, señor. My aunt got a sandfly stuck in her nose after travelling through the forest and it began to eat her nose away —'

'For God's sake, Ramon. I don't want to hear another story about your wretched aunt and her warts and nose sores.'

'Well, señor, I'm not sure to which particular humming noise, of the many that are going on around us at the moment, you are referring.' Ramon suspected he did know what the source of the mayor's disturbance was but he was reluctant to be the first one to raise his awareness of the presence of the Gringito in the plaza, having experienced before the retribution from his boss that followed the breaking of unpleasant news. Besides, the mayor had left explicit instructions that Ramon should inform him of any important happenings in the town during his absence. He now recalled that trying to get a message to the mayor to inform him of the arrival of the Gringito had been item number two on his list; and that trying to get the communications network to fix the phone lines so that he could *send* the message to the mayor had been item number three.

'How was your meeting with the district officer?' Ramon enquired, trying to change the subject. At which point the mayor exploded into a volley of abuse, completely drenching his assistant.

'Has that bloody doctor arrived yet?' he asked, finally pausing for breath.

'Oh, yes, señor,' replied Ramon. 'He turned up just after you left. I wrote and informed him that you would want to visit him on your return.'

'Well, why the bloody hell didn't you tell me he was here?'

And that, recalled Ramon, had been number four on the list.

*

The mayor had spent the morning reflecting on how the meeting with the district officer could have gone so badly. He had been so certain that the hiring of a doctor, and one from the city at that, would be a major political coup, enough to secure him preferential status in the eyes of the authorities. He had anticipated that his foresight in providing the town with its first ever doctor would ensure that any future requests to the authorities to support his plans would be met. It could bring his election onto the district council and even the departmental development committee. The mayor was determined that nobody, let alone a 'ragbag peasant group with no education', was going to stand in his way. As far as he was concerned, Valle de la Virgen had languished for far too long in its historic past. He was determined to put it finally on the tourist map.

The mayor had recently found himself in charge of a substantial amount of money, which by a stroke of good fortune and an enthusiastic piece of central government legislation had been deposited in the town council's bank account. The arrival of the money had been followed by some long and complicated official documents that set out the exact responsibility of the mayor's office in disposing of and accounting for the funds, and the respective responsibilities of the municipal and district councils, the canton, the department, the provincial secretariat, the prefecture, the Central Reforms Review Commission and the People's Popular Participation Vigilance Committee in overseeing their use. Having tried in vain to understand these various official missives, he had eventually consigned them to the rubbish bin, with the conviction that, as the departmental authorities had only in recent years discovered the exact location of Valle de la Virgen and they had never as yet actually managed to visit, they were unlikely to concern themselves with the affairs of the small and insignificant town.

The mayor had gleaned from the covering letter the district officer had sent to accompany the mounds of documentation that the authorities were most concerned to improve the health of the area. Apparently a large and costly survey had been carried out across the entire nation, using a very complicated set of questions and measures, and it had come to the conclusion that things were generally in pretty poor shape and that the country was not up to facing the challenges of the new millennium. It seemed that the province in which Valle de la Virgen languished boasted the worst statistics of all, having the least number of functioning health and education facilities, legitimate doctors and sensible teachers; the highest number of alcoholics; and the greatest proliferation of disease, pestilence, ignorance and indolence in the whole country. However, the note concluded, as several foreign governments appeared to be clamouring to spend money in the most impenetrable areas of the country, which the authorities presumed meant Valle de la Virgen, the mayor might be eligible for additional resources should he be able to make a convincing case for them.

'I am going to build a clinic,' the mayor announced triumphantly to Ramon one morning.

'Oh, good, señor. That's a wonderful idea,' Ramon replied. 'Who for?'

'The townsfolk, Ramon. Who do you think? If I am going to move this town into the twenty-first century, then we need to improve the health of the people here. At least that is what the authorities say.'

'Oh, very good, señor, very good,' Ramon agreed. 'Is someone sick?'

'I don't bloody care whether anyone is sick or not,' the mayor replied. 'If the authorities want us to build a clinic and hire a doctor, we will build a bloody clinic and we will hire a bloody doctor.'

'Excellent. I know,' Ramon said, entering into the spirit of the endeavour, 'we could have the clinic right here in the plaza. We have plenty of spare rooms in the town hall that the doctor could use.'

'Ramon,' the mayor said slowly and loudly, glaring at him. 'Let me make this very clear. I have no intention of being confronted by hordes of snot-nosed children and their scrofulous parents every time I step out of my office for a breath of fresh air. I want this clinic as far away from me as possible.'

It took some time to work out a suitable location for the project. At first the mayor decided that the only viable land on which to build the clinic, so that it was near enough to town, was on the edge of the estate owned by Doña Teresa. He resolved to make his aged aunt a long-overdue visit, not having ventured into the darkened and rotting estate that housed the cantankerous and morbidly revengeful old lady for some years. Despite his very best efforts, he failed spectacularly in persuading the old lady of the virtue of turning some of her land over to improve the health of the people, and his political career. He even magnanimously offered to have the building named the Doña Teresa Memorial Clinic, with an inscription suggesting that its benefactor had spent a life of selfless devotion to the needs of the common people. The visit ended in a stream of abuse, which the old lady sustained for a full ten minutes without hesitation or repetition, before she threw him out of the house saying that she would 'rather become a penniless whore than hand any of her precious land over to the thieving and stinking rabble who had mercilessly killed her husband.' After years of isolation, cared for by a handful of faithful staff, Doña Teresa had created a revisionist history of the events that fifty years ago had led up to the death of her husband, Don Pedro. In her mind, it had been a bloody and ruthless affair in which he had been ritually humiliated and then mercilessly slaughtered at the hands of a brutal and baying mob. She had long forgotten that he had died from a sudden heart attack brought on by the combination of years of overindulgence and an excessively large meal he had consumed just before hearing the news that the Great Dictator had been overthrown in a relatively bloodless coup.

The mayor finally settled upon a small and apparently useless pocket of water-logged land that nestled between the road and the edge of the swamp, half an hour's walk from the plaza. As the town was now apparently of interest to a number of foreign governments, he decided he would impress his future benefactors by declaring the clinic the gift of one of them. Placing a pin in the map of the world that hung on his office wall, he made a direct hit on Tokyo. He considered Japan to be an excellent choice, due to its exotic-sounding name and the fact that nobody in Valle de la Virgen would ever have heard of it, and inscribed the clinic a gift of the people of this nation.

Finding a doctor who was prepared to spend a year in solitude had not been as difficult as he had anticipated. Through the pulling of some not insignificant strings, which involved a high-up diplomat whom the mayor had encountered some years back in a compromising position in Consuela's guest house in Rosas Pampas, he had managed to secure the hire of a young doctor from the city. The acquaintance had a friend, an eminent surgeon, whose son had been annoying his father for some time with an unsuitable liaison. The acquaintance was sure the father would be delighted at the prospect of his son, who was due to leave medical school shortly, spending a year or two in a remote patch of swampland.

Proud of his achievements, and having cleared the bank account of every last peso, the mayor was ready to make his case for a second instalment of money. He dutifully filed a report to the district officer explaining that the town now had a brand-new clinic and that a doctor was due to arrive in the next few months. He also suggested in his report that, as he had important plans for the town, the authorities might wish to consider constructing a proper road into Valle de la Virgen as well as sending additional funds for the clearing of a landing strip and the purchase of a light aircraft to enable the mayor to go about his official business with greater ease.

A few weeks later, the mayor received an unpleasant and threat-ening note ordering him to come to the district headquarters in Rosas Pampas. The note implied that, as he had failed to submit legible and appropriate accounts for the previous year, a personal interview with the district officer was required to prevent the matter being referred to a higher authority.

*

The meeting with the district officer had not gone well. It had taken the mayor five days to reach Rosas Pampas, with several unneces-sary detours, so that when he finally arrived he was in a less than convivial mood and had the early symptoms of swamp fever. Having consoled himself for an evening in Consuela's Kitchen, he had turned up at the meeting with the district officer in a dishevelled and slightly inebriated state.

He was kept waiting for a good hour in the insufferable humidity before his interview took place. He was finally led by a bright young woman into a large room that contained nothing but a desk, behind which perched a diminutive figure in a smart, lightweight suit. The district officer greeted the mayor in an accent and tone that suggested he was not from the province and had little intention of staying there for very long.

'Señor, um, Ramirez, it is a pleasure to finally meet someone from your remote neck of the woods,' he simpered. 'How was your journey? A bit challenging, I detect.'

The mayor felt the eyes of the district officer running over him, taking in every detail. He was clearly a fastidious little man. His highly polished desk was devoid of anything that would give a clue as to his occupation, apart from a small pile of papers stacked in front of him. His hands, which rested neatly on the papers, were delicate and white with impeccably manicured nails. The mayor took a stained and rotting piece of cloth from his pocket and wiped his face.

'I suppose a big strong man like you is used to *fighting* his way through the forest,' said the little man. He emphasised the word 'fighting', making a limp swinging gesture with his right hand as if to imitate the use of a machete. The mayor attempted to speak, but only managed to produce a retching sound. The district officer proceeded, in a friendly and playful manner.

'My dear Señor Ramirez, the provincial authorities are most impressed by the speed with which you appear to have responded to their requests and spent all their money. Most impressed. None of the other municipalities seem to have achieved half as much in the time. Many of them are still struggling to decide where to begin. They clearly do not have your vision. I am sure that you'll be able to teach them a thing or two, hey? Oh, yes, I am sure a man like you could teach us all a thing or two.'

Despite the compliment, the mayor didn't like the district officer's tone. Had he not still been in a semi-inebriated state he would have sworn that the little man had just winked at him. He was beginning to feel most uncomfortable and had a sudden urge to throw up.

'It is remarkable that you managed to spend your entire budget for the year in a matter of months,' the district officer continued, 'although I am afraid my rather pernickety bosses in the department have voiced some concerns. Apparently, from the accounts you submitted they feel it is not possible to *track*, as they say, exactly what this money has been spent on. They've asked me to have a little word in your ear about the matter. Personally I'm sure you've done a grand job, and I'm looking forward immensely to making a visit to see for myself. I've heard it's a charming, quaint town, is that right?'

The district officer paused and took a swig of Coca-Cola. He continued.

'Look, I understand the problem you're facing. Things have moved on at rather a pace, haven't they? We have a change of government and everything turns on its head. It's enough to make you quite dizzy.' He raised his hand to his brow. The mayor nodded in mute agreement.

'The problem is,' the district officer continued, 'our friends on the People's Popular Participation Vigilance Committee have put in a complaint, and we have to be seen to take them seriously, if you know what I mean. Damn annoying really.'

The mayor yawned. 'What is this Popular Participation thingy anyway?' he asked.

'Oh, dear me,' clucked the district officer, clapping his hands with excitement. 'I see the problem. Someone hasn't been doing their homework, have they? Naughty,' and he tapped the mayor lightly on the hand. The mayor, who by now had decided he hated this little man, moved awkwardly in his seat.

'You see, Señor Ramirez,' the district officer continued, 'we all have our cross to bear. I, for my sins, have targets and I have to make sure that you reach them.'

'What do you mean, "targets"?' the mayor said, spitting again as he spoke. The district officer pointed limply at a whiteboard on the wall above his head. It was covered in criss-crossing lines.

'These,' he said. 'If we achieve them, then, my good friend, you will put Valle de la Virgen on the provincial map, so to speak, and we will all be happy.' The mayor stared blankly at the board.

'Look. I am sure we can sort this little problem out. All you have to do is make sure this clinic of yours is doing this.' The district officer waved an arm in the direction of the chaos on the board. 'You know, get those people of yours to see that doctor. Sick children, pregnant women, anyone you can find, the more the better.'

'How the hell am I supposed to do that? As far as I know, nobody in or around Valle de la Virgen has ever been to a doctor, and nobody has ever said they need one. I only built the blasted clinic because I thought you wanted me to!' The mayor was now shouting.

'Oh dear, we do seem to have a little misunderstanding,' the district officer said. 'I will soon be having a visit from the provincial authorities and I need to show them what progress we are making. I am counting on you. So you had better get the people on your side, and quick. Popular participation, you see, that's what we are all about now, isn't it?' And with that, the district officer abruptly terminated the meeting.

As he was about to leave the room, the district officer put his hand on the mayor's arm and whispered into his ear: 'Personally, I don't give a monkey's toss about Popular Participation Vigilance Committees, but we all have demands on us, don't we? You get me the targets I want or I'll make you pay back every penny you have spent from your own pocket, and with interest. Do I make myself clear?'

With that, the meeting was finally over.

Seven

The humming had grown louder.

'What the bloody hell is that noise?' the mayor bellowed again at Ramon, who took a step backwards and fell over the defunct ceiling fan lying on the floor behind him.

'It sounds as if it's coming from the plaza.'

Ramon, prostrate on the floor, was unable to prevent his patron from striding over to the window to discover the cause of the morning's disturbance. After a brief silence, the mayor nudged the quivering Ramon with his foot.

'What's going on?'

'We have a visitor,' Ramon replied. Ramon was then picked up by his shirt collar and dragged into the plaza to introduce the mayor to the stranger.

*

Nena and a few of her classmates had taken to sitting with the Gringito at the end of morning lessons to join him for a humming session, and were competing with each other to see who could hold a headstand for the longest without moving, while continuing to hum. The Gringito had explained to Nena that standing on his head was an integral part of his 'journey' and would enable him eventually to gain everlasting peace and inner tranquillity. Nena, doubting that everlasting peace and tranquillity could ever be achieved while living in her mother's house, thought it could be worth a go, and had also managed to sell the idea to a few of her more easily influenced friends.

When the mayor entered the plaza he was confronted by a circle of upside-down children, in the centre of whom was a bedraggled, upside-down foreigner. The mayor stood in silence. Finally, turning to Ramon, he yelled; 'What the bloody hell is this? You've let a madman into the town in my absence.'

'It's nothing to do with me. He's staying with Doña Nicanora,' Ramon replied, quickly passing the blame.

'Wretched woman,' exploded the mayor. 'I should have known she would have something to do with this.' Ramon moved a step away to try and avoid the inevitable spray of spit.

'I think he's a *hipi*,' Ramon said.

'A *hipi*?'

'Yes, a *hipi*.'

'Where does he come from?'

'I don't know. Apparently he was found in Puerta de la Coruña. There are a lot of them there.'

'How did he get here?'

'Ernesto brought him.'

'Ernesto?' the mayor replied. 'I thought we had seen the last of him.'

'Well, he's back, and he brought a *hipi* with him,' said Ramon. 'And I don't think he's as poor as he looks. Nicanora has certainly had a smile on her face ever since the Gringito arrived. Apparently he likes the peace and quiet here.'

'Peace and quiet? I have never heard such a racket,' the mayor said.

Nicanora suddenly appeared, crossing the square on her way home from the market. Seeing Nena, she shouted at her to get down unless she wanted what was left of her brains to run out of her ears. Clipping Nena lightly on the head, Nicanora took her daughter by the hand, telling her that if she could find no better use for her time than standing on her head she could help her with her chores. In her haste to avoid another scathing encounter with Don Bosco, Nicanora hurried across the plaza directly into the path of the mayor and Ramon.

'Doña Nicanora,' the mayor barked at her.

'Don Ramirez,' replied a startled Nicanora. 'It's good to see you have returned safely. When did you arrive? How is your good wife?' she gabbled. 'It's a long time since I have seen her. I heard she had her old troubles back again. Such a shame. I hope she's well.'

The mayor's wife, Doña Gloria, was a large and gregarious woman with an appetite for a good fiesta, young men and humiliating her husband. People still talked about the time when, during the last fiesta of the Virgin, Gloria had become so outrageously drunk that she had decided to do penance by divesting herself of an item of clothing at each of the fourteen Stations of the Cross. She had arrived in the plaza several hours later absolved of her sins and stark naked, to the horror of her husband, who was in the middle of his 'homage to the Virgin' speech. The mayor and several large men had had to chase Gloria several times round the plaza with a blanket before Gloria's humility was restored to her and she was led away to face her shame in the morning.

Doña Gloria had also given generously of herself during Ernesto's farewell party. Rumour had it that, following a night filled with beer and *aguardiente*, she had provided Ernesto with her own personal farewell present behind the church. Gloria's bouts of exuberance were generally followed by a rapid decline, during which time she was known to take to her bed in a fit of depression that could last for months.

'She's fine,' the mayor responded abruptly, not wishing to pursue the subject. 'Who is he, and where did he come from?'

'He's a tourist,' Nicanora replied.

'A *tourist*,' the mayor gasped. 'Is he really?'

The mayor, Ramon, Nicanora and Nena all stood in silence staring at the Gringito.

'I don't think so,' Nena replied finally. 'He doesn't have a camera.'

'Well,' said the mayor, 'we had better get him one then.' And he marched briskly back into the town hall, Ramon running along behind him.

*

'I don't understand why you want to open a café,' Ramon said. 'Run it by me again.' The mayor had been trying to explain the idea for the past hour, since discovering the Gringito in the plaza, and had finally lost patience.

'If I go through it with you one more time, will you then promise to do as I ask?'

Ramon nodded in agreement.

'Promise?'

'Promise,' Ramon said.

The mayor had arrived back in Valle de la Virgen a man with a mission. He was determined to show the authorities that he had his finger on the pulse, and now, as if it was a gift from the Virgin herself, they finally had their first tourist.

'What is it that you find so difficult to understand?' he asked.

'Well,' Ramon said, sitting down, his brow furrowed with concentration. 'You want to turn Don Bosco's shop into a café?'

'Exactly,' the mayor replied.

'Who for?'

'The tourists, Ramon. The bloody tourists.'

'What tourists? Do you mean that Gringito?'

'Yes, yes. I want to turn Don Bosco's shop into a café for the Gringito.'

'Is he hungry? I think Doña Nicanora is feeding him.'

'I don't care whether he is hungry or not. The point is, if we open a café others like him will come and stay here and start buying things.'

'What things?'

'I don't know – anything that we care to sell them. That's how it works, Ramon. That is why Rosas Pampas is rich and has telephone lines that work, and we don't,' the mayor replied picking up the defunct receiver and slamming it down again.

'But . . .' The mayor glared at Ramon, who continued undaunted. 'But how will they get here?'

'Ramon, if that hopeless *hipi* out there got here, others like him will. I will pay that good-for-nothing Ernesto to go in his truck and bring them here if I have to.'

'But will Don Bosco want to turn his shop into a café?'

'That, Ramon,' the mayor said, 'is for you to find out.'

★

It had been two years since the mayor's last visit to Rosas Pampas. He had always taken a perverse pleasure in visiting there, simply for the reassuring knowledge that there was at least one place on earth that was as apparently pointless as where he had just come from. As far as he was concerned, Rosas Pampas was a town built on opportunism and nothing more substantial than that. It was the last frontier between swamp and river, without even the glory of an historical past to boast about. It had grown out of wood, and existed solely for the purpose of the *peki-pekis*, the little motorised canoes, that buzzed up and down the river like oversized mosquitoes, transporting their cargo to Puerta de la Coruña and onwards to Manola.

Doña Consuela's Kitchen, with her lodging quarters above, was always the first port of call for the mayor when he arrived in Rosas Pampas and he always felt comforted by Consuela's hospitality. On his recent visit it was to Consuela whom he had turned to vent his fury at the sight that had confronted him. Rosas Pampas had in the time since the mayor's last visit quite simply reinvented itself. The town, and Consuela's Kitchen in particular, were now awash with foreigners. They were everywhere. The little shops surrounding the less-than-impressive central plaza, which even lacked a church, no longer offered the obligatory mix of tinned fish, dried pasta, beans, washing powder, candles, soap, beer, boiled sweets and unsavoury biscuits. Instead they boasted opportunities for the visitors to buy the rare handicrafts for which the region was now apparently renowned. Woven bags with *A gift from the historical town of Rosas Pampas* embroidered across them in blue and pink lettering; and bowls, cups and ashtrays with *I love Rosas Pampas* painted on them in gaudy lettering, now filled the shops.

What had really infuriated him beyond speech, however, was

shop after shop stuffed with brightly painted dolls. Small dolls, large dolls, dolls that winked, dolls with halos whose lights flashed, dolls with tears that streamed down their cheeks, dolls that repeated. 'Bless you, bless you,' when they were touched. Dolls that all claimed to be faithful replicas of the 'lost Virgin of the Swamp'. Some of the more enterprising young men had set up stalls on the edge of town selling bits of rock with postcards claiming them to be 'the last remains of the ancient town of the Virgin'. The accompanying literature told how the town had slid into the swamp years ago along with the treasured Virgin, and despite many expeditions into the forest – on which most of the brave explorers had apparently died – she had never been found. They also offered excursions by donkey to hunt for the remains of the town of the Virgin, which, judging by the maps that marked the various routes to be followed, clearly led the unsuspecting and intrepid tourists in quite the opposite direction to where the real Valle de la Virgen slept, oblivious to the slur on its existence.

'Bastards,' the mayor spat as he lamented to Consuela. 'Dirty, lying bastards.'

Consuela listened to the mayor's distress and then waved her hand in the direction of her assistant, who brought over two more cups of coffee.

'It isn't right, Consuela,' the mayor moaned, wondering why his usual order of beer had been replaced by the insipid coffee. 'They're stealing our business.'

'Oh Rodriguez, I doubt that really,' she replied, surveying her heaving establishment with pride. 'Let's face it. Nobody ever goes to your neck of the woods, apart from you people who live there, of course. Who is going to risk being eaten by the swamp to get to a small, forgotten place with nothing to offer them?'

'Nothing to offer them? Nothing to offer them?' the mayor repeated in indignation, spraying his coffee – which Consuela was now inexplicably and rather pompously referring to as *cappuccino* – as he spoke.

'No, Rodriguez, you have to face it,' she continued, 'if they were going to come to you, they would have got there by now.'

'But *we* are the town they have come to see,' the mayor said. '*We* are the real thing. We don't need to sell them fake dolls. The only problem is they don't know where we are. But I'll soon fix that.'

'But Rodriguez,' Consuela said, delighted to share her wisdom with her friend. 'What is it that you think these people come here for?' The mayor had been asking himself exactly the same thing ever since he had arrived.

'Well it's obvious,' he replied. 'They want to see the treasures of our ancient town.'

'Wrong,' said Consuela, watching the queues building up outside her café.

'They want to see the Virgin.'

Consuela shook her head.

The mayor was fast tiring of this game. 'They want to take photos of the Virgin weeping?' he said now more as a question than a statement.

'No, no, no,' Consuela said, banging the table with excitement as she directed her assistant with a nod of her head to make sure that the tables were being cleared quickly enough. 'Will they be able to take your precious Virgin home with them? No. You have it all wrong, Rodriguez. We are offering them the mystery of the lost town. They would much prefer that to trekking all the way to the real one just to find out that it is no more mysterious than where they just came from.'

'But –'

'And after they have seen your precious Virgin, what then?' she continued. 'You have to understand what these people want.'

'So tell me what that is,' the mayor said, defeated.

'Banana pancakes and computers,' Consuela replied. 'That's what keeps them here,' and she banged the table again with delight. The mayor only had to look around him again to see at last that Consuela was right. Doña Consuela's Cyber Kitchen was humming. He finally understood what made the foreigners come to the far-flung corners of the world. Consuela had the answer: pancakes and computers. These people would happily, willingly and diligently come to the depths of the remotest and most primitive regions as long as when they got there they could buy a cup of milky, frothy coffee and spend the rest of their day in a dank smoke-filled room sending messages home. Pancakes and computers they wanted. Pancakes and computers it would be.

*

Nicanora had been wondering for some time how she was going to raise the question of the hat shop with Don Bosco. The healthy wad of notes she had now saved from the rent money the Gringito was paying her was forming a lump under her mattress that was beginning to disturb her sleep. She had rehearsed the conversation with Don Bosco over and over in her head, never managing to get it to sound remotely acceptable or reasonable. 'Don Bosco, you are looking tired these days,' she would begin, or, 'Don Bosco, don't you think you have been a barber for quite long enough?' No matter how she imagined starting the conversation, it always sounded careless, contrived or downright rude. She had not planned when she would make her offer; when it happened, it could not have been done with less finesse.

Don Bosco had been standing in the doorway of his shop observing her conversation with the mayor and Ramon. As they left he beckoned her over to him. In recent weeks, Don Bosco's remarks had focused on the Gringito's antics in the plaza. 'Nicanora, it's such a joy to have a visitor to our town after all these years,' he would say, 'and it's all down to the efforts of your own dear son. I dare say that the mayor will one day dedicate a bench in the plaza to Ernesto for his endeavours in transforming our little town from a centre of peace and tranquillity to a place truly humming with eccentricity.' Or he would call her over on her way to the market and ask: 'Nicanora, I was just wondering, do you think a sensible girl like Nena really ought to be spending so much time standing on her head?' But today he took her off guard as he asked her in a more serious tone than usual, 'Nicanora, what do you really think this Gringito of yours is doing here?'

'I don't know,' she replied. 'He only talks to Nena. I still can't understand a word he says. Nena says she thinks he's lost.'

'Lost? Well he could be with us for some time then. I hope he's paying you handsomely for your hospitality,' he replied with a wink. Then, with a look of concern and kindness, he added: 'You do know what you are doing, don't you, Nicanora? You will take care, won't you?' And suddenly, standing in front her Nicanora saw the young man who had covered his shop in flower petals for her and she knew it was her moment.

'Don Bosco,' she replied, 'many years ago you offered me a share in your barber's shop, and I believe I did you a disservice in not considering your offer.'

Don Bosco dropped the razor he was holding and stared at her. He shook his head as if to clear the wax out of his ears.

'And so,' Nicanora continued, unable to stem the torrent of ill-chosen words streaming from her lips, 'and so I have been wondering whether you would be kind enough now to accept an offer of lunch at my house on Sunday.'

Don Bosco blinked, put his fingers in his ears to make sure all foreign objects were removed, and then said: 'Nicanora, have I heard correctly? Are you saying that, after twenty years of living in the shadow of my rejected offer, you now want to make up for it by inviting me to lunch?'

'Yes,' replied Nicanora. 'We're having chicken.'

'Chicken,' Don Bosco said.

'I'll get Ernesto to kill a plump one.'

'Chicken, you say,' he repeated again, staring at her as if his only consideration in accepting the invitation was what was on the menu.

'Yes, chicken,' she replied. There was a long pause, the silence between them filled only by the distant humming of the Gringito. 'Don Bosco, do you accept my offer or not?' she asked finally, anxious to bring the meeting to a close.

'Yes, Nicanora,' he replied at last, 'I gratefully accept your offer.'

Eight

All was not well in the mayor's house. The servants had been distracted during their employer's absence by the demands put upon them by his wife's increasingly erratic behaviour. Doña Gloria had taken to her bed after her sister and confidante, Doña Lucia, had generously shared with her the latest gossip circulating among Lucia's tea-sipping companions, and had refused all enticements from the servants to get up. The mayor, it seemed, had been seen in Rosas Pampas at a lodging house owned by 'a woman of questionable morals', as Lucia delicately phrased it to protect her sister's sensibilities.

'Screwing his bloody whores again — see if I care, the whore-loving bastard,' was Gloria's response to the news, and in a flourish of defiance she had locked herself in her bedroom refusing entry to everyone, including Lucia. Doña Gloria occupied her time writing long complicated daily menus, which she posted under the door for the servants, who left the requisite dishes on rows of trays outside her room to be devoured secretly in the middle of the night. Lucia, whose day could not progress without at least an hour's gossip at her sister's expense, adapted quickly to the situation by installing a chair in the hall outside Gloria's bedroom and shouting daily news updates through the keyhole.

'. . . And now there's a strange man standing on his head in the square humming to himself. He's a foreigner. Apparently Ernesto brought him here,' Lucia took great delight in informing her sister.

'What's Ernesto doing back here?' Gloria shouted. 'I thought he had gone for good. I expect he's going around spreading tales about me.' Recalling Ernesto's farewell party and her disgrace, Gloria descended into a flood of tears.

'Don't worry about Ernesto,' Lucia soothed. 'I'm sure he's forgotten all about it, as has everybody else. Anyway, he spends all his time with this new doctor now.'

'What new doctor?' Gloria enquired, calming down a little.

'The one Rodriguez found.'

'Don't talk to me about that whore-loving son of a bitch,' Gloria shouted through the keyhole, in another flood of tears. Then, after some time she enquired, 'So what's he like, this doctor?'

'I don't know. I've seen him sitting in the plaza. He's young, handsome. He seems shy. He has beautiful dark eyes though, sad eyes. He looks a bit like that film star.'

'Which one?'

'You know, the one in all those films. Remember . . . the one about the girl who falls in love with her brother's friend, but she can't marry him because he's married already, although he doesn't really love his wife, he just married her out of pity because she was poor and ugly – then his wife dies, but the girl has married someone else so she still can't marry him, even though he now realises he loves her. Then she kills herself. It made us cry, you remember.'

'Yes, I know, what's his name?'

'I can't remember. It will come to me. Anyway, he looks like him.'

'Hmm.'

'But Rodriguez won't be pleased when he gets back and hears we have a madman in the plaza,' Lucia continued, provokingly.

'Serves him right, the bastard,' Gloria screamed. 'Humiliating me like this again. Staying away for months while everyone knows he's sleeping with his whores.'

'Well, the man is a brute, I give you that. But don't upset yourself. Remember, Mother always warned us all men are brutes at heart, so there's no point in getting upset about it.'

'She was quite happy for me to marry him. She didn't think he was such a brute when he gave her all those presents of jewellery.'

'This is why I never married,' Lucia said finally. 'You can't trust any of them.'

'You never married because nobody ever asked you,' Gloria retorted, her vicious streak always stimulated by her sister's smugness.

'Don't you believe it,' said Lucia enigmatically. 'I always said: it is better to be mistress of your own house than play servant in the house of a man who has a mistress in another.'

'Well I tell you, the man is not born yet who can humiliate Gloria De Sousa Lozada,' Gloria announced loudly and resolutely. She then unlocked the bedroom door, ready to face her husband.

The mayor was somewhat shocked at the sight of the animated and defiant Gloria who greeted him on his return, and heeded the servants' warning to treat her with caution. On his first morning back home he took her a tray of fruit, freshly baked rolls, a selection of cold meats and cheeses and a pot of coffee to enjoy in the luxury of her bed.

'How are you this morning, my sweet?' he enquired in a simpering tone, which caused the tray to fly across the bedroom with the declaration:

'I am not your sweet, you whore-loving bastard. You think you can go off humiliating me with your screwing and your mistresses. Well I tell you, Rodriguez Ramirez. The man is not born yet who can humiliate Gloria De Souza Lozada.'

*

The mayor's threatened visit to the clinic did not happen for a few days after his return. Preoccupied with his sudden discovery of a foreigner in the plaza, and dealing with the problem of an increasingly difficult Gloria at home, his attentions were diverted elsewhere. When his visit did occur, it was unannounced and happened at a most inopportune moment.

Arturo, having decided to use Ernesto's time usefully, had embarked upon a programme of teaching him to carry out basic medical procedures in case his assistance should be called upon in an emergency. The plan included training Ernesto to give injections, in the event that a mass vaccination campaign needed to be mobilised against one of the many infectious diseases that plagued the country. Arturo had brought back from the market a large bag of oranges for the purpose, which he laid out in front of the clinic. Ernesto was enthusiastically making his way up and down the line of fruit, jabbing furiously with a huge syringe full of water, while Arturo observed the procedure with increasing horror.

Having tired of discussing the finer points of how to give an injection without causing permanent damage to the patient, the conversation had inevitably wandered to the kung fu films that

Ernesto had seen during his stay in Puerta de la Coruña. In an effort to widen Ernesto's knowledge of the cinema, Arturo was trying to explain the film that had just reached the city before he left.

'But if everybody knows that the ship is going to sink, I don't see where the suspense comes in,' Ernesto said, impaling another orange with vigour.

'Well, it's about more than just the ship sinking.'

'What else is it about, then?'

'Well, it's a love story really.'

'A love story? About a ship that sinks?'

'Yes, but it's more than that, it's also a comment on society. It's about how love transcends social class and social taboos. I suppose it's about the strength of love, especially forbidden love,' Arturo said, and his thoughts drifted momentarily to Claudia. 'You see there is a woman on the ship and she falls in love with a young man. The point is that she shouldn't really fall in love with him because she's richer than him and she's married, but she does anyway.'

'Does what?'

'She falls in love with him.'

'Then what?'

'They go dancing together.'

'Is that it?'

'Well, then the ship sinks and he dies.'

'Oh,' replied Ernesto, clearly unimpressed. 'I prefer a bit more action, like in *Fists of Glory* where the hero takes on a whole army and kills them using his bare hands. Did you see it?'

'No, I didn't,' Arturo replied. 'There's more to the cinema than the cheap kung fu movies they show in Puerta de la Coruña, Ernesto.'

'I know. I didn't just watch kung fu movies there,' Ernesto replied defensively.

'So what else did you see, then?'

'Well,' Ernesto said confidentially, 'I did see a film called the *Dance of the Lost Virgins*. I thought it was going to be about a town like ours, but it wasn't. They did a very interesting dance in it, though. Shall I show you?'

'No,' Arturo said firmly, 'we're supposed to be working,' but with no effect. Ernesto picked up two of the oranges and, holding them under his T-shirt, started prancing up and down the path, wiggling his hips in a bizarre attempt to imitate a belly dance.

'You shouldn't be watching films like that,' Arturo chastised in a serious tone, determined not to be drawn into Ernesto's foolishness; then collapsed into helpless giggles as Ernesto wiggled his way backwards and forwards in front of the clinic.

'I hope that's not my wife you're making fun of, you little bastard,' a voice cut through the hysteria. Ernesto leapt into the air. The oranges fell from his T-shirt, rolled down the path and landed at the visitor's feet. Ramon, who was running several steps behind the mayor, picked one of them up and started to peel it, offering the other to his patron.

'What the hell is going on here?' the mayor bellowed, dismissively knocking the orange from Ramon's hand.

Arturo, in a state of shock at the appearance of the uninvited guest, failed to immediately grasp the seriousness of the situation. In an effort to tidy up the entrance to the clinic, he started to pick up the other oranges. By the time the mayor reached the clinic door, he was standing with the bundle of fruit gripped firmly in his arms.

'So, you're the doctor who's been causing me so much trouble,' the mayor said, by way of an introduction. Arturo extended a hand to greet him, and the fruit cascaded like an offering at his feet.

'I have a serious bone to pick with you. I thought you were gone for good,' he said, addressing Ernesto. Then turning to Arturo said, 'Is this what I'm paying you for? To mess around with this bloody fool?' Arturo sensed that this was not the moment to point out that he had not yet received a single payment from the town and was still living off the small allowance that his mother had insisted his father give him before he left home.

'I'm very pleased to meet you,' Arturo said, attempting to regain some dignity. 'As you can see we have everything organised and ready to start work. Ramon has brought me all the necessary supplies, which I understand you kindly arranged to be sent by the provincial authority.'

'Never mind that,' the mayor replied brusquely, pushing past Arturo into the clinic, with Ramon close at his heels.

'How long have you been here exactly?'

'Exactly, I'm not sure,' Arturo said, looking at Ernesto for help. 'Over a month now, I think.'

'So where are they?' the mayor demanded, gazing around the empty and immaculate clinic.

'Who?' Arturo asked.

'The bloody sick and dying. The women and screaming children. I don't see anyone here.'

Ernesto cast a glance under the small examination bed, as if to hunt out any stray patient that might be hiding there. 'There aren't any,' he replied.

'What do you mean there aren't any?' the mayor said slowly.

'Well, nobody has been here yet,' Ernesto continued, 'except me.'

'What did you come for?' the mayor asked. Ernesto turned red and said nothing.

'So where are they?' he demanded of Arturo again, now standing so close to him that Arturo could smell the rancid tang on the mayor's breath.

'I don't know,' he replied quietly. 'I'm not sure they understand why I'm here. I was hoping perhaps that you could help, once you returned, with an announcement or something to the town, or maybe an official opening of the clinic, so that people can get to know me. Many people don't even know where the clinic is. Perhaps they're afraid to come here.'

'Afraid! Ignorant peasants, that's the trouble. I have to live in a town full of bloody ignorant peasants, like this one,' and the mayor waved his arm in the direction of Ernesto, who was now hovering in the doorway waiting for an opportunity to escape.

Arturo glanced at Ernesto, who looked down at his feet, and Arturo caught the fleeting glimpse of shame in his eyes. Arturo felt the same feeling of indignation rising in him that he had felt on behalf of Doña Julia all those years ago.

Quickly recovering himself, Ernesto replied in his usual playful tone as if no offence had been given or taken: 'I'm sure people will like the clinic eventually, Don Ramirez. You know how it is. People take time to get used to new things. The doctor here is making some good friends though, aren't you, doctor? He's been spending time at Don Bosco's.'

'And what has our good friend Don Bosco been telling you?' the mayor asked.

'Oh, nothing,' Arturo replied vaguely. 'He says that people don't really know why I am here, or what they are supposed to come and talk to me about. That is why I've been waiting for you to come back, Don Ramirez. As you invited me I thought you could help explain it. I'm eager to start work.'

'Well you'd better start soon. I'm expecting some important visitors, and you, sonny,' he said, pointing his finger at Arturo, 'had better not fuck up when they arrive.'

The mayor eased his sweating body into the small chair beside Arturo's desk, pulled a damp, grey piece of cloth from his pocket and began to wipe his face with it.

Arturo stared at his employer in silence, a shudder of repulsion running through him. He had felt the same sensation once before. It was on his first day at the senior academy when, full of the naivety and hope of a new student, he had enthusiastically offered the wrong answer to a maths question and had been called up in front of the class to receive a caning for his efforts. He had taken the caning stoically, intent on the teacher not seeing his fear and pain. As he was leaving the classroom at the end of the lesson, the teacher had crept up behind him and whispered in his ear: 'I have my eye on you, son,' and then, winking at him seductively, clipped him around the head for no good reason. The incident ignited a dormant spark of revolt in Arturo. Always an obedient and diffident student, Arturo now entered into a subtle and strategic battle with the teacher, a battle he eventually won by quietly convincing all the other students in his class to join him in his silent protest and refuse to respond to anything the teacher said to them. The silence of the maths class finally drove the teacher to take extreme measures such as singing and dancing in the middle of the classroom to stimulate a response. He was eventually led away on the arm of the principal in the middle of a lesson, following a particularly bad rendition of 'Don't Cry for Me, Argentina', never to appear before a class again.

'What visitors?' Arturo asked.

'The authorities,' the mayor replied. 'And you had better impress them. If you play your cards right there might be money to build yourself a hospital here before you know it.' An icy shiver ran through Arturo at the thought.

'You had better make sure,' the mayor continued, 'that when our visitors arrive this place is swarming with sick people. And I mean swarming.'

'How are we going to do that?'

'I don't bloody know,' the mayor bellowed. 'That's what I am paying *you* for, isn't it? I don't care how you do it. You can drag them here in handcuffs for all I care. This could be the most important visit our town has had for decades. The provincial authorities will be coming for the first time ever. We'll show them once and for all that this town is worth something, especially as we have a tourist here now.'

'Do we?' Ernesto said, with genuine surprise. The mayor looked at him as if he could eat him.

'The one making all that bloody noise in the plaza. I thought he was staying at your mother's house.'

'Oh, yes, he is,' said Ernesto, 'but I didn't know he was a tourist.'

'Well what the hell did you think he was then?'

'I don't know,' Ernesto replied.

'Well, what do you think, doctor?' the mayor said turning to Arturo.

'About what?' Arturo asked, distracted from the conversation by the vision of dragging the townsfolk to his clinic in chains.

'This Gringito. Who is he? Where does he come from? What is he doing here?'

'I don't know anything about him,' Arturo replied.

'Well, you had better find out and quick,' the mayor snapped.

'Check him out – make sure he's not a madman or something.' Then, pointing his finger at Ernesto, he added, 'And whatever the bloody hell he is, you had better have him walking around town behaving like a tourist by the time our visitors arrive. Otherwise your house guest will be out on his ear, do you get my meaning?'

The mayor stood up, shook Arturo's hand and made as if to leave. Then, thinking better of it, he took a step towards Arturo and whispered in his ear: 'One word of advice while you're here, son. Don't fuck with me. And you,' he said, now turning to Ernesto, 'never fuck with my wife again.' With that, he pushed past Ernesto and made his exit from the clinic as abruptly as he had arrived.

Arturo was silent for some time.

'He's right about one thing,' he said eventually. 'I have been too complacent. I'm a coward, Ernesto. I've been sitting here waiting for people to come to me. I justify it by saying that I need to take things slowly, build up their trust, when really I'm just scared to do anything.'

'Scared? What are you scared of?'

'People,' said Arturo, 'people and their problems. What can I do to help anyone?'

'Well, you helped me.'

'Yes, I did. But that was easy. What if people start coming to me with really sick children, with diseases I have never seen before that I don't know how to cure, or worse still with all their worries and fears? I can only let them down, Ernesto. I have nothing to offer them, nothing. What can I do for them? I don't understand anything about their lives.'

'You won't know though really, until you try,' Ernesto said.

'Well, that's true,' Arturo said, impressed by Ernesto's sudden insight.

'But don't worry, doctor,' Ernesto said, 'we'll come up with a plan. My mother may have some ideas. Why don't you come and join us for lunch on Sunday. You'll be able to observe the Gringito like the mayor said. See what you think, you know, see whether he's behaving normally for a gringo or not. You have seen more of them than I have. I find it hard to tell. You can also meet my sister, Isabela, she's been asking me a lot about you.'

'Well that would be nice, thank you, Ernesto,' Arturo said, genuinely touched at having received his first invitation to eat at someone's house. 'But will your mother mind?'

'No,' Ernesto replied. 'I'm sure she'll be delighted.'

Nine

Don Bosco had only one suit and he had worn that to Francisco's funeral. And besides, he said to himself, it's far too formal for Sunday lunch. He pulled his neatly folded collection of shirts from the drawer and stared at them. The blue one he had never worn and it was far too small; the two white ones were too frayed at the collar to be smart. That's because I wear them every day of the week. I must have something new, he concluded. 'But what is this all about? Could it be, could it be?' he asked out loud, and then stopped himself. 'Don't be a fool, Pepito, you were a fool once and see where that got you.'

Nobody now used his familiar name, 'Pepito'. His mother and brothers had always called him by it, but in recent years, since his family had one by one tired of life and left him to face the world alone, the name had been kept alive only in his solitary ramblings. He tried on the blue shirt just in case, and looked at himself in the dusty little mirror. A small, fat, balding man stared back at him in a shirt that was far too tight for any self-respecting barber to wear. He sank down on the bed and gazed at his feet. 'Fat old fool. Fat old fool,' he said softly, and threw one of the fraying shirts over the mirror in an effort to block out the truth. 'And why would she? After all these years why on earth would she?'

*

Don Teofelo had never seen his friend in quite such a state of confusion. The mood in the shop had been rather subdued all day. Don Julio had tried with limited success to draw Don Bosco into conversation and discover the cause of his dejection. The usual arguments and banter had been replaced by the drone of other people's sad stories being indiscreetly shared with the world in *Tia Sophia's Problem Hour*, through the voice of the small crackling radio in the corner.

'Our next caller, Maria-Lupe,' simpered the sugary tones of Tia Sophia. 'Tell us what is troubling you.'

'Hello, Maria Louisa?' Tia Sophia said again, a harsher tone creeping into her voice. 'You are through, please do tell us your troubles.'

'Yes,' a voice whispered in reply. 'I have many troubles, many troubles. I ask every day: "What have I done to deserve so many troubles?" I have seven children to feed and another one on the way, God help me.'

'God help you, indeed,' agreed Tia Sophia.

'But my husband is not a good man. He walked out of the house last week. He said he was going to buy some milk for the baby. He still hasn't come back. I pray to God every day that he may walk back in with the milk, but he hasn't.'

'Do you live a long way from the shop?' asked Tia Sophia.

'No, this is the problem, it's just down the road,' said the voice of Maria Louisa breaking down into deep uncontrollable sobs. 'He's left us with all his debts and now some men have come round and they say they are going to take all our furniture away. They're sitting here now drinking tea while I'm phoning you. I pray to God every day, please help us.'

'Well, your husband does sound like a bad man. Praise God, perhaps you are better off without him,' Tia Sophia suggested.

'But I have no money,' sobbed Maria Louisa. 'What am I to do about these men drinking my tea? What am I going to do about feeding the baby? Please, please can you help me?'

'This is a sad story,' Tia Sophia cut in. 'I will pray for you. We will all pray for you, for an end to your troubles,' she concluded as the soft music of *Tia Sophia's Problem Hour* drowned out the sobbing of Maria Louisa.

'I can't listen to any more of this,' said Don Bosco, wiping the corner of his eye with his old shirtsleeve. 'Why do people have such sad lives? Why? Can you answer me that, Julio? Sometimes I wonder, what's it all about when everywhere people are living such sad and desperate lives?'

'What is wrong with you?' said Don Julio, walking over to the radio and changing the channel. 'You've been acting like a hen that's lost her chickens all day. Pull yourself together, man.'

'The riots sweeping the city began two weeks ago,' the radio continued, now in a deep, confident, masculine tone. 'We are getting reports of a car bomb that exploded outside a police station this morning, killing two passers-by. Reports say it is believed to be the work of the People's Liberation Front. The army is beginning to gain control and the ringleaders of the riots, believed to be a group of students and teachers based at the university, have fled into the countryside. The President says he will not resign and that his decision is final.'

'The country is falling apart,' Don Bosco continued. 'Riots in the city, bombs going off, women and children without homes and food. You shouldn't joke about it, Julio. Why has the world become such a troubled place?'

'The world has always been a troubled place, Bosco, it's just that you have never bothered to take notice of it before,' Don Teofelo interrupted from the barber's chair. 'But right now I'm less concerned about the state of the world than I am about what you're doing with that razor. What's wrong with you?'

Don Bosco did not answer. He continued shaving the same patch of skin that he had been scraping at for the past five minutes. Then, suddenly catching sight of Nicanora hurrying across the plaza, he announced in a voice loud enough to drown out the radio, 'I don't have anything to wear.'

Teofelo turned abruptly in the chair, to make sure that the words had been uttered from his old friend's mouth. With the sudden movement, the razor, which had been hovering in anticipation below Don Teofelo's ear, cut a slice through the protruding organ. Teofelo, uncertain whether to be shocked more by his friend's sartorial announcement or by his effort to amputate his ear, was silent for a minute, then, seeing the stream of blood pouring down his face, screamed: 'Bosco, you've lost your mind and now you've tried to kill me,' and then passed out. Confusion continued in the shop for a good five minutes as the blood began to form a little pool at Don Bosco's feet. Don Julio ripped up a towel and tried to wrap it round Teofelo's head, for no better reason than that he could not stand the sight of blood and was about to pass out himself if he had to look at it any more.

As luck would have it, Arturo was passing through the plaza just at the moment when Don Julio rushed out of the shop shouting,

'Bosco has gone mad and has just sliced off Teofelo's ear, and he is lying in there bleeding to death as we speak.'

Arturo rushed to the scene, momentarily forgetting his own abhorrence for the sight of blood — just like a real doctor, he thought to himself afterwards. Don Bosco was standing staring into the mirror white-faced, the bloody razor in his hand.

'It was an accident,' he kept repeating, 'it was an accident. I didn't mean to kill him.'

Arturo placed a hand on Don Bosco's shoulder and led him over to a chair. 'Make him a cup of camomile tea,' he said firmly to Don Julio, who was running around the shop screaming, 'Oh, my Lord, there is blood on the floor and blood on Bosco's hands.'

The sudden authoritative tone of Arturo's voice brought Don Julio to an abrupt halt, in the middle of a sentence about how the blood flowing from the door of the shop was about to drown the plaza and sully the reputation of the town forever. Don Teofelo, who was slowly coming to his senses again in the midst of the commotion, let out a soft moan as he saw his bloodstained reflection in the mirror. Arturo gently unwrapped the towelling bandage that Julio had wound erratically around his friend's head in an attempt to mummify him, and revealed the offending wound. Don Teofelo sat compliant as the young doctor bathed the gash with warm water and then after some time announced that the cut, though deep, was neither life-threatening nor a cause for great concern.

'He's not dead, then?' Don Bosco asked suddenly, broken from his trance.

'No, I'm not dead, Bosco, no thanks to you,' Teofelo replied petulantly. 'But what about my ear, doctor, will I lose my ear?'

'Only if you lose your head as well,' Arturo replied in an attempt to lighten the mood as he re bandaged the ear. 'Both still appear to be firmly attached. You have no cause to worry.'

Don Bosco went over to Teofelo to offer his friend the hand of reconciliation.

'I'm so sorry, Teofelo,' he began. 'I don't know what came over me. I just didn't see your ear there.'

'Well, it was in the same place that it has always been, until you tried to remove it,' replied Teofelo, not quite ready to drop his indignation. 'I would have thought that, after thirty years of working as a barber, you would have discovered that your clients have ears attached to the sides of their head.' Then seeing the eyes of his old friend moisten, Teofelo stood up and embraced him. 'It was an accident, Bosco, I know that. I shouldn't have moved my head in such a hurry.'

Don Bosco sat down and put his head in his hands. 'I don't know what's wrong with me,' he said. 'I don't know what has come over me. I'm just not myself at the moment.'

Arturo sat down beside him and placed a comforting hand on his shoulder. 'What's wrong?' he asked gently.

'He doesn't have anything to wear,' said Don Teofelo.

Arturo stared at him.

'That's what is wrong with him, doctor. He's upset because he doesn't have anything to wear.'

Don Bosco hid his face in shame. 'It's true,' he said. 'It's true. I have nothing to wear and I'm a fat old fool.'

'Do you have a fever?' Arturo asked.

'I don't think so,' Don Bosco replied.

'What do you mean, you don't have anything to wear?' Teofelo asked finally. 'You're sitting there in a shirt and trousers as far as I can see, the same shirt and trousers that I've seen you in for the past ten years at least.'

'That's exactly it,' Don Bosco replied, his voice filled with anguish. 'That is exactly it, Teofelo. I have two shirts and they are both the same, and I've been wearing them for the past ten years. They are frayed at the collar and have holes in the sleeves, and I need something new to wear by Sunday.'

'Why, what's happening on Sunday?' Teofelo asked, intrigued.

'She has invited me to lunch.'

'Who has?'

Teofelo, Julio and Arturo now drew around Don Bosco in a tight confidential circle.

'Nicanora.'

'Nicanora?' replied Julio. 'Why?'

'I don't know. She just said that twenty years ago she did me a wrong and then invited me to have lunch with her to make up for it,' said Don Bosco. 'We're having chicken.'

'Chicken?' said Teofelo.

'I thought you were over her,' said Julio.

'So did I,' said Don Bosco hopelessly, 'so did I. But what do you think she wants, Julio? Why now, why after all these years should she invite me to lunch?'

'And you have nothing to wear,' said Teofelo, finally understanding the events of the morning and delighted that sanity had been restored to his friend. 'We can fix that easily. The clothes market will be near here in the next few days. We'll get there early and find you a new shirt, won't we, Julio? And a new pair of trousers for that matter.'

'Of course we will. What colour shirt would you like?' Julio asked brightly, looking at Don Bosco with compassion in his eyes.

'I don't know. I don't know anything about these matters,' Don Bosco said forlornly.

'Well, what do you think, doctor? You're a young man. What colour shirts are they wearing in the city these days?'

'All sorts of colours,' replied Arturo.

'Well what colour do you think would suit our good friend the barber here?'

'I don't know,' replied Arturo, uncertain why in his role as doctor he should suddenly be called upon to dispense fashion advice. 'Maybe blue. Men are wearing everything, even pink. Different-coloured shirts, shirts with jeans, you can get away with anything really.'

'I'm not going to Sunday lunch in a pink shirt,' Don Bosco said indignantly.

'Well, blue then,' said Teofelo with finality. 'We'll set off early tomorrow morning and find you the finest blue shirt in the market, and a new pair of trousers to go with it.'

'But what do you think it's all about?' Don Bosco asked. 'Why now, why after all these years does she suddenly want to make amends?'

'I don't know,' said Teofelo, 'but I'm not sure I trust her. Perhaps she's planning something.'

'You shouldn't judge her so harshly,' said Don Bosco. 'She's a good woman, Teofelo — a little impetuous, maybe, but a good-hearted woman.'

'Take care, that's all I am saying,' Teofelo said. 'Look what she did to you, Bosco. You're a forgiving man, but let's face it, she ruined your life.'

'All right, all right,' said Don Bosco, not wanting to pursue the subject further.

'Ernesto has asked *me* to lunch on Sunday as well,' Arturo said, suddenly remembering the invitation. All three men looked up at him. 'But I don't think I'll go,' he added, realising the inappropriateness of his announcement.

'You see,' said Teofelo eventually. 'She is planning something.'

'No,' said Arturo quickly. 'It was Ernesto's idea to invite me to lunch, but I won't go. I didn't realise that his mother had another guest.'

'It's all right, doctor,' said Don Bosco after a while, and he reached out to shake Arturo's hand. 'You can be my chaperone.'

Ten

A small, fat, balding man in a blue-and-pink striped shirt and a pair of tight jeans stood staring at himself in a mirror.

'I can't wear this,' he said at last.

'Why not?' said Teofelo exasperated. 'We've been through this already. They were a good price and it's all they had. Anyway, you don't have any choice, because you don't have anything else. You can either wear these or your old barber's shirt and trousers, now stained with my blood, I might add. You want to show her you're making an effort, don't you?'

'Yes, making an effort. Not deranged,' Don Bosco replied.

'It's a new look,' said Julio without too much conviction. 'You just need to get used to it, Bosco.'

'But do I look dignified?' Don Bosco asked.

'Let's say modern rather than dignified,' said Teofelo. 'Anyway you've been dignified all your life and where has that got you? Think of this as a new stage, a new phase in your life. You're a modern man now.' Don Bosco looked at himself again in the mirror.

'Come on, Bosco,' said Julio impatiently. 'You'll need to make up your mind soon. The doctor will be here in a minute,' and his friends left him to his indecision until the doctor arrived ten minutes later, wearing his smart white shirt and black trousers.

'What do you think, doctor?' Don Bosco asked timidly. Arturo stood open-mouthed.

'It's,' he began, 'you . . . it's . . . you look fine, just fine,' he stammered. 'Different, but just fine.'

Don Bosco sighed with relief at the doctor's approval, picked up the small bunch of flowers he had prepared as a thank-you gift for Nicanora, and left with the doctor for his lunch appointment.

*

The raised voices in Nicanora's house could be heard from the end of the street.

'*Now* you tell me,' Nicanora screamed at Ernesto. 'Now you tell me. Why today? Why did you decide to invite him today? He's been here for weeks. You could have invited him any time and you decide to invite him today.'

'You didn't tell me you were inviting Don Bosco,' Ernesto shouted back. 'You just asked me to find a plump chicken for Sunday lunch, so I thought it would be a good day to invite him to eat with us.'

'I don't need to tell you who I'm inviting to eat in my house,' Nicanora replied. 'And what have you got that on for?' she continued, turning her attention to Isabela, who had just walked into the kitchen wearing a low-cut sleeveless dress and displaying bright red nail varnish on her toes. 'You look like a hussy.'

'I want to make a good impression on the doctor,' Isabela said provocatively.

'Well, you can make a good impression by putting an apron on to cover yourself up and helping me.'

Nena had managed to escape the morning's hysteria by claiming that she had important books to read. She had taken herself off to find a quiet corner in the plaza from where she could observe the Gringito's meditations.

'Should I invite him to lunch as well?' she asked as she left the house in pursuit of her friend.

'You can invite the whole neighbourhood for all I care,' Nicanora replied, which Nena took to be an open invitation. The noise in the house had even driven Lucho from the yard. He had taken up his station at the end of the street in anticipation of the arrival of the guests.

'You had better make sure the chicken is well cooked,' Isabela said. 'You don't want to poison the doctor.'

'Why should I poison him? When have I ever poisoned anyone? And anyway it's been cooking for hours. Don't just stand there, you can give me a hand with preparing the table. They'll be here soon and nothing is ready.'

'So why have you invited Don Bosco?' Isabela asked, trying to provoke her mother again.

'He's an old friend. Do I need to have a reason every time I invite an old friend to lunch?'

'But you never invite anyone to lunch. And you have never invited *him* before. I was just wondering why?'

'Never you mind,' Nicanora snapped. 'And be polite to our guests. Don't you start teasing that poor young doctor.'

'Did you hear that?' Nicanora asked suddenly, turning to Ernesto as the distant sound of a dog snarling followed by a faint voice calling; 'Nicanora, are you there?' drifted into the kitchen.

'Did I hear what?'

'Nicanora, are you there? Could you come and get us?' the voice floated in on the breeze again.

'That,' replied Nicanora. 'Someone is calling,' and she ran into the street to find the source of the anguish. The doctor and a man in a blue-and-pink striped shirt stood with their backs against the wall of the neighbour's house. Lucho had his paws up against the stripy man's belly and was letting out a deep guttural growl at the sign of any movement. A small bunch of white flowers lay on the ground beside the dog, their petals cast like confetti around the man's feet.

'Get down at once,' Nicanora shouted, clapping her hands and aiming a small stone at Lucho's head, hitting it with expert precision. Lucho let out one last snarl to make it clear that he was still the boss and then, releasing Don Bosco, rolled over at his feet in the anticipation that his victim might now care to tickle his tummy. Don Bosco bent down to pick up what was left of the flowers, trying to dust the muddy paw marks off his new shirt at the same time. Nicanora stood staring at him.

'I didn't recognise you,' she said at last. 'You look, um, different.'

'It's the modern look,' Don Bosco replied.

'Oh, is it indeed?' said Nicanora. Never having seen Don Bosco lost for a quip at her expense she added, 'Well, modern or not, it certainly frightened the dog.'

*

Nicanora led her guests into the yard and disappeared into the house, returning a minute later with a chair for each of them. Arturo sat down and looked around. The little muddy yard was full of broken objects waiting for the owner to decide the next use for them. A chair with only two legs lay limply in the corner. Underneath it was stored a pile of old cans that had once contained cooking oil. In another corner a pile of rotting vegetables lent a sweet tang to the air. The chickens running around the yard filled the silence with their pointless squabbling. I hadn't realised they were so poor, Arturo thought to himself. Catching the look in Nicanora's eye, he was suddenly overwhelmed with the awkwardness of a man whose thoughts had just been detected by another.

'Isabela,' Nicanora shouted, disappearing into the house again, 'bring our guests something to drink.' Isabela appeared a few minutes later, nonchalantly swinging a bottle of beer in each hand.

'So tell me, doctor,' she said, handing the beer to the guests, 'how do you find our little town? I think my mother is worried that you're lonely up at that clinic there all by yourself. She doesn't think my brother is good enough company for you.'

Isabela leaned back and rested her foot against the wall of the house, her brown leg languishing seductively under her dress. Arturo's eyes were drawn to her perfectly formed limbs and she smiled knowingly at him as she waited for his answer.

'I don't know,' Arturo said. 'I suppose it can get lonely.'

'So why do you keep yourself to yourself? Isn't it odd for a young man to want to spend so much time on his own?'

'I don't really,' Arturo said, taking a rapid swig of beer.

'Perhaps you're just dedicated to your work. After all, it must be exciting being a doctor,' she continued. 'Tell me, what's the most exciting case you have ever seen?' Arturo took another large gulp of beer, desperate to think of a story to tell.

'Well I haven't really had any patients yet,' Arturo said, finally.

'Don't be shy, doctor,' Isabela said, 'you must have saved hundreds of lives before you got here. I expect you are one of those quiet sorts of heroes, aren't you?'

'Well not really,' Arturo said candidly, and was saved from the further humiliation of Isabela's probing by Nicanora, who reappeared in the doorway and asked everyone to follow her inside.

*

The table, laid with six places, filled the tiny room. Behind the table was an old wooden dresser that contained Nena's school books and a collection of plates and bowls, each still searching for its partner, covered in a variety of patterns.

'I don't know where Nena is,' Nicanora said, 'but we can't wait for her. She could turn up at any time, knowing her. Isabela, show our guests where to sit.'

'You can sit here next to me, doctor,' said Isabela, pointing to the chair in the corner and forcing Arturo to squeeze past her so that his arm brushed against her breast.

'And you should sit there next to my mother,' she said, turning to Don Bosco. 'You're looking very smart today,' she continued. 'Where did you get such a colourful shirt?'

'It's the modern look,' Nicanora said, placing a large bowl of stewed chicken on the table. Don Bosco, who had momentarily forgotten about his attire, turned pink at the attention.

'You look like a film star,' Isabela whispered across the table to him, making him blush bright red. 'One of those film stars who has got old and is trying to look thirty years younger than he is.' Nicanora caught the look of panic in the kind eyes of her old suitor.

'I have never seen you look so good,' she said. 'The colours are . . . they make you look . . .'

113

'Thank you,' said Don Bosco, staring at the table. Sensing that she had provided him with exactly the right degree of discomfort, Isabela turned her attention to Arturo again.

'So, do you have a sweetheart, doctor?' she asked.

'No. Yes. Well no, not really. I don't know,' Arturo replied.

'That sounds intriguing. You haven't come here with a broken heart, have you?' Isabela asked.

'No, no, it's nothing like that,' said Arturo, feeling the colour rising in his own cheeks.

'Well, whatever it is, we'll have to do something about it,' she said. 'Or are you another confirmed bachelor like Don Bosco here? That's right, isn't it? You are a confirmed bachelor, aren't you, Don Bosco?'

'Yes, that's right,' said Don Bosco looking at Nicanora.

'Isabela stop this silly prattle and help me serve the food,' Nicanora said. 'So how are you finding life here, doctor?'

'I like the town very much. It's beautiful, very quiet,' Arturo replied.

'So what do you do with yourself all day up at that clinic?' Isabela asked.

'Well, I haven't really done anything yet. I'm still waiting for some patients to come.'

'Where from?' Nicanora said, distracted as she served the food onto the plates.

'You've had one patient,' Don Bosco said. 'He saved Teofelo's life only the other day.' And he proceeded to tell the tale of how Don Teofelo had nearly bled to death in the barber's chair, leaving out only the crucial point about why Don Bosco had lost his concentration and inflicted the injury in the first place.

'It's not like you to be harming your customers,' said Nicanora.

'Perhaps you're losing your touch? Have you ever considered retiring and taking life easy?'

'Retire? Me? But why would I?' he replied, shocked. 'Why would I want to? What would I do with myself all day?'

'Oh, there are plenty of things,' Nicanora replied. 'There is so much more you could do. Why don't you give up that old shop of yours and do something interesting, while you still have the chance?'

'You never did think being a barber was very interesting, did you?' Don Bosco replied, looking at Nicanora, the old wound beginning to seep again. 'Why does everyone suddenly want me to retire? Maybe I just want to be a barber. Maybe I like being a barber,' he continued. 'Maybe being a barber is all I've ever wanted. Maybe I want to die in my barber's shop.' Everyone stopped talking for a minute, all struggling to find the words to move the conversation on. The silence was broken by Nena making her belated entrance with her bedraggled friend.

'What's he doing here?' Nicanora said turning to Nena, confused by how quickly she had found herself treading upon Don Bosco's fragile feelings again. 'Why didn't you leave him in the plaza like I told you to?'

'You said I could invite him,' Nena replied.

'But we have guests. We don't have room for everyone at the table.'

'But you said I could invite the whole neighbourhood, and I only invited him because I only like him.'

'Well, I didn't mean it. You don't have to listen to everything I say,' Nicanora replied. 'You'll have to squeeze onto the chair with Isabela, and go and get another plate for him,' she said, gesturing towards the Gringito, who was standing grinning at the assembled crowd. Don Bosco and Arturo exchanged awkward glances.

'I'm very happy to be introduced to your house guest, finally,' Don Bosco said after a while. 'He's been providing us with continual amusement for some time now. Perhaps it's time that we at least learnt his name.'

There was a pause.

'I'm not sure he has a name,' Nicanora said.

'But everyone has a name,' said Don Bosco. 'That's what makes us human.'

'That's not true at all,' Nena replied. 'Lucho has a name and he's a dog.'

'Well that's my point,' said Don Bosco. 'Even your dog has a name.'

'He does have a name, as it happens,' said Nena.

'Well what is it then?' asked Nicanora

'It's a secret,' said Nena

Ernesto leaned over to Arturo and whispered, 'So do you think he's mad?' as the Gringito lowered himself onto the chair next to Ernesto.

'And have you been enjoying the sun today?' Nicanora asked the flushed Gringito, trying out small talk for the first time since her house guest had arrived. Nena translated for her friend in the dialect that she had fabricated for his personal use, and he mumbled something in reply.

'That's just reminded me,' Ernesto said suddenly. 'The mayor came to the clinic the other day and he was very threatening about him. He said he might have to leave. He was very threatening to the doctor as well, come to think of it.'

'Why? Why would he want him to leave?' asked Nicanora. 'He isn't doing anyone any harm.'

'No, but according the mayor he isn't behaving properly,' said Ernesto.

'What are you talking about?'

'He isn't behaving like a foreigner.'

'Ernesto, what are you talking about?' Nicanora said again, exasperated by her children's wanton display of idiocy in front of her guests. 'Will you please make sense and stop speaking with your mouth full.'

'Apparently the mayor is expecting visitors from the authorities,' Ernesto continued in a conspiratorial tone. 'He wants to make a good impression on them. He wants to show them we have a tourist here. The problem is, the mayor doesn't think he's behaving like a proper tourist. And the doctor has to get some patients at the clinic by the time the authorities visit or he'll have to go back home as well.'

'Oh, we can't have that,' said Isabela, winking at Arturo, 'we can't have you being sent home when you've only just arrived.'

'What sort of patients do you need?' asked Nicanora.

'I don't know,' said Arturo. 'Sick ones I suppose.'

'I'm not sure anyone around here is sick at the moment,' said Nicanora. 'And if they were they would go and visit the medicine man.'

'What you need is a good business manager,' said Isabela. 'Since I've been helping my mother in the market the sale of her fruit has doubled. I would be a much better doctor's assistant than my hopeless brother. I've been thinking I may like to train to be a doctor. Perhaps, I could come to the clinic and you could show me how it is done.'

'Isabela,' Nicanora said, giving her daughter a warning look.

'I have a better idea,' said Ernesto. 'You could have a party, to christen the clinic. We haven't had a good fiesta here since my farewell party.'

'What a good idea,' said Don Bosco, amiably.

'So are we going to get to keep him?' Nena asked suddenly.

'Who? said Nicanora.

'The Gringito,' Nena replied. 'Ernesto said we may have to send him back. I don't want him to go. He's my friend.' Her eyes began to fill with tears.

'Don't you have friends your own age?' Don Bosco asked kindly.

'They're boring. They just want to do stupid things. The Gringito is more fun.'

'Well, if you want to keep him, you'll have to teach him how to be a tourist,' said Ernesto.

'OK,' Nena replied and she smiled at the Gringito, who was battling messily with a chicken leg.

Eleven

Don Julio and Don Teofelo had been waiting at the end of the street for at least three hours and they were beginning to get bored.

'I wonder what they're talking about?' Julio said again. 'At least it must be going well, otherwise they would have left by now. What do you think she wants with him?'

'For the last time, I don't know,' Teofelo replied. 'This was a silly idea. We could just as well have waited for him at home. Anyway she can't say much in front of the doctor even if she wants to.'

'Why do you think she asked him as well?' Julio continued. 'Do you think Bosco will tell us? You know what he's like, he's always so secretive.'

'Well, there's one way of finding out,' said Teofelo. 'We can go and listen for ourselves. You can creep into the yard and listen under the window for a minute, get the feel of the conversation.'

'But what if they come out?'

'You'll hear them moving from the table. That'll give you enough time to hide, and I can keep a lookout for you from the street.'

'Why me? Why do I have to go?'

'Because you're the one who is so impatient, and it was your idea to wait here for Bosco in the first place. Besides, you're nimbler than me, you could get away quicker if need be.'

'Oh no,' said Don Julio, 'I'm not falling for that one. We're both in this together or not at all.'

'Well then,' said Teofelo, 'we'll just have to wait here and then we may never find out what it's all about. Just like you said, Bosco will never tell us.'

★

All was clear in the yard apart from a couple of beer bottles that had been discarded on the floor. Muffled voices could be heard from the house.

'They must be inside,' Julio said. Teofelo shot him a look that was entirely wasted on him and Julio continued unperturbed. 'If I hide just around the corner from the window, I should be able to hear enough to make out what's going on, and then they wouldn't be able to see me if they came out,' said Julio. Then, seeing Lucho asleep on the mat by the door, he had a momentary second thought. 'What about the dog?'

'It's all right,' said Teofelo, 'it's too hot for him to wake up for a good few hours.'

Don Julio tiptoed slowly across the yard, stood round the corner from the door, waited there for a couple of minutes and then tiptoed back to Teofelo who was safely concealed on the other side of the fence.

'I can't hear what they're saying,' he said.

'Oh, for heaven's sake,' said Teofelo, who was growing edgier by the minute with the midday sun beating down on him. 'I'll come with you. But we need to get closer to the door.' As they shuffled quietly past Lucho, he let out a soft growl, dreaming contentedly of intruders tiptoeing across the yard.

Teofelo crouched under the window close to the door, with Julio behind him at his heels. 'What are they saying?' Julio whispered.

'Shh.'

'I can't hear.'

'You need to get the doctor to clear your ears out,' Teofelo snapped, 'and your brain.'

'So that's what we will do then,' Don Bosco was saying. 'Ernesto and Isabela will help with all the preparations – that'll keep you both busy.'

'They're planning some celebrations,' Teofelo whispered.

'You see,' said Ernesto, 'I knew everything would be sorted out.'

'It's a deal,' said Arturo, whose voice sounded unusual, slurred.

'And the doctor is drunk,' Teofelo said, into Julio's waiting left ear.

'So, he must have proposed again,' said Julio. 'They must be planning the wedding.'

'I'll make a large cake,' said Isabela. 'After all, it's not every day we get to celebrate at a clinic.'

'They're going to hold the celebrations at the clinic,' Teofelo whispered.

'Why?' asked Julio.

'I don't know,' Teofelo hissed into his ear, 'why don't you go inside and ask them?'

'But then they would know that we've been listening at the window,' Julio protested, and Teofelo, whose patience had finally left him for the day, turned around and gave his companion a sharp slap on the head. Julio let out a yelp that passed into Lucho's dreams, and he started a low growling by the door.

'What's wrong with Lucho?' Nena asked.

'Rats, I expect,' said Don Bosco, casting a glance at the window as he and Arturo stood to take their leave.

*

Julio and Teofelo were in the middle of an argument when Don Bosco and Arturo reached the end of the street.

'What are you two doing here?' Don Bosco asked without a hint of surprise in his voice.

'We just happened to be passing a minute ago,' Julio said, 'and we thought your lunch must be finishing soon, so we decided to wait here and walk back with you.'

'Most thoughtful,' said Don Bosco.

'Yes, most thoughtful,' Arturo repeated. 'That's what I love about the people here, they're so thoughtful, and friendly. It's a beautiful town really, beautiful people, look how beautiful it is today.'

'How much has he had to drink?' Teofelo asked.

'Not much, but I don't think he's used to it,' Don Bosco said. 'I didn't realise until it was too late. I should have kept an eye on him.'

'So, it went well then?' Julio said.

'You think so, do you?' Don Bosco replied.

'I was asking,' said Don Julio. 'How would I know?'

'How indeed. Well, yes, it went very well as it happens,' said Don Bosco.

'So,' Teofelo urged, 'what happened? Why did she invite you?'

'Does someone always need to have a reason to ask an old friend to lunch?'

'Oh, come on, Bosco, what did she want?' Teofelo said, putting a hand on his friend's shoulder.

'I don't know.'

'What do you mean, you don't know?'

'I mean, I don't know why she invited me. We had lunch. We made conversation. The doctor got drunk. We met the Gringito. The usual things and that is that.'

'You mean, you have spent three hours drinking beer and eating chicken while we have stood here sweltering in the sun waiting for you and you don't know why she invited you?' said Teofelo, irritated by his friend's enigmatic behaviour.

'Yes. That's true,' said Don Bosco, 'I have.' And he turned on his heels and walked back in the direction of Nicanora's house, offering no explanation to his friends, who were left to escort Arturo home.

'What's got into him?' Julio said.

'He obviously doesn't want to tell us. He can be so annoying. What's Bosco hiding from us, doctor?' Teofelo asked, slapping Arturo on the back.

'It's a secret,' said Arturo, putting his fingers to his lips.

'Well, we can play along with that if he wants us to,' Teofelo said as they led the doctor back to the plaza to sober him up.

*

Don Bosco tapped quietly on Nicanora's door. She was standing with her back to him, clearing away the remains of lunch from the table. At first he tapped so quietly that she didn't hear him. He cleared his throat, and then knocked again.

'Nicanora,' he said softly. She turned to look at him. His eyes, which always twinkled with unguarded softness and warmth when he spoke to her, now betrayed his vulnerability.

'I believe I may have left my hat here, I don't seem to have it with me,' he said, a gentle laugh in his voice, mocking his foolish-ness.

'You must be mistaken, Don Bosco,' she said. 'I don't recall you having brought your hat with you, and you certainly didn't leave it here.'

'Well, that has solved the mystery, then,' he replied, in a bolder voice. 'I am getting old. I never had my hat and, instead, I've lost my mind.' He made as if to go and then turned back. He stood for a moment, uncertain of his next step. His hand moved forward as if to touch her arm, before checking itself and finding a pocket in which to hide.

'Nicanora, something has been bothering me,' he said. 'When you invited me for lunch you mentioned what passed between us all those years ago. I, of course, have never forgotten it, but I thought perhaps you had. I have the feeling that you wanted to ask me something all day but couldn't. Am I right?'

Nicanora was taken off guard. 'Yes, you're right, Don Bosco,' she said. 'I do have something I want to ask you.'

He stepped forward and took her hand. The soft crinkle of his eyes as he smiled stirred long-buried feelings of remorse within her.

'Nicanora,' he said, 'we are old friends, are we not? Can you not call me Pepito again, like you once did? You are the only person left in the world who used to call me that.'

Nicanora blushed at the familiarity of the scene. She sensed, momentarily, that if she let her ambition go, she might still be able to find happiness with someone who cared deeply for her, and yet she knew with certainty that if she were to make her offer, this was the moment to do so.

'I have something to show you,' she said at last, breaking the spell. He stepped back and let go of her hand. 'It is something that I hope will make amends for what passed between us all those years back, so that you can enjoy your life now.' She left the room, returning a few minutes later with a cardboard box.

'Open it,' she said.

'Nicanora, what is this?'

'Open it,' she said again.

Don Bosco stood looking at the box and then removed the lid and peered inside. It was full of dollar notes.

'Where did you get this from?'

'The Gringito.'

'He gave it to you?'

'Yes, for staying here.'

'But Nicanora,' Don Bosco said, 'this is a fortune. Why would he give you all this money?'

'Ernesto said it's what he would pay to stay in a hotel in Puerta de la Coruña. He wanted to come here and as there is no hotel, he wants to pay me. There is nothing wrong with that,' she said, unable to remove the haughtiness from her voice.

'Are you telling me the truth, Nicanora?' Don Bosco asked.

'Why would I lie to you?' she said, shocked that he would not trust her.

'What are you planning to do with it?'

'I want you to have it,' she said.

'Me? Why? Why would I want it?'

'I have been saving it. For you. That's why I invited you to lunch. I wanted to ask you . . .' and she stopped, terrified that what she would say next would cut through the unspoken cord of affection that had existed between them for so many years, and yet unable to stop herself now that the moment had arrived.

'Ask me what, Nicanora?' he said, catching his breath, uncertain of what his eyes were seeing and his heart was feeling.

'I would like to buy your shop,' she said at last. The words clattered to the floor like painted pebbles.

'You want to buy my shop?' he said.

'Yes,' she said. 'Don Bosco, twenty years ago you offered me a share in your shop, and I refused you. I now want to ask you whether you would consider selling it to me, so that you can retire and enjoy your life.'

'You want me to take this money so that you can take my shop from me?'

'No, Don Bosco, it is not like that,' she replied. 'I want you to have this money so that you can be free to follow your dreams.'

'I have no dreams, Nicanora,' he replied. 'They left me years ago. My head is an empty vessel filled with shaving cream and nothing more. And you, what do you want to do with my shop?'

'I want to sell hats,' she said. 'I want to sell grand elegant hats like the ladies in the city wear. I want to make the plaza a centre of beauty. I want people to flock here from all over the province to buy hats more beautiful than they ever imagined. You know they say there is a hat for every dream, Don Bosco. I want to fill our town with dreams.'

He looked at her and saw again the impetuous young woman who had stolen his hope from him, and felt an almost uncontrollable need to take her in his arms and hold her and cover her with kisses. He wanted to tell her that it would be all right, he would do whatever she wanted just so that she would die a happy woman after a life of false starts and missed opportunities. Instead he said, 'A grand plan indeed. But where will you find such hats and who will buy them, Nicanora?'

'Times are changing, Don Bosco,' she said sharply. 'We have the Gringito here and he's brought money. We can get more of them where he came from. Even the mayor has plans now for the town and our Gringito can help him.'

Don Bosco was shocked by the harshness of her words. 'Don't tell me you're now supporting that man; the man whose family has drained our town dry for generations? Have you been selling your soul as well as your floor?' he said with unintended bitterness.

'What do you have against the mayor?' Nicanora asked, defiant as the brief hope that had flickered between them was snuffed out. 'Why do you dislike him so much? Why don't you have the courage to do something about it, to get rid of him if you don't trust him? Take this money. You can be free to do whatever you want, you won't have to work any more.'

'I don't want your money,' Don Bosco said, and for the first time Nicanora heard real anger in his voice. 'This is wrong, Nicanora, you don't know where this Gringito got it from, or what he wants. I won't take money from you, your Gringito or any other wandering soul who decides to make their home in our town. But I will give you my shop.'

'You'll give me your shop?' she said, astonished.

'Yes. On one condition,' he said.

'What condition is that?' she asked, half anticipating, half hoping for the proposal that had been made so many years ago.

'Make sure nothing bad happens to our town.'

'What are you talking about?' Nicanora said. 'All I want to do is sell hats. Why are you saying that to me?'

'Because, Nicanora,' he said, 'you have a gift. You know you have. Use it.'

'What are you talking about, Don Bosco?' she said in a whisper, her breath taken from her.

'You have a gift, Nicanora,' he said again. 'I have always believed in you, when nobody else has, you must know that. I think the time might be coming when you will need to use it. Keep an eye on our town is all I ask.'

'Don't be ridiculous,' she said, laughing off her fear and shame. He made to go and then looked back one last time.

'Nicanora,' he said. 'You must have known that if you wanted my shop, all you have ever had to do was ask and I would have gladly given it to you. There is one more condition on which I give it to you now. That you call me Pepito as you once did.' And he turned and walked away. She looked at his pink-and-blue stripy back retreating from her and felt lonelier than she ever had before.

Twelve

At the age of eighteen, a few months before she met Francisco, Nicanora was struck by lightning. She knew nothing about it until she woke in a darkened room two days later with her mother bending over her, asking her if she could tell her what would happen next week. Nicanora, without a moment's hesitation, and with no understanding of the significance of the question, sat up in bed, eyes wide open, and said: 'On Monday there will be showers. On Tuesday light winds will strengthen throughout the day to become stormy gusts by the afternoon. The winds will be so strong that Doña Felicia's knickers will be blown across the plaza and come to rest on the roof of the church. On Wednesday the rains will start again. The water will seep under the kitchen door and all precautions should be taken not to leave any items on the floor that could be damaged.' She then looked at her mother and asked, 'Where am I, what happened?' lay down, and fell asleep for another two days.

The lightning attack left burns down Nicanora's right arm that with the careful application of her mother's herbal ointments slowly healed, leaving only a darkened hint of misfortune on her skin. The effect of her uncannily accurate weather forecast left her with a deeper scar that she would spend many years trying to conceal.

'You have a gift,' her mother came home and informed her the following Tuesday afternoon, having just seen Doña Felicia's underwear take flight across town and ingloriously lodge themselves on the corner of the cross of the Church of the Virgin of the Swamp. 'And if my underwear were as grey and torn as hers, I'm sure I wouldn't have hung them out to dry in the first place,' her mother added as an uncharitable afterthought to the announcement that her daughter's auspicious survival had left her blessed by the ancestors. For several months following the incident, Nicanora's mother set her daughter a series of surreptitious tests to assure herself that the gift had truly been imparted.

'I wonder how much I will earn in the market next week?' her mother said absent-mindedly while peeling the potatoes, and before Nicanora had control of her senses her mouth replied, 'Next week will be a good one, you will earn at least fifty pesos a day. Be sure to get to the market early on Wednesday, as a travelling salesman will be passing through and will give you a good price for your oranges.'

Casual remarks from her mother such as, 'What should I wear tomorrow?' were enough to provoke an insightful warning from her daughter: 'I'd wear your new pink blouse, even though you are only going to the market, because by next week it will be ruined after falling from the washing line and being eaten by the goat.'

Despite her lack of control over her spontaneous predictions, Nicanora refused to listen to her mother's insistence that she was destined to become the town's next soothsayer and thereby fill a lucrative gap in the market that had been left by the untimely death of the old fortune-teller, Doña Nicolesa.

'You should set up a stall in the plaza,' her mother told her. 'People need to be able to hear it for themselves.'

'I'm not going to turn into an old hag like Doña Nicolesa,' Nicanora argued. 'She only told the future to earn money because she was too ugly to get married. Anyway, what good did it do her? It didn't stop her drowning in the swamp.'

'So, even a fortune-teller can have an off day,' her mother retorted. 'And since when have you been so proud that you are too good to tell fortunes? And don't speak ill of the dead or they will come back to haunt you, and mark my words the last person you want haunting you for the rest of your life is Nicolesa.'

The more her mother insisted that she had been blessed with the power of the ancestors the more Nicanora struggled to suppress her predictive insights. It took an enormous degree of self-control to hold her tongue and not provide passing strangers with a full weather forecast for the following month, or offer her neighbour a warning not to walk across the plaza on Tuesday morning as she would slip on a piece of rotting vegetation and sprain her ankle. Her efforts to remain firmly attached to the present were still not enough to prevent her mother's ambitions from getting out of hand.

'You could be a wealthy woman, if only you would apply yourself,' her mother scolded. 'People came from miles to see Doña Nicolesa, that's how she could afford to wear a new shawl every day. If you could just tell people something useful, they would come flocking to you.' And that was the problem: no matter how long Nicanora sat in a darkened room asking important questions such as where she would travel to or who she would marry and whether she would be a rich woman, the answers would come back blank, a avoid, denying her expectation.

She began to see some sense in what her mother was saying.

If she really was able to develop her gift she could use it to plan her escape from her backwater home. She could become anybody and anything that she wanted to be. She embarked on a concentrated programme, secretly trying to hone her skills. Sitting by the edge of the swamp, away from watchful eyes, she would burn offerings to the ancestors in the hope this would make them give her some useful pieces of information on which to build her future. 'Tell me, knowledgeable Mother,' she would mutter as she burned leaves and sweets and poured alcohol on the ground to loosen the tongues of the dead, 'how should I find a rich man to marry? Where will I live and what will I be doing in ten years' time? And what, after all, is the meaning of life?' The more profound the question, the more banal the response she received. After a furious argument with her mother one day, Nicanora fled to the swamp, poured in two bottles of *aguardiente* for good measure and then screamed at her ancestors, 'Please, please tell me something useful. Is there any hope for me? Will I ever leave this rotting, stinking place?' The request was met with a clear response: on Tuesday her mother had better take care of her oranges as a freak wind would whip up a minor tornado and wreak havoc in the market, making her fruit fly across the street and land in her neighbour's cauldron of fish soup. It wasn't the answer that Nicanora wanted or expected. She wondered momentarily whether feeding her ancestors two neat bottles of *aguardiente* before asking such an important question had been a good idea. In the end she had to face the truth. She had been blessed with the power to foresee the completely inconsequential, with a particular talent for accurate weather prediction.

Nicanora stormed home possessed of a fury the like of which she had never experienced before, fuelled by her ancestors' refusal to tell her anything remotely useful. She had made her decision. She was going to bury her gift and her mother's ambitions for her as a teller of mundane and banal fortunes once and for all.

'You're right,' she told her mother, 'I do have a gift and it is time that I proved it to all the gossips in the market and beyond.' She borrowed her mother's brightest shawl and an old crate that she used for packing her fruit and by six o'clock the following morning had set up a makeshift stall in the middle of the plaza. Above her head wavered a huge sign made out of a piece of rotting cardboard that she had mounted on a stick and on which she had scrawled: *Nicanora's predictions for the future — what everyone wants to hear. No matter is too small for my attention — weather forecasts a speciality.* Her mother had been right about one thing at least: the town certainly had a predilection for fortune-telling. By lunchtime the queue for her predictions had reached twice round the plaza and was beginning to stretch up the hill. Nicanora also gained some insights into why her ancestors remained firmly committed to imparting trivia to her. If the questions asked by her fellow townsfolk were anything to go by, it was because they had never troubled themselves to think about anything else.

'When will my goat give birth?' was the first question asked by her neighbour. It took Nicanora enormous control not to reply accurately that this event would be delayed for yet another two weeks and would be a trouble-free affair. Instead, she told her neighbour to go home immediately and not leave her goat's side as the event would be imminent, problematic and require her skilled attention to prevent her precious animal from dying.

'When will my Aunt Lola make her next visit?' asked another anxious neighbour, desperate to avoid the torrent of criticism that always accompanied the arrival of her relation at an unexpected hour in the middle of the night. 'You have nothing to worry about for another three months,' Nicanora reassured the exhausted woman as a vision of the tyrannical aunt making her way over the hill, ready to descend upon her well-meaning niece in the early hours of the next morning, appeared before her eyes.

'Who will win the football championship?' was the question on the tongues of most of the menfolk, who had recently set up an illicit betting club that met weekly beside the tree in front of the church, under the watchful eyes of the Virgin.

'It will be Don Aurelio's team, for sure,' Nicanora told one gullible soul, while reassuring the next that his hunch that Don Pedro's Jaguars would walk away with the title of Champions of the Swamp was the right one and worth the investment of a great many pesos. The task of giving false predictions was far more exhausting than imparting the very real tittle-tattle that was beginning to pass through her head. What Nicanora hadn't anticipated was that by inviting her neighbours to ask for her insights she had started to open her channel of communication with her ancestors, to the extent that she was becoming finely attuned to their continual quarrels. Nicanora began to be able to recognise individual voices, the loudest and most forceful of all belonging to her great-grandmother, Doña Alicia-Maria.

The story of the sad demise of her great-relation had been passed down the generations like a hideous family heirloom. Alicia-Maria had been born in a small, cold village in the mountains at a time when the tin mines were starting to clatter and boom. It was the same village that had been home to Nicanora's mother for the first twenty years of her life until a handsome young man from the lowlands passed through the mines and swept her away to the swamps with the offer of love, warmth and exotic fruit. Since then, not a day had gone by when Nicanora's mother had not bemoaned her impetuosity. 'If only I had stayed where I belonged,' she would mutter under her breath. 'Women didn't need to earn money where I come from. My mother got whatever she wanted for free. Milk, eggs, bread, she would go to the store and they would just give it to her. But here,' she spat the words out, 'everything is just money and work.'

'If it was so wonderful there, why on earth did you drag us here to this godforsaken piece of rat-infested swamp?' Nicanora asked.

'Don't you dare talk to me like that, you ungrateful child,' her mother snapped back. 'Your father and I have always done what is best for you and your sisters, even though we sacrifice ourselves for you every day. For one thing, I didn't want you to end up like poor Alicia-Maria.' And so the story of the demise of Alicia-Maria would be retold, each time with a new embellishment demonstrating the dangers of the mines and the future that would have lain ahead of Nicanora, had her mother contented herself with being a miner's wife.

Alicia-Maria had something of a passion for men. She was the godmother of many a riotous fiesta, and a local symbol of abundance and fertility, having given birth to fifteen children by the age of thirty-five, none of whom bore any resemblance to each other. Alicia-Maria had been taught by the missionaries that all men were equal in the eyes of God; taking a truly egalitarian approach to her pursuits, she considered any man fair game for her charms. Consequently she was adored by all the men in the neighbourhood, and despised by every woman within the twenty-mile radius of daily gossip. 'You have to understand,' Nicanora's mother explained to her, 'the mines are full of envy. There are people there who can make witchcraft with the devils that live deep in the caves.' Nicanora would sit enthralled by the tales of devils and witchcraft that her mother would then relay to her in defence of her departure from the village.

Alicia-Maria, while providing a joyous interlude in the lives of many men, made her husband's life a misery. She not only tormented him at home, but also shouted at him in public. Victor was a gentle man, and so completely bewitched by his wife's womanly allure that he could refuse her nothing, not even his humiliation at being the only man in the town's history to be sent out to fetch the eggs and milk on a regular basis. Victor would occasionally offer a mild protest against the unseemly challenge that carrying out such womanly tasks posed to his manhood. Alicia-Maria would respond with such enthusiastic confirmation that he was still a man where it mattered that he would forget his embarrassment and rush energetically from the bed to the market, brandishing a new shopping list.

Victor's mild manners were contrasted in every respect by those of his sister Genara. Genara was not only appalled by her brother's very public ridicule but eaten by jealousy at the popularity of her sister-in-law. She detested Alicia-Maria with as much passion as her sister-in-law adored men. Genara also harboured suspicions about where her husband disappeared to with such regularity on Tuesday evenings. 'Jealousy', Nicanora's mother informed her, 'is a ravenous beast. It grows like an overfed pig until it consumes everything in its path.' And so it was for Genara. The envy that had at first been a mere source of discomfort in her relationship with her sister-in-law grew over the years to such grotesque proportions that it finally filled every waking moment of her day and then started to inhabit the darker corners of her dreams. Genara finally could cope no longer. First she talked to her friends and confidantes, who consulted the coca leaves. Then she consulted the ancestors and the Mother

Earth. Finally, she consulted the *bruja* in the neighbouring town, renowned for her highly creative and innovative acts of witchcraft. The *bruja* listened to Genara's outpourings, brewed a cup of tea to soothe her agitated nerves and instructed her to return with an agile young toad and a handful of Alicia-Maria's hair. Capturing a young toad proved to be far less of a challenge to her ingenuity than surreptitiously clipping a lock of her sister-in-law's hair. For one thing, Alicia-Maria proudly wore her hair in two tightly plaited pigtails, which she was not in the habit of leaving lying around unattended.

Fortuitously, Genara's subconscious had started to work with as much malicious intent as her conscious mind and in one inspired dream the solution came to her. It so happened that it was soon to be the ceremony of the first haircutting of Alicia-Maria's youngest child. The first haircut was always a lavish affair. Friends and neighbours were invited to partake of as much alcohol as they could consume while a pair of large scissors was passed around the party for all invited to take a hack at the child's locks, on condition that they first laid down a large sum of money on its head.

Genara was the first guest to arrive for the haircutting, carrying a bottle of *aguardiente* that she had filled with water and from which she took ostentatious swigs. 'You watch your sister,' Alicia-Maria hissed at Victor in the kitchen, 'she's making a show of herself. She's taken to that bottle like a baby to the breast, and what's more, she isn't offering it to anyone else.'

Genara, who had mastered the art of acting at an early age, offered an impressive performance as a drunken aunt, and as the party progressed so did her good humour. Genara waited her turn as one by one her neighbours took their drunken swipes at the little boy's head until he could bear it no longer and ran bawling and clutching at his ears to the comfort of his mother's lap. Genara seized her opportunity. Lurching precariously towards her sister in-law, she swiped the scissors out of the hands of the priest, who had just taken his second drunken turn, and with uncanny precision chopped off one of Alicia-Maria's prized pigtails. Alicia-Maria stood silenced for a moment and then let out a scream, the like of which had only been heard before wrenched from the mouths of the devils deep under the ground. Dropping the child on his head she ran at her sister-in-law. In the confusion, Genara grabbed the dislocated pigtail and rushed from the room and on to the neighbouring town, stopping only to pick a bright young toad out of the watery green detritus by the side of the road.

The *bruja*, so the story was told, took a small doll and, placing a few drops of water on its forehead, christened it Alicia-Maria, and then buried it in a box along with the pigtail and the toad. Genara and Alicia-Maria never spoke another word to each other again, but at first all else seemed as it had been before. Then slowly Alicia-Maria began to notice small changes occurring in her body. First her legs began to swell; then her eyes grew bigger until they looked as if they were popping out of her head. She took herbs, she consulted the healer and the travelling doctor, but nothing helped her. Her legs grew so large and bent that she could no longer walk. Her skin covered in warts, turned hard and lumpy, and the only chastisements that she could offer her husband were harsh croaks in which the words were now indistinguishable. Alicia-Maria finally died of frostbite after she took to lying in puddles by the side of the road during the final months of her life.

'And so you see,' Nicanora's mother would finish the tale, 'I wanted to save you from the same fate as Alicia-Maria,' a decision for which Nicanora could only feel extremely grateful. Genara died of fright two months later, after meeting Alicia-Maria on a darkened path at night on her way back from visiting her bereaved brother.

Her mother hadn't told her the story for many years, but since Nicanora had started her predictions the story had begun to go round in her head. She could hear, at first dimly and then with increasing clarity over the following days, an argument between two unmistakable voices. 'Don't you believe any of it, my girl,' a croaky voice kept repeating, 'there never has been and never will be a toad in our family,' while a quieter and sharper voice would reply, 'It was the finest impression of a toad that I've ever seen.' The argument continued all day long with no change or interruption, only stopping occasionally when answers to the townsfolk's questions were required. By the end of her second week of giving predictions, the quarrelling had grown so loud that Nicanora could hardly hear her neighbours speak.

'That's enough. I don't care whether you're a toad or not,' she shouted at them finally, as her neighbour's niece approached to ask whether she was going to give birth to a boy or a girl. The woman burst into a flood of tears and, screaming 'Witch, *bruja*,' rushed home from the plaza to tell her husband. But it wasn't the arguing in her head that woke Nicanora the following morning, it was the sound of a large crowd of neighbours who had gathered in the yard of her mother's house to air their grievances.

'She put a spell on my niece,' her neighbour was saying. 'She told her she's going to give birth to a toad. She doesn't want a toad, she already has five daughters.'

'Well, I wouldn't count on what she tells you,' another shouted back, 'she's a fraudster. I've been waiting two weeks for my goat to give birth now. I haven't even left her side to eat. My chickens have all disappeared because I haven't been able to watch them, and even my husband is threatening to leave me if I don't return to my bed at night.'

'If you tell me about your stinking goat one more time I will go and strangle it,' one of the men shouted back. 'What do I care about your goat when I've lost a week's wages to a group of travelling vagabonds? She told me Don Aurelio's team would win for sure.'

'A week's wages?' another said. 'What is a week's wages to you when everyone knows you sleep with a stash of money under your mattress? And you still owe me a hundred pesos. I put my entire savings on Don Pedro's Jaguars.'

Through the chaos of voices Nicanora discerned that, so sure had each of the men been that their particular team would win, they had allowed a group of travelling Indians to enter the annual football contest, hoping to make a quick peso. For the first time since football had reached the town, the title of Champions of the Swamp had been carried away to the mountains by a group of itinerant pot sellers.

'And what were you doing, gambling away all our money?' a woman's tearful voice screamed back. 'We've lost everything. How are we supposed to feed our children now?'

Nicanora peeped out through the slats in the wall and saw the woman starting to hit her husband with her fists as some of the men tried to separate them. She lay down again and buried her head under her pillow to stifle the noise. She heard her mother's voice raised above the crowd, trying to appease her neighbours.

'I'm sure there must be some mistake,' she said. 'Even fortune-tellers need practice. She usually gets things right. You heard it for yourself, Doña Maria, when she predicted that Doña Ignacia would fall over in the plaza only last week.'

'Well, what does that tell anyone?' an angry man shouted back. 'Doña Ignacia falls over most days. Everyone knows she has a bottle of *aguardiente* hidden under her skirt.'

'Don't you talk like that about my mother,' Doña Maria replied.

'I only speak as I find,' the man said, belligerently.

'She told me to take all my fruit to the monthly market in Rosas Pampas,' a woman shouted over the din, 'and my donkey got stuck and tipped it all into the swamp. I've lost everything and your daughter is to blame. She must explain herself to us.'

The crowd started to chant, 'Nicanora, Nicanora.'

Nicanora was forced from the safety of her pillow by her mother, who grabbed her by the arms, pulled her to her feet and demanded to know the meaning of the chaos in her front yard.

'I don't know,' she said. 'I must have got some of the predictions wrong.'

'Wrong?' her mother yelled. 'How? How could you have got them wrong? You were getting them right before.'

'I told you I didn't have the gift,' Nicanora said defiantly. 'You're the one who forced me to do it. You told me to set up the stall.'

'You've made a fool out of me and all our family. I'm not getting you out of this. You go and explain yourself to them.' Her mother grabbed her by the hair and pushed her towards the door.

When Nicanora hit upon the idea of giving false predictions she hadn't considered the effect her answers might have upon her neighbours. At first she had planned to make slight mistakes, enough to ruin her mother's confidence in her gift but not enough to do any real harm. As the days wore on, she had become so bored with the monotony and predictability of her neighbours' questions that she had let her imagination have free reign and her fabricated answers had become more inventive and further

141

from the truth than she had intended. Now, it seemed, the crowd were discussing whether or not she had been practising witch-craft on them and whether or not she should be banished from the town forever. When Nicanora appeared on the front step, a hush descended on the crowd. 'I am truly sorry for any trouble I may have caused,' she began.

'Don't listen to her,' one of the women shouted. '*Bruja*, witch!'

'Be quiet,' Don Bosco called from the back. 'At least let her speak, let her explain herself.'

'It seems,' Nicanora continued, clearing her throat, 'that I may have made a few mistakes.'

'Mistakes – you call losing all my money a mistake?' Don Pedro heckled. 'You need to explain yourself better than that. If you offer your services as a fortune-teller, then we expect you to tell us the truth. You should have told us to beware of a group of vagabonds who would come and steal our cup from under our nose.'

Someone started to throw oranges at Nicanora and shouted 'Cheat, cheat,' while another demanded, 'She must be made to pay.'

'Pay for what?' Don Bosco shouted from the back of the crowd and he pushed his way forward through the flying fruit to stand beside Nicanora.

'She lied to us,' Don Pedro replied.

'How did she lie to you? She told you what you wanted to hear, which is all she promised,' Don Bosco continued addressing the crowd. 'It was you who chose to believe her, don't blame her for that.'

'What is it to you, Pedro Bosco?' one of the men shouted back at him. 'She didn't cheat *you* out your life savings.'

'Nobody cheated you but yourself,' Don Bosco replied. 'You took your chance because you thought you would make money out of your friends. She didn't tell you to let the pot sellers enter the championship, she only told you who might win.'

'But she told us all different things,' another man replied. 'From what she said, every team could have won, so what was the point of that?'

'Then she was right,' Don Bosco replied. 'Every team could have won. It was only because you thought you would make money from the travellers that you let them enter the competition.' The men started to look confused, unsure why they seemed suddenly to be losing the argument when they were so clearly in the right.

'She was wrong about my goat,' Nicanora's neighbour piped up.

'Not that bloody goat again,' an angry man replied, at which moment a young girl came running through the yard shouting, 'Mama, Mama, come quickly, the kid is coming, the kid is coming.' With the accusation fresh out of her mouth, the woman rushed from Nicanora's yard to see for herself if her goat was finally giving birth.

'You see,' Don Bosco continued, taking advantage of the situation, 'you didn't listen properly to what she was telling you, you were so eager to hear what you wanted to hear. Once she left its side, the goat has given birth just as Nicanora said it would. And you men, if you had listened to what she told you one of your teams would have won.'

'Well, why didn't *you* ask for a prediction, if you thought she was so good?' one of the men retaliated. Don Bosco looked at the crowd, then at Nicanora and then at his feet. The truth was that he had asked for a prediction of sorts. The previous evening, he had waited until all the townsfolk had gone home and had caught up with Nicanora as she packed up her stall. Taking her hand, he had looked into her eyes and asked her to tell him honestly if she thought he would soon find happiness and contentment. He held her gaze, so that she had no time to respond other than as her heart told her. She replied candidly that he would find happiness one day, that happiness comes in many forms and that he might not find it in the way that he wanted for a long time. Realising what she had said she blushed, apologised that she was tired and not thinking straight, returned home and decided that she was finally through with making predictions, true or false.

'How do you know that I didn't?' Don Bosco said to the crowd but looking at Nicanora, knowing in his heart that she had spoken the truth to him and to him alone. 'Why don't you all go home now and put this matter to rest.'

Nobody quite knew what else to say, the steam seemed to have been taken from their argument and people were beginning to want their breakfast. Slowly the crowd started to disperse, breaking up into the usual neighbourly quarrels. 'You didn't tell me you thought you were going to get such a good price for your oranges in Rosas Pampas,' a woman said to her neighbour as they left. 'Do I have to tell you everything?' the other replied. Finally, Nicanora and Don Bosco were left alone together in the yard.

'Thank you,' she said, not able to look him in the eyes.

'Tell me one thing,' he said, his eyes smiling. 'Did you really know what the true answers were?'

'Yes,' she replied.

'So why did you tell them lies?'

'Because I don't want to be a fortune-teller.'

Don Bosco looked confused. 'Well, setting up a predictions stall in the plaza is a strange way to go about not being a fortune-teller,' he said.

'I know it was wrong of me, but my mother kept telling everyone

I could see the future, and I wanted to put an end to it once and for all.'

'And can you?' he asked.

'I think so,' she replied.

'So, tell me one more thing. Did you lie to me when I asked you my question yesterday?'

'Yes, of course,' she said, looking at the ground. And she knew that with that she had told her final and worst lie of all.

'Good,' he said smiling again, and he squeezed her hand and arranged to meet her in the plaza the following Sunday for their usual stroll.

Thirteen

Nicanora sat staring at the letter that Don Teofelo had just handed to her. She had not yet been able to bring herself to read it, the very sight of it filled her with a deep sense of foreboding. She could not get from her mind the look she had seen in Don Bosco's eyes as he had walked away the previous day: the look that in one flicker of an eye had told her that, finally, the only man ever to have shown her any real kindness had given up hope.

Her first thought, immediately after it happened, had been to run down the street and beg him to forgive her foolishness. But her pride, which had been the cause of so many problems in her life, had prevented her and this time saved them both from more humiliation. Instead, she decided to pay him a visit the following morning to offer a simple apology for even suggesting he might want to sell his shop. She would thank him for the kindness he had always shown her and invite him to join her for lunch the following Sunday, this time unaccompanied. She went early, before the shop had time to fill up, to be sure to catch him alone. When she arrived the shutters were down and the door locked. She left, telling herself that maybe, for the first time in his life, he had decided to open late. When she returned a few hours later, the door was still locked, a dark silence seeping out through its closed blinds.

*

The quiet that hung over the plaza that morning was broken only by the commotion made by Don Bosco's friends, who turned up at the usual time to be met with the prospect that overnight their world had changed irrevocably.

'Bosco, are you in there?' Don Julio shouted through the shutters. 'Bosco, it's late, come and open up now, we're ready for our coffee.'

'For heavens sake, Julio, will you stop that,' Don Teofelo shouted back at him. 'Don't you think we've established by now that he is either not there or is hiding under the bed with a pillow over his head to get away from your noise?'

'What do you mean he's not there?' Don Julio replied. 'How can he not be there? He's never not there. Bosco, open up now,' he continued in a forlorn refusal to accept the evidence before his eyes.

'Julio,' Teofelo said quietly, 'if he were there he would have thrown a bucket of water over you by now.'

'Well, where can he be?' Don Julio said, his voice pleading with his friend to reassure him that everything was all right.

'I don't know where he is,' Don Teofelo replied truthfully. 'Perhaps he just wanted a change. Perhaps he's gone on holiday.'

'Holiday,' Don Julio said. 'He's opened up this shop every day for over twenty years, and he has never shown any signs of wanting a holiday. Why would he suddenly decide to take a holiday now, without telling anyone?'

'That is my very point,' said Don Teofelo. 'A man does exactly the same thing year after year, and tells himself every morning that he is doing what he wants and is happy and content. He tells himself the same thing day after day, until he finally comes to believe it. And then one morning he wakes and the world looks a little different. Some small thing has changed that nobody else would notice, but it makes him unsettled and he knows that he needs to do something new. Perhaps he opens his door at the same time he always does and suddenly in the flowers on the tree, which yesterday looked so fresh and hopeful, he notices the faintest hint of grey. Or he takes his cup of rich sweet coffee that he has brewed every morning for twenty years or more, and for the first time it leaves a bitter aftertaste in his mouth. Or . . .' Don Teofelo stopped, mid-thought.

Don Julio was staring at him open-mouthed. 'What are you talking about, Teofelo?' he said at last, and then resumed his banging. 'Open up now, Bosco, I want my coffee.'

'All I'm saying is that maybe our good friend Bosco has suddenly decided that after twenty years he doesn't want to open the shop today, or tomorrow come to that. He doesn't want to brew coffee for us any more or listen to everybody else's troubles, at least for a while. Maybe he just needs a break.'

'A break. You mean he's gone?'

'It certainly looks that way.'

'Well, what are we going to do? Where will we go? Who will we talk to?' Julio shouted, now running round in circles in a blind panic.

'We'll manage,' Don Teofelo said, patting his friend on the shoulder. 'After all, it may do us good. You can spend some more time on that neglected plot of yours, which is looking very overgrown these days. Perhaps that would be more useful than producing hot air to warm up Bosco's shop.'

'But what about Bosco? Where can he be? Aren't you even worried about him?'

'Julio,' Teofelo said, 'Bosco is a sensible man. He has taken care of himself for many years, I am sure he can continue to look after himself now.'

'Do you know something I don't?' Don Julio asked, after a moment's pause.

'Julio,' Teofelo said, placing his arm round his friend's shoulder, 'I have always known many things that you don't, but it has never worried you before.'

*

Don Teofelo did indeed know something, a good deal more than he was telling his friend, and he was far more worried than he was letting on. Don Bosco had arrived at his house well after midnight in a very agitated state.

'I'm going on a journey. I have a letter I want you to deliver to Nicanora,' Don Bosco had announced after waking Teofelo from a deep sleep. Bleary-eyed, Don Teofelo had tried to make sense of the sight in front of him. Don Bosco was standing on his doorstep in his new striped shirt and jeans, with his black Sunday hat on his head.

'It's to protect me from the sun, the rain, and unwanted thoughts,' Don Bosco informed his friend, as he handed him the letter and bent down to pick up a small frayed suitcase that he had placed at his feet.

'Now? You're going on a journey now, in the middle of the night, in that shirt and without a jacket?' Teofelo replied, taking Don Bosco by the hand and leading him into the comfort of his home.

'If I leave it until the morning I may change my mind, and my mind is made up,' Don Bosco said firmly as he followed his friend into the house.

'If you have made up your mind as you say, then that is that,' Teofelo replied. 'A good sleep and a change of clothes before starting your journey won't make any difference to your plans.'

It took Don Teofelo some time to persuade his friend that it did not make sense for him to start out on the first journey of his life by leaving his beloved town in the pitch-dark, when the night spirits wandered the swamp in search of lost souls and dejected barbers. After several comforting cups of sweet warm cocoa, Teofelo managed to convince him that no serious traveller would set out to the sound of hooting owls, and that the first birdsong of the morning was a much sweeter note on which to start his travels.

'But what has brought this on?' Teofelo asked.

'She was right,' Don Bosco replied. 'Do you know that? All those years ago, she was right about me.'

'Who?'

'Nicanora. I'm dull, Teofelo. I know you've been too kind to tell me. But I've done nothing with my life except cut hair and shave beards. And now I find I am dull.'

'Well, Bosco,' Don Teofelo replied, having listen with deep serious-ness to his friend's plight. 'If you are dull, what does that make me? I've spent a good many years of my life drinking beer and coffee with you, and have never found myself wanting anything more exciting than to pass my day in your company. I expect that must make me even duller than you. Should I pack my bags and leave as well?'

Don Bosco considered his friend's suggestion for a moment. 'I mean no offence to you when I call myself dull,' he replied. 'You are just too kind to notice that for years I have bored you senseless. You can't persuade me otherwise. I am going to make a journey so that I will have something interesting to say if I come back. Then, if I do return, at least I'll know why I'm here, and it won't be simply because I couldn't leave.'

'But isn't it good enough that this is your home?' Teofelo asked. 'We all need a home. This is where your friends are, where your work is, and this is where you will be missed if you go away.'

'You're very kind,' Don Bosco said meekly. 'Make sure you give the letter to Nicanora. Please don't let anyone else see it. I don't want to cause you or her any trouble. And if she asks for your help, will you give it to her?'

'Well, that would be a first,' Teofelo said. 'I've never known Doña Nicanora ask for help from anyone, although I know that you have helped her out more than once in your life. It was you who calmed everyone down after her ridiculous predictions, and you who welcomed her back after she married that good-for-nothing –' The look of sadness in Don Bosco's eyes made him stop and catch his words.

'Where will you be heading?' Teofelo asked, now realising the seriousness of his friend's intentions.

'I don't know,' Don Bosco replied. 'But I haven't seen my brother Aurelio since we were young men. He was the only one of us who had the courage to leave here. He's the only family I have left in the world. Perhaps it's time we saw each other again before we die.'

'Couldn't you invite him here? Surely he would come if he knew how you were feeling. Wouldn't he want to see the old town again, just once?'

'But that is hardly the point,' Don Bosco replied. 'I think you're trying to trick me. If he were to come here what would I have to say to him? I could say, here is the shop that I've worked in for a good part of my life, here is the plaza, there is the church and over there is the market. As you see, I've brought you all this way to show you that nothing has changed. And he would thank me politely and leave again in the knowledge that all is exactly as he left it. And besides,' Don Bosco added, 'I'm five years younger than he is. He's much too old to travel.'

True to his word, Teofelo woke his friend just as the first light was breaking. He made sure that Don Bosco ate a good breakfast of bread, eggs and coffee, and handed him a small parcel of cooked chicken, baked potatoes and fried plantain for the journey.

'So which way are you heading?' Don Teofelo asked again as he gave his friend a parting hug.

'I don't know yet, I will see which way the wind is blowing. I suppose it would be best just to follow the road,' Don Bosco replied. Don Teofelo stood in the doorway and watched his friend leave the house, his smart hat on his head and his battered old case in his hand. He watched Don Bosco walk across the plaza as he had done every day of his life, and then walk past the locked barber's shop and disappear out of sight as he had never done before. Don Teofelo poured himself another coffee, sat down and brushed the tears from his cheeks.

*

Teofelo wasn't sure what to say to Nicanora. He had never trusted her. She had broken his best friend's heart, that was certain, and now she had finally driven him out of town. Don Bosco had not told him what had passed between them the previous day, but clearly Don Julio's supposition that they had been making wedding preparations was incorrect. Teofelo now decided that Don Bosco had returned and offered his proposal to Nicanora, his hopes having been revived by the lunch date, and had once again been refused.

He's a fool, a silly old fool, he has only himself to blame. But a fool with a huge heart, Don Teofelo told himself, and the thought that Nicanora could refuse that heart made him more sad than angry. The truth was that although he knew he could not blame Nicanora for refusing Don Bosco's offer of marriage, he had never forgiven her for his own foolishness in betting his money away on Don Pedro's Jaguars and allowing the group of travelling vagabonds to win the Champions of the Swamp football trophy. And yet his best friend had sat there the previous night and trusted him, and him alone, with a letter for her, and had asked him to help her should she need it. Don Teofelo knew where his deepest loyalties lay. He waited for Nicanora in the plaza, and when he saw her approaching the shop he quietly took her to one side and put the letter into her pocket.

'Our good friend Don Bosco has gone on a little journey,' he said to her. 'He asked me to give you this, and to reassure you that should you need any help in his absence, you should not hesitate to ask me.'

'Where?' Nicanora asked. 'On a journey? What do you mean? How? On his own? He won't be able to get further than the edge of swamp.'

'You and I know that,' said Don Teofelo, 'but I expect he just needs to discover it for himself.'

'But why? Why would he do such a thing?'

'Because, Nicanora,' Teofelo replied, 'he has decided that at the age of fifty he would like to have something interesting to say.'

'To whom?' Nicanora asked.

'To you, I expect,' Teofelo said. At this, there was just the right look of concern in Nicanora's eyes.

*

Nicanora was still staring at the letter when Nena burst into the house later that morning, breathless with excitement, saying that there was a meeting in the plaza because Don Bosco had disappeared. Nicanora had still not been able to bring herself to read the note, and instead she handed it to Nena. If the words it contained came from her young daughter's mouth, she felt they might somehow be easier to swallow.

'Please read it to me,' she said, not able to meet Nena's eyes.

'Who's it from?' Nena asked.

'Never you mind,' Nicanora snapped and then, realising that Nena was about to find out anyway, said, 'Don Bosco.'

Nena drew in a deep breath.

'And he hasn't disappeared,' Nicanora added. 'He's just gone away for a few days. So don't you start spreading silly rumours.'

'It's not me,' Nena said, 'it's what everyone is saying. That's why they're having a meeting.'

'You'd better read it to me, then,' Nicanora said.

'"My dearest Nicanora,"' Nena began. 'Why does he call you "dearest"?'

'Nena.'

'"I would like to thank you, from the depths of my heart,"' Nena continued, '"for lifting the blanket under which I have buried my head for so many years. That I am a silly old fool, will, I am sure, come as news to nobody but myself."'

'I don't think he's silly,' Nena said. 'I think he's nice.' The look on her mother's face made her continue.

'"There are many things that I would like to have done with my life, for most it is now too late. I realise that you were right. Barbers are not very interesting people. So I have decided it is time that I took a journey to see something of the world before I die. I think your suggestion to turn my little establishment into a hat shop is an excellent one."'

'Hat shop? You're going to turn the barber's into a hat shop?'

'Nena,' Nicanora said sternly, 'will you please just get to the end. Where has he gone?'

'He doesn't say.'

'"I have been needing a new hat myself for some years now,"' Nena continued, unconsciously mimicking Don Bosco's voice, '"but have never had the time to make my way to Puerta de la Coruña to buy one. I have noticed that few people wear hats here, and when they do they are generally a battered and sorry sight. A hat shop will be of far more use than a barber's. I have left the key for you under the orange brick by the back door. I have always admired the way you have followed your heart (even when I have thought it has led you in the wrong direction). I am now following mine for the first time in my life. I hope you enjoy the little shop. It has made me contented for some years, and now I find it does not. Please take care of yourself. Your loving friend, as ever, Pepito."'

'"*Loving friend*,"' Nena said, her eyes wide with amazement at what she had just read. 'Why does he say that? Why has he gone away? Why has he given you his shop? Where are you going to get hats from?'

'Nena, that's enough,' Nicanora said. 'I can't listen to all your silly questions and think straight at the same time. You mustn't breathe a word of this to anyone. Do you promise me?'

'But why has he given you the key to his shop?' Then, suddenly piecing the possibilities together, she said, 'Oh no, is he in love with you? Has he kissed you?'

'Nena, that's enough,' Nicanora said, trying not to let tears well in her eyes. Then, taking Nena by the hand she left the house to see what trouble was brewing in the plaza.

Fourteen

The mayor had left home that morning in an unusually ebullient mood. The source of his good humour was a sound night's sleep in his own bed, with his wife, for the first time in weeks. What was more; he was convinced that when he returned that evening there would be no trace of his sister-in-law, Doña Lucia, anywhere in the house.

'She's like an overfed rat, infecting my wife with her rancid gossip,' the mayor confided to Ramon, 'lying there in my guest room like a great big cow that can't find its way home. Eating my food and getting fatter by the day.'

Ramon, not being a married man, was not used to being consulted on such affairs. He squirmed at this intimacy from his patron, before asking, 'Is there anything that you would like me to do about it, señor?'

'You can see if that bloody doctor has any poison,' the mayor replied. Ramon duly noted it on his 'To do' list.

*

Ever since the mayor's return from his disastrous meeting with the district officer and his stay in Rosas Pampas, his wife had refused him entry to the 'marital suite', as she now liked to call the bedroom, putting an emphasis on the word marital. Doña Lucia, who had supposedly only been staying for a few weeks during the mayor's absence, had taken up permanent residence in the guest quarters. The mayor had been reduced to sleeping in the sitting room, on an old chaise longue, a wedding present from his great-aunt, Doña Teresa.

'It's the only remaining trace of our family's European pedigree,' she had told him as she forced him to take away the hideous piece of furniture, 'since your father married that filthy *mestizo* whore.'

Doña Lucia was clearly relishing her status as her sister's confidante and marriage adviser, almost as much as she was enjoying the obvious discomfort it brought her brother-in-law. She prided herself on her skills as a solver of all problems marital, making a modest income from her activities as the town's matchmaker. On Lucia's advice, Gloria was now refusing to speak a word to her husband and was directing all communication through her sister.

'You know, her heart is in pieces,' Lucia confided to the mayor one evening, over dinner.

'I still don't know what I'm supposed to have done,' he replied.

'Rodriguez, we women are complicated creatures,' Lucia said confidentially. 'I'm afraid she has lost her faith. She is grieving for what you once were. You'll have to win back her trust.'

'Well, if she won't let me into the bedroom, how am I supposed to do that?' he asked, genuinely confused.

'Oh, Rodriguez,' Lucia replied with a hint of the coquette in her voice, 'you'll have to do better than that.'

On Lucia's advice, Gloria had been boycotting the dining room for a week and was living off sandwiches and titbits brought to her room by her sister. Seeing that the strategy did not seem to have brought about contrition from her husband, Gloria was desperately searching for a way out of the corner into which she had locked herself. In her self-imposed isolation, doubts about her sister's motives were starting to take hold. Gloria was beginning to feel that Lucia had manipulated her into this situation, and that Lucia now had free rein over the house. Gloria could not help feeling that she was the one being punished, banished to the bedroom while Lucia dined with *her* husband, at *her* table, in *her* house. In her darkest moments, Gloria was beginning to face a deep, painful and unspoken suspicion about Lucia's fidelity with her husband, which she was struggling to deny to herself. The subtle hints that Lucia had dropped recently tormented and tantalised Gloria, fuelling her dark moods. Yet, until now, she had never allowed herself to confront the possibility of this greatest betrayal of all, and she could not quite bring herself to believe it. She was desperate for her husband to do something to prove to her that her suspicions could not be true. Above all, she wanted him to make Lucia leave the house, as soon as possible.

'You've been so kind to me,' Gloria said to her sister. 'But I have started to wonder whether he has suffered long enough.'

'Never forget what he has done to you,' Lucia replied. 'Remember, he was seen with those two young women at that guest house in Rosas Pampas. And he hasn't even said sorry about it yet. Your dignity is at stake.' And with these words from Lucia the terrible stab of doubt pierced Gloria's heart again.

'But, Lucia,' she said, trying to find a defence for her husband's behaviour, 'you know he had to stay there all that time because he was suffering from a bout of the swamp fever. He couldn't even get out of bed.'

'I'm sure he couldn't, swamp fever, and the company of two young sluts,' Lucia said.

'Oh, but Lucia,' Gloria protested, 'we have no proof of that. It's just malicious gossip. Who could possibly have seen him there?'

'Even the trees have eyes,' was all Lucia would say on the topic.

*

With the thoughts of the previous night in his mind, the mayor gazed at the mounds of paperwork on his desk, sat back in his chair and smiled to himself. His strategy to win back his wife's affections had been executed with precision. He had resisted the urge to simply throw Lucia's belongings out into street and demand that Gloria stop all her nonsense, unlock the door and let him back into the bedroom. Lucia's influence had taken too firm a hold over his wife in his absence and he feared that unless he handled the situation with care, he might never have the house to himself again. It was imperative that Gloria should be the one to ask Lucia to leave.

Unbeknown to Lucia, in the past few days he had started delivering little breakfast trays to his wife. Setting them on the floor outside the bedroom, he pushed love notes under the door to alert Gloria to their presence. The previous night, having built up the anticipation, he had made his approach. He had ensured that Lucia was dead to the world by slipping some sleeping pills into the evening cocoa taken to her by the maid. He then sat outside the bedroom and started whispering soft lovelorn murmurings at the door.

'Are you there, my tender little peach?' he sang.

Gloria, who was sitting up in bed filing her nails at the time, at first thought she was hearing things, perhaps mice in the wardrobe.

Over their long and tempestuous marriage, her husband had called her many things, but a tender little peach had never been one of them. She decided she would make a visit to the handsome doctor that Lucia had told her about, to have her ears looked at. The singing continued. She got up and moved towards the door.

'My darling, my sweetheart. I can't bear this any longer, I'm aching all over with my devotion to you,' the voice continued. Gloria put her ear closer to the door as her husband's eulogy floated into the room.

'My darling, I'm wasting away. Please let me in and let me hold you close to me again, my soft little flower blossom.' Gloria felt a tear well up in her eye.

'My love,' he continued, holding his aching back as he crouched by the door. 'I know I've been a bad husband at times and a foolish man, but I'm falling apart.'

He tried to move into a more comfortable position. As he did so, a muscle in his back, which had been slowly tightening after weeks of sleeping on his European ancestry, went ping. He slumped to the floor in agony. With no warning, he started to sob. He had no idea where the sobs had come from. He hadn't even known that they had been bubbling in his heart, waiting to break out. Perhaps they were the result of the sudden pain in his back, perhaps of the growing tension he had been living under since his return home, or perhaps of the realisation that his life and marriage were a total disappointment to everyone involved.

He had married Gloria on a whim. He had not wanted to marry at all, especially not at the age of nineteen. Doña Teresa had tricked him into it with creatively vindictive flair, to ensure that he would never leave the town. He had been brought up in the small but elegant coastal town of Manola, several weeks' journey down river from the swamp in which he had languished for his adult life. His family had had high hopes for the young Rodriguez, the only boy out of their six children. His father, a respected lawyer, had devoted his life to establishing the family reputation in a town in which they were still considered to be relative newcomers, having lived there for only two generations. After many years of attending the right functions, wining and dining the appropriate people and having the most influential clients on his lists, he finally won his reward and was voted mayor, a position he had coveted.

It was entirely expected that Rodriguez would follow in his father's footsteps. Nobody had ever questioned the path his life would take. But the young Rodriguez did not choose his friends wisely. By the age of sixteen, he had taken to spending his evenings in the bars frequented by the sailors who came and went through the port. His parents, unaware of their son's pastimes, were content with their delusion that he was reading legal statutes in the library. Instead, his studies were teaching him how to hold down impressive quantities of beer without falling over or throwing up, and he was beginning to be able to win beer-drinking competitions with a panache that impressed even the most hardened of sailors. It was during this time that he was introduced to the women who made their living in the little rooms at the backs of the bars. He felt more at ease in their presence than he had in the company of anyone for years. They listened to him, comforted him when he got maudlin, laughed when he cracked jokes, and asked nothing of him except a very reasonable payment, at a discounted student rate, for the pleasure of the comfort of their bodies at night.

His father, unknown to him, was working on a plan to secure his son's future, through marriage to the daughter of his influential and highly esteemed business partner. While Rodriguez was discovering the meaning of pleasure, his father was ensuring that his future, life and liberty were all neatly sown up in a deal that would handsomely benefit both parties. Rodriguez had an inkling that something was afoot when the daughter of the business partner started to appear frequently at the house for afternoon tea. A pale, quiet, thoughtful young woman, she would look anxiously at her parents for approval every time she dared to open her mouth. After her visits, Rodriguez would disappear from the house, increasingly for several days at a time, seeking solace in the company of real women.

It was during one of these absences that he managed to destroy his family's reputation overnight. His father had fought and won his mayoral campaign under the banner of: *Keep Manola pure: a town built on clean hearts and sound minds.* As part of the purity campaign, his father had devised a plan to shut down all the brothels in the port area, which he considered a scourge on the town's wholesome reputation, if not its income. A series of secret raids were planned with the police, to take place on a particular night; the police having taken advantage of the notice they had been given to warn their favourite madams to get the best girls out of town.

On the day of the planned raid, one of the police officers, hearing that the mayor's son was a frequent visitor to one of the targeted establishments on the list, sent word to the mayor to make sure Rodriguez was not on the premises that night. The mayor, outraged at the insinuation, went to find his son among the law tomes in the library; but he was nowhere to be found. In growing fury, he decided to go to the brothel himself and remove Rodriguez before the raid took place. Unfortunately, the raid was brought forward two hours by the head of police, who was due to go on leave the following day and had a particularly early start planned. The mayor, who had gone to the brothel in disguise, was rounded up with all the other punters, having been caught in a room with a naked woman in the middle of an altercation with a young man. The police assumed it was a row between two regulars who had got their timings confused. Even more unfortunate for the mayor, the punter in the room next door was a journalist from the leading newspaper that had opposed his electoral campaign. The paper ran the story the following day with the headline: *Hypocrisy governs Manola: Mayor caught with his trousers down.*

The next week, Rodriguez was sent away from the family home, to tend to the affairs of his widowed great-aunt in a town at the end of the world, where he could do no more damage to the family name. Rodriguez had at first gone willingly, prepared to ingratiate himself with his wealthy relative with the aim of inheriting her fortune, having been led to believe that she was unlikely to last the year out. More than thirty years on she looked exactly the same, and gave no signs of being inclined to pass her fortune to anyone, least of all her great-nephew.

Doña Teresa had introduced the mayor to Gloria during his first year in Valle de la Virgen. Gloria was a very flirtatious and fulsome young woman, and he had instantly felt at ease with her. His aunt had introduced her as the daughter of the neighbouring estate owner, and Rodriguez swiftly calculated that, if he played his cards right, he could be heir to most of the land in the province by the time the year was out. What his great-aunt failed to tell him, until the day after the wedding, was that Gloria's father had played his own cards extremely badly. Having gambled his land away, he was desperately trying to marry off his daughters, who were becoming a drain on his dwindling resources and fragile nerves. What was more, Gloria was as good a match as any for the extravagant behaviour of her husband. And yet, over the years, despite all the failings of their lives and marriage, the mayor and his wife had found a way of accommodating each other, which at times was reassuring and comforting to both, and which, in brief moments of clarity, they recognised as love.

*

It was the sobbing that did the trick. It was exactly what Gloria needed to hear. Suddenly the mayor heard the lock click. The bedroom door opened slowly and an eye peeped through the crack. With the swiftness of a cat bolting from a trap, Gloria's head then poked out.

'Rodriguito, my dear,' she said softly. 'Do you really mean what you say?'

'Of course I do, my sweet,' he said, scrabbling to his knees. 'You are the world to me. Let me in now, my love. We have gone on too long with this, don't you think?'

'Say those beautiful things to me again,' Gloria said softly.

'What beautiful things are those, my sweet?' the mayor asked, already having forgotten the poetic phrases that had come to his mind in desperation.

'The thing about the peach,' said Gloria.

'What thing about a peach is that?' the mayor said.

'You remember,' Gloria said, 'the thing about me being a tender little peach.'

'Please, let me in, my tender little peach,' the mayor sang again, struggling to his feet. And for the first time since his arrival home, he was welcomed back into the bedroom. Before his wife had time to rearrange her hair, he lay down on the bed and fell into a deep sleep, his snores drowning out her tender words. He was woken in the morning by Gloria shaking him violently.

'Wake up, wake up, Lucia mustn't find you here,' she whispered, as if they were young lovers about to be caught in the middle of a clandestine tryst.

'It's my bloody bedroom,' he said, the husband of the night before having vanished.

'Let me deal with Lucia,' Gloria protested. 'If she knows you've slept here, she'll think you've forced your way in and will start spreading all sorts of rumours. Let me tell her today that I have forgiven you.'

'As long as she'll be gone from my house by tonight,' the mayor said. 'We need some time to ourselves, my sweet, my little peach.'

'I'll deal with her,' Gloria said, determined that this was finally the day when she would confront Lucia and put an end to her insinuations forever. 'I promise that by this evening she *will* be gone.' The mayor had then to face the indignity of climbing out of the bedroom window and creeping through the undergrowth and back into the sitting room, so that his sister-in-law would not know he had managed to have one good night's sleep in his own bed.

*

The mayor was so pleased with himself that he still knew how to win back his wife's favours after all these years, that he felt obliged to share some of his manly wisdom with Ramon, when he scuttled back into the office an hour later in an agitated state.

'Ah, Ramon,' the mayor said. 'How are things with you today?' Ramon was so flabbergasted by the unusual nature of the question that he was quite unable to answer it. Instead he busied himself tidying the mayor's desk and, in so doing, knocked the mounds of unread paperwork into a heap on the floor, burying the letter marked *Urgent* that he had placed there several weeks ago and had failed to tell the mayor about.

'There now,' he said, having rearranged the documents. Forgetting what had brought him to the room in the first place, he made to leave as quickly as he could.

'You're not a married man, are you, Ramon?' the mayor asked, stopping him in his tracks. 'Very wise, very wise. It takes a man of experience to really understand what makes a woman like my wife tick.' He winked knowingly. Ramon, horror-struck lest the mayor in his strange mood were about to divulge any more intimate details of married life, stood motionless in the middle of the room for a second, then suddenly recalled what had brought him there.

'There's a rabble in the plaza, señor,' he said.

'There's always a rabble in the plaza, Ramon,' the mayor replied. 'What do you expect from this bloody town?'

'No, there's trouble brewing,' Ramon whispered. 'Don Bosco's gone missing.'

'Missing? How can he go missing?'

'He's gone. Just like that. People are saying he may have been eaten in the middle of the night.'

'Good. Bloody annoying little barber,' the mayor replied.

'But I need a haircut,' Ramon said pitifully. Seeing the look on his assistant's face, the mayor began to take in what he was being told.

'Well, where is he? A man like that can't just go missing. Not at his age.'

'He has. The shop is locked. It's been locked since last night and nobody knows where he is. They are demanding that you come down and do something about it.'

'What can I do?'

'I don't know. Address the crowd. Reassure them that he will come back. Organise a search party. Find him.'

'I'll tell you what I'm going to do,' the mayor said briskly. 'I'm going to get that bloody shop back.'

*

As the crowd began to amass in the plaza, a storm was brewing in the mayor's house. Doña Lucia, who had been given notice to leave after breakfast, had broken down completely, confessing that over the years she had been engaged in a battle to fight off the mayor's advances and preserve the integrity of her sister's marriage. There was something in the tone of Lucia's voice that troubled Gloria, making her doubt her judgement. But when Lucia ingeniously managed to find conclusive evidence of the mayor's recent misdemeanours, Gloria could cope no longer with the humiliation of the apparent deception. A hurriedly scrawled love letter to an unnamed mistress and an extraordinary item of women's underwear were revealed to her, the latter having been bought by Lucia many years ago and never having found a use, until now.

'He has deceived us both,' Lucia said, melodramatically.

Gloria, stood in the middle of the dining room holding the offending items in her hand.

'What am I to do? What am I to do?' she said, over and over again to herself, lamenting the tatters of her marriage.

'Make him jealous, my dear,' Lucia said with a flourish of the hand. 'Shame him publicly. Make him realise the woman you are.

Show him that you can live without him. That is all there is for it.
I will be here to help you.'

Gloria got dressed for the first time in weeks, grabbed a bottle of
the mayor's finest whisky from the cupboard, and left the house,
uncertain where to go, and what her future held.

Fifteen

Nicanora had never seen the plaza so full. She had not realised that so many people lived in the town. Not even in her youth, when the vendors from the surrounding swamp villages made their weekly pilgrimage to set up their stalls in the Sunday market, had she seen the place so bubbling with life. She slowly made her way into the crowd, holding tightly onto Nena's hand. Men were huddled together in conspiratorial groups. As she pushed past them, she caught the rumours as they were being delivered fresh from the wagging tongues.

'I hear he's dying of a broken heart,' one man said to his neighbour, his tittle-tattle a bit too close to the truth for Nicanora's comfort. 'Apparently he's had a secret lover for years and now she has rejected him. Perhaps he's taken himself into the swamp to die, like the sly old dog that he is.'

'Yes, my dog did just that,' his friend replied. 'But that was because it had hurt its leg. It took me two days to find him. He was nestling under the roots of the old tree over there. Do you think perhaps that is where Don Bosco is?'

'At least some things never change,' Nicanora thought to herself.

'They are the most useless bunch of gossips that ever were.' She glanced warily over at the little shop. It remained dark and silent, the shutters down. A group of men stood forlornly outside like children who had lost their parents in the crowd, not knowing which way to turn. She spotted Don Teofelo in the middle of the group. He was talking to them and by the look on his face she supposed he was trying to calm the agitation among his friends. Teofelo's apparent ease at the situation did nothing to quell her own rising panic. She had a sense that something was unravelling, as if an unrecognised vital thread had suddenly been pulled from the town and its whole fabric was about to fall apart.

Women were now making their way from the market to the plaza, having left their fruit rotting on their stalls in the midday sun. It was the time of day when all self-respecting fruit vendors would normally slash their prices and take advantage of their clientele all gathered in one place. But nobody was trying to sell fruit today. Fidelia, having just spotted Nicanora, rushed up to her. 'I hear Don Bosco has gone missing,' she said, breathless with excitement. 'Do you know anything about it?'

'Why should I know anything?' Nicanora replied, alarmed that she was already starting to be the target of the town's gossip, and not for the first time in her life.

'Well, you used to be good friends, didn't you? That's all I'm saying. Such a shame about him. He always had a soft spot for you.'

But before Nicanora could answer, Fidelia's niece joined them. 'Have you heard? Don Bosco has disappeared. Apparently the *kachi kachi* came in the night and ate him.'

Nicanora left the pair to their gossip and tried to make her way to the middle of the plaza, keeping Nena close at her side. In the midst of the chaos she saw the Gringito sitting cross-legged under the tree. He was smoking a cigarette and quietly watching the proceedings, as if nothing unusual was happening. Nicanora shivered, remembering Don Bosco's words of warning. She had a deep feeling of discomfort that the arrival of the Gringito had somehow led to the events that were unfolding.

'We're going to have to do something about him,' she whispered to Nena.

'What do you mean?' Nena replied.

'He worries me. Something is not right about all this. First he arrives, then Don Bosco goes missing.'

'But you know why Don Bosco has gone missing, and it has nothing to do with the Gringito,' Nena said. 'He isn't the one who upset Don Bosco.'

Nicanora felt the thud of Nena's words against her heart. She squeezed Nena's hand tightly to silence any more words of truth that might be about to pour out of her child's mouth. One of the men from the group who had been standing outside the barber's shop also started to make his way to the centre of the plaza. 'We demand to know what is going on. We demand to know what is happening and where our barber has gone,' he shouted, to nobody in particular.

'Yes,' another from the group joined in. 'We've been waiting since this morning for the shop to open, and we want our mayor to explain where our barber has gone. We need our beards shaved.' And a handful of the men started to chant, 'We want the mayor, we want the mayor.'

Nicanora rolled her eyes. 'Is that all they are worried about?' she said to Nena. 'Is that all they think about? Is that what Don Bosco means to them? Do they think he is just a barber with nothing better to do with his life than shave their stupid beards?'

Nena looked up at her mother and said nothing. A small shrill voice piped up above the chanting men. 'Make way for the mayor — make way for the mayor please.' Nicanora saw Ramon running through the crowd like a dog in a frenzy, unable to find its master. Nobody paid any attention to him and carried on talking.

'I heard he's lost his mind,' a man standing next to Nicanora said to his friend. 'Apparently he attacked Don Teofelo with a knife only a few weeks ago. I think Teofelo has tried to hush it up to protect him.'

'Well, whatever has happened, Bosco is clearly not all he seemed,' his friend replied. 'I heard that he borrowed money from the mayor and can't pay it back and he's had to leave town in disgrace. Let's see what the mayor has to say about that.'

Nicanora turned to the men in a fury. 'How dare you spread such thoughtless rumours,' she said, her words dripping with indignation. 'Don Bosco is worth more than all of you put together. He has never done anything wrong or caused harm to anyone. How dare you talk badly of him.' But her words were drowned out by the pointless babble of the crowd. The men drifted off to test out their theories with their neighbours, none the wiser for Nicanora's lost words.

'What's going on? What's happening?' a familiar voice suddenly said in her ear. Turning, Nicanora was relieved to see the young doctor standing by her side.

'Don Bosco hasn't opened the shop today,' Nena said. 'And everyone is very upset.'

Arturo looked at her kindly and laughed. 'I see,' he said. 'Isn't a man allowed to have a day off once in a while without the town calling a general meeting about it?'

'No, it isn't that,' Nicanora said. 'He's gone. He's shut the shop up and he's gone. Nobody knows where he is.'

'He's gone on a journey, because he thinks he's dull,' Nena added.

'That's enough,' Nicanora said, giving her daughter's hand another tight squeeze.

'Well I'm sure he'll be back soon,' Arturo said, patting Nena on the head. 'But I don't understand why everybody is so upset, just because he has shut the shop for a day.'

'Because', Nicanora replied, 'he has never done anything like that before.' Arturo was silenced by the look of real anguish on her face.

Ramon, who was still running in circles through the crowd, started shouting again. 'Make way for the mayor. Make way for the mayor and the town council. The mayor is about to speak. Attention please. Attention please. Attention for the mayor.' The buzz of voices only grew louder in anticipation. 'Silence now,' Ramon continued, his voice audible only to those next to him. 'Silence for the mayor and the town council. Let the mayor speak. Let the mayor speak, I say.'

The mayor had by now made his way to the middle of the plaza to where Ramon had inspirationally placed a wooden box from which he was to make his address. Sweat dripped from the mayor's face as he attempted to mount the rickety podium. The crowd's attention was momentarily held by the impromptu balancing act being performed in front of them as the mayor attempted to steady himself on the box. He swayed backwards and forwards for a few seconds, before toppling into the awaiting audience. On the fourth attempt, having gained a precarious equilibrium, he seized the moment for an announcement.

'The town council . . .' he began, wobbling as he spoke. 'The town council . . .' and he lost his balance. 'The town council', he said again, trying to regain the podium for the fifth time, 'has called an extraordinary meeting . . .'

His words drifted aimlessly above the heads of the crowd, who by now had lost interest in what the mayor was saying and were instead involving themselves in a heated debate as to what he might be about to tell them. Ramon started running around again, kicking people on the ankles as he went. 'Silence now. Silence now, the mayor is trying to speak. Silence now for the town council. Have some respect please.'

'The town council', the mayor tried again, 'has called an extra-ordinary meeting.'

'No you haven't,' a man shouted back. 'We were here first.'

'Extraordinary indeed,' another shouted. 'I didn't even know we had a town council.' The crowd were loosening up and beginning to enjoy themselves. They started to laugh encouragingly at the participation from the floor.

'No heckling,' Ramon shouted, running up to one of the sniggering men and kicking him on the shins. 'No heckling now. No heckling at the back, I say. Silence while the mayor speaks.' The man brushed Ramon aside with a swipe of his hand, as if swatting an annoying fly.

'The town council has called an extraordinary meeting,' the mayor continued, the sweat drenching his shirt. 'Ramon, please could you read out the agenda for the meeting.' Ramon rummaged in his pocket and pulled out a crumpled piece of paper.

'Agenda item number one,' the mayor read, 'is occupancy of abandoned barbers' shops in the event of the disappearance of their owners.'

'What do you mean, "barbers' shops"?' the heckler shouted. 'We only have one. And now that is shut we don't have any.'

'The district officer has informed me that we will be having a visit from the provincial authorities in the next few weeks, and I', the mayor continued, 'intend to show them how we have developed our important tourist trade so that the town can continue to prosper.'

'What do you mean, "tourist trade"?' shouted the heckler. The mayor looked in direction of the Gringito, who was still sitting under the tree, quietly smoking.

'Oh no,' Nicanora whispered to Nena. 'I knew there would be trouble soon.' But the mayor's attention was deflected from the Gringito by the shouting man.

'Never mind all that. We want to know where Don Bosco is.'

'Yes,' another agreed. 'We demand to know where our barber is.'

'Well *I* don't bloody know,' the mayor replied.

But the men were no longer listening. 'We want our barber. We want our barber,' they chanted.

'Well, I haven't got him,' the mayor shouted over the noise, putting his hands into his pockets and pulling them out empty, as if by way of proof.

'I wish someone *would* bring him back,' the woman standing next to Nicanora said. 'I'm fed up with my husband already. He's been moping around the house all morning and he's really getting on my nerves.'

'You're the town council, you should do something about it,' one of the men said.

'Don Bosco's whereabouts are not my concern,' the mayor answered. 'This is a free town. A man can leave whenever he chooses. I can't stop him. I am only here to announce that if the barber's shop is not reopened by the keyholder by tomorrow, the shop will be taken over by the town council. We cannot allow prime business premises to remain empty, especially in our central plaza.'

Nicanora held onto the key in her pocket as the mayor spoke.

'But it's Bosco's shop. We need Bosco. We need a barber,' a man shouted, and to Nicanora it seemed that he was directing his accusing words at her alone.

'He'll be back by tonight,' she told herself. 'He will be opening the shop again tomorrow. He must.'

'If you are all so concerned about the whereabouts of Don Bosco, then you find him,' the mayor challenged. 'I now formally announce that the town council is looking for volunteers to go into the swamp and bring back our missing barber. Ramon will lead the search party.'

There was silence. Ramon turned white. 'But señor, what about the *kachi kachi*?' he whispered into the mayor's ear.

'Do I take it there are no volunteers?' the mayor continued, ignoring Ramon. 'I see that when it comes to it, our good friend doesn't mean as much to you as you all say.'

'Don't believe that for one minute,' Don Teofelo said, stepping forward at last. '*I* will lead the search party, and it will be made up of people of *my* choosing. Julio here will accompany me, for one.' Julio looked as horror-struck as Ramon. He had always harboured the deepest fear of and respect for what lay in the depths of the swamp and had never troubled himself to venture in to find out what it may be.

'I need at least two more volunteers,' Teofelo shouted. 'Who will come with us to find our friend?'

The silence was broken by a voice at the edge of the crowd. 'I will,' Arturo said raising his hand. 'You may need a doctor with you,' he added.

177

Ernesto, who had just joined the crowd and had missed most of the previous discussion, was swept away by the drama of the moment and shouted, 'Wherever the doctor goes, I'll go.' He had heard similar words spoken in the adventure movies in Puerta de la Coruña and liked the sound of them coming from his own mouth.

'Oh Lord,' Nicanora whispered to Nena. 'If this is Don Bosco's search party then the poor man is lost forever.'

'You have until tomorrow,' the mayor replied. 'If our barber is not returned to us by then, I am officially notifying you that the property will come under the auspices of the mayor.'

He then turned and left, with Ramon running behind him muttering, 'Señor, señor, if I get eaten by the *kachi kachi* my mother won't like it, she won't like it at all.'

Sixteen

Arturo had been in a state of confusion all day. The previous evening a visitor had come to the clinic, the thought of whom sent a feverish and guilty tingle through his limbs. He had been taken home after the lunch party by his new friends with the elation of a man who finally feels he belongs, and had fallen immediately into a deep, alcohol-induced mid-afternoon sleep. He had woken several hours later with the feeling that a vice had been clamped to his head and that someone was watching him.

'It's good for hangovers,' Isabela said as he woke, and she handed him a cup of warm sweet herb tea. 'My mother made me come to make sure you were all right. I was worried that she might have poisoned you.'

'Why?' Arturo asked, laughing in surprise. 'Is that what she was planning to do?'

'You can never be too sure with my mother,' Isabela replied in the flirtatious tone that formed her defence against the disappointments of the world, and then continued: 'I was worried about you. My brother thought that you are not used to drinking.' The seductive warmth of her voice sent a shiver through Arturo's veins. He tried to remain formal and polite with her at first, but soon found himself giving in, relaxing in her company as she entertained him with her rendition of the afternoon's events. He laughed helplessly at her uncannily accurate impersonations of all the leading characters at the lunch table, especially her mother and Don Bosco. She had the same engaging manner as her brother, and a quick wit that Arturo sensed was still waiting to find its direction.

'You should be an actress,' he said, as she gave a perfect imitation of her mother's interactions with the hapless Gringito.

'Oh, I will be one day,' Isabela said with absolute seriousness. 'I don't want you to think that I will stay here forever. I'm not going to spend the rest of my days selling my mother's oranges. She may have been content to do that with her life, but I want to make something of myself. I'm going to be a film star.' Arturo heard the echo of another's words and spirit as Isabela spoke, and he instinctively moved away from her to put a safe distance between himself and the temptation of the attraction that he was trying to deny. In Isabela, he sensed an energy that was waiting to be unleashed on the world. In the company of Isabela and her family, he felt for the first time in his life that he was with real people. He tried to refocus the emotions that had been awakened by Isabela to thoughts of Claudia, and an icy anxiety gripped his heart.

'I must go,' Isabela said, standing up to leave, as if she had detected the shift in the flow of his thoughts, 'my mother will be wondering where I am. I'm pleased that you're all right, though. I'm sure you will be very good for us here. As I said, I think you are probably a quiet kind of hero,' and she leaned over and gently kissed him on the cheek as she said goodbye. It was Isabela's kiss that gave him the confidence to take the dramatic action and offer his services to the search party.

*

Arturo and Ernesto hurried back to the clinic, with the excitement of men preparing for a mission. For the first time since his arrival, Arturo felt a sense of purpose.

'What exactly is this *kachi kachi*?' he asked Ernesto as they walked up the path.

'Oh nothing to be concerned about,' Ernesto replied. 'People believe that it wanders the swamp at night and has an appetite for lost and lonely travellers. That's why it's not advisable to go out there alone.'

'What does it look like?'

'Many things. Sometimes an owl, sometimes a snake, sometimes a cat. Whatever it chooses to be.'

'Do you believe in it, Ernesto?' Arturo asked, with a detectable note of concern in his voice.

'No,' Ernesto replied. 'I did see it once when I was a child. It chased me through the forest. But now I've stopped believing in it, I haven't seen it for years.'

As soon as they reached the clinic Arturo busied himself gathering the necessary supplies, ticking off his hurriedly prepared checklist. 'Cream for mosquito bites, plasters, bandages . . .' Ernesto disappeared into the darkened consultation room in search of the ointments and injections he had safely stored under the bed. Two minutes later he ran out screaming. Arturo rushed to see what had happened, and found Ernesto standing shaking on the step of the clinic.

'What is it? Are you hurt?' Arturo asked. Ernesto said nothing. He stood shaking and pointing at the door.

'What is it? What's in there? Is it a snake?'

Ernesto shook his head.

'It isn't the *kachi kachi*, is it?' Arturo said only half joking.

'No. We have a patient,' Ernesto replied.

Arturo gave a yelp of surprise. 'A patient? Are you sure?'

'Yes, she's in there and she wants to talk to you,' Ernesto said, looking in the direction of the small room.

'Who is it?'

'Doña Gloria. Pretend I'm not here.'

'Doña Gloria?'

'The mayor's wife.'

'Why does she want to talk to me?'

'Because you're the doctor.'

'Oh heavens,' said Arturo.

'I'll come and get you if you're not out in ten minutes,' Ernesto said, as Arturo disappeared into the hitherto unused room.

Doña Gloria, who had made her way to the clinic determined to make her acquaintance with the handsome young doctor, had by now arranged herself on the consultation bed in anticipation of the meeting.

'Is that you?' Gloria's voice drifted from the bed as Arturo entered the room. Arturo walked over to the window and lifted a small shutter to allow some light to filter in.

'I'm Dr Aguilar,' he said at last, introducing himself with un-necessary formality.

'I know,' Gloria replied in a deep throaty voice, 'that's why I'm here. I wanted to see what you look like.' Arturo coughed nervously.

'What's wrong?' he asked, sitting down on the little stool in the corner of the room. 'Can I help?'

'I hope so,' Gloria said.

'What's the problem?'

'I have a dislocation.'

'A dislocation? Where does it hurt?'

'All over,' Gloria replied. 'I have a dislocated soul. It walks two yards in front of me, taunting me. It keeps trying to trip me up. I nearly twisted my ankle on the way over here.' Arturo leaned back against the wall and closed his eyes.

'Can you cure me?' Gloria asked.

'I'm not sure. What do you think has caused your soul to become dislocated?'

'It's because I'm sick,' Gloria said.

'How long have you been feeling like this?'

Gloria sat up in the bed and slowly looked Arturo up and down. 'Since before you were born,' she said. This was exactly the sort of consultation that Arturo had been dreading. One in which he found himself with no skills to treat, no power to console and no capacity to comprehend.

'Would you excuse me for a minute,' he said and went outside to consult Ernesto.

'What am I going to do? Apparently she has a dislocated soul. I don't know how to cure that.'

'It isn't lost then?' Ernesto said. 'That's easy. You only really have to worry if it's lost; it can creep up behind you and make you die of fright. It's simple. It just needs to be enticed back. They can be very capricious,' Ernesto continued, lowering his voice. 'Especially in women of her age.'

'And how do you entice a soul back?' Arturo asked, with some genuine interest.

'Well, different things can work. Sweets, alcohol, love . . .'

'I think perhaps she's had enough alcohol,' said Arturo. 'I don't suppose aspirin will help will it?'

'Does she have a headache?'

'I don't think so.'

'Well, then, no, I don't think aspirin will help.'

'What am I going to do with her, Ernesto?' Arturo said. 'We're supposed to be meeting Teofelo outside the barber's in half an hour. I can't let him down. What about Don Bosco? We have to go.'

'You see, I said you would soon be in demand,' Ernesto replied, and they went back inside the consultation room to try and devise a cure for their patient. Fortunately, in the time it had taken to discuss her course of treatment, Gloria had descended into a deep sleep and was snoring loudly.

'I know,' Ernesto said. 'Let's cover her with a blanket and leave her to sleep it off.'

'Can you sleep off a dislocated soul?' Arturo asked. 'She's my first patient, apart from you. I can't just abandon her. She's the mayor's wife.'

'You aren't abandoning her really,' Ernesto said. 'You're giving her a place to rest. Rest is often the best cure, isn't it? What more can you do?'

Impressed by Ernesto's sudden flash of brilliance and anxious not to let down the search party, Arturo did not stay long enough to discover that the cause of Gloria's dislocation was her husband, her marriage and everything else about life as she knew it.

*

Nicanora waited until the crowd in the plaza had disbanded. She saw several men go up to Teofelo and shake his hand and commend him on his bravery before making their excuses as to why they would not be able to join him in his search. She approached him as he stood alone outside the barber's shop. 'You will find him, won't you?' she asked. 'He won't have gone far, will he?'

'I'll do my best,' Teofelo said. 'To be honest, I expect we will find him sitting under the nearest tree, waiting to see how long he can respectfully stay there before he comes back. I was giving him another day and then I was going to look for him, until all this fuss happened. One thing is for sure, it has certainly been good for his business, he's now more in demand than ever,' and Teofelo winked at her reassuringly, confident that normality would be restored to the town by the following day.

Nicanora felt so comforted by Teofelo's calm reassurance that she left the plaza certain that he would return with Don Bosco in time for dinner. After some careful thought she decided against preparing chicken, as this might stir up more sad and unwanted memories for Don Bosco and before she knew it he would be lost to the swamp again. It occurred to her that even in her thoughts she could not refer to the man who had pursued her with such love and tenderness, and who had clung to those feelings for all these years, in any other way than by his formal name. She had not wanted to let him know that his parting request to her to call him Pepito, as she once had, was founded on a false memory. She had never in her life called him by that name. She would rather have used any name other than such a familiar one for the man who had always made her feel safe and secure, and who now refused to leave her thoughts for fear that she had finally driven him from his beloved home.

She immediately set about preparing the welcome fare, including fresh bread for its warm, homely smell, the smell of her mother's house before the world became filled with worry. Fish stew, rice, fried plantain and mango slices will add to the feast, she decided. After all, she told herself, they will be famished from a day wandering through the swamp. Don Bosco has been out there for a whole night and he won't have had any breakfast. She did not consider that she was being presumptuous in assuming that the first place the search party would come to would be her home, and that she was being even more presumptuous in thinking they would return at all.

The emptiness of the house made her nervous. Nena had stayed in the plaza with the Gringito after the crowd had dispersed, refusing to go back with her mother. 'But he has to finish his lessons,' she had protested and Nicanora had been so distracted that she had not even thought to ask her daughter what she was teaching him. Isabela had been nowhere to be seen through all the commotion of the morning. She had no idea where the girl was. One thing was certain, she would not be in the market selling fruit as she had promised her mother she would be. I really must talk to her as well, Nicanora said to herself. But the biggest gap in the household that day was left by Ernesto. When she thought of him going off with the doctor to look for Don Bosco she felt a sensation that she had never experienced before. She was proud of her son. Nicanora turned on the radio to fill the vacuum left by her children. Immediately, the comforting tones of *Tia Sophia's Problem Hour* entered the room. Tia Sophia never failed to reassure her listeners that no matter how miserable their lives, somebody out there had it worse than them.

'I understand that you recently lost your husband,' she said gently to a caller.

'Yes . . .' a sobbing voice said on the other end of the line, but was unable to continue.

Tia Sophia left a slight pause into which the woman shed her tears, before asking, 'How long ago did it happen?'

'Just two days ago,' the woman replied, making a great effort to control herself.

'Two days ago,' Tia Sophia repeated. 'You must still be in shock.'

'I am,' the woman whispered, 'it has come as a great shock.'

'It wasn't expected?'

'No,' the woman said, 'we've been there many times before.'

Tia Sophia allowed some silence to follow the non sequitur, before asking softly, 'To the hospital?'

'No, to visit my sister,' the woman said.

'He died on the journey?' Tia Sophia asked.

'I don't think so,' the woman said, her voice quavering with tears.

'You don't think so,' Tia Sophia said, an edge of irritation creeping in. 'So where is he?'

'I don't know,' the woman replied. 'As I said, I've lost him.'

'Let me get this clear,' Tia Sophia said, the sympathetic tone having vanished from her voice. 'You have lost your husband, as in you have misplaced him?'

'Yes,' the woman said. 'I can be very careless. God forgive me.'

'Don't be ridiculous,' Tia Sophia snapped. 'You can't just lose a grown man.'

'Oh yes you can,' the woman and Nicanora said in unison.

'It was in a crowd,' the woman tried to explain. 'We went to market on the way to my sister's. He was hungry so he went off to buy something to eat. But the market is very large and we just lost each other. He's probably still wandering around looking for me.'

'Surely he'll find his own way home,' Tia Sophia said.

'You don't know my husband,' the woman said enigmatically, and was instantly cut off by an advertisement offering the slime of snails to lighten the skin.

Nicanora finished her preparations and sat down at the table. It was true. You could, indeed, be careless enough to lose a grown man. She felt as helpless as Tia Sophia's caller. She had no idea how to rectify a situation that seemed to be getting worse by the hour. For now, all she could do was wait. Lost in her thoughts for some time, she suddenly became aware that *Tia Sophia's Problem Hour* had been replaced by the voices of knowledgeable city folk, arguing stridently.

'The issue is with the rural provinces,' a man was saying loudly. 'These remote places have been left to fester for too long. They are the root cause of all the problems in this country. This is where these groups like the People's Liberation Front are recruiting from, the uneducated and simple-minded peasants. They will follow anybody.'

'But these demonstrations haven't been started by the peasants,' another argued. 'The riots were led by the teachers and students at the university. This was a well-planned operation. Apparently the PLF is being financed by an international group. But they won't be able to mobilise the peasants here. They don't even speak their language.'

'I don't agree,' the other replied. 'They have the support of the peasant unions. The perpetrators of these crimes are being harboured in the remote countryside as we speak. The *campesinos* believe they are fighting their cause. These people are just a bunch of foreign opportunists.'

Nicanora listened for a while and wondered who these uneducated peasants were. It's a shame that people have to live like that, she thought to herself. But her mind wandered from the state of the country to worrying once again about the lost husband. Would he really be doomed to spend the rest of his life walking round and round a market, hoping that he might eventually bump into his wife? She supposed she would never find out whether the couple were ever reunited.

The table was laid, the stew bubbling, but no guests appeared. Nicanora sat waiting. She had lost track of for what or for whom. After all, she had spent a lifetime waiting. She was waiting for Don Teofelo so that she could thank him for his friendship even when she felt she did not deserve it. She was waiting for her son to return as the man she had always hoped he would be. She was waiting for Don Bosco, to know that he was safe, and she was waiting for the life that she had never known but always wanted finally to start. But nobody arrived.

It occurred to her that maybe the search party had already returned and that Don Bosco was sitting at home waiting for someone to notice he was back. After all, he probably had more than one key and Ernesto might have gone straight back to the clinic with the doctor. She had sat holding the key for the whole day, waiting until the market had closed so that she would be able to slip in unseen and at least have a little look around the shop.

*

As Nicanora approached the plaza, she felt an uncanny quiet hanging over the town. The doors on a couple of the small shops were swinging lazily open, the owners asleep under the counters. Everything looked just as it should. A couple of men, too old to worry about having their hair cut, were sitting on the benches talking. The shutters on Don Bosco's shop were closed. And yet, there was a life about the old place. Although the shop was clearly locked, the usual table and chairs had been set outside and a man was sitting there writing on a piece of paper. Taking in the scene, Nicanora's heart missed a beat and then raced a little. She rushed over to see what was going on and in the blindness of anticipation did not realise until she was almost upon him that the man sitting at the table was the Gringito.

'What are you doing?' she shouted at him. 'What on earth is going on?' The Gringito looked up at her and smiled. Nena appeared from around the corner carrying one of Nicanora's bowls filled with cold soup from breakfast.

'What are you doing?' Nicanora said, this time to Nena. 'And what is *he* doing?'

'Writing a postcard,' Nena said.

'He's doing what?'

'He's writing a postcard,' Nena repeated. 'In a café,' she added in case her mother had not understood.

'A postcard? A café?' Nicanora repeated.

'Yes,' she said. 'The mayor said all the tourists write them and send them home.'

'A postcard?' Nicanora said again, and picked up the piece of paper that had been laid on the table in front of the Gringito. On one side Nena had drawn a picture of the plaza. It showed the church on the corner, a tree in the middle and a rather oversized barber's shop with an arrow saying: 'I am here.' Her daughter was certainly enterprising, Nicanora had to give her that.

'And what are you doing with that bowl?'

'The mayor said that tourists write postcards in cafés,' Nena explained. 'We don't have a café, so I'm using Don Bosco's table while he is away, to pretend.'

'And where did you get the table from?'

'Don Bosco keeps it in the backyard.'

'But you can't do that,' Nicanora said. 'What will he say when he comes back later today and finds you have turned his shop into a café?'

'He won't mind,' Nena said confidently.

'You put the table back where you got it from right now,' Nicanora said firmly. 'People will think we have no respect for the missing.'

'OK, I'll take him round the plaza to start taking photos,' Nena said, pointing at the obliging Gringito, and then she reached into her bag and pulled out a camera.

'Where did you get that from?' Nicanora asked, astonished.

'The mayor gave it to me.'

'The mayor? He gave it to you?' Nicanora was now so stunned at what she was hearing that she was simply repeating everything her daughter said. 'Why?'

'I don't know. But he said if I make the Gringito behave like a proper tourist in front of the visitors I can keep it. Ramon said the mayor is going to turn the barber's into a café, if Don Bosco doesn't come back tonight,' and Nena pointed to a small note pinned to the door of the shop. 'Ramon put that there after the meeting.' Nicanora peered at the note. It was so small that she had not even noticed it as she approached the shop. She tried to make out what was written in the near illegible scrawl. '"The mayor,"' Nena read out helpfully, '"on behalf of the town council, formally announces intention to change the lease of this premises to make it a tourist shop and a, a . . . something café due to vacant occupancy by the barber." That's not fair,' she said turning to her mother, 'I had the idea first.'

'A tourist shop?' Nicanora said.

'Yes, and a something café,' Nena repeated.

'What do you mean "a *something* café"?'

'I don't know,' Nena said. 'I can't make the word out. It looks like "kyber café".'

'He can't do that,' Nicanora said. 'Have you been putting ideas into the mayor's head?'

'No,' Nena replied.

'But what is he talking about? We haven't got any tourists,' Nicanora said. With perfect timing, the Gringito, who had been fiddling with the camera while Nicanora and Nena had been trying to read the notice, stood up and pointed it in their direction, made a clicking noise with his tongue and then grinned at them. 'He is going to have to go,' Nicanora said to Nena. She then sat down on the chair next to the Gringito and put her head in her hands, feeling that she no longer comprehended the world in which she lived. Nena placed a postcard in front of her mother and asked her what she would like to order.

*

Nena, the Gringito and Isabela returned home for supper, drawn by the smell of the freshly baked bread that had made its way down the street and into the plaza, where it lingered in an enticing, welcoming cloud.

'Are we expecting guests again?' Nena asked, staring at the burgeoning dinner fare, which replaced the usual fish soup.

'I expect it's for Don Bosco?' Isabela teased her mother.

'Is he back already? I didn't see him,' Nena said, and she reached out to grab a slice of bread.

'Never mind that. Where have you been all day?' Nicanora said, turning to Isabela and trying to change the subject. 'There is a stack of washing to be done and the fruit is piling up on the trees for picking. What did you do with the oranges that I asked you to sell this morning?'

'I sold them,' Isabela said, and she placed a pile of money on the table in front of her mother.'

'So quickly?' Nicanora asked, astonished. 'How did you manage to sell so much so quickly?'

'You have to understand your customers,' Isabela said. 'You have to make them want to buy your fruit,' and she flashed her mother a coquettish smile that she usually saved for special occasions and followed the Gringito out into the yard. Nicanora had had a growing sense lately that there was more to Isabela than she had ever given her credit for, and she felt a pang of guilt that she had always underestimated her eldest daughter's talents.

'He's learning very quickly,' Nena said, pointing at the Gringito. 'Soon he'll make a perfect tourist. The mayor will be pleased.'

Nicanora had been waiting for the right moment to tell Nena that she had finally made her decision. She did not know quite how she was going to tell her that their house guest, who had been nothing but pleasant to them, had now outstayed his welcome. All she knew was that the Gringito had to go, and soon, to prevent any more damage being done. When she looked at him now, all she could feel was shame. She had been so overwhelmed by the money that he had given her that she had not considered how Don Bosco would feel when she made her offer to him. She had genuinely convinced herself that he would welcome the chance of giving up the shop, and would enjoy his new-found freedom. In so doing, she had driven him from the town, and the only home he had ever known. And now the mayor was also using the Gringito as the reason to take Don Bosco's shop from him and turn it into a *something* café so that he could impress the provincial authorities, and encourage more Gringitos to visit. There would be no end to the troubles that she seemed to have started. The main difficulty, she now anticipated, lay in convincing Nena to tell her friend he had to leave.

'Do you think Don Bosco will be coming back?' Nena asked her mother as if tapping into her thoughts.

'Of course he will,' Nicanora replied. 'Why on earth wouldn't he? Don Teofelo will know where to find him.' But the words sounded strangely hollow to her ears as she spoke them.

'What are you going to do about the shop?' Nena said.

'Nothing,' Nicanora replied. 'It's Don Bosco's. He was just being foolish. I'll give the key back to him as soon as he comes home tonight and the mayor won't be able to do a thing about it. But I need to talk to you,' she said, 'about the Gringito.'

'What about him?'

'I think it is time he went,' Nicanora said in her usual blunt manner.

'Why?'

'He has been here long enough. This is a small house and it's very cramped.'

'But that's not fair,' Nena said, 'he hasn't done anything wrong. Are you angry with him for sitting at Don Bosco's table?'

'No, it isn't that,' Nicanora said. 'I'm worried about him, Nena. I don't think it's good for us to have a stranger staying here for so long. After all we don't know who he is or why he's here. I should never have let him stay in the first place.'

'It hasn't bothered you until now,' Nena said petulantly. She

194

looked at Nicanora as if she were about to say more, but they were both silenced by the sound of men's voices and footsteps in the front yard.

'It's them,' Nicanora said, 'they're back,' and she ran to greet the search party. A group of men were standing in front of her as she opened the door. At first she could not make out their faces as they stood in the unlit yard. She counted five figures. Five darkened shapes on her doorstep and her heart leapt with relief. She searched for Don Bosco among the group, wondering whether she could run up to him in front of his friends and tell him how pleased she was that he was safe. As her eyes adjusted to the dark after the light of the house, she realised that one of the men she had counted in the group was the shadowy figure of the Gringito, who had slipped out into the yard after dinner to smoke a cigarette. She suddenly felt overwhelmed with hatred for him. There were four other familiar faces looking at her. Finally, Ernesto stepped forward out of the darkness. 'We're back,' he said quietly and walked past her into the house. Don Teofelo stood in front of her, his head bowed. The two other men, whom Nicanora now recognised as Don Julio and the young doctor, turned to leave, patting Teofelo on the shoulder as they did so. Don Teofelo stood alone in front of her. The Gringito had retreated into a corner of the yard.

'Where is he?' Nicanora asked, searching Teofelo's face for an answer. Teofelo said nothing. He just stood with his hands behind his back, staring at the ground.

'Where is he? Please tell me. Where is Don Bosco? Where did you find him?'

'We didn't,' Teofelo said finally, not meeting her eyes.

'But . . .' Nicanora said, and stopped herself from saying, 'you promised you would.'

'I was so sure I knew where he would be,' Teofelo said. 'I thought he would be waiting for us by the road. But he wasn't there.' He was talking more to himself than to Nicanora. 'We searched the swamp as far as we could go.'

'So where is he?' Nicanora asked again, refusing to hear what Teofelo was telling her.

'I don't know,' he said. Then, stepping into the light, he brought his hands forward and handed her something. 'We found it by the old tree,' he said. Nicanora reached out and took hold of Don Bosco's hat. It was battered and covered in mud.

'He wouldn't go anywhere without it,' Teofelo said quietly. 'I think he would have wanted you to have it,' and he quickly turned his face away and bade her goodnight.

Seventeen

The shop smelt cold and lonely, as if it had been left alone for much longer than a day. The key that Don Bosco had given Nicanora only worked in the back door. She wondered whether he had kept the front-door key for himself, knowing that he would soon be coming back. The candle in her hand cast an outsized shadow over the small back room, which looked as if it contained years of old bric-a-brac. I hadn't taken Don Bosco to be a hoarder, Nicanora thought to herself, as she tripped over the wheels of a broken bicycle. She was still not sure what had driven her to the shop in the middle of the night. Perhaps it was to pay homage to the man who in her heart she simply could not believe was gone for good. Maybe it was the hope that the shop would hold a clue to where he was and, more importantly, when he would be returning. Or perhaps it was simply her curiosity getting the better of her after a day of holding the key, an opportunity to find out more about the man who had been there in the background of her life for as long as she could remember and who had provided her with a steady, secure sense that somebody really cared about her.

When Nicanora thought about Don Bosco, she realised that she did not really know him at all. Even in their more intimate days she had felt that he held something back from her, which at the time she had put down to him being older and wiser. She had never really had a conversation in which he had revealed anything of himself to her that would explain why he had chosen the life he had, the life that he had now so suddenly walked out on. Perhaps she also harboured a hope that the shop that had been offered to her once with so much love still held her future happiness at its heart.

It was clear that Don Bosco used the back room as a store cupboard. The shelves were cluttered with old pots and jars, which Nicanora supposed contained the alchemic secrets of the barber's trade. The floor was covered in bits of old scrap metal and wood. I wonder what he was planning to use all this for? she thought to herself as she picked her way through the mess. She banged her elbow on the corner of a little wooden cabinet as she went, knocking some of the bottles and barber's brushes that had been piled on top of it onto the floor. It suddenly seemed strange to her that she had never in her life stepped inside the shop, apart from on that one occasion many years ago when it had briefly turned itself into an expectant marriage parlour. The memory of that day filled her with so much regret that she had to sit down and draw her breath. She could not bear to think about how deeply she had hurt Don Bosco in her careless rush, all those years ago, to discover the disappointments that were awaiting her in life.

She wondered whether any other woman had ever been inside the shop, she had certainly never seen a woman go nearer than the doorstep to peer in to look for a lost husband. What would Don Bosco say if he knew she was here now? With that thought she was overcome by an unsettling anxiety. What if Don Bosco was upstairs asleep in his bed? Maybe he had just been playing a trick on his friends and had been waiting to see whether they would come and get him. What would he say to her if he found her snooping around? What would he think of her? Could it be any worse than what she supposed he thought of her already?

Nicanora reached across, picked up the candle and carefully made her way from the back storeroom into the front of the shop. It had the smell of yesterday's washing, left neglected in a corner to go damp and mildewed. In the dim light it took her a while to focus on what was really unsettling. The shop looked exactly as it would in the middle of a busy working day, as though it had been left in suspended activity, waiting for Don Bosco to pick up where he had left off. The sink was full of stale water, with foam floating on the surface. The barber's razor was lying on the tabletop, open and ready for use. An old damp towel hung limply on the back of the chair, and cuttings of hair lay scattered on the floor as if freshly hewn from their owner's head. I would have thought he would have swept up after him before disappearing like that, Nicanora said to herself as with her foot she pushed the curly grey bits of human debris, which from the look of them were offcuts from Don Julio's hair. This was certainly not the shop of the fastidious man Nicanora had known – or thought she had known – for all those years. And yet Don Teofelo had not given her the impression that Don Bosco had left in a hurry. At least he had given enough thought to what he was doing to have packed a small case. It was only then that Nicanora realised that she was standing in the middle of the shop still clutching Don Bosco's hat in her hand. It felt strangely intimate, even more intrusive somehow than having broken into his property in the middle of night to make critical comments about the state of his cleaning. But he did give me the key, she reminded herself. 'He must have known that I would come here. And Nicanora carefully put the hat on the pole that Don Bosco always left outside the shop to show he was open, placed the candle in a jar on the table, rolled up her sleeves and set about clearing up.

Momentarily lost in the task, Nicanora forgot about her unease that Don Bosco might be asleep in bed upstairs, until she became aware of a gentle tapping coming from the room above the shop. She stopped what she was doing and listened. The tapping stopped. She went over to the window and peered through the shutters, to see if anyone was outside. The familiar plaza, the plaza she had known all her life, looked uneasy in the dark. The church on the corner assumed gigantic proportions in the middle of the night, and the vegetation covering its front gave the appearance of the forest trying to break in and take the Virgin as its own. The trees cast unholy shapes around the building, which was buried in a deeper tone of dark to the rest of the night. She felt overcome by an inexplicable terror.

With a shiver of foreboding running through her, Nicanora quietly made her way up the rickety staircase at the side of the shop, to where the tapping had come from. She stopped at the door that she supposed led to Don Bosco's bedroom, and listened carefully. She could hear nothing that hinted of a human presence. The tapping started again. She slowly opened the door and looked in on the most private corner of Don Bosco's life. This was certainly not the bedroom of the man who had left the shop downstairs in such an untidy state. A neatly made bed nestled in the corner. The few books on the shelves were all lined up in order of size. A pair of shoes was tucked under a chest of drawers; the heels exactly level with each other. The tapping that had assumed such portentous meaning in Nicanora's mind could now be attributed to a simple source. It was the only indication that Don Bosco had departed from this room in an untidy state of mind. The window beside the bed had been left slightly ajar and the shutters were banging against the frame with the ebb and flow of the night breeze. Nicanora could not contain her curiosity. She opened one of the drawers. Don Bosco's old white barber's shirts were still there, carefully folded. They smelt of starch and fresh ironing. In the wardrobe there hung a single pair of trousers. Suddenly, she had an unwashed, sullied feeling, looking through a lonely man's paltry possessions.

She ran down stairs with the fury of guilt rising inside her. What have I done? she said to herself. Where could he have gone? It felt as if the comforting eye that had watched over the town for years from its unassuming home had now shut, and without it anything could happen. With that thought the little shop was suddenly overwhelmed with the scent of wild rose blossoms and a vision of the room as it had been the last time she had stepped foot in it filled her senses. She knelt down on the floor, put her hands among the phantom petals, and wept.

Nicanora knew exactly what she needed to do. It was Don Bosco who had reminded her of it. What had his parting words been – before asking her to call him Pepito? 'Make sure nothing bad happens to our town,' that was what he had said. 'You have a gift. Use it.' What had he meant by it? She had never mentioned 'the gift' to her children, hoping that all traces of it and the early humiliation it had brought her had been buried alongside her mother. Indeed, she had never given her ancestors any thought since her teenage years and had never again tried to make contact with them. They, for their part, had also left her well alone. But since Don Bosco had uttered those words she had felt a deep disquiet at the core of her being. The feeling was difficult to describe, but she was sure some-body was trying to tell her something, and that it was something that she really did not want to hear. She had a sense of a familiar voice saying to her very faintly, over and over again: 'There is trouble ahead, Nicanora.' What made her most uneasy was that this thought had come to her with greatest clarity while she was standing in the plaza with Nena, watching the Gringito writing the postcard. Don Bosco had never seemed comfortable with having the Gringito in town. Did he know something that he had not told her? It felt as if the Gringito, simply by being there, had altered a delicate and imperceptible balance in the life of the town, so that all the unseen strands of the web that had held things in their place for years had been shaken, and an unpredictable force was entering. Did Don Bosco know the Gringito in some way? 'That is absurd,' Nicanora said out loud. 'Don't listen to yourself. This is the night talking.' Whatever the questions were, Nicanora knew there was only one answer. The Gringito had to go.

Certain of what she had to do next, Nicanora went into the store-room and searched among the shelves. It took her some time to find what she was looking for, but eventually hidden in the midst of the dusty jars she found a small bottle of neat alcohol. She supposed that Don Bosco used it for cleaning his razors, or at least she hoped that was what he used it for, but it would do for the purpose. She went back into the shop, the ghostly waft of rose petals having now been replaced by the fresh smell of soap from her cleaning efforts. She pulled some leaves out of her pocket, placed them on the ground and poured the alcohol over them. She then knelt down and whispered: 'I am very sorry not to have been in touch for so long. I hope everyone is keeping well.' Even to her ears the words, once spoken, seemed rather ill fitting to the occasion. She then waited. There was no reply. After some time the faint tapping in the room above started up again, as if it were an obscure sign from the ancestors. Nicanora waited patiently for a few minutes and then she shouted at the top of her voice: 'Where has he gone? Why won't you tell me? Is he ever coming back? Why have you never told me anything of any use?' Suddenly, out of the deep fug that now filled her brain, she heard a very faint, but familiar voice.

'Well that's a fine way to talk to us.' The tone clearly indicated that the voice was perturbed. 'Over twenty years and we hear nothing from her. Not so much as a birthday call. But now she's in trouble, it's a different story.' It was, quite obviously, Genara.

'Well, it's only to be expected,' croaked a voice in reply. 'She always was a thankless girl just like her mother.' Nicanora jumped from the bed in shock, uncertain whether to be delighted to hear from her long-lost ancestors again, or to be angry at the abuse they were so ready to hurl at her. The critical tone certainly ran through the family.

'And what is that supposed to mean?' came another voice. 'She is headstrong and always has been. She will never listen to advice from anyone, least of all me. I told her at the time she should have married him. Now look at her.'

'Hello Mama,' Nicanora said. 'How are you?'

'Fine. Thank you for asking,' her mother replied. And Nicanora was certain that if she could see her mother's face, her lips would be pursed very tightly. 'It's only taken you fifteen years to get in touch. I suppose you've been too busy to say a quick hello, although goodness knows what with.' Nicanora decided that it was best not to answer. Strange, she thought, how after all these years one can slot back into such a familiar argument.

'Strange indeed,' her mother agreed. Nicanora now remembered why she had so purposely lost touch with her ancestors: the problem with having such direct communication with them was that her thoughts were never her own.

'I'm sorry,' Nicanora replied, deciding that conciliation was the best tactic. 'But I really need your help. Do you know where Don Bosco is? Can you tell me whether he will come back safely?'

There was silence at the other end. Nicanora sat waiting for a reply. Nothing happened. She sat down in the barber's chair and waited, until she finally drifted into a half-sleep. She lost track of how long she had waited, until she saw the first light of dawn appearing through the shutters. The silence continued.

'Are you there? Can you tell me where he is?' she whispered at last. She waited some more. Then, sobbing, certain that she had been given her answer, Nicanora cried out. 'He's dead, he's dead. I know he is. And I've killed him.'

'Well you should have married him when you had the chance, instead of going off with that good-for-nothing.' It was her mother.

'Where have you been?' Nicanora shouted. 'I've been waiting for hours. Can you answer my question. Do you know where he is?'

'We can't know everything.' It was Alicia-Maria's voice. Then in a slightly more comforting tone she said, 'But we have had a consultation and we don't think you have cause to worry, yet. You just need to make him *want* to come back.'

'How do I make him want to come back?'

'Make up for old hurts,' her mother said. 'Find the tears to wash away old sorrows.'

'How?'

'Ask the Virgin for help,' Alicia-Maria said.

'The Virgin?'

'We have had a long consultation and our advice is to get the blessing of the Virgin. Hold a fiesta. She might help bring him back.'

'But I need to bring him back today. What can I do?'

'We have to go, we are late for a committee meeting,' Alicia-Maria replied, her voice now faint in Nicanora's head.

'Stop, please don't go,' Nicanora said. 'What did you mean by telling me there is trouble ahead?'

'There is always trouble ahead,' the voices said as they faded away.

*

Once again Nicanora was left alone. With dawn breaking, there would soon be activity in the plaza. She hurriedly gathered up the leaves to remove all signs that she had been in the shop and made her way towards the storeroom. As she placed the bottle of alcohol on the shelf she once again banged her arm against the small cabinet in the corner. It seemed out of place in the broken chaos of its surroundings. Taking a closer look she saw that it was engraved with delicate flowers and leaves, clearly made by the hands of a master craftsman. In the early light the red wood shone with a deep lustre. She tried opening the top cabinet drawer. She had now intruded so far into Don Bosco's world that looking into one more small corner of his life seemed almost inconsequential. The drawer was locked. Certain that the key must be kept somewhere near, Nicanora started hunting among the bottles, jars, tins, cans and other junk. In her haste she knocked the bottle of alcohol onto the floor. It smashed and the pungent vapour of the spirit filled the dusty room. She went back to the cabinet and on the top, behind the jars and brushes, quite obvious now, she saw a little tin.

She knew that it contained the key before she even took off the lid.

The cabinet was as untidy as the room that housed it. Her first instinct that it would be full of more barber's junk had clearly been correct. The top drawer was stuffed with broken implements: scissors that had lost their handles, old brushes and rusting razors, a collection of keys, green with age, that had long since forgotten which door they belonged to, old pens, broken watches and clock faces. There appeared to be some system in the disorder. The second drawer was obviously used for storing old bits of paper. On the top were some blank writing pads, some newspaper cuttings and a pile of brown tinted photographs of Don Bosco and his brothers as children. Beneath the photographs was an envelope. Nicanora instantly recognised the writing on the front as Don Bosco's: *To my love*, was all it said. No longer aware of the time, or concerned about who might be passing through the plaza to catch her, she sat down on the stool in the corner and opened the envelope. It was full of single sheets of paper on which were written love poems unashamedly describing the virtues and failings of the woman to whom they were written. Some of the poems were less than flattering, but all were written with the compassion and tenderness of a man who loved consistently, despite the shortcomings of the object of his affections. Each poem was inscribed with little drawings of flowers of the forest, birds with multicoloured plumes and trees from a mystical land dreamt up in Don Bosco's lonely imagination. Each sheet of paper was separated from its neighbour by a dried rose petal. Nicanora took one of the petals in her hand and it crumbled into dust, adding to the film on the floor.

Were these poems really meant for her? She certainly recognised herself in some of the narratives, especially the more descriptive passages. Had he intended her to find them? Perhaps that was why he had given her the back-door key. Had she entered through the front of the shop she would most certainly not have stepped more than one foot into the messy storeroom. At the very back of the envelope, tucked in behind the poems, was a sheet of paper that looked fresher than the rest, as if it had been recently placed there. She carefully took it out and read it, certain that it had been put there for her to find. It was not a poem like the others and had no drawings on it. *My only real sadness*, it said, *is that you have not yet known what it is to be loved and may now never find out.*

Nicanora could not help herself now, she delved further into Don Bosco's secrets. There were answers inside this cabinet, she knew it, and her search was quickly rewarded. Beneath the envelope was a letter, clipped to a photograph of a young man and woman. The woman was small and slight. She was wearing a light summer dress, her shoulders covered by a shawl and her long hair tied back so that the sun fell on her delicate Indian-looking face. Nicanora was struck by the uniqueness of the woman's beauty and the honest expression in her dark eyes. The couple looked unselfconsciously happy. The young man was saying something to make the woman laugh. It was Don Bosco. Nicanora stared at the photograph and was clutched by a pain that she had not experienced since the early years of her marriage to Francisco. She was overtaken by a deep and unexpected jealousy. Her mother's words of warning echoed in her head: Jealousy is like an overfed pig, consuming everything in its path. She did not know what to make of the scene she was looking at. There was no doubting the radiance of love in Don Bosco's eyes. She could not make out from the photograph exactly when it would have been taken, but judging by Don Bosco's age, it must have been about the time she had left to try and make her life with Francisco. She felt foolish and cheated. She had spent her whole life assuming that she had been the only object of Don Bosco's affections. She was not afraid to admit to herself now that it was the conviction that he still loved her, after all these years, that had given her the strength to face her life. Now, she held in her hands the evidence that he had given these feelings to another, and probably more deserving, woman.

The letter to which the photograph was attached was dated twenty years previously and had been sent by Don Bosco's brother, Aurelio. She opened it and read it. She no longer felt as if she was intruding into someone else's private affairs, but rather that some hidden secrets of her own life were revealing themselves to her. The letter began with Aurelio counselling his younger brother on the ways of fickle women and suggesting that he leave behind his humiliation and the tatters of a broken heart and join him as a partner in the new export business he had established in the city of Manola. Inside the envelope was a ticket for the boat from Puerta de la Coruña. It was Don Bosco's passage out of town, a ticket to the life of hope and success that he had never had. His brother had offered him the chance to start again and for some inexplicable reason Don Bosco had chosen not to take the risk and had stayed tied to his tiny barber's shop. Perhaps she was not the only woman to have destroyed his dreams. To have your heart broken once is sad; to have it happen twice in the space of a few years is something that a person would never recover from. In her careless offer to buy the shop from Don Bosco, Nicanora now knew she had tried to take from him his reason for being. He had faced the harsh reality of his existence with enough clarity not to bother to sweep its sad remains from the floor. The ticket, being out of date, had been left in the drawer and Nicanora supposed that after all his years as a barber he had now managed to save enough money to buy his own boat ticket to Manola, if that was where he was heading.

As she gently placed the evidence of a lost life back from where she had taken it, her hand brushed against the corner of a larger, sturdier envelope. It had been carefully tucked away at the back of the drawer. Dislodged by her fumbling, it had edged its way forward, into her hands. Believing there could not possibly be any more secrets to discover, she pulled out the envelope. Don Bosco had written on the front: *Shop lease and agreement*. She opened it. There were two documents inside. The first was largely unreadable, the language was so obscure. She turned the document to the last page and there were the signatures of Don Bosco and Don Ramirez, proof that the mayor had handed the property over to Don Bosco. This, she realised, was her chance to do at least one good deed in return for all the damage she had caused. She would pin the lease to the front of the shop so that everyone could see that it right-fully belonged to Don Bosco, and so prevent the mayor from doing anything to take away his business.

The second document was entitled 'The Agreement'. It too was signed by Don Bosco and Don Ramirez, and dated the same day as the lease of the shop. *I, Don Pedro Bosco,* the letter stated, *agree that in return for the lease on the barber's shop I will assist Don Rodriguez Ramirez in all his political activities. I give my solemn word in front of the Virgin that I will never stand against him in his efforts to become mayor or support any other individual who stands against him.* It continued: *I, Don Pedro Bosco, understand that the lease is granted to me on condition that the keyholder will have full and unrestricted use of the premises on the plaza for as long as I desire, as long as the property is never closed for more than one working day in a week.*

Nicanora had to read the paragraph several times to make sure that she had really understood what had been written there. Don

Bosco had signed away not only his integrity but his freedom: his right even to close his business for longer than a day. That at least had explained his dedication to his work. But why had he not just walked away from it now, as the mayor must have expected him to do years ago when he asked him to sign such a ridiculous agreement? It was now clear to Nicanora that he had stayed because the shop, with all its sad memories; had been his purpose, his hope and his home. Perhaps he had been waiting all these years for the woman he loved to come back and join him. He had left now because he no longer felt he belonged.

Eighteen

Arturo returned to the clinic more dejected than he had felt since his arrival. He had failed everyone, not just himself. He had failed Don Bosco. He had failed Teofelo. He had let Doña Nicanora down and he felt he could no longer look Ernesto in the eye. Above all, he had shown himself to be far from the hero that Isabela believed he could be. Teofelo would have continued leading the search party into the swamp and risked all their lives if Arturo had not stopped him. Was it fear for his own life that had held him back? Perhaps Teofelo was right. Perhaps it would only have taken a few more paces into the darkness and they would have found Don Bosco, dead or alive. Arturo had stood there, in front of Julio and Ernesto, and persuaded Teofelo to call off the search after only eight hours. They were pushing deeper and deeper into the treacherous bog and Arturo feared that he was allowing Teofelo to lead them all to their deaths. It was Arturo who, as they turned back, had seen the hat floating on a deep patch of bog, almost hidden in the undergrowth near the old tree. A sign to all that Don Bosco had been swallowed by mud. He did not know how Teofelo was going to break the news to the town that the search party had brought back certain evidence of Don Bosco's death. It was too awful to contemplate.

He turned on his little radio to try and fill his overwhelming emptiness, and immediately tuned into a heated argument. 'We will hunt them down,' a man said stridently. 'We will stop at nothing until we find them. We will not tolerate insurgents threatening our country and democracy. We will hunt the PLF down, I say. We will stamp them out.'

'But with due respect,' a voice replied, 'don't you think that sending the army into the countryside is an unnecessary response? After all, we are talking about a small group, who by all accounts are mainly students and intellectuals. Don't you think the army will just cause more disquiet among the peasants?'

'We will not tolerate this form of intimidation,' the politician continued. 'An army officer has been killed. A car bomb was placed close enough to the presidential palace to blow the windows out, and the *campesinos* have been looting shops in the city centre. There is mayhem in our streets and if we do not stamp on it now our country will descend into chaos. We must defend our democracy from the evil forces within.'

'But with all due respect,' the interviewer continued, 'can we really call it a democracy when we do not let people speak out freely? After all, this began as a peaceful demonstration. People on the streets are saying that it only escalated into violence after the demonstrators were fired on with tear gas and rubber bullets. There was no intention for it to become violent before that.'

'That', the politician said, 'is because most of the people on the streets are ignorant. Our country is full of uneducated peasants. That is the biggest problem we face.'

'Isn't that', the interviewer interjected again, 'because the government has neglected the people's needs for so long? After all, that is what the demonstrations were about in the first place. Our country is selling its natural resources to increase the wealth of foreign nations rather than investing in the welfare of its people.'

'You have clearly not been doing your homework,' the politician continued. 'We have the welfare of our people very much at heart, very much at heart. Haven't we brought in reforms to make sure foreign investment goes to the poorest provinces?'

'People are saying that is just a sop, a way to appease the peasants with the elections coming. Most rural communities don't even know the money is there or how it is being spent. It is simply disappearing into municipal bank accounts.'

'I say to those people', the politician said, 'that our spending in health and education is greater than any government before us. We have the support of our foreign friends who are investing in the development of our nation, and our provincial authorities are doing all they can to show the benefits of that investment.'

'And what do you say to those who accuse you of dancing to a foreigner's tune?'

'I say I chose my dancing partners very carefully.'

*

Arturo listened to the debate with a growing sense of unease. He turned the radio off and lay awake with only the ghostly call of owls for company. Claudia was coming. He had known it for some time. His thoughts immediately turned to Isabela, and it felt as if a fresh, light breeze had floated in to calm his nerves. He drifted off into a disturbed sleep and woke suddenly in the middle of the night in a cold sweat. There was someone in the room with him, staring at him. The dream of Claudia still lingered in his subconscious. But it was not excitement or desire that thrilled through him at the anticipation of Claudia's arrival: it was a sort of dread. He had no idea what trouble she was bringing with her, but whatever it was, his dream filled him with a sense of foreboding. Claudia had stood in front of him, a gun in her hand and a bullet hole in her chest, and told him she was on her way. Blood had tricked down her shirt at a slow and steady pace. Arturo had tried to reach out to her but he had been unable to move. He called to her but his words hovered in the air above her head and then floated away.

'Well, you're not much use, are you?' Claudia said at last.

'What's happened to you?' Arturo asked.

'It's nothing,' she said.

'You're bleeding. Claudia, what have you done? What are you doing this for? It's crazy, Claudia, you're hurt.'

'At least I'm trying,' she replied. 'What are you doing with yourself? What good are you to anyone here? From what I can see you are just drifting, Arturo. You couldn't even find the barber.'

'I tried,' Arturo said, the guilt of his failure turning his limbs cold. 'Well at least I'm not letting people get shot, that's for sure. Claudia, you need help.'

'You're a doctor, aren't you?' she said, challenging him. 'Why don't you help me?'

Arturo reached out to her again, but she was too far away for him to touch her. He tried to stand but his knees buckled under him. He crawled across the floor until he reached her feet. She towered above him so that he could not see her face and her blood fell on him like a thick, warm waterfall.

'I must stop the bleeding, I must stop the bleeding,' he repeated to himself.

'You can plug the hole,' Claudia said in a matter-of-fact tone. 'You can plug the hole with glue.'

'It's not as easy as that, Claudia,' he said. 'Things are not as easy as you say they are. You can't just glue people back together again. If it were that easy there would be no need for doctors. We would only need modelmakers.'

Claudia looked down at him and then spat a large clog of leaves into her hands and stuck them into the hole in her chest. 'There,' she said, 'I'm fixed,' and the blood immediately stopped flowing. 'You're no good, Arturo,' she said. 'When I need you, you can't help me. You're weak. You will never be anything other than weak and pampered,' and she disappeared.

Arturo sat up in bed peering into the darkness. He heard a faint rustling noise and then silence.

'Is that you?' he said softly. There was a pause.

'Yes,' a voice whispered back.

'Is that really you?' Arturo asked again.

'I think so,' the voice replied. It sounded thick and hoarse.

'How did you get here?'

'I walked.'

'So far? You must be exhausted.'

'I am. I am exhausted. You are the only person who has noticed.'

'Are you in danger?'

'I don't think so.'

'Are they following you?'

'No. But they mustn't find out that I'm here.'

'Are you sure they don't know where you are?'

'No, we will have to keep it a secret.'

'Who is after you?'

'The mayor.'

'The mayor,' Arturo exclaimed. 'How do you know the mayor?'

'I'm married to him.'

Arturo leapt out of bed and fumbled for his trousers. He grabbed a small box of matches from the pocket and lit one. There, perched on the end of the bed, was Doña Gloria. He had completely forgotten about the patient he had deserted the previous day in his search for Don Bosco.

'What are you doing?' he asked. 'You can't come here in the middle of the night. What will your husband say?'

'He won't find out,' Gloria replied. 'As I said, we will keep it a secret. Who did you think you were talking to?'

'Nobody,' Arturo said. 'I was dreaming. I thought you were a friend.'

'I am a friend,' Gloria replied. 'You sounded frightened.'

Arturo lit another match and searched in the small cupboard next to his bed for a candle. In the light he felt exposed, standing in front of Gloria with no shirt on. She was taking in every aspect of his being with her keen eyes.

'I can help you,' she said softly.

'I don't need help,' Arturo replied.

'I think you do,' Gloria said. 'You look sad.'

'I'm fine.'

'I can smell sadness when I am near it,' Gloria said. 'If you are not sad, then tell me, what are you doing hiding yourself away here in the full bloom of your youth?'

'I'm not hiding,' Arturo said. 'I've come to help.'

'Help who?'

'Well, you,' Arturo replied.

'And why do you want to help me?' Gloria asked, with genuine interest.

'Because', Arturo replied, 'your husband said you need a doctor.'

'Well, he's right about that,' Gloria said. 'I do need a doctor.'

'No,' Arturo replied, 'I meant everybody here. The townsfolk.'

'Why?' Gloria asked. 'What's wrong with them?'

'Nothing. Nothing at all,' Arturo said, suddenly feeling exhausted.

'Well, never mind that. I'm here now,' Gloria said. 'And I need your help.'

'I'm sorry,' Arturo said, sitting down on the bed. 'Don't you see? I'm no good to you. I shouldn't have been sent here. It was a mistake. I'm sorry, but I just can't help you. I don't have what you need. I don't understand anything. I certainly don't understand ailments of the soul.'

'I'm sure you do,' Gloria said. 'After all, you have one yourself.'

'I do?'

'Of course, it's obvious. You are dislodged.'

'Am I?' Arturo asked.

'You're not at one with yourself, are you?'

'I don't know.'

'You see, the difference between you and me', Gloria continued, 'is that you haven't yet discovered who you are. I expect that is what has driven you here, to find out. Whereas I once knew exactly who I was, or I thought I did, and now I have lost it.'

'I wish I could help you, Doña Gloria,' Arturo said, the sadness in his patient's voice filling him with empathy. 'I really, really wish I could help, but you see, I'm a fraud. I'm not the doctor you need. I am not the person that this town needs. I only have pills and potions. I have nothing to give you that will be of any help and nothing to teach anyone. What knowledge I have comes only from books. I don't have anything that will give you peace of mind. I don't know how to bring your soul back.'

'It's easier than you think.' Gloria said. 'You're making things far too complicated. You young people always do. You're coming to it all from the wrong direction. I need my husband to feel what it really means to be without me. Just as the town is feeling what it means to be without their barber. That is the only way I will discover the truth.'

'I don't understand. How can I be of help?'

'I need to stay here, with you, of course.'

'You can't do that,' Arturo said in horror.

'Why not?'

'Because your husband will kill me,' Arturo said.

'But he won't find out. It will be our little secret. I can't go back home,' she said defiantly.

'But you can't stay here,' Arturo said again. 'Really, Doña Gloria, think about it. It just wouldn't be right.'

'If I can't stay, I can't be cured. And if I am not cured, I can't go home,' Gloria said stubbornly. 'So you are stuck with me either way.'

'No, I have a better idea,' Arturo replied. 'Why don't we see whether you can stay with Doña Nicanora. She is very kind and she likes looking after people. She has that Gringito with her after all. That would be very proper and you would be much more comfortable there. I know she would keep it a secret if you asked her to.'

'Stay with Doña Nicanora and Ernesto,' Gloria said, mulling the idea over in her mind. 'That could certainly do the trick. That is not a bad idea, not a bad idea at all.' And Gloria went back to the little consultation room a consoled woman, leaving Arturo to contemplate how he was going to convince Doña Nicanora to take in another house guest.

Nineteen

Everything had suddenly been put to rights. As the townsfolk awoke and started to make their way across the plaza, the disturbing strangeness of the previous day had passed over. Life was back to normal and all was exactly as it should be. The shutters on Don Bosco's shop had been lifted once again. Don Julio was the first to see the new dawn break on the barber's. He knocked several times, calling Don Bosco's name. 'Bosco, are you there, are you home?' He peeped through the window slats: a figure was moving in the shadows at the back of the shop. The door remained firmly locked. In his excitement he rushed to his friend Teofelo to tell him the good news.

'He's back,' Don Julio shouted, banging on Teofelo's door. 'He's back, Teofelo, come and see.' Teofelo, who was not an early riser, came to the door bleary-eyed, afraid that the noise would awaken his wife.

'What's the matter with you, Julio?' Teofelo said, irritated. 'You will wake the whole town if you carry on like this. What's wrong? Who is back?'

'Bosco of course,' Julio replied. 'Bosco is back. The shop is open and everything. Come and see for yourself.'

'Bosco is back?' Teofelo said confused. 'Are you sure? Have you seen him?'

'Yes, yes. I've seen him,' Julio said. 'He hasn't opened the door yet but he has opened the shutters and I saw him moving around inside.'

'I can't believe it,' Teofelo said, 'I almost thought we had lost him for good.' And when he stepped forward into the morning light Julio saw that Teofelo's eyes were swollen and red-rimmed.

'He must have returned in the middle of the night. I wonder where he was hiding, the old dog. Well let's at least leave him to settle in for half an hour, we don't want to overwhelm him,' Teofelo said, still not quite believing that their friend was back. 'You know what Bosco is like. We don't want to intrude on him too early in the day.' And Julio settled down to a welcome breakfast, ready to pick up his life where it had left off two days earlier.

By the time Teofelo and Julio reached the plaza, a small group of men had gathered outside Don Bosco's, just as they would have on any normal working day. The pole had been placed in front of the door to indicate that the shop was now open, and the table and chairs were exactly where they should be.

'Do you know when he got back?' Teofelo asked Don Alfredo, who was sitting tapping his fingers impatiently on the table.

'I've been waiting for over an hour now and he still hasn't appeared,' Alfredo replied. 'You would think having left us in the lurch for so long that he would at least open on time.'

'Come now,' Teofelo said, anxious to prevent a quarrel the moment Don Bosco opened the door. He knew his old friend well, and he was sure to be feeling shamefaced about his uncharacteristically impetuous behaviour. 'It has only been one day after all, and Bosco has been going through a hard time lately.'

'*He's* been going through a hard time,' Alfredo replied. 'I've had to put up with this stubble on my chin since Sunday. I really don't think that he's running a very good business these days.'

'I agree,' said Don Arsenio, who had joined Alfredo at the table. 'It was very irresponsible of Bosco to shut up shop without even telling any of us. It is a barber's after all. It's an essential service. He doesn't have the right to just go off like that. It's downright irresponsible of him and I have a good mind to tell him so myself. Once he finally opens up.'

Ramon, who was sleepily crossing the plaza, late for his administrative duties yet again, saw the barber's pole out of the corner of his eye and made a mental note to go later in the day and get his hair cut. He then stopped in his tracks, realising what it meant, and gave a yelp. He went running towards the crowd of men who had gathered on Don Bosco's doorstep to find out what was going on.

'Don Bosco has returned,' Julio replied triumphantly. 'No thanks to you,' he added.

'Oh no,' Ramon said, remembering the notice that the mayor had asked him to place on the shop the previous afternoon. 'The mayor will not be pleased. He will not be pleased at all.' Ramon knew he was now in for a very difficult day at the town hall. 'Where did you find him?' he asked, somewhat in awe of the search party. 'Did you have to go far into the swamp? Did you see the *kachi kachi*?'

'We went as far as we needed to go,' Teofelo said quickly.

'Some of us', Julio replied, 'are not afraid of the *kachi kachi*. At least we would not let it stop us from going where we need to, to find a friend. And as it happens we did see it –' and Julio was about to start a long description of how the *kachi kachi* had followed them, first in the guise of a large water rat and later as an owl, when he was stopped mid-speech, by the door of the shop slowly opening. At first it opened only a crack, wide enough for Don Bosco to peep through and see who was waiting for him on the doorstep.

'Come on, Bosco,' Alfredo said, 'we aren't really going to give you a hard time for deserting us. Let's get the day started, there are plenty of beards here waiting to be trimmed.'

'Yes, come on, Bosco,' Julio joined in. 'We are just glad to see you back, you know that. Hurry up and open, and I hope you have the coffee brewed.' There was a hesitation behind the door, suddenly it opened wide, and someone who certainly was not Don Bosco stepped out and put a sign next to the barber's pole.

Under temporary management, it read, *until the return of Don Bosco.* There on the doorstep, with a razor in one hand and a shaving brush in the other, stood Doña Nicanora. 'So which of you is first?' she asked, welcoming her clientele. The men stood open-mouthed, every one of them lost for words. Never in the history of the town had such an audacious event occurred. Nicanora left them to their silence and disappeared back inside to return a minute later with Don Bosco's hat, which she placed on the barber's pole.

'Don Bosco', Nicanora began, with as much authority as she could muster, 'is temporarily unavailable for business. Due to personal reasons,' she added, 'as I am sure you are all aware.' Word had spread fast across town that Don Bosco had returned, and more and more men were now gathering outside the barber's as Nicanora spoke.

'What is *she* doing here?' one of the newcomers to the crowd shouted, astonished at the sight of Nicanora standing on the doorstep wearing Don Bosco's apron. 'Has she gone mad?'

'As you all know,' Nicanora said again, 'Don Bosco is temporarily unavailable for work and has requested in his absence that I should take care of his business. I am sure you are all very anxious to have your beards shaved. So let's get on with it. Who is first?' There was a silence in the plaza, the depths of which had never been heard before. Nicanora looked at the faces before her, and realised that this time she had gone too far.

'Where is our barber? What have you done with him? How come you have his hat? Witch,' Don Dionisio shouted, pointing at the battered black trilby. Nicanora felt a panic rise inside her.

'Don't be ridiculous,' she said. 'I have done nothing with Don Bosco. He has simply asked me as a friend and neighbour to take care of his business while he is away. What is so surprising about that? Now, who is first? There are a lot of you to get through and you all look as if you need a good shave, so let's begin.'

'How dare she,' another man shouted. 'Teofelo, what are you going to do about it? She has stolen the key to Don Bosco's shop. We should take her to the mayor. She needs to be stopped. Witch, witch . . .' And the chanting man from the previous day started to try to agitate the crowd.

'Take me to the mayor if you like,' Nicanora challenged, her indignation at the suggestion fuelling her courage. 'Take me to the mayor and see what good that does you. For one thing you will lose your precious barber's shop forever. You heard him yesterday. If the shop is not opened by the keyholder today then by the terms of the lease he will claim it back and you will never be able to have your beards cut again. Within a few months you will be tripping over them. Don Bosco has faithfully run this service for years and now I am taking over for a while.' And Nicanora passed to the crowd the note in Ramon's scrawled handwriting that had been pinned to the door the previous evening.

'But you aren't the keyholder. Bosco is,' someone said.

'I am for the time being, until Don Bosco returns. I ask you once again, who is first? Don Julio, you look as if your beard needs a trim.'

'Witch! Liar!' Don Dionisio shouted, trying to whip the crowd into a fury. Teofelo, who had said nothing up to this point, stepped forward.

'She is speaking the truth,' he said. 'I was witness to it. Don Bosco did indeed leave the key with Doña Nicanora for her to look after his shop until he returns.'

'You know where Bosco is?' Don Alfredo asked, astonished.

'No,' Teofelo replied. 'All I know is that he has gone on a journey because he needs a break from all of you. But he thought of you enough to ask Doña Nicanora here to kindly look after his shop while he is away.' Teofelo, who was as stunned by the scene being played out in front of him as anyone, was also beginning to enjoy the proceedings and, despite himself, was filled with admiration for Nicanora's courage.

'He's gone on a journey because he wants to find something interesting to say,' a small voice piped up from the back of the crowd. Nicanora shot a look to silence Nena, who had stopped on her way to school to see what was happening.

'Well,' Don Teofelo said to Nicanora sternly, the crowd parting to let him through.

'That's right, Teofelo,' Don Dionisio egged him on. 'You sort her out.'

'If this is to remain a barber's shop,' he continued, loud enough for all to hear, 'then you had better behave like a barber and start shaving.' There was silence again from the watching men.

'No woman is going to shave my beard,' Don Dionisio said at last.

'Well,' Teofelo said, turning to address him, 'you had better get used to growing it then.' The crowd looked on aghast as Teofelo stepped inside and sat himself in the barber's chair, ready for Nicanora to begin her work.

*

Ramon raced straight to the town hall to alert his boss to the events unfolding in the plaza. When he got there, the mayor was nowhere to be found. In his anxiety, Ramon, decided to busy himself with tidying the paperwork that had now abandoned the desk and was lying in mounds on the floor, making entry to the mayor's office a complicated procedure. Devising a fail-safe plan for cutting through the piles of letters and forms, he decided to throw away anything that was more than one month old, and he was making excellent progress, managing within the space of an hour to clear almost the entire pile.

He was so pleased with his efficiency that he had already forgotten the extraordinary events of the morning and was starting to sing with the satisfaction he was deriving from his work when his gaze was drawn to an envelope with large red lettering on it: *For the Urgent Attention of Mayor Ramirez.*' Ramon froze and his stomach lurched. He looked at the date. It had been sent just under four weeks ago and was stubbornly defying his sorting system by demanding that it still be attended to. Ramon suddenly recalled having received the letter in the donkey delivery from Rosas Pampas a few days after the mayor's arrival back in town. Life had become so busy recently, what with the doctor and the Gringito, that it had quite escaped him to make sure the mayor had seen the letter. He was also reminded of the phone call he had received a few days previously in which an officious voice on the other end had informed him that he had an urgent message for the mayor – and was then cut off before the message could be given. There was nothing to be done. Ramon opened the letter and then let out another yelp.

★

The mayor's house was empty. Ramon knocked on the open door and called out. There was no answer. He went round to the back and found his patron walking about the garden looking confused.

'Señor, are you all right?' Ramon asked, and then, not waiting for a reply, added, 'Señor, you must come quickly, there is trouble in the plaza.'

'Not again,' the mayor replied. He sounded distracted and was not really paying attention to what Ramon was saying. He turned away, and got down on his hands and knees and started looking under a bush.

'What's wrong, señor?' Ramon asked, slightly disturbed by his patron's strange behaviour. 'Have you lost something?' And he also got down on his knees and started looking for the lost object.

'I can't find Gloria,' the mayor said at last, sitting back on his haunches.

'Gloria?'

'My wife.'

'Do you think she is hiding under the bush?' Ramon asked.

'I don't know,' the mayor replied. 'I've looked everywhere. I haven't seen her since yesterday morning. You don't know where she is, do you?'

'I don't think she's in here, señor,' Ramon replied. 'What is wrong with everyone? Nobody leaves town for years and then suddenly they all start disappearing.'

'So what's going on?' the mayor asked. 'What's the problem now?'

'Well it's not a problem as such,' Ramon said, trying to break the news gently.

'If it's not a problem why have you come here to disturb me? Can't I leave you to carry on with things for one morning while I sort out my business at home?'

'It's just that I thought you would want to know,' Ramon said.

'Know what?'

'That it's open again,' Ramon answered, getting to his feet.

'What is?'

'The barber's.'

'The barber's? Bosco is back? Bloody annoying little man. He can't even disappear properly,' the mayor said, stumbling to his feet.

'Well, no, not exactly,' Ramon continued.

'What do you mean "not exactly"? Is the barber's open or not?'

'Sort of,' Ramon said.

'How can it sort of be open? Either it is open or it isn't. Ramon, is Bosco back?'

'No,' Ramon answered.

'Ramon,' the mayor said, stepping towards him so that there was only a hair's width between his face and Ramon's. 'Let's get this clear. I am not in the mood. So let us start again. Have you come here to tell me the barber's shop is open?'

'Yes.'

'Are you telling me that Don Bosco is back?'

'No.'

'So what are you telling me?'

'That Doña Nicanora has become a barber,' Ramon said.

The mayor gazed at him, mouth open.

'Apparently Don Bosco gave her the key to his shop, and so she has become a barber,' Ramon said.

'She can't do that,' the mayor replied. 'It isn't proper.'

'Well, apparently it is,' Ramon said. 'She is shaving Don Teofelo as we speak.' And then taking advantage of the mayor's apoplexy, he said, 'And the visitors are arriving tomorrow.'

Twenty

Nicanora caught sight of herself in the mirror. She was covered from head to toe in Don Bosco's apron, she held his razor in one hand, his barber's brush in the other, and his best friend was sitting in the chair in front of her. In the space of a day she had quite simply taken over his life. It had certainly not been her intention to do so when she had gone to the shop the previous evening. But she refused to believe that he would not be coming back. After everything Don Bosco had given up, she could not bear to think that she had tried to take what little he had from him, and she was determined to protect it for him now. What was more, without the barber the town seemed to be losing its cohesion and its whole structure was about to fall apart.

Nicanora stood transfixed with fright as the crowd outside the shop watched her. 'Why don't you start?' Teofelo whispered from the chair. Having sat in anticipation for the past couple of minutes he was now rapidly losing his nerve. The memory of Don Bosco's recent debacle with the razor was still painfully fresh in his mind and Don Bosco had thirty years of experience behind him.

'I don't know what to do,' Nicanora replied.

'What do you mean you don't know what to do? Just start shaving.'

'I can't.'

'You have to. We've committed ourselves. Everyone is watching. If you back out now we will both look ridiculous.'

'I don't know how to.'

'It's simple,' Teofelo said. 'Just cover my face with soap and then run the razor over it. Only make sure that you don't cut my throat.' Nicanora took a deep breath, dipped the shaving brush into the bowl of warm water and began covering Teofelo's face in foam. As she lifted the razor, a hush fell over the chattering crowd. She slowly put the implement to Teofelo's neck and paused. Teofelo drew in a sharp breath, made the sign of the cross, asked the Virgin for forgiveness and then shut his eyes tight. Nicanora started to shave. Five minutes later, Teofelo emerged a renewed man. Nicanora stood back and took the towel from his shoulders as if unveiling a great work of art. Teofelo opened his eyes and ran his hand over his chin. The crowd looked on.

'That is as smooth a shave as I have ever had at the hands of our dear friend,' Teofelo whispered in Nicanora's ear, 'but don't ever tell him that, he would be mortified.' Nicanora felt tears of pride well up in her eyes. 'Tell me,' he said to her. 'Why are you doing this? Why are you putting yourself on the line like this?'

'I think we both know that I owe it to Don Bosco,' Nicanora replied. 'The least I can do is safeguard his business for him until he comes back. You heard what the mayor said, if I don't, Don Bosco will lose this shop forever.'

'Nicanora,' Teofelo said, gently placing a hand on her shoulder. 'You, I and the rest of the townsfolk will have to face up to our loss eventually.'

'Don Teofelo,' Nicanora replied, 'I don't know where Don Bosco is, and I don't know whether he will ever be coming back. But I can tell you one thing for certain. He is not dead.'

'And how can you know that?' Teofelo said, his gaze involuntarily turning to the hat on the pole.

'The same way I knew all those years ago, without a shadow of a doubt, that you would lose the Champions of the Swamp trophy to those wandering pot sellers.'

'You really knew that?' Teofelo said, now laughing at the memory of his foolishness. 'In that case you owe me fifty pesos. And you really know that our good friend Bosco has not been eaten by the swamp?'

'I do,' Nicanora said.

'I am so pleased,' Teofelo said mildly. 'We all have our time. I accept that. But he would not have liked to go that way, swallowed by mud. He always hated to get his clothes dirty.'

'You talk as if he is never coming back,' Nicanora said.

'And is he?'

'That I don't know. But I will do what I can to make sure he has something to come back to.' Nicanora desperately wanted to ask Teofelo about the photograph she had found in the drawer and whether that might be a clue to Don Bosco's whereabouts. She felt certain he had placed it where she would find it. He obviously knew her well enough to suppose that given the key to the shop she would not be able to resist snooping into the dark corners of his life. Could she confess to Teofelo that, having been in the shop for less than a day, she had started going through Don Bosco's secrets? Teofelo must know something about it, and she suspected that he was hiding something from her. What she really wanted to tell Teofelo was that she had not realised until Don Bosco was no longer there how much he meant to her and how much she missed him. She felt as if she had been playing a game with herself, never prepared to admit that she had looked love in the face and scorned it. She had committed the greatest betrayal of all: she had denied herself the chance of happiness. But the discovery that Don Bosco had been, and possibly still was, in love with another woman had now made her reassess her whole life. It all made sense to her now, Don Bosco had finally gone off in search of his lost love, and if he found her, he might never come back. She had turned him away, cruelly, when she had the chance of happiness with him and had never allowed herself to admit that it was the kindness and warmth of Don Bosco that had drawn her back home and enabled her to live there in peace for all these years. She felt now that she had been extraordinarily arrogant in assuming that she had been the only woman for whom Don Bosco had ever felt affection.

'Don Teofelo,' she said. 'Where do you think he is heading?'

'I don't,' Teofelo replied, 'I didn't believe he would actually go. He just told me that he had some unfinished business that he had to attend to.'

But before Nicanora could continue, a voice rose above the murmuring of the crowd, breaking through her thoughts: 'Three cheers for Nicanora, three cheers for Nicanora.' Nicanora turned to see Dona Gloria making her way towards the door of the barber's.

'I have come to offer you my help. I am an expert in these matters,' Gloria declared, stepping inside, and with one magnificent flourish of her hand, she pushed Teofelo out of the shop.

*

The mayor was not sure which way to turn. He simply could not comprehend how life could change direction so dramatically in the course of one day. He had returned home the previous evening an utterly contented man. Everything, for once, was working in his favour, and well, he thought, he deserved it. He had exerted his authority before the townsfolk, he was master of his house again, and this time Lucia would be gone for good. He had regained his place in his bed, next to his wife, who, for all her faults, he knew to be a very forgiving woman. He found it hard to admit quite how much he had missed Gloria on his recent visit to Rosas Pampas. He had missed the comforting familiarity of her body next to him at night, he had missed the playful glint in her eye when she was trying to humour him, and he had missed the inevitability of their bitter arguments and sweet reconciliations. But most of all he had missed the smell of her, the indescribable smell of the person who had lain beside him night after night, year after year, and knew him for exactly who he was.

After thirty years of marriage, he had to confess that he had become accustomed to Gloria in the way that he was accustomed to his legs being attached to his body, or to his eyes allowing him to see which path to take every morning. He felt deeply hurt by her accusation that he had been engaged in anything other than utterly official business during his absence. It was true, in the past he had been guilty of such excesses on more than one occasion. He now deeply regretted that it had caused Gloria pain and regretted even more that she always found out about his misdemeanours thanks to Lucia's highly proficient network of salacious gossips.

He had never really understood why Gloria was so perturbed by his careless meanderings. He had told her on many occasions that they meant nothing more to him than a simple release of his passions. He felt that she should have been proud of him for having so much masculine drive, but he had never quite been able to put this argument across lucidly enough. Gloria could never see his point of view on this. He consoled himself that she was not an entirely innocent party, and that she was certainly not averse to a public flirtation or two, as her drunken display with Ernesto had made quite apparent to all, only a few months previously. He had never chastised her for these bouts of self-expression, as they were always followed by the deep and painful depressions that it took him months to coax her out of. It was the depressions that in the past had been the reason for his many absences, allowing himself a short respite to glimpse a carefree side of life. He had never understood what prompted Gloria's melancholy, but he was convinced that her darkest moods often followed an extended stay from Doña Lucia, who, for his own reasons, the mayor strongly tried to discourage from visiting the house.

What had mortified him most about Gloria's accusations was that on his recent visit to Rosas Pampas he had no longer felt any desire for younger womanly companionship. He had simply longed, every night, for the familiarity of his bed and his wife. It was not just that with the passing of time he had lost confidence that he could perform his part effectively, a shortcoming that happened with alarming frequency these days, and which his wife accepted with stoicism and good grace. It was simply that he derived no pleasure from even the thought of being next to anyone other than Gloria. I have been a good husband, he told himself on reflection. I still am a good husband, no matter what Lucia may say. I have always had my Gloria's best interests at heart.

With Gloria foremost in his mind he had stopped at the little shop in the plaza to buy some of the *sublime* chocolate bars that she so enjoyed and a bottle of *aguardiente* with which to toast his good fortune. As he left the square, he raised the bottle in salute to the liberation of the barber's shop and was immediately overwhelmed by an acute pang of guilt. He was, he had to admit, the only person in the town with a reason to celebrate the shop's closure. But he certainly did not wish any harm to Don Bosco, quite the opposite. He wished him well on his travels and truly hoped that he would find happiness now that he had finally taken his life into his hands. He poured a splash of *aguardiente* on the ground and asked the Mother Earth to take good care of their absent friend. He had become as accustomed over the years to his unspoken battle of wits with Don Bosco as he had to his marriage to Gloria, and he had a grudging admiration for the little man.

Very soon after his arrival in town, the mayor had identified Don Bosco as the only real rival to his ambitions. He had initially encountered him during a meeting of the townsfolk when the first elections for the newly created town council were being discussed. Don Bosco had argued lucidly for the rights of the peasants to a greater allocation of the estate land under the statutes of the recently passed Land Act, which he had clearly understood, having read it from cover to cover, which was more than the mayor had been able to do, despite his legal training. The mayor had sniffed the intelligence of the man and despised him for it.

Over all these years, Don Bosco had remained an enigma to him. He had never understood why the barber had remained in the shop for so long, especially as he had made the terms so unreasonable. He had done so simply to exert his authority over a man who he knew could thwart his own plans with a wink of his eye. He had sensed the barber's regret at signing the agreement almost as soon as he had done it. The change in Don Bosco had happened almost immediately, as if the man were mourning a part of himself that had died overnight. The thought that he had been the cause of the diminishment of another man's soul had played slowly on his mind over the years. He felt an odd kinship with the barber. In him he saw a man just like himself, a man who had thrown his life away on a whim. In Don Bosco's frailties he saw his own failings starkly reflected.

What aggravated him most was that he had never really wanted anything more than to gain Don Bosco's respect, which was something he had never achieved. It infuriated him, how Don Bosco would stand in the doorway of his shop and tip his hat whenever he saw the mayor crossing the plaza, in some ridiculous parody of deference. It made him uncomfortable, knowing that behind the closed doors of the shop he was the object of ridicule at the hands of the barber's quick wit and good-natured humour. After the history between them, he had never really felt comfortable taking a seat in the barber's chair. Doña Gloria looked after his hair cutting needs, and so he was excluded from the very centre of male town life, which only added to his sense of isolation. And yet Don Bosco had come to his rescue on more than one occasion and had offered him help when he had feared that the town and his position within it were under imminent threat.

It had come to Don Bosco's attention a few years previously that a group of antiquity hunters were roaming the forest in search of the church and the precious Virgin, housed within it. Don Bosco had alerted the mayor to the threat and he had without hesitation allowed Don Bosco to send a group of reliable men to drive the treasure hunters into the swamp and to ensure that the rumour was kept quiet so as not to alarm the townsfolk. In return, the mayor had made Don Bosco keeper of the Virgin, to make sure she was protected under siege. From that day on the church had remained locked, Don Bosco and the mayor being the only people to hold the key. The mayor was able to stop worrying about his most precious charge, secure in the knowledge that she slept safely under the protective gaze of Don Bosco.

In recent years, the quiet influence that Don Bosco exerted over the town had begun to play on his mind. He felt the steady eye of the barber watching him, as if in passing over the charge of the Virgin he had handed Don Bosco a greater power than he could ever have. Don Bosco knew all the important affairs of his clientele, and all the really serious disputes were resolved within a beard's whisker of his razor. It had become very apparent to the mayor that he held his position in name only; it was Don Bosco to whom the towns-folk turned when they were in trouble, and it was Don Bosco they listened to when they needed advice. Don Bosco quite literally had at his fingertips the ears of all the men.

The mayor had known what he had to do ever since his return from Rosas Pampas. Above all, he needed to convince Don Bosco to give him the shop back so that he could start his plans to develop the town. He had taken his time to think through how to deal with the situation and had finally approached Don Bosco just as he was closing on Sunday morning, Don Bosco having in recent years taken to opening for a few hours even on his day of rest, due to popular demand. Don Bosco had clearly been in a strange state of mind and was very distracted when the mayor had knocked on the door. It was true, in all their years living side by side the mayor had only stepped over the threshold of the shop on a handful of occasions, once to seek advice regarding the protection of the Virgin, and on the others for some counselling on how best to deal with Gloria's fits of depression. Indeed, Don Bosco knew more about the ups and downs of living with Doña Gloria than he probably cared to.

The mayor had never encountered Don Bosco in such a state of

237

agitation before. He was pacing up and down the barber's shop as if he had no idea where he was, dressed in the most outrageous set of clothes. As the mayor entered, Don Bosco turned to greet the visitor and, on seeing who it was, froze on the spot.

'Not a bad time to catch you is it?' the mayor asked. 'I see you have been splashing out on new clothes.' Don Bosco visibly winced at the reference to his appearance.

'Yes,' Don Bosco replied. 'I have an engagement.'

'Oh,' the mayor said, still trying to make sense of the sight in front of him. 'Your shirt is very, very . . .'

'Modern,' Don Bosco replied, providing him with the word for which he was most certainly not searching.

'Modern, indeed,' the mayor agreed. 'You are looking very modern today.'

'To what do I owe this unexpected pleasure?' Don Bosco asked. 'It is some time since we have had one of our chats, but I am afraid today we will have to be brief. I am expected elsewhere very soon. Everything is how it should be at home, I trust? I heard that Doña Gloria has not been herself of late.' He said this with such sincerity in his voice that the mayor was momentarily taken off his guard. He had certainly not come here today to discuss his own troubles, much as he would have welcomed the opportunity.

'All is as it should be, thank you for asking,' the mayor replied. 'But I haven't come here today to discuss my wife's health, although I appreciate your concern.'

'And so to what do I owe this honour?' Don Bosco asked again, looking anxiously at his watch, awaiting the doctor's arrival.

'I realise you are busy,' the mayor replied, 'so I will get to the point. I have come to make you an offer. An offer to which I hope you will give due consideration. Don Bosco,' the mayor continued, 'for all these years, you and I have been bound by an agreement, an agreement that on reflection I feel has brought neither of us much joy. You have been true to your side of the bargain and have diligently provided this town with your services for six days of the week.'

'Seven,' Don Bosco corrected him.

'Indeed,' the mayor said, 'seven days a week. And the townsfolk are most grateful to you for doing so.'

'I know they are,' Don Bosco replied.

'And now I want you to be a free man.'

'A free man?' Don Bosco replied. 'I am as free as I chose to be.'

'You have been bound to this wretched shop for over twenty years because of the lease I asked you to sign,' the mayor replied. 'I want you to be free from it before it is too late,' and he reached inside his shirt and handed Don Bosco an envelope.

'Who are you to give me my freedom?' Don Bosco asked. 'Do you think I could not have walked away from here any time I wanted?' and he took the package, looked inside and then handed it back.

'It is a very reasonable sum,' the mayor continued.

'And what are you asking in return?' Don Bosco said.

'Nothing,' the mayor replied. 'Only that I have the shop back and that you enjoy your retirement. Every man deserves to find happiness in his life.'

'And why would I go in search of happiness now, after all these years? It can come and find me should it so wish.'

'Don't be a fool, man,' the mayor replied. 'I am making you a very good offer.'

'Why?' Don Bosco asked. 'You still haven't answered my question. Why do you want my shop?'

'Because', the mayor said, 'times are changing whether you like it or not. Haven't you seen? We have tourists here now, the old ways are going, Bosco, and people like you need to move aside to let that happen. Even you, after all, are now going for the modern look.'

Don Bosco stared at the mayor and then at his feet. 'I think you should leave,' he said at last.

'Just think about it,' the mayor said, and he placed the envelope on the stand next to the sink on which Don Bosco kept his brushes and razors. 'This should help you make your decision. The money is yours, if you shut up shop.'

As the mayor stood in the plaza contemplating the events of the past two days he reflected on how smoothly things had worked out. He had not expected Don Bosco to make a decision quickly and certainly did not anticipate that he would leave town without a word to anyone. But he was convinced that the barber would simply see sense, declare an end to their battle and would not be able to stay and look defeat in the eyes. He raised a toast to Don Bosco again to wish him well on his travels and returned home to find Lucia reclining on the chaise longue eating a box of chocolates, his wife nowhere to be seen.

Twenty-one

The mayor was so distracted by the loss of Gloria that, at first, he did not pay too much attention to what Ramon was telling him. He simply could not understand where Gloria could have gone, or why she would have left like that. He had methodically searched the house from top to bottom, looking for her in all the cupboards, under the beds, in the servants' rooms. The only place in which he had not been able to look was Lucia's room, the door having remained firmly locked since their altercation of the previous evening.

'Don't worry, I will stay and keep you company until she is back. I could not dream of leaving you alone,' Lucia had reassured him as he entered the house. He was not sure what had horrified him most, the sudden departure of Gloria or the apparent permanence of Lucia in his home.

'I don't understand. We were getting on so well again,' he said. 'We only just made up. Why would she have gone just like that?'

'I can't think,' Lucia said, stuffing another chocolate into her mouth. 'She is very up and down these days, just like dear Mother.'

'You don't think she might have done something foolish, do

you?' the mayor asked, and in voicing his deepest fear he was over-come by a terrifying anxiety. Over the past couple of years his wife's black moods had increased with frequency and intensity, and they seemed to overtake her with no apparent warning. 'Have you been saying things to her again, Lucia?' he asked, seeing the look on Lucia's face. 'I swear to God, if I find out that you have anything to do with this I will not be responsible for my actions.'

He reassured himself that Gloria would not have gone too far. She was not an adventurous woman and he was certain she would not have strayed much beyond the confines of the house. He had just begun his search of the garden that morning when Ramon found him on his hands and knees under the bushes. He had listened to Ramon's ramblings with only half his mind on what he was being told and the other half occupied with how he was going to throw Lucia out of the house and ensure that she never stepped foot in it again. He decided he would not leave for work that morning until he had at least accomplished that task.

He must have got the wrong end of the stick, the mayor told himself as Ramon beat a hasty retreat after imparting his news. I will wait for Lucia to come back and then see what is going on. I expect it is just that wretched Nicanora woman creating a stir about something or other again. She gets herself into everything these days. I must keep my eye on her – she is a troublemaker that is for sure. He was, he had to remind himself, grateful to her for having brought the Gringito to town, just when he needed something to show the visitors. Whatever she is up to, he told himself, that shop is now rightfully mine and I have the authority to take it. Bosco has given me that, and I will do so as soon as I am good and ready.

As for the visitors, he was certain that Ramon was getting himself in a state over nothing as usual. The district officer had assured him during their meeting that he would be given at least a month to make all the preparations for the visit. After all, there was a good deal at stake for the authorities, the district officer had made that quite clear. 'You had better not screw up,' had been the exact words he had used. 'You show them that our money has been well spent, and before you know it, you will have your own private helicopter in which to leave town.' The district officer had suggested that there may even be foreign dignitaries among the party, and they were to be received with a full official welcome. The mayor had not felt it politic to ask what a full official welcome might entail.

He had drawn up his plans as soon as he had arrived back in town, he knew exactly what he needed to do. He had decided that even though he had not yet received word from the authorities, the time was right to start to prepare the townsfolk for the changes that were afoot, and that meant removing Don Bosco from the shop on the prime site in the plaza. He had certainly not envisaged that it would be quite so easy to convince Don Bosco to leave. He is an intelligent man after all, the mayor said to himself. He simply realised that he could not stand in the way of progress. It was, nonetheless, unfortunate with the visitors coming that he was having such trouble with Gloria again. He was sure that a full official welcome would at the very least entail a reception hosted by the mayor and his wife and it would not look seemly to say he had lost her. I am sure I will have time to sort it out before they arrive, he told himself, and with Gloria in mind he went back into the house.

As he entered, he noticed that the door to Lucia's room was slightly ajar. He had seen her leaving for her morning stroll just before Ramon arrived. He knocked gently on the door to make sure she had not returned unnoticed, and then opened it and peered inside. Lucia's possessions were neatly laid out, as if she had been resident in the house for years. Photographs of her mother and father were placed on the little dressing table, and numerous pink cuddly toys were laid out on the bed. 'Gloria,' the mayor called softly, 'are you in here, my sweet, my little peach?' There was no reply. He stepped inside and rapidly started to search the room. He looked in the wardrobes, now stuffed full of Lucia's clothes, in the cupboards, in the drawers, and finally in the bed. And there it was, the thing he knew he had been looking for all along: the evidence of Lucia's treachery. Hidden under the sheets was a ridiculous set of women's underwear the like of which he had never seen in his life and a sheet of paper torn into pieces. Carefully placing the fragments together he read the note, apparently signed by him and written to a young lover. The evidence of Lucia's untamed jealousy was shocking enough, but what really disturbed him was that Lucia would go to these lengths to risk her sister's health and delicate frame of mind just to get her revenge on him. After all these years, Lucia had never forgiven him for refusing her advances. He had never been able to disclose to his wife the reason for his distaste for Lucia, convinced that it would threaten Gloria's stability if she knew that her sister had tried, on several occasions, to betray her with her husband. Besides, he was concerned that if he were to accuse Lucia, Gloria would be more prone to believe her sister's lies over his honesty in this matter, his integrity having been rightfully called into question on so many other occasions.

The ludicrous picture now conjured up in his mind, of being cornered in his own house by his over bearing sister-in-law, would have made him laugh out loud had it not also been so pitiful. He had never really understood what possessed Lucia to make her lascivious propositions to him. Perhaps it was loneliness that inspired her, although Lucia had a confidence and zest for life that made this hard to believe. Perhaps it was an untamed sibling rivalry, inherited at birth, that continued to play itself out in increasingly adult games. Or perhaps it was simply that Lucia still wanted her younger sister as her own, her possession, her shadow that she could control with nobody coming between them, just as it had been in their desolate and unloved childhood. For the sake of his marriage, and his sanity, he knew he could no longer risk having Lucia in the house. He packed her possessions into the cases piled in the corner of the room and placed them outside the door with a note asking Lucia kindly never to return, and then gave instructions to the servants to change the locks and under no circumstances to allow Lucia to step foot in the house again. With the underwear still in his pocket he made his way to the town hall to see what trouble was brewing there.

*

Everything looked calm as he approached the plaza. There was no commotion, no crowd waiting to bombard him with questions about the whereabouts of the barber. Everything seemed perfectly under control. The Gringito was asleep as usual under the eucalyptus tree.

'Bloody *hipi*,' he said under his breath. 'The first foreigner to make it here in years and we get one who can't stay awake for longer than ten minutes.' And he made a mental note to put an official notice on the tree banning people from sleeping under it. 'I will have him behaving like a bloody tourist before the day is out, whether he likes it or not,' he muttered under his breath. From the direction of his approach, the front part of Don Bosco's shop was obscured from view by the corner of the town hall. As far as he could discern there were no signs of activity coming from it. He decided to go straight to the town hall to find Ramon and gather the equipment he needed for the next stage of his plans. He had plenty of time to get everything under way. Even if the letter had been a little delayed getting to him, the district officer had promised he would telephone him to give him ample warning of the visitors' arrival. Then he stopped in his tracks with a gut-churning realisation: the telephone lines had been down for weeks.

*

'Where is it?' the mayor shouted as he stormed into the building. There was no sign of life in the deserted offices, apart from the scurrying of a family of rats who, recently dislodged from their home, were making their way down the corridor. He looked into the little room in which Ramon was supposed to perform his administrative duties, as usual it was empty. He then went straight to his office, took one look inside and bellowed, 'Ramon, I've been burgled.'

Ramon, certain that the mayor would be waylaid at the barber's shop, had not expected his patron to arrive at the town hall quite so quickly and was under the desk at the time sorting through the remaining paperwork. He leapt up, banging his head as he did so. 'I've had a little tidy-up, señor,' he announced, rubbing his head.

'For heaven's sake, Ramon. How many times have I told you not to do that?' the mayor said, clutching his heart. 'Where is everything? Where have all my things gone?'

Ramon looked round the room at the empty desk and chair. 'What things are those, señor?' he asked.

'My things. My files. My paperwork. My official business. Where has it all gone?'

'Well, señor,' Ramon replied, 'I decided that there was no space in here to file everything, as a lot of the paperwork was quite old. I thought it was becoming a health hazard, gathering all that dust. Some rats had even made a nest in the corner of one of the piles of folders. So I decided that perhaps it was wise to reorganise.'

'So where is it?' the mayor said, glaring at Ramon.

'It was all getting a little out of hand,' Ramon continued.

'Where is it? And where is the letter?' the mayor asked, walking towards Ramon, who took a step backwards. He pointed at the empty desk on which now lay a single sheet of paper. The mayor picked it up.

'This was sent nearly a month ago,' he said, looking at the date on the letter. 'Why didn't you tell me it had arrived?'

'I did, señor,' Ramon replied. 'At least, I remember putting it there on your desk in the "To be urgently attended-to pile". But with things being so busy I think it must have got overlooked.' The mayor had stopped listening. He was reading the official notification of the planned arrival of the visitors. He stared at the letter, then at the calendar on the wall, and then at Ramon.

'It's tomorrow,' he said.

'Is it? Already? How can that be?'

'The visitors, Ramon. The date in this letter. Their estimated arrival time. It is lunch-time tomorrow. "We are giving you due advanced notification,"' the mayor now read out loud, '"as we will expect you as leader of your esteemed town council to host the official welcome according to the protocol that has been sent to you ahead of this notice."' Enclosed was a brief itinerary of what was to follow the official welcome, and included a tour of the town to take in the antiquities, the tourist attractions and all the recent developments in which the provincial authorities had invested their money.

'Protocol documents? Ramon, where are the protocol documents?'

Ramon scanned the empty room. 'I can't be certain,' he said, 'but I think I may have filed them with all the old paperwork.'

'And where is that?'

'I burnt it.'

By the time the mayor reached the backyard of the town hall there was little remaining to show for years of unattended-to official business but a pile of smouldering ashes.

*

'What is it?' Ramon said, staring at the black box on the mayor's desk.

'It's the future, Ramon,' the mayor said.

'Really?' Ramon said, taking in a breath, and he reached out to touch it. 'It looks like a television. Like the one in Don Bosco's shop. Can we watch football on it?'

'I expect so,' the mayor said. 'That and much, much more besides.'

'What does it do?'

'It will connect us to the world,' the mayor said, borrowing the phrase he had learned from Consuela and her bright young assistant.

'How?' Ramon asked.

'What do you mean "how"?'

'Well, how will it connect us to the world?' Ramon asked, pressing a button on the lifeless black box.

'Through the superhighway,' the mayor replied.

'The superhighway? So they are going to build a road after all?' Ramon said.

'They will when I am done with them,' the mayor replied. 'At least I'm prepared. Good thing you didn't have the key to my cupboard otherwise you might have destroyed this as well.' Ramon looked shamefaced and stared at the ground.

'We will just have to make it up as we go along,' the mayor said. 'But I tell you, this will impress the visitors, official protocol or not.'

'So where is the superhighway?'

'It's in the computer, Ramon. It is the pathway to the rest of the world. Through this, we can get any information we need.'

'About what?'

'About things, Ramon.'

'What sort of things?'

'Many things. Anything. About the places where the foreigners come from, for a start.'

'Where did you get it from?' Ramon asked.

'Doña Consuela sold it to me. Have you any idea how difficult it is carrying a computer by donkey through swamp? The days will soon be gone when I will have to make a trip like that again. This is what I have invested the remainder of the money in. Ramon, can you believe it? Consuela's business is doing so well that she was getting rid of these old computers and having new ones sent to her by boat from Manola.'

'Where does she get all that money?'

The mayor took Ramon by the arm and led him to window. 'What do you see out there?' he asked.

'The plaza of course,' Ramon answered, wondering why the conversation had suddenly changed direction.

'And what else?'

'The eucalyptus tree. Oh yes, and Doña Nicanora having an argument with Don Pedro.'

'Wretched woman,' the mayor said, gazing out of the window. 'I'll sort her out in a minute. Look again. What is the most valuable thing that this town possesses?'

'Oh, the church and the Virgin,' Ramon said, suddenly feeling ashamed, and he crossed himself.

'No, Ramon I didn't mean the church. I meant the bloody *hipi*.'

'The *hipi*?'

'Yes, Ramon. Don't you see? He is our future. What do you think he is doing here?'

'Sleeping,' Ramon said.

'Well, yes, I think we got a bit of a faulty one there to be honest,' the mayor said. 'The ones I have seen do things.'

'What sort of things?'

'They wander around buying things. And they sit and eat food, drink coffee and use bloody computers. Ramon, we need more of them here, lots of them. But better than the one we've got at the moment. I want this town to be rich, like it was in the days of our ancestors. I want it to be the centre of the province again. I think that is the least we deserve.'

'Señor,' Ramon said, now really confused and trying not to undermine his boss's enthusiasm. 'What has the computer got to do with it?'

'That is what they will come here for.'

'Why? I'm sure they have them in their own country, señor.'

'I know they do, Ramon. That is the point.'

Ramon, who had been trying to hold his own in the conversation, now floundered. 'Señor, there is something I really don't understand. Why would they want to come here to use a computer to find out information about the places they have just come from? I know,' he said with a sudden flash of inspiration. 'Nicanora said she thought the Gringito was lost. Is that why they need computers? To find out how to get home?'

'They talk to people, Ramon. That's what they use them for. They talk to other gringos, in other countries. They talk to other people like themselves, when they are travelling.'

'Don't the telephones in their country work either?'

'No, they like to talk to people they don't know. People they have never met and never will meet, anywhere in the world, in other parts of the world.'

'So let me get this right,' Ramon said. 'They will travel all the way here to talk to someone they don't know, who is somewhere else altogether?'

'Yes.'

'Why?'

'I don't know, Ramon,' the mayor said, sitting down. 'Probably to stop them feeling so alone. All I know is that there is money to be had from it.'

'So how does it work?' Ramon asked, pressing a button again and waiting expectantly for the screen to burst into life.

'I have no idea,' the mayor said. 'But you had better find out by tomorrow.' And he handed Ramon a small book, a bag of cables and a set of round discs that looked like little saucers, given to him by Consuela's assistant.

'Right,' the mayor said, getting up from his seat. 'We have business to attend to. I am going to sort out that Nicanora woman once and for all, and you had better make sure all the arrangements are made and everything is in order by tomorrow morning.'

Ramon was left standing with a list headed 'Visitor Protocol

Arrangements' in one hand, and a booklet entitled 'Instruction Manual' in the other. He sat down in the mayor's chair, opened the drawer of the desk and for the first time in his life helped himself to a large glass of whisky.

Twenty-two

It was mid-afternoon by the time the mayor reached the barber's shop. Don Julio and Don Teofelo were sitting at the little table and chairs playing dominoes, Don Teofelo absent-mindedly scratching at his chin.

'I wish you would stop doing that,' Don Julio said. 'You've got me started again now.' Don Teofelo placed a double six, followed by another five pieces.

'Your turn.'

'I thought you said she gave a smooth shave,' Julio complained.

'I just thought she needed some help to get started. She is doing this for Bosco, after all.'

'Is she?' Don Julio said. 'How do you know she's telling the truth?'

'I trust her,' Teofelo said.

'You've changed your tune,' Julio said. 'But Teofelo, what if she just saw this as an opportunity to steal Bosco's property? I still don't understand how she got the key. Bosco has never given anyone the key to his shop before. You know what he's like, he's so secretive. Why would he just hand it over to her? She's a woman, Teofelo.'

'I had noticed,' Teofelo replied, laying down another string of dominoes. Being true to his promise he had not breathed a word to Don Julio, or anybody, about his parting conversation with Don Bosco, nor about the letter he had been entrusted to hand to Doña Nicanora. He had also not told Julio of the promise he had made as he bade his dear friend farewell. 'If she asks for your help, will you give it to her?' Don Bosco had said. It was true, Doña Nicanora had not, strictly speaking, asked him for help, and nor, he suspected, would she. She was very like Bosco in that regard, too proud for her own good. But he knew that now was the time she really needed him as a friend, and he was determined to be just that until his faith was proved unfounded.

'My face feels as if a swarm of bees has been playing on it all afternoon,' Julio complained.

'Stop making such a fuss,' Teofelo replied, finishing off the game. 'I think, perhaps, she didn't use enough soap. She will get the hang of it soon. After all, we were her first customers.'

*

Nicanora had been as astonished by Gloria's sudden arrival at the shop as she had by Teofelo's bravery in front of the crowd. 'Doña Gloria,' Nicanora said after Teofelo had been pushed from the shop, 'it is delightful to see you up and about again, but your husband will be very unhappy if he finds you here. It will be bad enough when he finds me, without your help.'

'Good. Let him stew in it,' was Gloria's response.

Don Julio had just entered the shop, encouraged in by Teofelo, and had placed himself in the barber's chair ready for Nicanora to begin her work. Gloria, seated in the corner, was filing her nails and watching as Nicanora slowly and meticulously started to scrape the razor over Don Julio's chin.

'If you carry on like that,' Gloria said to Nicanora, 'your customers will have no faces left. You will frighten everyone away.'

I'm not sure who she thinks she is, talking to me about frightening the customers, Nicanora thought to herself. It seemed to Nicanora that Gloria had not paid too much attention to the detail of her attire as she had left the house that morning and she was looking decidedly off-putting. Her lipstick was smeared across the lower part of her face, her hair was piled in a makeshift knot on her head, and her dress looked as if it had been slept in. Which, Gloria confessed to Nicanora later, it had been. At the clinic.

'You stayed at the clinic, last night. Alone?'

'No, with the doctor.'

'You slept at the clinic with the doctor?'

'I was sick,' Gloria explained. 'We slept in separate rooms of course,' she added. 'After all, I have only just made his acquaintance. But he made me feel very welcome.'

'Did he indeed.'

'Anyway,' Gloria continued, 'he was very kind. Do you know, he is the first person who has ever really listened to me. I mean, properly listened to me. He made me feel that I was not a useless person. I do have something to offer. And so this morning I realised what was wrong with me. After all these years, I think he has finally discovered a cure for my problem.'

'And what is that?' Nicanora asked, busying herself tidying the shop in preparation for her next customer.

'I need a purpose.'

'A purpose?'

'Yes, I need to give my life meaning. The doctor said everyone needs a purpose, otherwise there is no point in getting out of bed in the morning.'

'Doña Gloria,' Nicanora said. 'I have been getting out of bed every morning for the past forty years and I have never once had a purpose.'

'Of course you have,' Gloria said. 'You just haven't realised it. You go to the market, you come home, you peel potatoes, you wash clothes, you listen to your children squabbling, you wash the dishes, and then you go to bed.'

'And that is a purpose?'

'Yes.'

'My dear Doña Gloria, I wish you had come to me and told me so years ago. I would gladly have moved out of my house and let you take over.'

'Maybe I don't want to do what you do exactly. But I need something to do with my days other than worry about where my husband is, and who he has been with.'

'I'm glad we have brought a doctor all the way from the city to tell you that,' Nicanora said.

'Yes,' Gloria agreed, 'he's a very clever young man, and so handsome. It has all worked out extremely well.'

'What has?'

'Well, you see, I was crossing the plaza on my way to find you, as the kind doctor had suggested that it might do me good to stay in your house.'

'He did, did he? So that you can see what my life is like to make you more contented with your own?'

'And then I saw what was happening here,' Gloria said, ignoring the possibility that she might just have given offence, 'and I realised that this is exactly the purpose I need. I said to myself, I will help Doña Nicanora become a barber.'

'Why?'

'Because', Gloria said, 'I have been shaving my husband's wretched beard for years and I know exactly how not to give him a shaving rash. There we are,' Gloria said, pointing to Don Alfredo who, egged on by Don Julio, was now hovering in the doorway of the shop. 'Your next customer.' Nicanora picked up the razor to start. 'More soap,' Gloria instructed from the chair. 'And quicker with the razor. No, not like that, watch me,' and she snatched the implement out of Nicanora's hand and with short, precise movements cleared Don Alfredo's face of any sign of stubble before he had a chance to open his mouth to protest.

'I will make a deal with you,' Gloria said triumphantly, as Don Alfredo leapt from the chair a free man once again. 'I will teach you how to give as good a shave as Don Bosco ever has, and I won't ask for any payment, if you in turn let me work here with you, and perhaps sleep at your house, for the time being at least.'

'But I don't need any help,' Nicanora said. 'Don Teofelo was very happy with the shave I gave him.' Then looking out of the window she caught sight of Teofelo helplessly scratching at his face.

'He was just being kind, wasn't he?' she said turning to Doña Gloria. 'We have a deal.'

*

After the initial excitement of the morning, word spread quickly that Teofelo and Julio were looking decidedly red in the face. The men started moving away from the plaza, worried that if they hung around for too long they would be forced to take their own place in the barber's chair. Don Alfredo had been dispatched by Don Teofelo to persuade a few of his friends that the service had improved dramatically, but custom had been very slow for the best part of the morning. It was only after Nicanora came up with the ingenious idea of a two-for-the-price-of-one promotion, offering a free haircut with every shave and unlimited quantities of coffee for her clientele, that business began to pick up. Doña Gloria was also proving herself not only to be adept with a razor, but highly proficient with a pair of scissors.

'I have always thought this would make a lovely little salon,' she said to Nicanora. 'I have told my husband over the years, it was such a shame it was allowed to become a crusty little barber's. No disrespect to Don Bosco, of course,' she said, hastily looking at the hat on the pole, and then she crossed herself.

Don Pedro, encouraged by Teofelo, had been the first to take up the offer of the free haircut. 'Not too much off,' he warned, as Gloria approached his thick hair with the energy of a wild beast.

'And how is business these days?' Nicanora asked Don Arsenio, who had taken his place next to his friend in the barber's chair.

'Not too good I am afraid,' Don Arsenio replied. 'What with the price of coffee falling it is hard enough to make a living, and with the rains being so temperamental this year, I'm afraid that my crops on the slopes won't even ripen properly for the harvest.'

'Oh dear,' Doña Nicanora replied, her instinct getting the better of her. 'That is a worry for everyone. But don't be too concerned – the rains will start by the end of the week. And how are things at home?' she asked her next customer, who was watching in astonishment as lumps of Don Pedro's hair cascaded to the floor.

'Not so good I'm afraid,' he replied. 'My wife has been a little off colour. I think she's going down with the swamp fever again.'

'I wouldn't worry,' Nicanora replied. 'I'm sure it's just a cold. When you go home this evening she will be right as rain, you'll see.'

'What have you done? What have you done to my lovely thick hair?'

Don Pedro suddenly screamed from the chair, his reflection having just been revealed to him.

'I saw it in a magazine. It's apparently how all the men in the United States are wearing their hair these days,' Doña Gloria said as Don Pedro rushed out into the plaza with Nicanora following behind in an effort to calm him down. It took her some time to convince the small group of lingering men that they were being given not only a free haircut, but the very latest style to have reached the city from abroad. By late afternoon, the word had spread so effectively that by the time the mayor reached the premises a queue had formed and was stretching round the corner.

Don Julio was the first to see the mayor approaching. 'He doesn't look too happy,' he whispered to Teofelo, who rushed inside the shop to warn Nicanora. Doña Nicanora had been expecting a visit from the mayor, but had become so absorbed in her burgeoning business that she had almost forgotten about him. She suspected that none of the townsfolk had been brave enough yet to inform him of the whereabouts of his wife, especially as a good many of the men were now rather diffidently sporting Gloria's creations on their heads.

'Don't you worry any more about your chickens,' Nicanora was telling Don Amelio as Teofelo burst in, 'they just took a fright and are hiding. They will be back in your yard by the time you get home this evening.'

'What the hell is going on here?' the mayor shouted, storming into the shop and halting any further conversation about lost chickens. 'Where is Bosco?'

'He isn't here,' Nicanora replied. 'He hasn't yet returned from his travels. Were you wanting a tidy-up?' Nicanora heard a stifled snort coming from the back storeroom.

'What on earth are you doing, woman?' the mayor demanded. 'Have you gone quite mad? You are trespassing on municipal property and I demand you leave it this minute.'

'Municipal property?' Nicanora said calmly. 'But this is Don Bosco's shop.'

'Haven't you seen my notice? Don Bosco gave up rightful possession of this shop the minute he left. It is now the property of the town council, as my notice has made quite clear.'

'What notice is that, Don Ramirez?' Nicanora asked.

'The notice that was pinned to the shop door yesterday evening and that you appear to have removed. I have already given warning that if Bosco is not back today, razor in hand, then under the terms of the lease this shop comes under my jurisdiction. And you, madam, now appear to be trespassing. I warn you if you do not leave peacefully, I will have you removed by force.'

'By whom?'

'By whom?'

'Yes, by whom?' Nicanora asked. She looked into the plaza at her hovering clientele. She caught sight of Ramon peeping round the corner of the town hall. 'Who exactly will you get to remove me?' she asked. 'I see nobody here who would be either willing or up to such a task, especially as I am quite within my rights to be here.'

'How dare you?' The mayor was spitting as he spoke. 'How dare you contradict the town council? The terms of the lease for this shop were drawn up between Don Bosco and me. He knew exactly what our agreement was, and he has now of his own volition agreed to hand the shop back to me, and for a very tidy sum I might add.'

'Don Ramirez, I believe there has been a misunderstanding,' Nicanora said. 'Don Bosco has handed the keys over to me while he has a short break, as you will see from this note. Do you have anything in writing that contradicts his wishes stated here?' and Nicanora handed to the mayor the letter that Don Bosco had given her, with a few key passages blotted out.

The mayor looked at the letter and then at Nicanora. 'Hat shop?' he said. 'What's he talking about? A hat shop?'

'Never mind that,' Nicanora said. 'That was a mistake. This is a barber's shop, and that is how it will stay, at least while under my management.'

'I have come to tell you that we have very important visitors coming tomorrow and I need this shop back, *now*,' the mayor said, almost stamping his feet, as Gloria chose this as her moment to make her presence known.

'Gloria,' the mayor said. 'What are you doing here? I've been worried sick about you. I've been looking everywhere for you.'

'How sweet,' Gloria replied.

'Gloria, what do you think you are doing?'

'Helping Doña Nicanora,' she said.

'Helping Doña Nicanora do what?'

'Cut hair and shave beards,' Gloria replied.

'Gloria,' the mayor said. 'That just isn't seemly. I demand that you come home this minute.'

'I am sorry, Rodriguez,' Gloria replied. 'You're just going to have to do without me.'

'Gloria, my love,' the mayor pleaded. 'This is all Lucia's doing. It's all a lie. Whatever it is that Lucia has been telling you, I can assure you, it is a lie.'

'That's what I am afraid of,' Gloria replied.

'Gloria, come home and talk to me. I will make Lucia confess what she has done. She has always hated me because I married you and not her. I can prove it's all a lie.'

'I don't need you to prove what I already know,' Gloria said. 'Prove to me instead that it has not been a lie – our marriage, our life together. In the meantime, I have work to do,' and she disappeared to the back of the shop.

'I think we have nothing further to say to each other for the moment,' Nicanora said, 'unless you would like a shave.' And then she whispered in the mayor's ear, 'I know about your agreement. I know where Don Bosco has kept it all these years, and I am sure you would not want me to make it public, especially not with visitors arriving. Or would you like me to pin it to the door so that everyone can see what sort of agreement it is that gives the town council the right to take a man's property from him?'

Nicanora turned and left the mayor standing dumbstruck as one of the men from the crowd approached her. 'Excuse me. Is that hat for sale?' he said, pointing at the barber's pole.

'Of course it isn't,' Nicanora replied. 'It belongs to Don Bosco.'

'Yes, but it doesn't look as if he wants it any more. Anyway, he won't be needing it now, will he? How much do you want for it?'

'I have told you, it is not for sale,' Nicanora replied, furious. 'This is a barber's, not a hat shop,' and she went back inside and put the 'Closed' sign on the door.

Twenty-three

Nicanora was feeling the full weight of the responsibility of having Doña Gloria to stay. As soon as she had put her new house guest safely to bed, Nicanora sat down with Ernesto.

'We need to talk. I want you to take him back where he came from,' she said pointing in the direction of the Gringito, who was sitting in the front yard, smoking as usual.

'But I don't know where he came from.'

'I mean I want you to put him back where you found him,' Nicanora said. 'I need you to go to Puerta de la Coruña tomorrow in your pickup truck. Will you do that for me? I have thought about it all day and I know what I have to do to put everything to rights again. I need to ask the Virgin for her forgiveness and for her blessing to bring Don Bosco home. If you go to Puerta de la Coruña, you can get rid of the Gringito and bring back the beer we will need for the fiesta at the same time.'

'Are we having a fiesta?' Nena said bursting into the room. 'Can we have fireworks? You can't have a fiesta without fireworks.'

'Nena,' Nicanora said, exasperated that it was impossible to have any privacy in her own house. 'I don't want either of you to breathe a word of this yet, do you understand? I will announce it tomorrow when everyone is gathered for the visitors. That way the mayor will not be able to stop me.'

'Can you do that?' Ernesto asked. 'It has only ever been the mayor's family who have hosted the fiesta before.'

'That's because they are the only ones who have ever been able to afford to pay for it before,' Nicanora said. 'I have the Gringito's money now and this is how I want to use it.'

'Why?' Ernesto asked. 'Why do want to get rid of him suddenly?'

'Because,' Nicanora said. 'So far he has only brought us bad luck, and this way at least the whole town will benefit from his money. Don't you see? The Gringito's money is the reason that Don Bosco left. And now these visitors are coming. If they find the Gringito here, it will change our town for good, and it will be my fault for letting him stay. The mayor will convince them to build a road, more tourists will come, and before long everything will be out of control. Now I understand what Don Bosco meant when he said don't let anything bad happen to our town. I have to stop the visitors seeing we have a foreigner here.'

'What's wrong with foreigners?' Nena asked.

'Nothing,' Nicanora said, 'that's not what I meant.'

'He isn't a foreigner once you get to know him,' Nena mumbled. 'You've just never tried to talk to him.'

'Well, I can't understand what he says,' Nicanora replied.

'You haven't listened hard enough.'

'That is not the point,' Nicanora said, knowing that she was never able to win an argument with her daughter.

'What is the point then?' Nena asked, defiant.

'He's different, that's all,' Nicanora said. 'And it worries me.'

264

'We're all different,' Nena mumbled.

'Nena, have you talked to him yet?' Nicanora said.

'Yes. He says he doesn't want to go.'

'Why not? I thought he would be pleased. I thought he didn't know how to get home.'

'He says he doesn't want to go to Puerta de la Coruña. He doesn't like it there.'

'Why not?' Nicanora asked.

'It's full of people like him. He finds them boring.'

'I can see his point there,' Ernesto said.

'He says he's happy here.'

'How can he be happy here?' Nicanora said. 'He doesn't know anyone. He doesn't do anything. I don't understand why he wants to stay, it isn't his home.'

'He says he's found himself.'

'Found himself?' Nicanora said. 'So he was lost then?'

'He's worried that he isn't paying you enough. He said that he will pay you more if he can stay for another few weeks.'

'More?' Nicanora said. 'The whole point of the fiesta is to spend his money, not to make more out of him.'

'But can't he just stay for the fireworks? After all, if he's paying for the party he should be able to be there. Perhaps I can persuade him to leave after that.'

'Nena, he has to leave by the morning and that is that. I'm not going to argue with you about it any more. I've made up my mind. Ernesto, do you think you will be able to get to Puerta de la Coruña and back by Saturday? We must have the fiesta this Sunday, the sooner the better.'

'I'll do my best,' Ernesto said.

'You will be careful on that road, won't you?' Nicanora said, and she pushed a small doll into Ernesto's hand. 'She will make sure you are safe.'

'I'll be fine,' Ernesto said. 'I've done it before. I'll take the doctor with me for company. And I'll bring you back a special box of fireworks,' he said, winking at his sulking sister.

*

The town awoke the following day ready to receive some very important guests. The word had spread quickly that unexpected visitors were on their way and would be arriving at lunchtime, by helicopter. The conclusion had been reached, through a chain of whispers, that the mayor had kept the visit a secret until the last minute for security reasons. The visitors, it had been concluded, were a party of foreign dignitaries, very possibly including the head of state of a neighbouring country with whom the president had been in dispute for some years over land matters; he was now trying to make amends by hosting a visit to the humble town. A helicopter had been spotted in the early hours of the morning by some farmers who had seen it hovering in the distance over a remote patch of swampland. 'They must have been looking for a place to land,' the excited farmers had decided and had rushed back to tell their friends. A competing rumour had been circulating that had gained slightly less favour, which was that one of the visitors was the Gringito's father, who was coming to take his son home at last.

Nicanora had not slept at all, worried that the mayor might take it into his head to try to break in and claim possession of the barber's shop in the middle of the night. When she opened the shop in the morning she almost tripped over the body of the sleeping mayor

266

snoring in the doorway. A small group of men who were waiting eagerly outside immediately rushed up to her. 'I'm very sorry, we're not quite ready for business yet,' Nicanora said, stepping over the sleeping mayor and placing the barber's pole outside the shop.

'No, no, it's not that,' one of the men said. 'I just want you to tell me what to do about my sick goat.'

'You see, I went home last night,' Don Amelio explained, 'and my chickens had returned, just as you said they would.'

'And my wife has made a miraculous recovery from the swamp fever. By the time I got home all she had to show for it was a red nose.'

'Can you tell me whether I should go to the slopes to harvest my coffee next week as I planned, or leave it for another few weeks?'

Nicanora stood listening to the men's requests with a sinking heart. A wise woman, her mother had always told her, will learn from her mistakes.

*

Nicanora was not the only person not to have slept that night. Nena had been waiting for the early dawn to break before waking the Gringito. 'I'm taking you to visit a friend for a few days,' she explained as she led him out of the house. 'You can come back on Sunday for the fiesta. I know somewhere you will be safe. I'll take you to the medicine man. He'll ask the ancestors for help, so that you can make this your home if you want to.' Then she added as an afterthought, 'You will have to pay him in pesos.'

As Nena made her way back home in the morning light having accomplished her mission, it seemed to her that the forest had suddenly given birth to a new creature. Distant figures moved through the undergrowth, human in form, foreign in being, leaves covering their heads and faces. They were quietly talking into little black boxes that they held in their hands.

*

Ramon, under the mayor's instructions, had been busy all morning preparing the plaza with the help of a few of the more obliging men of the town. A large banner made out of old sheets had been hung above the town hall saying: 'Valle de la Virgen welcomes all visitors.' In order to make the point as clearly as possible, Ramon had also pinned a large notice to the eucalyptus tree with the words 'Tourist spot' written on it. A makeshift podium had been erected in the centre of the plaza out of orange boxes. On top of the podium sat the lifeless computer. An impromptu flagpole had been erected, which towered over the plaza like a watching antenna.

Ramon raced into the mayor's office red in the face, his preparation list in his hand. 'Where have you been?' the mayor demanded, making last-minute amendments to his speech. 'They will be here in an hour.' Ramon was about to answer and then took another look at his patron.

'Señor,' he said, 'I hope you don't mind me asking, but have you had a shave this morning?' He did not want to say too much on the subject, but even by the mayor's standards he was looking decidedly dishevelled. The mayor had not told Ramon about his night sleeping on the doorstep of the barber's shop, and his last bid to stop Gloria from entering. As he had seen her approaching he had tried to bar the doorway and had only relented and let her past after Gloria had threatened to welcome the visitors chained to the barber's pole. He had then adopted a softer and far more effective

268

tactic. 'But my dearest,' he had pleaded. 'This may be the greatest honour you will have in your life. Surely you don't want to miss such an opportunity because of a silly argument, and Lucia's malicious lies. You still have time to go home and put on your best dress. You will be the star of the show.' He had been so persuasive that he had almost succeeded in breaking Gloria's resolve, until disastrously he reached inside his pocket for a handkerchief with which to wipe his face and brought out the offending underwear. From that moment on, war on the visitors had been declared very loudly from behind the barber's chair.

'Are we running to schedule?' the mayor asked Ramon.

'We are, señor. We are indeed,' Ramon said walking around in circles, reading from his preparation list. 'Exactly to schedule, exactly to schedule. The school band is ready. They will be assembling soon. The podium is constructed and we have finally managed to make the banner stay up. I just have to get the gourds.'

'Gourds?'

'To hang around the visitors' necks.'

'Hang around their necks?'

'I think we have to give them a gift.'

'You can't hang bloody great gourds around the visitors' necks, Ramon. You will decapitate them.'

'Oh,' said Ramon, 'what shall we give them then?' and he rapidly crossed gourds off the list.

'I don't know. Something unique. Something they will remember us by. I thought you said you had it in hand.'

'Not gourds then,' Ramon said.

'Think, quick. What do we have that we can give to them, that symbolises what is really important about the town?'

'How about a bit of the church wall?'

'We are not giving our visitors a bit of crumbling old wall to go home with, Ramon.'

'I know,' Ramon said, quick as a flash. 'Don Bosco's hat.'

The mayor took a step towards Ramon as if to hit him. 'Go and get one of the schoolchildren to pick some bunches of wild flowers, Ramon. Have you got that bloody computer working yet?'

'I'm working on it, señor,' Ramon answered. 'The problem is we need to plug it in.' 'Well of course we need to plug it in, Ramon. How did you think the bloody thing works?'

'I mean we need a cable, señor; that is long enough to stretch from the town hall to the podium. We can't run it from the barber's shop as Doña Gloria is currently blocking the door, although she has put up a nice banner above the shop.'

'Has she indeed?' the mayor said.

'And is the doctor ready?'

'The doctor?' Ramon said, as if it were the first time he had thought about him.

'Have you got a group of women and children ready to be at the clinic?'

'Yes, Señor, yes, I have done that. I went to the market this morning and paid them all just as you asked me to.'

'So the doctor is ready at the clinic?'

'Well, señor,' Ramon said, wondering how he could avoid telling the mayor that, in all the rush of preparations he had so effectively put into action, it had slipped his mind until an hour ago to make the visit to the doctor to warn him of the guests' arrival. When he had got there, the doctor had been nowhere to be seen.

'I am sure he is. I am sure he is,' Ramon replied, but the mayor was distracted and had wandered over to the window to look at the final preparations. 'I'll show that bloody Nicanora woman that she can't steal my thunder,' he said. 'By this time tomorrow, I will have her out of that shop. I just don't want Gloria making a fuss in front of the visitors. We can use this to our advantage —' And then he screamed, 'Where is the bloody *hipi*?'

'What bloody *hipi* is that?' Ramon said. The mayor looked at him as if he wanted to kill him.

'How many bloody *hipis* do we have in this town, Ramon?' he bellowed.

'One,' Ramon replied, and rushed to the window to stare at the vacant spot under the eucalyptus tree. 'He's gone,' Ramon said, horrified.

*

Nicanora stood next to Gloria, observing the proceedings in the plaza as the time of the planned arrival approached. The exasperated mayor was still trying to raise the flag, which was as defiant in its determination not to move up the pole as Gloria was in her resolve not to leave the shop. Suddenly the waiting crowd started to clap as the national emblem ascended in uncertain, jerky movements.

'I'm sure it shouldn't be red,' Nicanora said to Gloria. The mayor turned and glared at Ramon.

'It was the only colour I could find,' Ramon explained. 'I painted one stripe on the top and then I couldn't find any yellow paint for the next stripe. I hung it out to dry overnight, but it seems to have run a bit.'

'Well, it will have to do. They will be here any minute now,' the mayor said. And the townsfolk gathered to welcome their foreign guests as the red flag flew high above the town of Valle de la Virgen. The school band started up as the clock struck eleven, which everybody knew meant it was noon. Nicanora suddenly saw Nena rush across the plaza ready to take her place in the welcome party. Nicanora called her over.

'Where have you been?'

'I just went for a walk,' Nena said.

'Nena,' Nicanora said. 'I hope you haven't been into the swamp alone again. What were you thinking of?'

'It's all right,' Nena said. 'I didn't go far.' She was about to go off and join the band when she turned back with a worried look on her face and said to her mother, 'There are green men in the forest and they are talking to themselves.'

Twenty-four

Arturo received a visitor in the night. He had been half anticipating the knock on the door, although he was not sure from whom it would come. He had never become used to the dark of the forest nights, darker than any of the childhood tales that Doña Julia had spun for him and which now retold themselves in his dreams with the terrifying rationality of an adult mind. Alone in the dark, his sleep was visited by the spirits that invaded the slumbering bodies of unsuspecting souls. He dreamt of the pregnant woman who gave birth to an anaconda after having taken fright one morning when she woke to find a snake in the bed beside her instead of her husband. He saw himself attending the labour as the unending body of the serpent progeny tore the woman's womb apart and then consumed everything in its path.

He sat up in a cold sweat, his thoughts involuntarily turning to Don Bosco wandering alone in the forest night. The haunting image of the barber's half-submerged body appeared in his mind, not for the first time. He was no longer sure whether it was the product of nightmares or whether he had truly seen it lying there covered by the undergrowth, floating face down, bloated, swarming with flies, mud oozing from its pores. He had heard about such things in his medical training. Shock can make a liar of an honest man, obliterating all sense of what is real in the world, turning facts into fiction and fanciful stories into God-sworn truths. He tried to push the vision of the body from his mind and to think more comforting thoughts. The picture of the hat on the barber's pole floated in front of his eyes. He had seen it as he walked through the plaza earlier that day, a totemic representation of all that was good and precious about the town: to him it symbolised the very being of the place. He wondered how long the townsfolk would go through a period of denial before the grieving process would really begin. What a brave, kind woman Doña Nicanora is, he thought. He did not have the heart to tell her that he was certain that a man like Don Bosco could not have survived lost in the swamp for days. He fell, once again, into feverish dreams, this time plagued by the apparition of Doña Gloria teasing him with her ghostly ailments.

He lay drifting in and out of sleep. Earlier that evening he had allowed his body to be washed by the freshness of Isabela's touch, and his mouth had tasted the sweetness of her kisses. She had come to him, the night of his return from the search party, and she had sat and listened to him, and consoled him, comforting him that if it was not Don Bosco's time to be found, nobody could have done any better. Isabela's visits were now a frequent, and eagerly antici-pated, occurrence. She would arrive just after her brother had left, with some tasty titbits from her mother's kitchen, and help Arturo prepare a meal for two on his lonely gas ring. She was not now the playful, flirtatious young woman with whom he had been confronted at first: she was quickly becoming his confidante, his soulmate. 'It doesn't really matter to me if you aren't a hero,' she had told him as she left that evening, 'I like you just as you are.'

Then, as she rose to go home so that her mother would not miss her from the house for too long and start asking questions, she turned and said to him, 'You know, you are the only person who listens to me without judging me. You are the only person who sees me for who I really am.'

*

Arturo lay thinking about Isabela, consumed with the guilt of his infidelity. And then came the knock on the door. As if called by an unknown duty he got out of bed, lit a candle and went to let in the visitor. A young man in an army uniform stood in front of him. In the candlelight, Arturo could make out the shape of a gun slung over his shoulder.

'Are you the doctor?' the young man asked.

'Yes,' Arturo replied.

'My name is Carlos,' he said and reached his hand out to shake Arturo's. Then he raised his gun. 'You're coming with me,' he said.

*

Carlos stood grinning sheepishly at Arturo, not sure what he was supposed to do next, as if he had obeyed his orders but had no idea how to enforce them. 'I've heard a lot about you, comrade,' he said, filling the awkward silence as Arturo stood staring at him. 'We need medicines. We need your help. She said to tell you to bring your things. It is time now. Time for you to leave. Your work here is over,' he said, giving a disparaging glance around the little clinic.

'How did you know where to find me?' Arturo asked.

275

'It wasn't hard. We followed the road. It has taken us weeks to walk here. We've been training for it. There aren't too many doctors from the city in these parts, word travels fast. We've been here for a couple of days, watching you.' Carlos looked no older than eighteen. He had the naive enthusiasm of youth written all over his face, a look that had only recently been washed from Arturo's own features. He spoke with a cultured voice, not dissimilar to Arturo's. He was certainly not a product of these parts, Arturo recognised another pampered city boy when he met one. Arturo hesitated for a moment.

The young man smiled warmly, shrugged his shoulders and then nudged him with his gun. 'I'm under orders,' he said, diffidently. 'We need everything you have.' Arturo showed him to the medicine chest in the small room in which his meagre supplies were kept. Useless potions, he thought, as he watched Carlos empty the contents. What good are they to the likes of Doña Gloria or Doña Nicanora? How will they bring Don Bosco back from the dead?

'Where did you get the uniform?' Arturo asked, as he packed his paltry belongings into a small bag, just as Carlos had instructed him to do.

'It isn't real,' Carlos said proudly. 'It's a good copy though, isn't it? We made one for each of us, to look like the real thing. So that people would think we are regular army.'

'Are you at the university?' Arturo asked. Carlos looked unnerved by the familiar manner in which Arturo was addressing him, like an indulgent older brother. He nodded.

'What are you studying?'

'History. I'm at the end of my first year,' Carlos replied. Then, as if embarrassed by the inexperience in his voice, said, 'I am through with that now. I am ready to do real work.'

'Real work?' Arturo said. 'And what is that? Are you perhaps thinking of training to be a barber?'

Carlos looked uncertain whether to laugh at the joke or to be angry at the insult, and so he lightly prodded Arturo with his gun again. 'We must go now,' he said.

Arturo picked up his bag and took one last look at the little room that had been his home for the past few months and said a silent goodbye. He wondered whether the room would miss him. It already looked as if it had never known he had lived there.

*

It did not take long to reach the clearing in which the little impromptu camp had been set up. It was only half an hour's walk from the clinic and close enough to the road that it could easily be seen by anyone who chose to venture along that bit of track, which fortunately they did not. Arturo thought it seemed rather an inept place to hide. Two young men were standing in the clearing, their backs to Carlos and Arturo, guarding a sleeping body that Arturo immediately recognised as Claudia. As he approached, the memory of a love, slightly faded and yellowed at the edges but achingly familiar, caught him at the throat.

'Is she hurt?' he asked Carlos as he made his way past the young guards, knelt down beside Claudia and started to take her pulse. All three men instinctively put their hands to their guns. Claudia opened her eyes and smiled.

'Did we give you a surprise?' she said as she tried to sit up, wincing as she did so. 'It can't have been that unexpected. You knew we would be coming soon.'

'I wasn't sure what I was expecting,' Arturo replied. 'I certainly didn't think you would be accompanied. Not in this way.'

Claudia looked at the three young men, their guns trained nervously on Arturo. 'They're harmless,' she said.

'I don't understand this. Claudia, what is it that you are involved in?' Arturo whispered.

'Don't you know anything about what is going on in the world, Arturo?' Claudia said. 'Things are happening out there. The people of this country are no longer willing to accept the old ways. They're finally taking control.'

'With your help?' Arturo asked.

'You can't stay locked in your safe little haven forever, Arturo,' Claudia said, the harsh challenge in her voice bringing back memories of the thrill of the fear that she used to instil in him. But now her words had a different quality from the seductive tones of her youth, they had a harsh, sharp ring that echoed painfully in Arturo's heart. He slowly opened Claudia's shirt to reveal the wound, exactly where he knew he would find it.

'Can you fetch me some boiled water?' he said looking up and addressing Carlos directly. Carlos looked at Claudia, who nodded, and he immediately left.

'Can we be alone for a moment?' Arturo said to Claudia, as the two other men remained, their guns still trained on him. Claudia signalled with her hand and they too vanished into the forest.

'Are they your students?' Arturo asked. 'This is certainly an interesting way of teaching them. Isn't it against college rules?'

'Don't be so precious,' Claudia said. 'They're not children, Arturo. They know what they're doing.'

'Do they? Do you? Do any of us?' Arturo asked, as he examined the wound, frowning as he did so. 'You need help,' he said at last.

'It isn't too deep, but I think it's infected and you've lost blood. I need to get you to a hospital. You have a fever.'

'Well, you're not much use, are you?' Claudia said taunting him. 'I thought you were supposed to be a doctor. That's why I came to you.'

'So you didn't come because I'm a friend?' Arturo said. 'There is nothing I can do for you here, Claudia. I need to get you to the nearest hospital. I need to take you to Puerta de la Coruña.'

'Puerta de la Coruña,' Claudia said, laughing bitterly. 'I'm not on holiday, Arturo. I haven't come to you because I want you to show me where I can buy postcards. Don't you understand how serious the situation is? You once swore you would always be there for me if I needed help. Well I need your help now.'

Arturo could feel the irresistible pull of Claudia's magic working on him. It was true, he had made a commitment to her in his youth, before he knew anything about the realities of the world that lay beyond the confines of his parents' garden.

'This is a bullet wound. How did you get it?' he said, gently bathing the wound with the water that Carlos had put in front of him.

'I'll explain on the way. It's nothing. We need to go now. Just give me some antibiotics and I'll be fine. Are you ready?'

'For what?' Arturo asked.

'To come with us.'

'Where to?'

'The border. It's not far from here. We have worked it out. It's only another couple of days' walk through the swamp and we'll be there. We have friends waiting for us,' Claudia replied, the heat of her fever now chilled by the coldness of her voice.

'Are you mad?' Arturo said. 'Claudia, you have no idea what

you're talking about. The forest is impenetrable in that direction. This is too desperate. What are you running away from?'

'I am not the one who is running away, Arturo,' Claudia said. 'We can make it with your help. You know the locals by now. The people here trust you. We will take one with us as our guide.'

'Even the locals never go into the swamp, Claudia. They know better than to do so,' and as he spoke the image of Don Bosco's half-submerged body reappeared in his mind.

'What about the young man who has been helping you at the clinic?'

'Ernesto?' Arturo said. 'He may be local, but he has never been far into the swamp.'

'Arturo,' Claudia said, her voice now turning cold. 'Why are you being so difficult? When are you going to stop playing your little games? When are you ever going to grow up and stop trying to please your father? Wake up to what is real in the world. You have the chance to do something useful with your life, at last. Why do you think I sent you here? Not because I thought your little box of pills would do any good for anybody. It was me who asked my mother to help your father find you this post. Do you know why? So that when the time came we would have a place to hide and a way to get out if we needed it. We will need a doctor with us, even though you are useless,' and as she said this there was the slightest hint of familiar teasing in her voice.

'What is all this for, Claudia?' Arturo said softly. 'What are you doing this for?'

'Do you really think you can help the people here with your injections, Arturo? Do you really think people like you will make any difference at all to the lives of the majority of people in our country? So you spend a year here and then what? You know you will never belong here. You will never be a part of these people's lives. They are different from us, Arturo,' and as she said this Arturo heard the echo of his mother's words in Claudia's. 'You're just playing at living, Arturo, with your little infatuations and flirtations with the local girls,' she continued with bitterness. 'You're fooling yourself. When your year here is up, what is there for you if you don't come with me now? You'll return to the city to live the life of the pampered middle classes like your father, with your private practice and your wealthy patients and your housemaids. And you will be using these people here to justify it all to yourself. You will tell yourself you deserve it because you once spent a few months in some piece of forgotten swampland trying to help the poor. They don't even want you here.'

Arturo stood up, reeling from the punch of Claudia's words.

'And what good do you think you can bring to the people of this town?' he asked. 'What do you know of their struggles, Claudia? Tell me, exactly how will your fight help Doña Nicanora save the shop in the plaza? How will it help Doña Gloria stop her soul from tormenting her? How will it help the town find the barber they did not realise they loved so much until it was too late? Will your fight help the people here to sort out these troubles?'

Claudia looked at Arturo as if he were the one with the fever. 'It's no good is it, Arturo?' she said at last. 'You just don't get it, do you? You never have and you never will. You're lost. But Arturo, if you won't come with us willingly, I have the power to make you.' And she clapped her hands and the three young men stepped out of the trees, their guns pointed at Arturo's head. He took a step backwards. In the far distance he could hear a very familiar sound: the slow rumble of wheels on the dirt track.

'Claudia,' Arturo said, 'you're too sick to make it to the border.

281

And even if you weren't, I wouldn't come with you. This is not my fight. This is your battle with yourself and your mother. I will help you as I promised, but not in the way that you want. I will take you to Puerta de la Coruña, to the hospital, if you choose to come with me. But you have no power to make me do anything against my will, guns or no guns. Maybe you're right. Maybe this is the right way. But it isn't for me. If you want to instruct your students to shoot me in the back as I walk away, then so be it. It's your choice. I'm going now, to find a friend who can help you.' As Arturo turned to make his way out of the clearing he heard the click of three rifles preparing to shoot, and then he walked down the track to meet Ernesto.

*

Ernesto was uncertain whether the figure walking towards him was the doctor or a form borrowed by the *kachi kachi* in the night to trick him. It had appeared as if from nowhere, and was approaching, waving, with a small bag slung over its shoulder. It looked like the doctor, but it had an alien quality to it, a confidence and assuredness in its step that he had never seen in the doctor before. It was certainly the doctor's voice calling him.

'Ernesto, Ernesto, am I pleased to see you,' Arturo said as Ernesto slowed the vehicle down. When he stopped, Ernesto thought he could detect a film of tears in the doctor's sad eyes.

'Where are you going so early in the morning?' Arturo asked as the vehicle came to a halt beside him.

'Puerta de la Coruña,' Ernesto replied. 'I was looking for you to see whether you would come with me. I am taking the Gringito there, except I can't find him. And I need to buy beer and fireworks for the fiesta of the Virgin, to bring Don Bosco back.'

'I think it will take more than beer and fireworks to bring Don Bosco back,' Arturo said, and then he checked himself. 'I'm sorry, Ernesto, if you feel that is what is needed, then that is what you must do. But I need your help, Ernesto. I have a sick patient.'

It took Arturo some time to persuade Ernesto to walk back into the forest clearing with him. 'It's an old friend of mine, from my childhood. She came to me in the middle of the night. She's in trouble. She's very sick,' Arturo said by way of an explanation. When he looked at Ernesto he saw a look of concerned incomprehension on his face. It was the same look that Arturo had so often shown to Ernesto in their first weeks together. Arturo led the way down the little grass track from where he had just come. When they reached the clearing there was no sign that any human form had been lying there only an hour ago. Arturo stood at the spot where Claudia had lain.

'Do you think I could have dreamt it, Ernesto?' he asked at last. 'Do you think I could have been drawn here by some apparition from my mind?'

'The forest can play tricks on all of us, doctor,' was all that Ernesto would say.

'She was here, Ernesto,' Arturo said at last. 'It was no dream. She came to offer me a choice. A way forward and I couldn't take it.'

'I'm sure she did,' Ernesto said and he laid his hand on Arturo's shoulder. 'What do you want to do now?' he asked.

'Come with you,' Arturo replied. He did not tell Ernesto that he had all his worldly possessions packed in his little bag. One thing was certain. Whether he had been lured into the forest by a wayward ghost or not, Claudia had been right. He was a weak man and he had nothing to offer the little town or the young woman who now owned his heart.

Twenty-five

The road started its journey as a gentle track. As it climbed upwards, the tangle of forest gave way to small orderly clearings of banana groves. Young children scrambled down hidden paths to greet the little pickup as it edged its way slowly up the hill. The plan was to follow the road to the top of the valley, where it then divided. The most dangerous stretch, Ernesto assured Arturo, was the upward fork that wound its way to the city. The gentler route, which they would take, carved a path along the other side of the valley into the steamy depths of the lowlands where Puerta de la Coruña lay. Arturo closed his eyes and allowed the freshness of the morning air to fill his lungs. He felt a deep pang of guilt as he thought about Isabela, and wondered what Ernesto would think of him if he knew what he was running away from. This is for the best, he told himself, Claudia is right, I can never belong there. What happiness could I possibly bring to her? It is best for everyone that I end it now. As they continued upwards the whirring noise of a helicopter grew louder, ebbing and flowing across the forest.

'What is it?' Arturo asked.

'The army I think,' Ernesto replied.

'What are they doing flying over here?' Arturo said.

'Looking for coca crops,' Ernesto said, pointing to the green terraces they were now approaching. The men working the fields stood alert as the pickup passed them by. The truck continued to climb, holding tenaciously to the side of the mountain. Occasionally it halted and slid a few yards backwards before gathering control again and forging another small path onwards. The steeper the incline, the narrower its path became, until the pickup was finally edging its way along a precipice so narrow that when Arturo glanced out of the window he was unable to see any road beneath them. Instead, he looked over a mist-filled ravine so deep that it was impossible to see the bottom. 'It gets much steeper soon,' Ernesto said. 'That's why we have to reach the brow of the hill by nightfall.'

Arturo shut his eyes and crossed himself. The tiny figure of a plastic Virgin with a posy of flowers in her hands bobbed on the windscreen. The small radio that Arturo had brought with him picked up a stray signal and crackled into life. 'We have intelligence of a terrorist camp close to the border,' a man said. 'We believe they are a group of peasant communists who are receiving training from outside sources. We understand there is a connection to the recent riots and the People's Liberation Front. We cannot reveal our sources, but suffice it to say that we have the situation under surveillance.'

Arturo felt a cold chill wash over him as he strained his ears to listen. The commentators were arguing about whether insurgents were supporting the terrorist group and if so what the government should do about it. So that was where Claudia was heading. One thing at least was reassuring about the news: Arturo was now certain that Claudia's visit had not been a creation of his imagination. The problems that the country was facing all seemed insignificant to him in the light of the troubles of the little town that he was leaving behind. He wondered why the newsreaders were not discussing how a barber could become lost in a swamp in which he had lived all his life. But of course they did not know that Don Bosco was lost, and nor, he suspected, would they ever find out.

*

The band in the plaza played the national anthem for the tenth and final time. The clock on the town hall struck five, which meant it was six o'clock, and exactly on queue the light began to fade. Within half an hour the little town would be lost in darkness again. The computer sat on the podium drenched in a pool of water. The slow drizzle of the afternoon had ensured that the flag was entirely covered with an even coat of red paint.

'I don't think they're coming,' someone from the crowd said at last, breaking the tension that had been building for the past few hours.

'Just give it ten more minutes,' the mayor pleaded to the wet and agitated crowd. 'They must have been delayed. The letter from the district officer clearly states that they will be here by noon.'

'Well, they clearly weren't here by noon, were they?' the man shouted back.

'Show us the letter,' another demanded. 'How do we even know that you are telling the truth?'

Ramon and the mayor both put their hands in their pockets and looked at each other, each convinced that the other was the last to have seen the document.

'I've had enough of this,' someone said. 'You've completely wasted our time.'

'And our money. Why would the visitors want to come all this way to see an old television anyway?'

'It isn't a television. It's a computer,' the mayor said, for the twentieth time.

'What are we going to do with a computer?' someone asked.

'Travel the superhighway,' Ramon said, but the crowd was not listening any more. No longer were the townsfolk standing as one united group drawn together by the anticipation of the honour of receiving foreign guests. People had broken off into small clusters, murmuring and arguing amongst themselves as to why the mayor would play such a trick on them and make them stand in the rain for six hours looking ridiculous. Scuffles began to break out as neighbour accused neighbour of spreading false rumours and wasting each other's time. As the townsfolk stood there in the plaza, wounds that had healed over years ago slowly began to reopen. Friends turned on friends, neighbours on neighbours, each blaming the other for the disappointment of the afternoon, the previous week, month and year, and finally for all the mistakes they had made in their lives. The mayor, having lost control of the situation, took refuge with Ramon under the eucalyptus tree, ready to make a break from the plaza should a riot erupt. Nicanora stood watching the scene from the barber's shop. The time has come, she said to herself, and with her last remaining drop of courage, she made her way through the crowd and mounted the podium, taking her place beside the drowned computer.

'Shame on you,' she shouted, 'shame on you all.' The crowd continued with their arguments, oblivious to her. 'Shame on you,' she shouted again, and this time her voice resounded around the plaza. 'What would our friend Don Bosco say if he could see you all now?' and as she spoke a quiet descended on the agitated crowd.

'I believe that our mayor was acting in good faith, even if he was misguided. He truly believed we would have visitors today,' she continued.

'You know, we should listen to what she says,' Don Amelio said to his neighbour, 'she gave me very good advice about my chickens.'

'After all,' Don Arsenio agreed, 'she is looking after Don Bosco's shop until he returns.'

'I believe that for too long we have neglected our duties to each other,' Nicanora said, now with the full attention of the crowd. A clap of thunder sounded overhead and the sky darkened as if a curtain was being drawn over the town. 'I believe', Nicanora continued, 'that Our Lady of the Swamp will help us. She will reunite us as the friends we all once were before money, greed and personal ambition started to take over our lives. I stand here before you to ask you the honour to host the fiesta of the Virgin. It has been too long since we have held the fiesta for the Virgin, and I now wish to ask her blessing to return our lost friends to us. I know you may be thinking that I have no right to be saying this to you. I am nobody. I am not from one of our wealthy families. But times and fortunes are changing. I have had the pleasure of having a foreign guest in my house for some months now, and due to his generosity, I am able to pay the tribute required of the host,' and Nicanora looked in the direction of the bedraggled and dejected mayor as she spoke.

'The procession,' she continued, 'will leave from Don Bosco's barber's shop on Sunday evening. It will not be the grandest procession the town has ever seen. But it will be the people's procession and I hope that is how it will remain in our hearts and in our memories forever.' The crowd drew in a breath as she spoke. People started to brush stray tears from their eyes, and then in one corner of the plaza somebody began to clap. 'She's good. I'll give her that,' a man said to his neighbour. And then another joined in with the clapping, and another, and soon the whole crowd were cheering and stamping their feet.

'People's procession?' the mayor grumbled to Ramon. 'Where the hell did she get that from? She sounds like some bloody third-rate politician.'

In the deserted town hall the silence was broken by the ringing of a telephone. At the other end of the newly restored line the district officer was trying to get a message to the mayor to tell him that the visitors had been unavoidably delayed due to inclement weather conditions. The telephone rang intermittently in the empty office for over an hour, until a small landslide in a far away part of the province cut it off again, for months to come.

*

It was just before midnight when Arturo and Ernesto finally reached Puerta de la Coruña. Arturo, curled up in a deep sleep in the passenger's seat, was suddenly shaken into life.

'We're here,' Ernesto said, 'we've made it.' Arturo opened his eyes. Lights winked on the hill in front of him, seductively welcoming him to the town. The pickup made its way down the steamy backstreets that led towards the town centre. The smell of stale urine mixed with rotting food rose from the gutters to welcome them. As they turned a corner into a side street, the darkness was lifted by a bright light streaming from a house, from which also spilled the sounds of salsa and shouting.

'Where are we?' Arturo asked

'This is my aunt's guest house,' Ernesto replied. 'We can stay here for the night.' Arturo read the lettering in pink lights above the door: *Dolores's Karaoke Bar. The Hottest Hot Spot in Town.* Before he could gather his thoughts to protest, a large woman ran out to greet them, shouting with delight at the sight of Ernesto.

'Well if it isn't my favourite nephew,' she said as she scooped Ernesto up in her arms in a bear hug and then placed him back on the path next to Arturo.

'And who is this?' she said, touching Arturo gently on the arm.

'This is my esteemed friend and colleague, Dr Arturo Aguilar,' Ernesto replied, his voice puffed up with self-importance. 'Doctor, may I have the pleasure of introducing you to my Aunt Dolores.'

'He looks too small to be a doctor,' Dolores whispered to Ernesto. Then she turned on her four-inch pink stilettos and led her guests inside the house.

'Aunt Dolores?' Arturo whispered into Ernesto's ear as they passed through a small courtyard in which a group of men sat drinking beer at plastic tables. 'Since when have you had an Aunt Dolores?'

'Found yourself some new young friends, Dol?' one of the men shouted, provoking a burst of exuberant laughter from his companions, which was swiftly silenced by an elegant gesture of Dolores's hand. She led Ernesto and Arturo into a room lit with sporadic flashing lights, and sat them at a table covered in cigarette ash and beer stains. With a click of her fingers she summoned a young woman with a tray of beer and then sat down next to Arturo.

'So you're a friend of Ernesto's,' she said in a voice as rich and deep as molasses. 'You are most welcome.' Arturo gazed at their hostess. Huge hoops of metal hung from her ears, making large circular movements as she turned her head to speak. Her dark brown thighs spread out liberally over her bar stool, and her skin glistened with bright succulent beads of sweat. She said something to Arturo that he could not hear over the noise of the bar, her eyes laughing as she spoke. Arturo watched her red lips mouthing words: they looked as if they could suck him in.

'You look like a child,' she said warmly into Arturo's ear as the music died down for a moment. There was another burst of laughter, followed by shouting and breaking glass from the front yard. Arturo watched as Dolores moved through the smoke-induced fog towards the commotion. The bar throbbed with discordant waves of music. Salsa was being piped through loud speakers, while a drunken old man was singing, '*Dónde están mis zapatos blancos?*' through a karaoke machine in the middle of the room. A small mariachi band roved in and out of the courtyard, competing with the karaoke and barking out a ballad about a woman who met a sad and bitter end because she had failed to make her husband's heart sing and his shoes shine.

Arturo could hear the men in the front yard shouting and swearing as he peered through the haze. Several young women moved with efficiency between the tables, serving beer from battered tin trays, winking and laughing in response to the cursing and barbed banter of the men. One of the men had risen to his feet, grabbed one of the young waitresses around the waist and was dancing with her between the tables. The girl, taken by surprise, had dropped a tray of beer, soaking the man's drinking compan-ions. Arturo caught a brief glimpse of her face. She was smiling and laughing, trying to appease her impromptu dance partner, but her eyes were unable to hide the fear that flickered behind them. The soaked man rose to his feet and grabbed his friend by the ear.

'*Hijo to puta*,' he shouted. 'She is my girl. Put her down – and you have soaked my pants.'

'Don't blame me for your pants being soaked, you horny old

bird,' his friend laughed as he continued to salsa roughly around the tables.

The karaoke came to an end. A hush descended on the bar as Dolores moved languidly towards the scene. The girl had started to struggle slightly with the dancing man, trying to get free from his grip. 'Enough, Don Carlos,' she said, 'we have danced enough now. I will go and get you some fresh beer.' The dancing man grabbed her tightly around the waist and swung her, knocking his friend on the head as he did so. The man with the wet pants stood up again.

'I'm warning you, Carlos,' he shouted, 'put her down.' And without giving his friend a second chance he thrust a clenched fist into the middle of his face, bringing the salsa performance to an abrupt end. The dancing man, blood streaming from his nose, picked up a bottle from the table and was about to bring it down on his drinking companion's head when he was grabbed from behind and raised from the floor, his legs kicking in mid-air. Dolores, towering over him, carried him out of the bar, into the street and placed him in the gutter.

'I will have no more of your cursing in here tonight, Carlos,' she said.

'Don't you worry. I mean what I say this time,' he shouted at her retreating figure. 'I won't come back to this stinking hellhole of whores.' And then he broke down weeping, holding his bleeding nose.

'Be certain that you don't,' she said over her shoulder. 'Or I will be sure to shave your moustache off this time,' she added as a last insult to his manhood. The karaoke started up again, with a slow, sad rendition of 'I am No Longer the Man I Used to Be'.

'Don't worry, they're just writers,' Dolores said, returning to Arturo, 'they get over-wrought sometimes. Pay no attention to them. Their problem is they have nothing useful to do with their lives, so they get drunk and talk rubbish. So tell me,' she said, now addressing Ernesto, 'what brings you so far from home again? We have another visitor here from your neck of the woods. Have you come to take him back with you?'

'A visitor? From our town? Is it the foreigner I met here?' Ernesto asked, realising that somehow the Gringito must have managed to make his own way back to Puerta de la Coruña.

'Well, he's not our usual sort of customer, that's for sure,' Dolores replied. 'But he's certainly not a foreigner. One of our regular punters brought him here last week. Apparently he had hitched a lift with him on the road.'

'What's he like?' Ernesto asked.

'He's very polite and quiet. I'm a bit concerned about him, to be honest. He keeps himself to himself. He goes out in the morning and comes back every evening with some boxes. He takes a beer and a bite to eat and then goes to his room and refuses any company from my girls. I asked him whether he wanted me to find him a quieter, more suitable establishment for him to stay in. But he said that he was perfectly comfortable and enjoying his visit. He told me he's on a journey to find out about life. He seems a bit too old for that, if you ask me.'

'What does he look like?' Ernesto asked, not believing what Dolores was telling him.

'He's quite small, tubby, balding, with kind smiley eyes,' Dolores said. 'He's a real gentleman. Shall I take you to meet him?'

*

The mayor slowly unlocked the church door for Nicanora. It was only the third time in her life that she had been taken to see the Virgin. Nicanora had gone to the mayor with her tribute as the crowd had dispersed from the plaza. 'Please, will you take me to see her?' she said, as she handed him the shoebox. 'This will pay for the fiesta and for the upkeep of the church for the next few years.' The mayor had opened the box and then looked at Nicanora, and his eyes had told her that he was finally defeated. The computer and the flag remained in the plaza, symbols of his unfounded hope. 'Maybe she will be able to help you as well,' Nicanora said to him gently as he unlocked the door of the church and let her in.

The air in the church smelt of damp feet and lost time. In the dim candlelight, Nicanora could see the outline of the Virgin at the foot of the crumbling altar. Bats circled overhead, their dark sanctuary disturbed by the intrusion of the visitors. Nicanora, over-whelmed by the occasion, allowed the mayor to slowly lead the way between the crumbling pews, until they stood in front of the Lady. 'It's some years since I've been in here myself,' the mayor confided to Nicanora. He crossed himself and knelt down in front of the statue. As he did so, his hands pressed lightly on the feet of the Virgin and she sprang into life. Lights flashed on her halo, tears streamed down her cheeks, and an unearthly voice rang out from a dark corner of the church: 'Bless you, bless you, bless you.' The mayor clutched at his heart. Nicanora ran forward with the candle and gazed at the Virgin in dismay, and then at the mayor. Clearly written across the plinth on which the statue was standing were the words: *A gift from Rosas Pampas.*

Twenty-six

Don Bosco sat in the front of the pickup, wedged between Arturo and Ernesto.

'Well that was quite an adventure,' he said at last. 'I still can't believe you turned up and found me, just like that.'

'It is a very strange coincidence,' Arturo agreed.

'I'm touched, touched,' Don Bosco said, 'that everyone would be so concerned that they would think of having a fiesta to bring me back. I do feel a bit of a fool, though, returning after only a week. Do you think people will mind after all the trouble they have gone to?'

'No. no, not at all,' Ernesto and Arturo said together, concerned to reassure him in case they lost him again.

'I hope I will live up to expectations after all this fuss,' Don Bosco said. 'You know what it is like. A person disappears, and for a time they become somebody else in people's minds. All their irritating features turn into the most endearing traits overnight – until they are brought back to life to annoy everybody again, that is.'

'Are we agreed?' Ernesto said. 'We'll keep you a secret until after the procession. The fiesta is sort of in your honour and we don't want to spoil it.'

'I suppose, though,' Arturo said, 'that strictly speaking it is because of the Virgin that you are returning anyway. If Ernesto hadn't come here to buy the beer and fireworks, we wouldn't have found you.'

'Indeed,' Don Bosco agreed. 'It was starting to trouble me how I would get back home. And then from nowhere you arrived. So perhaps the Virgin did send you.'

'I still can't believe we found you at Dolores's Karaoke Bar,' Ernesto said. 'It's the last place in the world that I would ever have looked for you.'

'But what I don't understand,' Arturo said, 'is how your hat came to be in the middle of the swamp.'

'Well,' Don Bosco said, at last enjoying the opportunity to tell at least one interesting story. 'To be honest I set out uncertain in which direction to go. I had thought of perhaps walking through the forest to Rosas Pampas. As I was sitting on a tree stump taking a bite of breakfast, a wind blew up from nowhere and took my hat clean off my head, over the trees and into the mud, just out of arm's reach. I am not really a person who takes guidance from the ancestors, but this seemed to me to be a sign if ever there was one. It was clearly telling me that I was going in the wrong direction. And so I started to wander along the road, my head bare, thinking about what to do next, when out of nowhere a truck appeared. It was apparently going to Puerta de la Coruña and the driver kindly gave me a lift all the way here. It couldn't really have been easier. He stopped at your Aunt Dolores's lodgings. I thought, well if this is where chance has brought me, this is where I will stay. And you see I was right to have followed my instinct. Just when I had finished my business here, you arrived to take me home.'

'And so what have you been doing?' Ernesto asked, looking at Don Bosco's boxes. He was still slightly irritated that it had taken an hour to load them all into the back of the pickup and that they had taken up so much room he had been forced to leave one crate of beer behind with Dolores.

'Buying supplies,' Don Bosco said.

'What sort of supplies?'

'For the barber's.'

'So that is it?' Ernesto said.

'That is what you have been doing?' Arturo asked.

'Yes,' Don Bosco said.

'Shopping,' Ernesto and Arturo said.

'Yes,' Don Bosco replied. 'I've been on a little shopping trip.'

*

The three men sat in silence for some considerable time as the pickup made its way slowly out of Puerta de la Coruña and along the upward bend of the valley. As it reached the fork where the road split, one path heading for the city and the other for the swamp, the truck came to a halt. Arturo sat staring ahead, not moving, his mind wandering between Isabela, Claudia and the radio reports of the army closing in on the PLF. Where was Claudia heading? Where was the army following her to? What would life be like without Isabela?

'So have you decided what you are going to do?' Don Bosco asked, breaking through his thoughts. 'Which way is it to be?'

'I don't know,' Arturo said.

'Why do you want to leave us?' Ernesto asked.

'It's not that I want to leave you,' Arturo said. 'It's just that I can't stay.'

'Why? Is it because we bore you?' Don Bosco said. 'Because I have some very interesting things to talk about now.'

'No, no, not at all,' Arturo said. 'Of course not.'

'Haven't we made you feel at home?' Don Bosco asked.

'Quite the opposite,' Arturo said. 'When I think about it now, I've felt more at home in the past few months than I've ever felt.'

'So why then? Are you lonely?'

'No,' Arturo said. 'Not at all.'

'Is it because of your friend?' Ernesto asked.

'What friend is that?' Don Bosco said.

'He dreamt he had a visit from a childhood friend in the night and she asked him to go with her.'

'Where to?'

'A troubled place,' Arturo said.

'Oh,' Don Bosco said, not really understanding. 'And you don't want to go?'

'I can't,' Arturo said. 'That is the problem. I just don't know where I should be. I see where she is heading and I can't follow.'

'I see,' Don Bosco said. 'No, you certainly don't want to follow someone in life. If you go with them, you must go as equals.'

'The problem is, I have nothing to offer you if I stay,' Arturo said. 'I'm a fraud. I'm not even a good doctor.'

'I see,' Don Bosco said again. 'You don't need to give us anything to be with us, you know. Do you want to go home?'

'No,' Arturo replied. 'If I go home, what then? I will go back to my parents' house and live my parents' life, the life that I've only just broken free from. I will never be myself.'

'You do have a dilemma,' Don Bosco said. 'Interestingly, it is similar to the one that I have recently faced.'

'Oh,' Arturo said. 'What was that?'

'Well,' Don Bosco said. 'When I first set out on my journey it did cross my mind that I was perhaps looking for a new life, a new beginning – even at my age it is possible to start again you know. Some people even change their name and create a whole new identity for themselves. It's a thought, isn't it? It is within our power to become somebody different, to become anybody we want to be.' Don Bosco was silent for a minute. 'And then I arrived quite by chance at your Aunt Dolores's guest house, Ernesto. I have never been anywhere like it in my life. And I thought what better place to reinvent myself? And do you know what happened?'

'What?' Arturo and Ernesto asked, now intrigued by the story.

'Nothing,' Don Bosco said. 'Absolutely nothing. I woke in the morning and found that I was still the same Don Pedro Bosco that I have always been. I still wanted my cup of strong sweet coffee. I still wanted my chat with Don Teofelo and Don Julio. I still needed my shirt to be ironed and my trousers pressed, and I hated all the noise and exuberance going on around me, even though your Aunt Dolores was very kind. They looked after me very well, someone knocked on my door every night to see whether I would like any company, but I was quite content to sit in my room on my own. And although I realised that I was just as dull as I have ever been, I felt comfortable with it. The truth is I realised that this is who I am, and who I will always be.'

'Oh,' said Ernesto, deflated by the unpromising trajectory of the tale.

'So do you know what I thought next?' Don Bosco asked. Ernesto looked at his watch, wondering how long it would take Don Bosco to get through this story, and whether they would make it back home in time for the procession. He had never heard Don Bosco so eloquent.

'What?' Arturo asked, before Ernesto could stop him.

'I thought, well, I have come all this way and probably for the first and last time in my life. The least I can do is take a boat trip to Manola and visit my brother Aurelio as I planned to do over twenty years ago, just before I lost my heart and then my mind.'

'So why didn't you go?' Arturo asked.

'I very nearly did,' Don Bosco replied. 'I bought the boat ticket. I went with my bag packed to the quay and was about to board. Then I was struck by another thought – what will happen when I get there? I have not seen Aurelio in over thirty years and you know we never really did get on. I will always remain his younger brother no matter how many years there are between us and our child-hood toys. After a day of hugs and kisses we would be arguing about the same things. Who really was the cleverest at school? Who was Mother's favourite? And who put the toad in my father's soup? And I would be straight back where I started, only having travelled many unnecessary miles to get there.'

'And so what are you saying?' Ernesto asked, trying to hide his irritation.

'I am saying', Don Bosco replied, 'that when a man reaches a point in his life when he cannot go forward and does not want to go backward, there is only one thing for him to do.'

'And what is that?' Ernesto and Arturo asked.

'Stay exactly where he is,' Don Bosco said. 'It means that he has found the right time and place to be, for the moment at least.'

The three men sat for some time in silence contemplating Don Bosco's words. Then Ernesto turned the key of the engine, and the little pickup truck started its journey on the downward hill, taking them back home.

'Ernesto,' Don Bosco said after some time. 'Is Dolores really your aunt?'

*

The pickup reached the town by night fall on Saturday, just as Ernesto had promised. An unusual light covered the plaza, spreading like a warm blanket from the barber's: Candles had been set in rows outside the shop and the square was covered with fronds of the forest, laid like a carpet for the Lady to walk on, should she come to life. Offerings had been placed outside the barber's; sweets and flowers from the children, little dolls made from woven strips of banana leaves. The scent of warm berries, mangoes, oranges, coconut milk and bread lingered over the plaza, making a feast of the night air.

'It looks like a shrine. You don't think somebody has died, do you?' Don Bosco said.

'You have,' Arturo replied.

'Oh dear,' Don Bosco said. 'I feared as much. How very inconvenient.'

'We must be careful that nobody sees you,' Ernesto said, as Don Bosco made his way across the plaza to peer into the barber's.

'She has done all this for me?' Don Bosco said, and his voice cracked slightly with tears seeing his hat perched on the barber's pole.

'She has been looking after the shop until you come back,' Ernesto said.

'She is a dear, kind, woman,' Don Bosco said.

In the dim candlelight Don Bosco could make out the figure of the Virgin, Doña Nicanora asleep beside her. Don Bosco suddenly froze to the spot.

'The Virgin,' he said to Ernesto and Arturo. 'I had quite forgotten. When does the procession start?'

'Tomorrow evening. I will prepare the truck tonight. My mother will be the guardian of the Virgin until then,' Ernesto said proudly.

'It is all too late. There is nothing I can do now,' Don Bosco mumbled to himself.

'Do you think it will be all right if we drive her in the pickup, rather than my mother having to carry her in the traditional way?'

'Of course,' Don Bosco said, 'why not? Times are certainly changing and I am sure that if our ancestors had had a pickup truck at their disposal, they would have done exactly the same thing.'

*

The townsfolk woke in the morning to the vision of the Lady, standing on a bed of petals and banana fronds in the back of the pickup truck, parked in the middle of the plaza. She was covered from head to foot in a fine shroud, so that nobody could glimpse her face. The pickup had been decorated to look as if the Virgin were standing on a hill of flowers.

Nicanora looked proudly out of the window at her fine work. The soft drizzle gently moistened the town, filling the air with the perfume of damp petals. The mayor lay, as he had for the past few days, asleep under the eucalyptus tree. As Nicanora approached him he moved uncomfortably in his sleep and groaned. She gently shook him and placed a cup of hot coffee beside him. 'Drink this,' she said. 'It will do you good.' He opened his eyes, bringing into focus first Nicanora and then the covered statue.

'What are we going to do?' he asked. 'If they discover that she has been stolen, and that this is an impostor, they will drive me out of town. And you as well,' he added, 'once they find out that you knew it was a fake and went ahead with the procession.'

'If Our Lady really is missing,' Nicanora said, 'that is even more reason for us to hold a fiesta in her honour. Let's think of this as a fiesta to bring back not only lost souls but also stolen statues. If she knows we are genuine, she will come to us.'

'And if she doesn't come back?' the mayor said.

'Then we are both in serious trouble,' Nicanora agreed.

*

The tension had been building all day. The townsfolk gathered in the plaza in anticipation of the long-awaited fiesta. As the sun began to fade Nicanora finally walked out of the barber's shop ready to lead the procession into the night. She was dressed in her mother's finest silk shawl, the one her mother had been married in and which Nicanora had been promised for her own wedding day. Nicanora had come across it after her mother's death, when sorting through her possessions. It had been wrapped in paper and attached to it was a note saying: *For Nicanora, to wear when she finally sees sense.* Nicanora knew that day had come. On her head she wore the straw boater the travelling salesman had tricked her with. She had kept it for all these years as a trophy of her naive youth. The salesman's fake plastic flower had now been replaced with a delicate tiara of fine wild blossoms that Doña Gloria had threaded round it. In her hand, Nicanora was holding Don Bosco's hat.

303

Don Bosco stood watching from his hiding place at the corner of the barber's shop, his boxes of supplies now lined up against the wall and covered by a large cloth. As Nicanora made her way towards the Virgin and the pickup, the crowd stood in silence. Don Bosco drew in his breath as he watched Nicanora mount the truck, astonished by her radiance. She looked more beautiful to him in her ageing years than in her youth. Nicanora stood beside the Virgin and poured the contents of a bottle of beer on the ground, asking the Virgin to bless the town once again and bring back lost souls. She then placed Don Bosco's hat at the feet of the statue. Don Bosco felt tears of humility stream from his eyes. The engine started up and the pickup began making its journey around the plaza, the townsfolk following, the school band playing: everyone singing, shouting and banging drums.

After fourteen turns of the plaza the pickup drew to a halt. The townsfolk lined up once again, each placing their small gifts and offerings beside the truck. When the last gift had been given, Nicanora beckoned the mayor to come forward so that he could place his personal offering to the Virgin. 'This gift', Nicanora announced as the mayor and Ramon stepped forward carrying the dripping computer, 'represents our mistakes of the past and our hopes for the future, and is presented today to Our Lady to do with as she wishes. I now hereby invite all gathered to take part in our people's fiesta.' Ernesto, on his mother's command, lit the fireworks to mark the start of the party. One by one they whizzed over the Virgin's head and were extinguished in a series of sharp explosions.

It seemed to all who spoke about it in the months to come that there was a momentary pause in which all thoughts and action were held in abeyance. As the last firework lit the sky, it was answered by a shot from the forest, as if the spirits of the swamp were replying with their own firework display. Arturo was the only one among them to understand – too late to warn anyone what was taking place. In that second, he realised exactly why Claudia had visited him in the night, and to where she had led her pursuers.

At the moment the shots from the forest were fired, Nena, who was standing beside her mother, looked across at the barber's shop and saw a familiar face in the crowd. 'He's here, he's here, he's come back!' she shouted. As Nicanora looked up, she too saw the hatless figure of Don Bosco appear from round the corner of the shop. Nena let go of her mother's hand and ran to meet him. She did not make it past the feet of the Virgin.

As Don Bosco stepped forward, his face beaming with delight at the expression of joy that covered Nicanora's, the computer screen burst into life. According to the onlookers, it first flickered and then shimmered, as if it had collided with another world, before it shattered into tiny pieces. The shroud fell from the Virgin, lights momentarily flashed around her head before she, too, disappeared in a shower of minute fragments. Nena fell to the ground at the Virgin's feet, a small pool forming under her that slowly trickled across the plaza in a delicate red stream. Bottles of beer smashed to the ground, their contents mixing with the debris now filling the plaza as the sound of explosions echoed across the town. Don Bosco tried to make his way through the chaos to the place where Nena had fallen, grabbing at people as they ran in panic-driven circles and pushing them in the direction of safety and cover. He saw the doctor running into the centre of the crowd, tears streaming from his eyes, waving a white handkerchief above his head, oblivious to the risk he was taking. When Don Bosco finally reached the spot where the broken Virgin had stood, he found the Gringito kneeling, weeping, holding Nena in his arms.

As the mortars hit their target, the boxes at the side of the barber's shop flew into the air and then fell apart above the spot where the impostor Virgin had stood. Those who remained in the plaza stood still, watching, as a cloud of feather-plumed hats gently floated down, covering the destruction beneath.

Twenty-seven

The little town was filled with visitors, more visitors than had ever been thought possible, visitors who were fast outstaying their welcome. Word quickly reached the city through the commander, who radioed to the general to report that the carefully planned assault on the rebel town had been executed, a mistake had been made, and then a miracle had occurred.

'It seems', the commander informed the general, 'that we have the wrong location.'

'The wrong location?' the general replied. 'How can you have the wrong location? You've been watching it for weeks. I thought you said they had the rebel flag flying.'

'It seems it was meant to be the national flag,' the commander said. 'Apparently they didn't have any yellow paint.'

'What about the communications equipment?'

'A computer. Some idiot had the idea of starting an Internet café.'

'But the rebels? You told me a few days ago you had tracked the group to a camp outside the town. What about the foreigner who's leading them?'

'Turns out he's the wrong one,' the commander said languidly.

'Wrong one? How can he be the wrong one? Who is he? What's he doing there?' 'Nobody seems to know. Just hanging out apparently.'

'Hanging out?' the general said. 'Why would anybody want to hang out in a place like that?'

'Beats me,' the commander said.

'And the van? The man you saw leaving the town, followed by the van a few days later? I thought you had them under surveillance.'

'We did,' the commander said. 'According to the locals in the villages it was most unusual to have all that coming and going. The van was carrying suspicious packages.'

'So,' the general shouted through the crackling radio, 'have you found any of the weapons of destruction that they were transporting?'

'We made a direct hit on the target,' the commander replied.

'I told you not to fire unless absolutely necessary,' the general said. 'Why did you mortar?'

'It was self-defence,' the commander said. 'They fired rockets.'

'Rockets,' the general confirmed. 'So they did have weapons stockpiled then?'

'Not really,' the commander said. 'Turns out they were letting off fireworks. They made a hell of a bang.'

'So what was in the packages?'

'Hats,' the commander replied.

'Hats?' the general said.

'Yes, hats,' the commander confirmed. 'Hundreds of the bloody things.'

There was a silence on the other end of the line.

'What a total fuck-up,' the general said at last. 'The media will love this.'

'Quite,' the commander replied.

*

Helicopters had been arriving all day and the plaza had turned into an impromptu landing pad. Television crews sat drinking coffee at the little tables outside the barber's shop, preparing for the day's filming. Doña Nicanora and Doña Gloria rushed back and forth trying to keep up with the orders.

'Do you do banana pancakes, love?' one of the crew asked Nicanora as he walked into the barber's to set up the scene for the interview. Large cables criss-crossed the plaza as the satellite equipment was installed for the live broadcast. Don Bosco stood waiting patiently to tell his story. The barber, it seemed, had the most interesting tale of all and everyone wanted their share of it to sell. He had saved the lives of many of the townsfolk as he pulled them out of the range of the mortar fire. He had also been, apparently quite by chance, the first person to witness the reappearance of the Virgin.

The preparations for the broadcast had been going on for some hours. Every time the television interviewer began to speak into the microphone he was stopped by a man with a set of headphones, who kept repeating the words, 'Alpha-brava, alpha-brava, testing, testing,' before bursting into a stream of swear words. 'The bloody rain isn't helping,' he grumbled to the interviewer, who was also fast losing patience with the stubborn equipment.

'I wonder what has happened to that foreigner,' Don Bosco heard one of the journalists say to his colleague as they sat at the little tables.

309

'According to the people I've spoken to he was staying with that waitress over there,' his friend said, pointing at Nicanora, and he called her over. 'Any chance of another coffee, love?' he asked.

'Yeah, that's what I heard,' his colleague replied. 'Nobody seems to know where he's gone. Bloody annoying he's just disappeared like that, the day we get here. Would have been good to get his side of the story – put an interesting angle on things having it from the mouth of a foreigner. It would give the story that extra bit of credibility.'

'Yes, bloody annoying, a lost opportunity,' the other journalist agreed. 'I wonder what he was doing here.'

*

The mayor sat under the eucalyptus tree, watching the visitors. Ramon was running around trying to make himself useful to the cameras crews, fiddling with cables and any stray piece of equipment he could get his hands on. 'Will somebody get rid of this bloody annoying little man,' the sound recordist shouted to nobody in particular, as Ramon helpfully started to play with the buttons on the sound mixer.

Don Bosco stood patiently in the doorway, awaiting further instructions. The film crew were busy trying to fix a new sign above his shop. 'I can't get the damn thing to stay up,' the man who was balancing precariously on a chair grumbled as he tried to hammer a nail into the antique fascia of the barber's. 'The wood is too rotten to hold it.'

'Looks much better though,' one of the men in the plaza shouted back. 'You may just have to stand there and try to balance it from the side, if we can get you out of shot. Makes it much clearer to viewers that it's a barber's shop now. Looked more like some old junk shop before with all those hideous hats in the window.' Nicanora and Gloria came and stood beside Don Bosco, watching the proceedings.

'I don't know why he's looking so glum,' Gloria said, pointing to the mayor under the tree. 'He's got exactly what he wanted.'

'Be careful what you wish for,' Don Bosco said.

'I feel sorry for him,' Nicanora said. 'He's been sitting out there for days now.'

'Serves him right,' Gloria said, but with no conviction in her voice.

'He can't do without you, Gloria,' Nicanora replied. 'Don't you think you've punished him long enough?'

'I don't want him to think I've forgiven him too easily,' Gloria said with a hint of petulance.

'Well don't leave him out there too much longer,' Nicanora replied. 'You don't want him to shrink in the rain.'

*

Suddenly someone shouted to Nicanora and Gloria, and one of the crew stepped forward and pushed them out of the doorway. A camera swung round and pointed at Don Bosco, who assumed the pose he had been instructed to hold, his razor held high to make it clear to the world that he was the town's barber. As Nicanora looked at Don Bosco poised ready to tell his interesting story to the world, she saw a radiance emanating from him that she had never seen before.

'He has a glow about him,' she whispered to Gloria.

'He's standing in the bloody light,' the camera man shouted. 'Get that barber out of the light, quick, make him move to the left,' and Don Bosco was roughly grabbed from behind and repositioned so that the camera could get the best shot.

'Here I am,' the interviewer began, walking slowly round the plaza with the camera following him, 'on the corner of this little plaza, in this humid, isolated, mosquito-infested swamp town quite forgotten by time. The townsfolk here are a simple and honest people, going about their business trying to eke out a livelihood in this hostile and inhospitable environment.' The camera panned to a shot of the mayor sitting under the eucalyptus tree and Don Teofelo and Don Julio taking coffee at one of the little tables outside the barber's, which had now been cleared by all the film crews for the sake of the integrity of the image. 'The townsfolk have lived for years in peace and tranquillity, with few outsiders even knowing that the place existed,' the interviewer continued. 'Suddenly, they have become the centre of a quite extraordinary case of mixed identity after a series of unfortunate blunders by the army, who believed them to be hiding the ringleaders of the rebel People's Liberation Front. Despite the town having been under surveillance for several weeks, and no evidence of any terrorist connections, yesterday they came under sustained mortar fire during their very rarely celebrated fiesta of the Virgin. A little girl was hit, the Virgin was destroyed, and then a miracle apparently took place. I am standing here outside the unassuming little barber's shop that was the scene of so much activity yesterday. We will pick up the story now from the mouth of the barber himself. Mr Forest,' the interviewer said turning to Don Bosco. 'Tell us first about the foreigner who was staying here. It seems the army mistook him for the one leading the rebel group. But what do you really know about him?'

Don Bosco bristled slightly as the camera swung around to point at him. He did not like the accusatory tone of the interviewer's question.

'Nothing,' Don Bosco said.

'Can you tell us what he was like,' the interviewer encouraged.

'He was very polite,' Don Bosco said.

'Yes, yes,' the interviewer continued. 'But who was he? What was his name?'

'I really don't know,' Don Bosco said. 'He was a gringo.'

'I understand he was here for quite some time. Didn't you find out anything about him?'

'No,' Don Bosco replied, 'nothing at all.'

'Why not?'

'Because I had no reason to,' Don Bosco said, agitation showing on his face.

'So where is he now?'

'On his way back home, I expect,' Don Bosco replied.

'Why has he gone home now?'

'To take up where he left off.'

'So what do you think he was doing here?'

'I think he needed a different point of view for a while.'

'So tell me about your own recent journey,' the interviewer said, changing tack to see whether that would help to get more useful information out of the obstinate and, frankly, annoying little barber. 'I understand you went to Puerta de la Coruña recently.'

'I did,' Don Bosco said.

'So tell me, why did you bring back all those hats?'

'Because', Don Bosco replied, 'I had grown tired of cutting hair. So I thought I would buy a hat for everyone to cover their heads instead.'

'And you really had no idea that the army was watching you?'

'Why would I?' Don Bosco said. 'You see, I know we are far from the centre of things here, but I hadn't realised that in our country today a man no longer has the right to buy hats should he wish to.'

The camera moved in on Don Bosco as Doña Nicanora and Doña Gloria edged closer to hear what he was saying. 'He really has become very interesting these days,' Nicanora whispered to Gloria.

'You see,' Don Bosco continued on live national television, 'I hadn't realised that an ordinary man going about his business was such a threat to our national security. That he would find himself unwittingly under surveillance and that the powers that be could misunderstand his innocent motives so much that they would risk his and others' lives by indiscriminately shooting at him. Troubled as this country is, I had understood, until now, that a man still has the liberty to do as he wishes, as long as he is not harming others. I had not realised that the army would take such an interest in my personal affairs.'

'So tell me, Mr Woods,' the journalist said, trying to change the tone of the interview, 'tell me again what happened that day, exactly as you saw it,' and Don Bosco relayed once again the story of how the Virgin had been destroyed, the little girl had been felled by a bullet and the townsfolk had been brought down by fear and grief as box after box of hats had exploded over the plaza.

'So how did you feel?' the interviewer asked quietly, with apparent emotion in his voice.

'How did I feel?' Don Bosco said.

'Yes,' the interviewer said slowly and slightly louder, so that the

314

barber would understand. 'How did you feel when you saw the little girl being hit? How did that make you feel?'

'How did that make me feel?' Don Bosco asked, lingering over the question. 'You, an educated man, have come all this way to ask a simple man like me how it feels to see his town destroyed and have his feet washed by the blood of a child whom he has loved all her short life? Isn't that a question that all humanity would immediately know the answer to? You certainly don't need to come here with your cameras to ask me that.'

The journalist was silent for a moment before deciding to wrap up the interview. 'So tell us about the miracle,' he said.

'Do you mean the miracle of the Virgin, or the miracle of life?' Don Bosco asked.

*

Nena had lain cold and motionless in the bed above the barber's shop. The sobbing Gringito had carried her there, away from the mayhem in the plaza. Nicanora kept vigil over her daughter, begging the Virgin, the ancestors, the doctor, the Gringito, whoever might have the powers to help, to give her daughter life. Arturo worked quickly and without hesitation, stemming the flow of blood, Isabela never far from his side, helping him throughout the night, changing blood-soaked bandages, until there was nothing more for anyone to do but hope. Only the faintest sign of breathing indicated that for the moment Nena was still in the tenuous clutches of the present.

'It is my fault,' Arturo confided to Don Bosco as he left the room, allowing Nicanora time alone with her daughter.

'How can that be?' Don Bosco asked. 'If that child lives it will be thanks to you; and you alone.'

'No,' Arturo said. 'You don't understand. It's my fault that the army were here in the first place. I see it now. They were led here on purpose. The friend that I told you about, the one who came to me in the night, it wasn't a dream. They were looking for her. She brought them here to put them off her scent. I thought she had come because she needed me, but she came to me for quite another reason.'

'Who was she?' Don Bosco asked.

'Someone I once thought was very dear to me,' Arturo replied. 'Someone I once believed I could not live without.'

'Were you her lover?' Don Bosco asked.

'No,' Arturo replied sadly, 'I was her decoy. I always have been.'

★

While Nicanora sat beside her lifeless daughter, the frightened townsfolk disappeared to the safety of their homes as a quiet calm descended on the town. Don Bosco and Don Teofelo worked alone into the night to clear the debris from the plaza, keeping watch for the forces encroaching on them from the forest. As all the hats were collected, the splinters of glass and plastic swept up, the leaves and petals removed, Don Bosco and Don Teofelo knelt silently side by side.

'How could a child lose so much blood?' Don Bosco said at last, trying to remove the last stains of the night from the stones of the plaza. 'Yesterday we were preparing for a procession of the Virgin, with so much hope. Now I fear, come daybreak, we will be making preparations of quite another kind.'

Teofelo said nothing, but placed his hand gently on his friend's arm.

'How are we going to bear this, Teofelo?' Don Bosco whispered at last. 'How will Nicanora survive it after all she has been through? It is my fault.'

'How so?' Teofelo said gently. 'How do you come to that conclusion, Bosco?'

'Because I cheated everybody,' Don Bosco replied. 'I cheated the town, and I cheated Nicanora. You know that, as well as I do. I knew the Virgin was a fake and I said nothing. I let the procession go ahead and now Nicanora is being punished for my mistake.'

'I didn't take you for a superstitious man,' Teofelo said. 'I thought you were a modern man like me. I'm sure there is quite another explanation for what took place tonight, which we will find out soon enough. But you were acting in good faith. Surely that is as much as any man can do. And besides, don't you think Nicanora would have realised herself that it was a fake?'

'It was a foolish trick, Teofelo,' Don Bosco said. 'I should never have asked you to buy such a thing in Rosas Pampas, and I should never have tried to trick the mayor.'

'I think the opposite,' Teofelo said. 'Whatever happened out here tonight, you saved her from destruction. Remember, Bosco, you only did it because you didn't trust him to safeguard our Virgin in the first place. You seem to have lost your memory suddenly. You thought he was going to sell her to the antiquity hunters.'

'No, Teofelo. I just thought I was better than him. And look where my lack of trust has got us. But do you know what the real shame of it is? I have quite forgotten where I hid her, it was so long ago.'

'Well, we had better start looking then,' Teofelo said, 'before whoever it is who is out there finds their way to us.' He picked up one of the hats as he stood. 'These really are quite beautiful,' he said.

'Yes,' Don Bosco replied. 'Puerta de la Coruña, it seems, is a town of expert milliners.'

*

Nicanora and the Gringito sat in the bedroom above the little shop, neither speaking, barely breathing in the silence of the room, oblivious to all that was happening in the plaza below. The young doctor knelt beside the body of Nena, unable to take his hand from her wrist for fear of letting go forever the faint hope of the echo of a pulse. Nicanora felt a surge of hatred for the little bedroom that, with no apparent struggle, was so readily transforming itself into a funeral parlour. Her anguish let out its objection to the night in an unguarded moan of tears. 'My little girl,' she said as she rocked gently backward and forward, 'my own little girl.'

Isabela clutched her mother's hand, and then pressed her face into Nicanora's shoulder, just as she had done as a child when she was too shy to speak to a neighbour, or when trying to deflect a scolding. The Gringito made a sound as if his voice were about to break in two in an effort to speak out and halt the movement of time. Nicanora looked up. 'What did he say?' she whispered to Isabela.

'I don't know,' Isabela replied. 'Perhaps he is trying to tell us that Nena is the only one who has ever really been able to understand.'

*

Don Bosco and Don Teofelo sat in the refuge of the church.

'Think, man,' Teofelo said. 'She must be here somewhere.'

'I'm trying,' Don Bosco replied. 'I'm doing my best, but we've looked in all the possible places.'

'Well, perhaps he did sell her after all,' Teofelo suggested.

'Perhaps he did,' Don Bosco agreed. 'But somehow I think not. Either way I've failed everybody, and Nicanora most of all.'

The two men sat in silence as the rain that had been politely tapping on the windows started to thump on the decaying roof of the church in an effort to be let in. The sound of boots crunching on stones could now be heard in the distance, replacing the deathly silence of the plaza. As Don Bosco rose to greet the visitors for whom they had been waiting, he noticed a door at the side of the church swinging open with the winds of the impending storm. A small trickle of water, which had made its way down the centre of the pews and had been seeping through the holes in the toes of his shoes, ran from under door. A faint memory stirred in his brain.

'I remember where she is,' he said at last.

*

As Don Bosco and Teofelo made their way through the dark recesses of the church and retrieved the sad, lonely figure of the rain-soaked statue from her resting place in the cupboard at the end of the forgotten corridor, the ghostly sound of the voices of strangers echoed through the pores in the church walls.

The two men gently placed their charge in her rightful position at the front of the church, and with a renewed strength went out to face the visitors. Nicanora, the doctor and the Gringito, who had all been caught in a brief moment of sleep, woke up with a start at the sound of the strange voices below. As they did, a more familiar voice drifted across the room.

'You had better make sure that you close all the windows and doors,' Nena mumbled as if from the depths of her sleep, 'the heavy rains are about to start and will not stop for at least a month.'

In the plaza, the commander surveyed the town of his captives. 'There's nobody here,' he complained through the crackle of his radio.

'Well, why did it take you so long to get there?' a voice barked back at him. 'It's been at least eight hours since the operation began. Why has it taken you so long to move in on them?'

'We got stuck in the goddamn swamp,' the commander explained, forlornly.

'Well what can you see?'

'Nothing of interest,' the commander replied. 'Just two old men hanging around in the plaza, and a church with a statue in it. It's strange, though, it's raining so hard I could swear it makes the statue look as if she's crying.'

*

As dawn finally broke over the plaza, the townsfolk awoke to the miracle. The church doors were open for the first time in years. There in the central aisle stood the Virgin, the gentle rain leaking from the roof washing the stains from her cheeks.

Don Bosco led Nicanora down the stairs into the shop, leaving the Gringito to say his goodbyes to Nena, who by now was sitting up in bed chattering. When they reached the bottom of the stairs, Don Bosco turned to Nicanora and took her by the hand. 'I want you to close your eyes,' he said, memories of a time long gone

320

echoing in both their hearts. He led her by the hand into the centre of the shop. 'You can look now,' he said.

There, in front of her were hats of such beauty that she could not at first comprehend what she was seeing. Purple hats with the feathers of peacocks from distant lands sat on the barber's basin. Hats that looked as if they had grown the wings of the condor and were about to take flight stood elegantly in the window. 'There is a hat for every dream, or so I was once told,' Don Bosco said as he picked one up and handed it to her. It was made of fine silk woven into strands. As Nicanora looked at the hat in the morning light, its colour changed, slowly passing through the shades of the rainbow. Then Don Bosco got down on his knees in front of her.

'Everything you see here is yours,' he said, 'regardless of whether you will have me, or not. But you would make me the happiest man in the world if you would reconsider my offer of twenty years ago.'

Nicanora said nothing, the words silent in her throat.

'Will you have me?' he asked again.

She was still silent.

'I can't,' she said finally in a whisper.

'Why not? I'm no longer a barber,' Don Bosco said, standing up and brushing the dust from his trousers and indignation from his voice. 'And you are, and it doesn't worry me.'

'It's not that,' Nicanora said, and she took Don Bosco by the hand and led him to the back storeroom. 'I need to make sure of something. I don't think it is me who will really make you happy,' she said. 'If you love somebody else you must try and find her, no matter how far away she may seem right now. It's the least you deserve.' Don Bosco was now the one who was speechless as Nicanora opened the drawer to the little cabinet.

'It was made by my father,' he said, running his hand gently over the surface.

Nicanora handed him the photograph. 'I know I should never have looked in here,' she said. 'But you should try and find her before it is too late.'

'I've been trying most of my life,' Don Bosco said, staring at the photograph. 'I had quite forgotten that I had kept this.'

'Did you love her?' Nicanora asked.

'I did,' Don Bosco replied. 'Very much. We can't help who we fall in love with, Nicanora, however unsuitable the person may be for us.'

'What happened to her?' Nicanora asked, and then anticipating the answer said, 'Did she die?'

'Not in my heart,' Don Bosco said. 'Take a closer look, Nicanora. Don't you recognise that shawl? Don't you see yourself?'

Nicanora stared at the picture. 'I have never seen a photograph of myself before,' she said at last.

'No,' Don Bosco said, 'and you have never seen yourself as I see you.'

*

Don Bosco lay in the warmth of his lover's bed, snoring the snore of a contented man. After a lifetime of emptiness and longing he had felt for the first time the warmth and comfort of a woman lying beside him, breathing softly, her leg wrapped over his. He put his hand on Nicanora's head and smoothed her hair, afraid that she would fade away. The last of the television crews had finally disappeared, having received warnings to evacuate quickly or risk being stranded in the little town for months as the storms started. Don Bosco drew Nicanora closer to him.

'It's raining, my sweet,' he whispered in her ear, 'and we are going to drown.'

'So be it,' she said dreamily and turned to hug her aged lover. 'I was wrong about the Gringito, you know,' she said after some time. 'He was really very kind and generous. I see that now. I hope he will get home safely in this weather.'

'We were both wrong about him,' Don Bosco said. 'You can mistrust a man simply because you don't understand him.'

'And that is really why you left?' Nicanora said.

'It is,' Don Bosco replied. 'It occurred to me in the middle of the night that a person cannot open a hat shop if they don't have any hats to sell. I'm sorry about the mess I left, I had quite forgotten it.'

'And the mayor?' Nicanora asked. 'Weren't you worried that he would take the shop from me?'

'No,' Don Bosco said, 'I knew you would be able to deal with him. He's quite harmless really.'

'Tell me,' she said after a pause. 'Do you really think it was a miracle? It had crossed my mind that maybe somebody had played a trick on the mayor.'

'Surely not,' Don Bosco said. 'Who would have done such a thing? And anyway, you would have noticed if it had not been the real statue. After all, you were host of the fiesta.'

'Of course I would have noticed,' Nicanora said. 'So a miracle it was then?'

'Absolutely,' Don Bosco agreed. 'What other explanation can there be?'

'I do hope the mayor and Gloria will make their peace soon,' Nicanora said, listening to the rain from the comfort of her bed. 'If she leaves him under that tree much longer he will float away.'

'I think they may just need a little help,' Don Bosco said. 'Why don't we invite them both to Sunday lunch?'

'What a lovely idea, Pepito,' Nicanora said, as she kissed him. 'I'll tell them we're having chicken.'